A DAUGH
LOVE

Nancy Revell is the author of twelve titles in the bestselling Shipyard Girls series – which tells the story of a group of women who work together in a Sunderland shipyard during the Second World War. Her latest books, *The Widow's Choice* and *A Secret in the Family*, feature some of the characters from the world of the Shipyard Girls series in a new County Durham setting. Nancy's books have sold more than half a million copies across all editions.

Before becoming an author, Nancy was a journalist who worked for all the national newspapers, providing them with hard-hitting news stories and in-depth features. She also wrote amazing and inspirational true-life stories for just about every woman's magazine in the country.

A DAUGHTER'S LOVE

Nancy REVELL

PENGUIN BOOKS

PENGUIN BOOKS

UK | USA | Canada | Ireland | Australia
India | New Zealand | South Africa

Penguin Books is part of the Penguin Random House group of companies
whose addresses can be found at global.penguinrandomhouse.com

Penguin Random House UK,
One Embassy Gardens, 8 Viaduct Gardens, London SW11 7BW

penguin.co.uk

Penguin
Random House
UK

First published 2026
001

Set in 10.4/15pt Palatino
Typeset by Falcon Oast Graphic Art Ltd

Printed and bound in Great Britain by Clays Ltd, Elcograf S.p.A.

The authorised representative in the EEA is Penguin Random House Ireland,
Morrison Chambers, 32 Nassau Street, Dublin D02 YH68

A CIP catalogue record for this book is available from the British Library

ISBN: 978–1–804–94511–7

Penguin Random House is committed to a sustainable future
for our business, our readers and our planet. This book is made from
Forest Stewardship Council® certified paper.

To Paul,
I do love you so
x

God grant me the serenity to accept the things
I cannot change,
Courage to change the things I can,
and Wisdom to know the difference.

Karl Niebuhr, theologian (1892–1971)

Acknowledgements

As always, a huge 'Thank You!' to all my lovely readers who really are the best any author could ever wish for.

To the lovely Emily Griffin, Publishing Director of Century Fiction, who has been a huge support and gifted me so much confidence during my journey as an author.

To my editor Susannah Hamilton, who made working on the edits of this book so seamless.

To 'Team Nancy' at Century, who always work incredibly hard and with such professionalism.

To my super copy editor Caroline Johnson.

To the forever supportive Katy Wheeler, journalist at the *Sunderland Echo*, and Booklover Beverley Ann Hopper.

To Phil Curtis and Linda King of the Sunderland Antiquarian Society.

To Ian Mole and his much lauded Shipyard Girls Walking Tour.

To my cousin Allison McDonald and her daughter Chloe, Kath and Ray Thirlwell, Pauline Stevenson and Elena Notarianni, who have all helped me in so many different ways.

To my sister Jane Elias and her wonderful, inspiring family – husband Siôn and children, Ivor, Matilda and Flynn.

And to my husband, Paul, who is always there for me.

Prologue

Cuthford Manor, Cuthford, County Durham

October 1953

Standing alone by the large floor-to-ceiling windows in the grand front reception room of Cuthford Manor, a flute of champagne in her hand, Marlene Boulter watched as her brother and his new bride quietly slipped away from the party, despite it still being in full swing. Officially it was a wake, but it had turned out to be much more of a colourful celebration of life and love – not only because that was what Ida Boulter had demanded of her children for her send-off, but also because her son Danny and his love had turned up out of the blue and announced that they had just returned from Gretna Green and were now man and wife.

There had, naturally, been much excitement, especially when they had arrived in a beautiful, brightly painted horse-drawn Romany Gypsy caravan. Marlene had thought it 'amazingly romantic' and told them so. She was over the moon that her older brother had been able to have his happy ever after with Lucy Stanton-Leigh. Something that had seemed highly improbable before the pair had eloped, for Lucy's parents would never in a million years have given permission for their daughter to marry Danny Boulter, who, despite living in one of County Durham's most splendid and certainly most unusual manor houses, with its castellated turrets and tapered towers, was still, at the end of the day, the son of a coalminer. A working-class boy from the shipbuilding town of Sunderland, he had only ended up at the manor because their elder sibling, Angie, had married the heir.

When the newly-weds left the hustle and bustle of the party, Marlene watched her brother take his bride's hand. As they made their way across the mosaic-tiled hallway to the bottom of the sweeping staircase leading up to the makeshift honeymoon suite that had been prepared earlier, Marlene thought there was something incredibly intimate about a couple holding hands. Perhaps it was the sense of unity. Of togetherness. Of strength. That whatever life threw at them, they would deal with it together. And they would *have* to be unified when Lucy's parents found out what their daughter had done. There would undoubtedly be another war on as there was so much more at stake than their daughter simply choosing to marry someone they didn't approve of.

As Marlene looked around the rest of the guests, she caught a glimpse of herself in the French gilt-framed mirror hanging on the wall opposite. She knew she looked very glamorous in her figure-hugging red dress, something her mother would have approved of as she had forbidden anything dark or dour for her wake. Marlene was just a few months shy of her seventeenth birthday, but she looked much older. *Felt* older. Had always *been* older than her age. Scanning the room, she saw Angie and her husband, Stanislaw Nowak, whom she had married two years previously. They were both glowing with joy, having announced that they were expecting their first child together.

Next to them were Angie's father-in-law from her first marriage, Lloyd Foxton-Clarke, and his wife, Cora, the former housekeeper. The two helped run the manor, which was no longer just a home to them all but also their livelihood, following its conversion into a small and exclusive country house hotel. Marlene caught Lloyd and Cora exchanging looks and smiling, communicating in that way couples did when they knew what the other was thinking.

Hearing a loud burst of laughter, Marlene glanced over to the buffet, where a gaggle of guests were chuckling. Clemmie Sinclair, adopted auntie to Marlene and her siblings, was holding court and no doubt being outrageous and quick-witted, as was her way. Next to Clemmie was her partner, Barbara. Unlike the other couples in the room, they might not be able to show their feelings for one another in public, but any fool could see the love they shared.

Surveying the rest of the room, Marlene suddenly became conscious of being on the periphery of the party. Of standing on her own. And of *being* on her own.

'Penny for your thoughts?'

Marlene clapped her manicured free hand to her chest.

'Oh, God! Thomas! You made me jump out of my skin. *And* nearly made me spill my champers!' She looked at him and thought how handsome he looked in his black suit, especially as he had a slightly dishevelled look due to his loosened tie and the open collar of his starched white shirt.

Thomas smiled at Marlene. *Forever the drama queen.* A very gorgeous drama queen.

'Are you all right? It's unlike you to be on your own at a party. I'd normally have to fight my way through the hordes to get to speak to you.'

Marlene tutted, batting away the compliment, but a half-smile played on her lips. She liked the image Thomas had painted of her as the belle of the ball.

'You looked,' Thomas continued, 'as though you were lost in a sea of your own thoughts.'

'*Lost in a sea of your own thoughts*?' Marlene said, eyeing him mischievously over the rim of her champagne glass as she took a sip. 'You're being a tad poetic today.'

'What? Can't a stablehand be poetic?' Thomas retorted, slipping into the verbal ping pong they had fallen into of late. He took a sup of the pint of beer he was holding, leaving a thin foam moustache on his upper lip. He wiped it away. 'Actually, I thought you looked a bit sad – and a little lonely . . . ' This time his tone was serious. Since Marlene had returned from her traumatic trip to London three months previously, she had changed. Not obviously so, though. The change had been subtle, and Thomas still hadn't worked out exactly what it encompassed.

'Well, I'm entitled to be sad, aren't I?' Marlene huffed a little theatrically. 'I mean, my mother *has* just been buried.'

Thomas conceded the point with a nod and another sip of his pint, although they both knew that while Marlene was sad at her mother's death, she was not distraught. If anything, she felt lucky to have been reunited with her mam before her passing – and to have bonded with her. For the first time ever, Marlene had told him, she had felt that she did actually have a mother. And, moreover, one who loved her, cared for

4

her and had tried to help her as much as she could before her time was up.

'But as for lonely,' Marlene said, 'nearly everyone here is family, or as good as family.' She lifted her glass to indicate those in the room. 'I'm about the unloneliest person you can get.'

Thomas gave her a sceptical look.

Seeing it, Marlene turned away. Thomas had always been able to see right through her, even though she prided herself on being quite the expert in masking her feelings from the outside world.

'Actually, if you must know, I was thinking about love,' she admitted, throwing Thomas a sidelong glance.

Her comment was met by a bark of laughter. 'The ice maiden has a heart after all!'

Marlene flashed Thomas a look of annoyance. He might well be able to read her like a book, but when it came to her feelings for him, he was as blind as a bat. Or perhaps he *did* know and was intentionally ignoring it. Which was far worse.

'Well, unlike some, I don't wear my heart on my sleeve for all to see,' Marlene said, making a show of looking behind Thomas. 'Oh, what a surprise!' She raised a perfectly pencilled eyebrow. 'No Mabel hot on your heels.'

Thomas deliberately ignored the bait. Marlene loved to jibe him about Mabel, one of the staff, and the fact that she was sweet on him. What really rankled him, though, was that Marlene was under the misapprehension that those feelings were reciprocated. *Surely, she knew exactly where his heart lay?*

'She told me she was having an early night,' Thomas said. 'I think she was exhausted. She was working until late last night prepping everything – and then was up at the crack of dawn getting ready for today.'

'And you know that because . . . ?' Marlene again raised an eyebrow.

'I know that *because she told me*,' Thomas said, shaking his head.

Shortly after ten o'clock that night, one mile away as the crow flies, in a bedroom on the first floor of the very stately and renowned Roeburn Hall, the mistress of the house, Elise Stanton-Leigh, ended her phone conversation and hung up.

She sat immobile for a few seconds, hand still on the receiver, her grip so tight that her knuckles had gone white.

She then lifted up the black Bakelite receiver from its cradle and smashed it down, again and again.

When she finally stopped, she raised her face to the high, ornately plastered ceiling and let loose a muted scream that caused her face to turn an unhealthy shade of crimson and her head to feel as if it was going to explode.

Jumping up from the chair by her dressing table, she stormed out of her bedroom suite. Still in her heeled shoes, she stomped along the carpeted corridor, turned right and headed down another equally long passageway before she eventually reached her husband's living quarters.

She burst into the room with such fury that the heavy oak door smacked against the wood-panelled wall.

'*Wake up, Edward!*'

She reached for the light switch.

'What the hell!' Her husband sat bolt upright, the whole room suddenly illuminated. He hadn't actually been asleep, but the violence of his wife's entrance and her shrill, nigh-on hysterical voice had still taken him by surprise.

'I don't believe it! *I just don't believe it!*' Elise had her hand clasped to her throat as though the words she was about to speak might strangle her.

Edward reached for his cigarettes and lighter, which were on his bedside table, and watched as his wife paced up and down the room, her breathing heavy. She opened her mouth to speak, but nothing came out.

'For God's sake, Elise, just spit it out. It's not like you to be at a loss for words.' Edward lit his cigarette and blew out smoke.

His wife shot him a daggered look that could have killed him several times over.

This was all his fault.

'Your daughter . . .' Elise gasped. 'Your daughter . . .' Another gasp of incredulity. 'I can't believe I'm actually saying this . . . Your—'

'*Our* daughter,' Edward interjected.

'Oh, no,' Elise hissed. 'Lucy is *your* daughter. Always has been. The perfect embodiment of a proper little Daddy's girl.' Elise took a breath. '*Your* deceitful, devious, back-stabbing daughter' – the words came out like the peppering of a machine gun – 'has not actually been in Devon these past few weeks with her so-called *friend*, preparing for her wedding to Anthony Hetherington . . . *Oh, no!*' Elise shook her head a little manically and again started pacing the room like a tiger in a cage. 'She's actually been just seventy miles away, over the border in Scotland. *In Gretna Green!*' Her voice notched up an octave.

Edward creased his brow as though not totally under-standing what his wife was trying to tell him, which he did, but he was not going to tell her that as she would demand he explain how he was already privy to such information within hours of their daughter and her new husband's return.

'She got married there?' Edward continued to feign ignorance.

'*Yes*, she got married there!' Elise would have screamed had she not wanted to keep the scandalous news under wraps. She did not want any of the staff to hear before they had to.

'*Why else does anyone go to Gretna Green?*' God, she felt like strangling Edward and getting rid of all her pent-up anger. 'She's married that bloody Boulter boy. That upstart of a street urchin from Sunderland. The son of a *coalminer*! And by all accounts, our daughter will be living with him at the Cuthford Country House Hotel – with the rest of the mon-grels there!'

'Oh dear God!' Edward tried to sound as shocked as he would be if he had just found out such catastrophic news.

Elise stopped dead in her tracks. '*God! The shame of it!* Living with a load of social pariahs. Everyone knows the boy's sister, Marlene, is illegitimate and went off to London to find her real father, only to get herself mixed up with a load of gangsters. And then topped it all by bringing back another waif and stray – her *married* mother's fancy piece! You couldn't make it up! And don't get me started on the Polish refugee who married the eldest sister when her first husband's body was barely cold.'

Edward knew this to be something of an exaggeration

as there had been nearly a three-year gap between Quentin Foxton-Clarke, the original owner of Cuthford Manor, dying and his widow remarrying. And what he'd heard others say about Marlene did not concern her illegitimacy but rather her hourglass figure and drop-dead gorgeous looks. As well as the fact that she was not beholden to anyone. And how whoever put a ring on her finger would be marrying into a family whose foray into the hotel and hospitality business had gone from strength to strength.

Edward threw his quilt aside and got out of bed. Pulling on his dressing gown, he walked over to the dressing table, where there was a decanter of Scotch. He pulled out the stopper and poured them each a drink, quickly checking himself in the mirror to make sure he had assumed a suitably shocked expression.

'How did you find out? This isn't some kind of Chinese whispers, is it?' he asked.

'If only!' Elise spat the words out. She took her drink. 'No, I heard it from a reliable source.'

'Gertrude?' Edward guessed. Gertrude Fontaine Smith was their nearest neighbour and also a good friend of his wife's.

'Yes, although the information came via her son, Jeremy. He'd apparently been over to see one of the workers there about something or other.'

'I'll bet,' Edward mumbled. Jeremy Fontaine-Smith's penchant for young, physically fit labourers was well known, though never spoken of.

'Apparently, Jeremy was just leaving,' Elise continued, 'when our daughter and her new husband turned up in a

Gypsy caravan, of all things.' She took a sip of her drink. 'As if it couldn't get any worse.'

'So, Gertrude's confirmed that they've definitely got married?' Edward asked, not that he needed the confirmation. He'd had a first-hand, blow-by-blow account just an hour earlier. His own penchant for young, working-class lovers, albeit female ones, had also given him a heads-up.

Elise nodded. 'Yes, *married*. Good and proper.'

'Well, this is disastrous. A catastrophe, no less!'

'It is!' Elise spoke her words through gritted teeth. 'By marrying that halfwit, she's sounded the death knell for this place. Our home. Our heritage. *Our everything.*'

Edward thought his wife of eighteen years was wrong in referring to Danny Boulter as being intellectually challenged. Judging by the growth in popularity of the Cuthford Manor Riding School, he had good business acumen. Elise was, however, spot on in declaring that their daughter had just signed the death certificate for Roeburn Hall. He gave a defeated sigh, which was genuine.

'She has. There's no doubting that,' he agreed solemnly. 'I don't know what I'm most shocked about – the thought of losing this place, or the fact that Lucy has done what she's done.'

'I know!' Elise blustered. 'That girl has never crossed you once! Not once! She's *always* done as you've asked.'

Edward knew his wife was right. He had always been able to steer Lucy.

Elise took another drink. Her adrenaline almost spent, she sat down in the armchair by the open fire, which was now just smouldering embers.

'What the hell are we going to do?' she said, staring into the orange glow of the dying fire. It felt symbolic. The end of a part of her life.

Edward stood, one hand on the marble mantlepiece, the other clutching his cut-crystal tumbler of Scotch. 'There is only one option.' He looked at his wife, knowing this was her worst fear. 'We'll have to sell. Our daughter's actions have left us with no other choice. Without the injection of cash from the Hetheringtons, we're done for. No marriage, no money.'

'No more Roeburn Hall,' Elise grieved. She took a sip of her drink and grimaced at the harsh burn of alcohol and the painful thought of no longer being the lady of the manor. This was certainly going to destroy her social standing. She could foresee how quickly those in her circle would go from looking up to her to peering down their noses at her. *Damn her daughter! And damn Edward for being an incorrigible gambler – not just on the horses, but with all of the unsound investments he'd made over the years.*

Husband and wife were quiet, both trying to work out what to do next.

Elise couldn't drag her eyes away from the dwindling fire. She would not end up a mere nothing. *Like hell she would.* She would rise like a phoenix from the ashes of this disastrous marriage and start again. It wasn't as though there would be much love lost. Theirs had always been a marriage of convenience, after all. Though it had worked well up until now, which was why she was so angry at Lucy. God, she'd even spelled it out to her before she'd gone off on that imaginary trip to Devon. Women, she'd told her, could have their cake and eat it. Lucy could have saved her ancestral home by marrying a self-made millionaire's son – and not a bad-looking one at that – and still kept her horse-obsessed son of a coalminer. *But no*, her daughter wouldn't listen.

Elise sat back. She'd stayed married to Edward because of Roeburn Hall – the oft-lauded 'jewel of the county'. But as soon as they had a buyer, she'd be off. She would leave Edward. She would divorce him. It would be easy enough. She would cite his adultery. It would not be hard to prove. They had an unspoken agreement to ignore each other's indiscretions. She would easily be able to find out his latest conquest. After which she would find herself another husband. A rich husband. And one who didn't have a gambling habit.

Edward finished his drink and went to pour himself a refill. He knew what was probably going through his wife's mind. Just as he knew he'd probably be able to convince her to stay until a buyer had been found. Elise had never made any bones about the fact that she had married him because of his long line of ancestors with tenuous connections to those with blue blood flowing through their veins, and, of course, because of Roeburn Hall. The Stanton-Leigh name and their ancestral home gave her the prestige she had been denied, coming from a family that had made its vast wealth through manufacturing cough sweets.

In some ways, he blamed Elise's parents for the situation in which they now found themselves. When he'd agreed to marry Elise, it had been on the understanding that money would never be a problem. There'd always be plenty in the pot when needed. But Elise's parents had gradually let their vast wealth dwindle to next to nothing after the business had been sold. And to top it all, they had died without having had the foresight to put measures into place to prevent the government from nabbing a large percentage of their daughter's already diminished inheritance.

Lucy's arranged marriage to the Hetherington boy had been their last chance saloon. Just as Elise had married Edward for his heritage and he had married her for money, so it had been for Anthony and Lucy: the Hetheringtons had wanted status, and the Stanton-Leighs a windfall that would not only replenish their coffers but save Roeburn Hall.

Now that this option was well and truly scuppered, Edward would have to think of another way out of the financial quagmire he'd found himself in.

He took a large mouthful of single malt and swallowed.

No matter what, goddammit, he'd find a way. He'd do whatever it took to save Roeburn Hall. And himself.

Chapter One

Cuthford Country House Hotel

Ten months later

August 1954

Angie looked around the dining-room table as they all started to tuck into their game pie, home-grown vegetables and mashed potatoes. Although Alberta had now taken on the role of nanny for baby Juni, she still liked to keep her oar in downstairs in the kitchen. The delicious pie and melt-in-your-mouth shortcrust pastry had all the markings of their former cook's input. And although Angie didn't want Alberta, who was now past retirement, to be doing too much, she was glad of her meddling. This past year, they'd taken on more staff, who needed the oversight and guidance of an older, more experienced person, especially as the manor's original workforce had, on the whole, taken on more responsible roles within the business.

Mabel had been one of those employees who had risen quickly through the ranks. She had gone from scullery maid to working alongside Cook, before then making the leap to work as Cora's assistant. Angie looked at Cora, who was making sure the children ate their vegetables and meat, not just the pastry. Cora, who likened her job as hotel manager to being a skipper on a ship, had not disguised her relief at gaining an assistant and could often be heard singing Mabel's praises for being very 'cool, calm and collected' and for 'knowing what needs to be done and just getting on with doing it'.

Pouring herself a glass of water from the jug, Angie saw that Marlene was deep in conversation with Lloyd and Clemmie, presumably about the plans for renovating the third-floor attic space, which had been left empty for as long as anyone could remember. Angie knew Marlene was particularly enthused as it had been her idea to turn it into a honeymoon suite to beat all others. The idea had come to her after she had helped create a make-do-and-mend suite for Danny and Lucy when they had unexpectedly turned up at Ida's wake as newly-weds. As Marlene had pointed out, it made sense since it would be a great selling point for the hotel, and it would make it more likely that betrothed couples would also want to book the hotel for their wedding breakfast and evening do. For relatively little outlay, she'd declared, it would boost profits and grow the hotel's reputation still further.

Watching Marlene talking instead of eating her dinner, Angie knew that her younger sister's excitement was also because she was an incorrigible romantic – and this gave her the opportunity to indulge that side of her character. Naturally, Marlene tried to play down her deep-seated and long-held love of romance in all its forms, whether on the silver screen or in the real world, and insisted that the attic conversion was purely a savvy business move.

'I must say,' Clemmie's voice boomed, 'the way our government is spewing out all this reprehensible marriage propaganda, the success of your honeymoon suite is a *sure thing*, as the Americans would say.' She took a quick drink of her wine. 'We women were given a brief sniff of freedom during the war, but ever since there's been a relentless campaign to push us back into the kitchen – to "baking and breeding", as Angie's friend Dorothy likes to say.' Clemmie blew out a puff of air to express her exasperation.

Angie caught Stanislaw's eye and they smiled at yet another burst of feminist outrage from Clemmie. Being the new parents of a two-month-old baby girl had them floating on a cloud, although that other-worldly feeling was also down to a serious lack of sleep.

'So,' Clemmie's voice again rose above the general chatter, 'what goings-on have I missed today while I have been working myself to the bone, nose to the grindstone, *trying* to educate a load of eighteen-year-olds who seem more intent on filling their heads with what's the latest fashion, or debating who is the most swoon-worthy Hollywood heartthrob.'

Marlene chuckled, thinking of Thomas, who had recently started to style his hair in a quiff. She'd ribbed him about it no end, even though she really thought he looked rather gorgeous. Very Montgomery Clift.

'Dare I ask about Roeburn Hall?' Clemmie looked across at Lucy. 'I saw that it was still in the window of Durham Estates when I was in town today.'

'But I thought you had your "nose to the grindstone"?' Marlene quipped.

'When you work at the coalface of education, you need

your sustenance, and the estate agent just so happens to be next door to the most amazing new bakery.'

Clemmie turned her attention back to Lucy.

'I rode past today,' Lucy said, shaking her head. She sat back, giving up on eating. 'And the sign's still up. I don't know if I'm glad they haven't sold or not.'

'Because,' Clemmie surmised, 'if and when it sells, you'll feel as guilty as sin, since you perceive yourself to be the cause? Wrongly, of course.'

Lucy took a sip of water and nodded. 'But if it doesn't sell, what will happen then? Will Mother and Father be reduced to living like paupers, eating husks of bread and drinking water, having sold everything just to keep a roof over their heads?'

Angie tutted, trying not to show her irritation at her brother's young wife. 'Honestly, Lucy, I'm pretty sure it will never come to that. What an imagination! I think you've been spending too much time with Marlene.' This was true. Since Marlene's best friend Belinda had moved away, the two had become more like sisters than mere sisters-in-law, despite their differing natures.

Lloyd shook his head. He still couldn't believe that Lucy had been expected to marry someone for money so her parents could keep their ancestral home. And, moreover, that they had disowned her for doing the unthinkable – marrying someone she loved.

'How long has it been on the market now?' Stanislaw asked. Since becoming manager of the estate, he had learnt why people were reluctant to buy stately homes with expansive grounds. The upkeep was very costly. And they provided little to no income.

'Eight months – they put it on the market at the beginning of the year,' Danny answered. He knew Lucy had never had a moment's regret about marrying him. They couldn't be happier as a couple, running the newly named Cuthford Manor Equestrian Centre together, but when it came to Roeburn Hall and her parents' predicament, there was no dispersing the dark cloud of guilt that continued to loom over her.

Clemmie squinted at Lucy across the table. 'You're looking a bit peaky. You must not let this get you down. I think what you need is a little glass of Carl's amazing home-made fortified wine.' She looked at Carl. 'Honestly, I don't know why you don't sell it. It really is quite something.'

Carl smiled to show he appreciated the compliment. Since he had arrived at the manor a year ago, when he had brought Marlene back from her ill-fated trip to London, he'd started working in the grounds to pay for his keep. Despite never even mowing a lawn before, he'd discovered that he was a natural gardener and could grow just about anything he planted.

'This will put some colour in your cheeks,' Clemmie said, reaching for the bottle in the middle of the table.

Lucy shook her head. 'No, honestly, I'm fine.'

Knowing that Clemmie would pour her a glass anyway, Danny put his hand over the unused wine glass by his wife's place mat.

Clemmie looked questioningly at Lucy and then at Danny.

'It *is* rather tasty,' Clemmie said, topping up her own glass.

'Oh, it's not that I don't like Carl's wine.' Lucy looked apologetically at the man, who, they all knew, was still quietly grieving Ida's death. 'It's just that wine's been making me feel very nauseous lately.'

Everyone turned their attention to Lucy.

'You're not?' Marlene gasped, her face alight with excitement and expectation.

Lucy broke into a wide smile on seeing Marlene's reaction.

'Yes, I am,' she said, a flush spreading across her pale face. She turned to Danny, whose eyes were sparkling.

There was a short, stunned pause before everyone started bombarding the couple with questions.

Once the younger ones had realised why the adults were getting so excited, they too started firing questions. Jemima, twelve, and Bonnie, eight, were excited as they loved playing with baby Juni, who Jemima had declared was their 'real-life doll.' Bertie, on the other hand, now thirteen, remained nonchalant, saying he would only get excited if it was a boy.

Angie forced out the expected congratulations, again holding back her opinion that she thought this was far too early to start a family. Lucy had only just turned eighteen and Danny nineteen.

'Congratulations!' Stanislaw reached over the table to shake Danny's hand. He knew well how his wife's younger brother would be feeling, having only recently experienced the joy of becoming a father for the first time himself.

'Well, I think we need to celebrate with a bottle of champagne from the cellar?' Marlene suggested. She looked at Lucy. 'You can have the tiniest of sips just to mark the occasion.'

'Hear! Hear!' Clemmie agreed. 'One must always toast the miracle of a new life-to-be.'

'Good idea!' Lloyd agreed, getting up and pulling the long corded servants' bell. 'I'll get one of the staff to fetch us a bottle of Bollinger. We had a case delivered the other day.'

By the time Lloyd had sat back down, the new maid, Shirley, was bustling into the room. She had only recently been taken on and was out of breath, having rushed to the dining room from the kitchen, wanting to impress her new employers with her speed.

After Lloyd told her what was needed, where exactly in the cellar to locate the champagne and that perhaps she should bring an extra bottle 'just in case', Shirley turned to leave. But as she did so, she walked straight into Mabel.

'Sorry, sorry . . . ' Shirley was still apologising as she scuttled from the room.

As Mabel walked in, Marlene felt her skin prickle, which had become normal whenever Mabel was about, especially lately. And especially since she had taken to wearing dresses very like those Marlene wore.

'What is it, Mabel?' Cora asked.

'I'm so sorry to interrupt like this,' Mabel said, 'but I've just taken a phone call.' Her eyes found Lucy, who was leaning into Danny as he put his arm around her and pulled her close. Despite what she was about to impart, she thought the pair annoyingly lovesick. 'A phone call from the hospital. Dryburn Hospital. They asked me to tell you, Mrs Boulter –' she kept her eyes on Lucy '– that your mother has had an accident. A bad accident. They've suggested you get there as soon as possible.'

'Oh God!' Lucy broke away from the comfort of her husband's embrace.

'Did they say anything else?' Danny asked. 'About what happened?'

Mabel shook her head. 'Only that it was serious. And that Mrs Boulter should get there as quick as she could.'

'I'll drive you!' Marlene said, standing up and putting her napkin down by the side of her plate.

Lucy looked from her sister-in-law to her husband.

'You don't mind if Marlene takes me, do you?'

She didn't have to say why; Danny understood. There was undisguised ill-feeling between him and his in-laws. His presence would not be appreciated.

He shook his head.

'Of course not.'

Chapter Two

Marlene and Lucy were quiet as they drove to the hospital. Marlene was concentrating as it was now pitch-black – a deep, penetrating inky darkness. The kind only found in rural parts. The absence of any kind of lighting, even in the small mining villages dotted along the route to the city, was exacerbated by the night's waning moon, which barely afforded even a modicum of light. But it wasn't just the darkness that had Marlene watching her speed and being extra vigilant for any foxes or other nocturnal animals caught in the glare of the headlights, it was her precious cargo – her pregnant passenger.

Even though time was of the essence, Marlene kept her speed down as she negotiated the five miles of winding country roads; it was only when her mind drifted to Mabel that she found herself automatically pressing a little too heavily on the accelerator. It irked her no end that Mabel was quite the golden girl since becoming Cora's right-hand woman. Marlene loved Cora dearly, but she felt annoyed at her for not seeing through Mabel's 'sugar and spice and all things nice' veneer. Or perhaps all Cora was really bothered about was Mabel's ability to do her job. Marlene had to admit, begrudgingly, that Mabel was indeed very good. And incredibly efficient. Like this evening, when, as soon as Marlene had said she was taking Lucy to the hospital, Mabel had swung into action, instructing Jake, the chauffeur, to fetch the car and telling him to make sure it had enough petrol and was warmed up, ready to go. Then, in the blink of an eye, she had got their coats and had given them to Wilfred, their elderly butler-cum-concierge, before heading off to the office, telling them she would ring the hospital to inform them that they were on their way.

Marlene slowed down on approaching a T-junction and indicated, although she didn't have to since there was not another car on the road. As she turned right and went through the gears, Marlene had to admit that Mabel would not have vexed her so much had she not – loath though she was to admit it – viewed her as her rival in love. In her love for Thomas. Seeing the distant city lights as they drove over a slight hilly incline, Marlene was glad that she had never told anyone – bar Lucy – how she felt about Mabel.

Pulling her concentration back to the here and now, Marlene looked at Lucy. Her face looked even more ghostly white when contrasted with the surrounding darkness.

'Are you okay?' she asked, taking one hand briefly off the wheel and squeezing Lucy's, which were knotted together as though in prayer.

'No, not at all okay,' Lucy answered, letting out a garbled half-laugh, half-cry. 'I just wish I knew more – what happened, what *kind of* accident, how bad Mother is.' She let out a choked sob. 'God, I feel so guilty. The number of times I've wished her dead for what she did that day.'

'What *they* both did that day,' Marlene added. For it had been Lucy's father as much as her mother who had dragged her sister-in-law into an emotional pit so deep it had taken a long time for her to claw herself out of it.

'Yes, both of them,' Lucy murmured as she stared at the road ahead, which was only just visible in the car's bobbing headlights. The day she had gone to see her parents after she'd returned from Gretna Green had been the most upsetting one of her entire life. She'd left it a week before she had ridden over there on her horse, Dahlia. She hadn't wanted Danny to go with her in case it inflamed the situation. In hindsight, she wished he had been by her side, for she had never seen her mother or father so fury-filled or so hateful towards her – so devoid of love for their only child. It had been shocking to hear the venom spewing from her mother's mouth, but even more to see and hear her father viciously berating her for what she had done. She had never thought the man she adored could be so angry, or so cold and unfeeling.

She had realised this past year that in many ways she did not really know her parents. They had packed her off to boarding school as soon as they were able to, when she was five, and it was only when she was fourteen and had pleaded and begged for them to let her go to a day school in Durham that she had started to find out what they were really like. Her mother, she'd soon learnt, did not have a single maternal bone in her body. Her father, on the other hand, was always kind and loving towards her, which had been some solace – until the day she had gone to Roeburn Hall a newly married woman. It was then she realised that she really did not know him. He'd been like a different person. She would never forget the hardness in his voice when he told her that she was never to step over the threshold of their home ever again.

It had been his disappointment in her that had hurt the most, although, as Marlene had told her many times, it should be *Lucy* who felt disappointment in *her father* for not wanting her to be happy and marry the man she really loved.

Danny had been apoplectic when she returned home and told him, in between uncontrollable sobbing, how heinous her father had been towards her, and how it had been like seeing a different person. He'd said something that had struck a chord: 'It's because you've never stood up to him before.' Lucy had thought about those words many times since and realised Danny was right. She had never had reason to argue with her father before.

As they drove into Durham, Lucy was pulled out of her reverie by the towering outline of the city's historical castle and Romanesque cathedral, but then plunged back into the quagmire of fear and dread that her mother might die. Might already be dead.

Thankfully, there was little traffic on the road as they made their way from the east of the city, across Framwellgate Bridge, over the wide stretch of the winding River Wear, then onto North Road, where the former Dryburn Hall, now Dryburn Hospital, stood.

As soon as Marlene had driven through the stone-pillared entrance and parked, Lucy was out and hurrying up the steps to the entrance. Marlene quickly caught up and they strode through the main doors together. As they did so, the receptionist waved them over.

'Mrs Boulter?'

Lucy nodded.

'Your mother is in the Critical Care Unit,' she said, her

voice grave. 'Go straight down this corridor and turn right and you'll see it signposted.'

Lucy and Marlene rushed down the corridor, the tapping of their shoes on the shiny vinyl flooring the only sound. It was late and the hospital was quiet.

Turning right as instructed, they immediately spotted Edward Stanton-Leigh.

He was pacing the short breadth of the corridor, brushing his thick dark brown hair away from his face.

Sensing movement, he turned.

On seeing his daughter, he flung open his arms and strode towards her.

'Oh, my darling LuLu!' he said. He was tall and his long legs needed to take only a few strides before he reached his daughter.

Marlene watched as Edward Stanton-Leigh folded his daughter in an embrace.

'I am so sorry, my darling girl,' he said, kissing her forehead before freeing her from his hold, 'but it does not look good for your dear mama.'

Marlene watched as the reality of what Edward was telling his daughter hit home.

'She's going to die?' Lucy's voice was shaky. Tears had started to fill her pretty blue eyes, and her lips began to tremble. Her father wrapped her in his arms once again and Marlene could see that her friend was sobbing from the shuddering of her body.

Standing only a few feet away in the shadow of the corridor where a light was out, Marlene felt like an onlooker. Not part of the scene. And with that came a short, sharp shock of envy. Lucy might well have been ostracised by her parents, but it was clear that she and her father shared a strong bond. And in this time of need, everything that had gone before had been swept aside. Forgotten.

Marlene allowed herself a moment of sadness that she had never experienced a father's love. The man who had brought her up had never shown her or any of her siblings an ounce of love or affection – or even much attention. And the man who had fathered her, the man who had charmed her mam into his bed and then left her high and dry, was a feckless man. Not a bad man, but one who had no interest in being a parent.

Guilt pushed back Marlene's covetousness as she reminded herself why they were there. How could she feel jealous of Lucy's relationship with her father when her mother's life hung in the balance? Marlene might like to have a father who loved and cared for her, but she would not want to be in Lucy's shoes if her mother died. Lucy, she knew, would be distraught, not just because she had lost her mother but because they had not had the chance to make up their differences, as Marlene had been able to do with her own mother.

'Ah, Miss Boulter, I didn't see you there.' Edward released his daughter and stretched out his hand to Marlene. 'What awful circumstances in which to make your acquaintance.'

Marlene stepped forward and shook his hand, which felt soft and uncalloused.

'Indeed, it is awful,' Marlene replied. 'Although we don't really know what has happened. All the hospital said over the phone was that Lucy's mother had had an accident.' She paused. 'And to get here quickly.' Marlene's tone was clipped and cold. Lucy had been inconsolable for days on end after her mother and father had disowned her. She might have momentarily forgotten this, as all she could think about was whether her mother would live or die, but Marlene hadn't.

Edward looked at Marlene. She was sure she saw a flicker of amusement in his eyes at her chilly tone before his expression turned deathly sombre.

'I'll explain as we walk. The unit's just a bit further along this corridor. I have a feeling there really is no time to waste.'

Edward did not go into detail about the accident, other than to say he'd come back to Roeburn Hall early in the evening to find his wife lying in a pool of blood at the bottom of the stone stairs to the cellar.

'It actually took a little while to find her as I presumed she was out,' Edward relayed.

'But what was Mother doing going down into the cellar?' Lucy asked. 'She never goes down there.'

Edward stopped as they reached the main doors to the ward. He took a deep breath and cupped his daughter's hand in his own.

'She has been doing so since we had to let most of the staff go, my darling girl.'

Lucy looked horrified and guilt-ridden.

'Oh my God.' She withdrew her hand from her father's and put it to her mouth. 'This is all my fault.'

Edward gave his daughter and then Marlene an apologetic look, showing his reticence over having to tell the truth about the circumstances surrounding his wife's potentially fatal accident.

'LuLu, don't blame yourself,' Edward pleaded. 'Your mother had been drinking.'

Lucy widened her bloodshot eyes.

'Drinking?'

Edward nodded. 'A lot. It was why she was going to the cellar. This isn't anyone's fault.'

'But of course it is, Father! If it wasn't for me, Mother wouldn't have taken to drink and wouldn't have been going into the cellar.'

Any more self-recriminations were brought to a halt when the nurse, having spotted them through the portholes of the swing doors, came out to see them.

'One visitor at a time. And family only,' she said.

Edward nodded to Lucy, who took a shuddering breath and allowed the nurse to take her through the ward doors.

'Is there any chance she might pull through?' Marlene asked Edward as she looked through the small window into the unit and watched as the nurse took Lucy over to where her mother was lying in a bed, surrounded by tubes, a drip and a small monitor.

Lucy sat down at her mother's bedside, nervously taking her hand. There was no movement from Mrs Stanton-Leigh. She remained inert, cocooned in starched white sheets, her head in a bandage, eyes closed.

Marlene brought her attention back to her friend's father and saw that his eyes were red and puffy, and suddenly she was the one who felt guilty for being so hard and uncompassionate towards him.

'It's unlikely she'll pull through,' Edward said again, pushing his hair away from his face. As he did so, Marlene was suddenly struck by how young he looked, then remembered Lucy telling her that he had only been eighteen when she was born. The same age Lucy would be when she had her baby.

'The doctor said that Elise fractured her skull during the fall and they believe she has a bleed on the brain,' Edward explained.

'And there's absolutely nothing they can do?' Marlene asked.

He shook his head. 'Nothing. It's just a case of wait and see. There is a remote possibility that Elise might regain consciousness, but my understanding is that my wife does not have long to live.'

Lucy remained by her mother's bedside for a short while before being ushered out by the ward nurse, after which Edward was given time to be with his wife.

'Oh, Marlene, it was ghastly.' Lucy sank down onto the chair next to her sister-in-law. 'It didn't feel like the person lying in that bed was my mother. She looked so different, so pale, so old and fragile, which is ridiculous as Mother isn't old, she's only thirty-seven.' She choked back tears. 'She looked so vulnerable, and that's not something I'd ever have thought I'd say about Mother.'

Marlene took her hand. 'Were you able to say anything to her?'

Lucy let out a garbled sound. 'Oh, God, I didn't know what to do other than hold her hand, and then I just started telling her how sorry I was – and that this was all my fault.'

Marlene tutted and shook her head.

'Then I started justifying what I'd done. Telling her that I wasn't like her, I couldn't have married Anthony. I couldn't *have my cake and eat it*, as she told me I could.'

Marlene's eyes widened. This was something Lucy hadn't told her.

'It would have made me sick,' Lucy carried on, 'and Danny would never have even talked to me again if I had forsaken him and married Anthony, never mind agreed to carry on an affair.' Lucy stopped, took in a deep breath and exhaled. 'And then I just started crying and told her that I loved her. Which was when the nurse came over and coaxed me away.'

Marlene gave her friend a cuddle as she cried yet more tears.

'The truly terrible thing,' Lucy said, drawing breath in between her tears, 'is that I didn't feel it in my heart.'

'You didn't feel what?' Marlene asked.

'*Love*. I said I loved her, but I didn't feel it. How unnatural am I? Not feeling love towards my own mother.'

Marlene was just about to reassure her, tell her she was not *unnatural*, that she'd never been close to her own mother, when Edward re-entered the room.

'God, that was hard,' he said as he went to sit next to his daughter.

'I'll go and ring Cuthford Manor and give them an update, now you're here,' Marlene said, getting up. She had not wanted to leave Lucy on her own. 'They'll be worried.' She cast a look at Edward. 'About Lucy.' The words she didn't speak conveyed what Marlene wanted to say. *Unlike you and your wife these past ten months.*

Marlene had just opened the door to go and make the call when they heard a commotion down the corridor.

Chapter Three

Elise Stanton-Leigh started to regain consciousness, causing the monitor on the table by her bed to start bleeping.

Nurse Jones quickly left her station and hurried over to the partially curtained-off bay, her rubber-soled shoes creaking on the linoleum floor.

'Mrs Stanton-Leigh, can you hear me?' Nurse Jones asked, trying to keep her voice steady and calm as her eyes flicked from the dial on the monitor to her patient, who was now moving her arms and trying to speak.

The nurse pulled out a pen torch from her breast pocket, gently holding her patient's head still before pulling open one eyelid and then the other and shining a light into them.

Both times, her patient's head moved slightly, as though trying to avoid the bright ray of light. All the while, she was mumbling incoherently.

Placing the palm of her hand on her patient's forehead, she realised there was no need for a thermometer. The heat coming off her brow told her that her patient's body temperature was dangerously high.

Suddenly Nurse Jones felt her patient's hand grab hold of her wrist, making her jump.

'Mrs Stanton-Leigh, can you hear me?' she asked, the tremor of anxiety in her voice audible.

With her free hand, Nurse Jones checked her patient's neck to feel her pulse.

It was rapid.

Too rapid.

Her patient's mouth moved, but all she could hear was a low mumble.

'Mrs Stanton-Leigh, I didn't hear – try and say it again.'

The nurse moved her head nearer, her eyes once more going to the monitor on the bedside table.

Panic set in on seeing that her patient's blood pressure was dropping quickly.

Too quickly.

She tried to move to call for a doctor, but Mrs Stanton-Leigh had a vice-like grip on her arm.

'This . . . is . . . *his* . . . fault.' Elise finally managed to get the words out.

'Who? Whose fault?' the nurse asked, torn between calling for help and listening to her patient.

'Edward . . . ' Elise swallowed hard. 'This . . . is *Edward's* doing.'

Suddenly the nurse felt her patient's grip loosen, then the alarm on the monitor sounded out and all hell broke loose.

The nurse started chest compressions just as the doctor rushed into the ward.

Nudging Nurse Jones aside, the doctor continued the attempts to resuscitate.

And kept trying.

But it was no good.

Life had left Mrs Stanton-Leigh.

She had spoken her last words.

Chapter Four

On hearing the news from the duty doctor, Lucy was inconsolable and cried gut-wrenching tears into her father's chest as he held her tightly in his arms.

Marlene sat quietly, again the onlooker and glad of it. She knew her sister-in-law well and guessed that her grief would also be heavily laced with guilt. Marlene had watched her own mother die but had been untethered from the burden of guilt, which so often seemed to go hand in hand with death, because her mother had made amends. How different was Lucy's situation. Her mother had died suddenly, with no time for any kind of reconciliation. Seeing her now, Marlene knew that Lucy would not have this salve while dealing with her mother's demise. The last words Lucy and her mother had spoken to one another had been ones of hate, not love. Lucy, she knew, would suffer because of her mother's wrongdoing.

Something told her, though, that Lucy's father would not be one to flagellate himself with any kind of self-recriminations or guilt. From Marlene's understanding of the Stanton-Leighs' marriage, it had not been based on love, but rather was one of mutual benefit. Still, it was the loss of a life – the life of a woman who had been his wife, the mother of his daughter, someone he had lived with for almost two decades.

Marlene wondered what Edward must be thinking and feeling. Unusually for her, she was not able to read his expression as he held his distraught daughter in his arms. Was it indifference she saw in him or was he trying to be stoic for his daughter's sake? Or was it relief?

After a little while, Marlene stood up, straightened her skirt and manoeuvred herself around the small coffee table. She bent forward and squeezed Lucy's hand.

'I'm so sorry, Lucy,' she said, looking at Edward to show that her sentiments were also directed at him. 'I'm going to get us some tea. I won't be long.'

Edward mouthed 'Thank you' as Lucy let loose another burst of tears.

Gently shutting the waiting-room door behind her, Marlene turned to find herself face-to-face with Elise's allocated nurse, Miss Emma Jones.

'I heard you mention tea,' Nurse Jones said with a sad smile. 'Let me take you to the staffroom. I'm guessing you'll also need to make some calls?'

'Yes, yes, please,' Marlene said.

Stepping into the small room, Marlene was hit by the smell of stale smoke and old polished wood. It had a homey feel, with a few chairs around a small table with an ashtray in the middle. She knew the hospital had once been a stately home, but if she hadn't known, she would have guessed.

After ringing Cuthford Manor from the grey phone on the wall and informing Lloyd of Mrs Stanton-Leigh's death, Marlene hung up.

'Sit down and have a quick cuppa before you go back in there,' Nurse Jones said.

Marlene was surprised to see there was a tea tray now on the oval-shaped table.

'There's no one from the deceased family you need to inform?' she asked as she poured out two cups and added a splash of milk. 'Sugar?'

Marlene shook her head and smiled her thanks as Nurse Jones handed her the cup of tea.

'I don't believe so,' Marlene said. 'I don't think Lucy's mother had any other living relatives. Her mother and father passed away a few years ago. And they only had the one child, so there's no brothers or sisters.'

Nurse Jones, who Marlene guessed to be in her early thirties, added sugar to her own cup and stirred.

'And how do you think Mr Stanton-Leigh is taking his wife's death? Silly question, really,' she said, shaking her head and taking a sip of her tea. 'It must be such an appalling shock?'

'I'd guess so,' Marlene said. 'Although, to be honest, I don't really know Lucy's father. You see, my sister-in-law became estranged from her parents some time ago.'

'Oh?' Nurse Jones said, surprised.

'I don't think they were very happy about her marrying my brother.'

'Ahh,' she said, nodding her understanding.

They both drank their tea.

'Well,' Nurse Jones said, 'death can also heal rifts, so hopefully that will be the case for your sister-in-law.'

Marlene nodded but didn't say anything.

Why did she feel that healing rifts might not necessarily be a precursor to happier times?

*

Ten minutes later, when Marlene took a tea tray into the relatives' room, she was relieved to see that Lucy had stopped crying and was wiping her tears away with a large starched white handkerchief embroidered with the initials *E.S.L.*

They both looked up when Marlene entered.

'I was just telling Lucy what her mother said only the other day,' Edward related, looking at Lucy and then up at Marlene.

'Oh, yes?' She put the tray down on the little wooden coffee table.

'Mum was going to come and see me,' Lucy said, her voice raspy with all the tears she had spent. 'To apologise for being so horrible that day.'

'As was I,' Edward chipped in.

Marlene looked at Edward. Her instinct told her he was lying, but looking down at Lucy's face, so relieved and devoid of the expected guilt, Marlene thought that if it was a lie, it was a lie told out of kindness. A lie he knew would bring some comfort to his daughter.

'And,' Edward added, 'I was just telling Lucy that the doctors didn't pussyfoot around the fact that if Elise – God rest her soul – had regained consciousness, she would undoubtedly have been severely brain-damaged.'

Marlene nodded. So that explained the relief she had seen on his face.

God, sometimes she had such a low opinion of people – a lack of trust that had become worse since her trip to the capital.

Chapter Five

At Cuthford Manor, having received the news that Lucy's mother had died, Angie, Cora, Lloyd and Danny congregated in the large flagstone-floored kitchen-cum-scullery for a cup of tea or a glass of brandy, or a mixture of both. The black-leaded range had been in use all day, so the air was warm and there was still the lingering smell of the freshly baked bread and breakfast buns that had just come out of the oven and were cooling on the side, ready for the morning.

All were in agreement that Mrs Stanton-Leigh's death was terribly tragic and incredibly sad, but their concerns were primarily for Lucy and how she would cope with her estranged mother's sudden death.

'Only time will tell,' Cora said, holding a bulbous brandy glass into which a good measure of cognac had been poured. 'But I do know that she will be all right because she has us, and we'll make sure she is.'

'Without a doubt,' Lloyd agreed. He thought the world of Lucy and had naturally felt paternal towards her in light of her father's abominable behaviour. Lloyd could not imagine how a father could even consider marrying his own daughter off for money. And then disown the poor girl when she refused.

'As long as her father doesn't try and worm his way back into Lucy's life,' Danny said, finishing his tea.

'Especially,' Angie added, getting up to prepare a bottle for baby Juni, 'as he hasn't any other family, from what I can gather – or any he's close to.'

'Well, he can try all he wants . . . ' Danny murmured, the look on his face taking away the need for any more words. He stood up to leave. 'I'll be back in a while. I want to see how Stanislaw and Thomas got on with fixing that damn fence.'

He'd just shut the back door when Mabel bustled into the kitchen.

'Everything's in order for tomorrow,' she told Cora. 'The first guests are due to arrive at midday, which will give the maids enough time to turn the Primrose Suite around after the Campbells check out at nine thirty. Jake's due to take them to the station for the ten-thirty train, so they won't be dilly-dallying.'

Cora nodded, thankful that Mabel had taken charge.

'Do you want me to take that up to Alberta?' Mabel asked, seeing Angie shake the bottle of formula and knowing that if she was not with her baby girl, then 'Nanny Cook' would be.

'No, I'm going up now, but I'll be down again when Lucy and Marlene arrive back,' Angie informed them, taking a final sip of her tea and chucking the dregs into the ceramic sink.

Cora and Lloyd, brandy glasses in hand, followed suit, leaving Mabel in the kitchen with Winston and Bessie, the two elderly Bullmastiffs, who were snoring contentedly in their baskets.

Chapter Six

'Right, my dear girl, you look like a veritable ghost. It's time for you to get yourself home, pronto. I'll sort everything out from now on.' Edward paused as they stepped outside. 'Funeral arrangements and the like.'

Marlene looked at Lucy's father. *Damn right he would.* He and Elise had united against their daughter, so there was no way Lucy should have to do a thing. Although she did wonder how he was going to afford to pay for it. If he and his wife had needed their daughter to marry for money a year ago, she'd be surprised if they weren't now even more deeply in hock. Unless they still had some family heirlooms stashed away.

'Are you going back to Roeburn Hall?' Lucy asked.

'Oh no,' Edward said, shaking his head. 'I couldn't go back there this evening. God, no. I just couldn't cope with . . . well, I couldn't deal with the aftermath.'

He didn't need to say more – the vision of a short flight of stone steps and a pool of congealed blood at the bottom had already appeared in both women's minds.

Edward looked around the car park.

'Besides, I came with Elise in the ambulance, so I don't have any transport. Which really is the least of my worries.' He took a long inhalation of air. 'I still can't quite believe she's gone.'

'So, where are you going, Father?' Lucy asked.

'My dear, do not worry yourself about me. I shall check into the County for the night – and get a taxi back home in the morning.'

Lucy turned away from her father and tugged at Marlene's arm.

'Oh, Marlene, I can't leave him like this,' she said. 'I really don't think my conscience would let me.'

Marlene glanced at Edward. 'Mmm, don't forget that he let you leave Roeburn Hall that day in the most dreadful state.'

'Yes, but I had Danny to come home to – and all you lot. Father's got no one now.'

'I suppose so,' Marlene acquiesced. Lucy did have a point.

'Do you think it would be all right for Father to come and spend the night at the manor? I just can't bear to think of him alone in some ghastly hotel – probably drowning his sorrows in a bottle of Scotch.'

Marlene looked at the time. It had just gone eleven o'clock. She glanced back at Lucy; her eyes were pleading. There was no way she could deny her request.

'Okay, tell him while I go and get the car,' she said.

As she walked away, the words of the nurse came back to her about death healing familial rifts. Marlene worried the opposite might well be the case for Lucy and that her mother's demise would instead cause new and greater divisions amongst those she now considered family. Taking Edward back to Cuthford Manor was undoubtedly going to put the cat among the pigeons. Marlene's own reticence about taking Edward in – even if it was just for the one night – was nothing compared to how she knew the rest of those at the manor would feel.

Danny and Angie in particular.

Chapter Seven

After Mrs Stanton-Leigh's body had been taken down to the morgue, Nurse Jones went back to her office next to the Critical Care Unit. She had already completed the handover to the night nurse and was looking forward to getting home, but something was holding her back.

She looked at the phone on her neatly organised desk. Should she call the local constabulary and tell them about Mrs Stanton-Leigh's final words?

This is his fault . . . This is Edward's doing.

The words kept revolving around her head.

Nurse Jones stood up.

She was tired. It had been a long shift. She was reading too much into it.

If the husband with the double-barrelled name had tried to kill his wife, wouldn't she have said something along the lines of '*He tried to kill me*'? Or '*My husband pushed me*'?

Nurse Jones chewed her lip, then picked up her handbag and coat.

Her friends were always saying she had a rampant imagination and that she read too many trashy whodunnits.

She'd sleep on it.

See what she thought in the morning with a fresh head.

Chapter Eight

When the car pulled up outside Cuthford Manor, it was late, but there were still lights on downstairs. It went without saying that Danny would be up, waiting for Lucy's return, but Marlene guessed that Angie and Cora would also have stayed up, wanting to check she was all right, or as all right as could be, considering the circumstances. Marlene just wished she'd had time to ring and forewarn them that they would be returning with Edward in tow.

'Looks like someone's stayed up,' Marlene mumbled as she pulled on the handbrake and turned off the ignition. She was glad to be back, as Lucy had insisted her father sit in the front passenger seat, which had made her feel uncomfortable. He'd felt too close. He was quite a tall man and he seemed to take up more than his fair share of the car. Marlene had told herself not to be so sensitive. She was also aware that the attack she'd been subjected to when she'd gone to London to find her biological father was still affecting her. Her mam had told her that the feeling would pass, but it would take time. Marlene had thought that time might have been and gone; obviously not.

'Goodness, I had forgotten how magnificent this place is,' Edward declared as he pulled his tall but lithe frame out of the confines of the Ford Anglia, his eyes on the wonderful Gothic-styled manor with its castellated design.

'*A manor with aspirations of being a castle.*' Marlene quoted the description her sister's first husband, Quentin Foxton-Clarke, had used of their incredible home.

Seeing the main door open and Danny appear, Marlene watched as Lucy ran to him. He held her tight as she buried her head into the crook of his neck and cried.

Looking over his wife's shoulder, Danny stared across at his father-in-law. It was very evident that his presence was not expected – or welcomed.

Marlene saw Edward raise a hand to wave to the son-in-law he had never been properly introduced to, but his attempt at conviviality was met by a look that was the complete opposite.

Suddenly Winston and Bessie came charging down the front steps and made a beeline for Marlene and Edward, their tails wagging frantically. Their slightly staggering gait told Marlene they had just woken up.

'At least someone's glad to see me,' Edward muttered as he made a fuss of the dogs.

'You can't blame anyone,' Marlene said, her voice taut. She wanted to say more but didn't. His wife had just died, after all. This was not the time to have a go at him about the trauma and upset he and his wife had put Lucy through.

As Marlene and Edward made their way towards the manor's entrance, a dog on either side of them, Danny threw his father-in-law one last scathing look before ushering Lucy into the house.

Walking into the main hallway, Edward and Marlene were greeted by Angie and Cora. Their reaction on seeing Edward was only slightly less shocked as Danny had given them a few moments to take on board the arrival of their impromptu guest. Their faces were grave, not only because this man now standing in front of them had just become a widower, but because, like Danny, their opinion of him was so low as to be irretrievable.

Angie held out her hand. 'We're all very sorry for your loss.'

Cora stepped forward and shook his hand. 'Mrs Foxton-Clarke, but you can call me Cora.'

Marlene watched as Edward clasped Cora's hand with both of his to show his deep gratitude. His eyes, she thought, appeared anguished and grief-stricken. This was the saddest she had seen him since he'd been told his wife had died. Perhaps, she thought, because he no longer had to keep a stiff upper lip for his daughter.

'Thank you.' He looked at Angie and then at Cora. 'Thank you for your words and for taking me in for the night. I really was unsure, but Lucy insisted.'

He looked to Marlene, who nodded, confirming that this was the case.

'It's late.' Cora stepped forward. 'Follow me and I'll show you to the guest room. I'll get one of the staff to bring you some sandwiches and tea and a drop of whisky.'

'And Lucy? Will she be all right?' Edward asked, concerned.

'She'll be okay. Danny will have taken her back to the cottage,' Angie said, trying to add some warmth to her tone and failing.

'They live in a cottage in the grounds,' Cora explained.

'Will you tell Lucy that I am here if she needs me?' The question was directed at Marlene. 'I know we've had our differences in the past, but I do love her. Dearly. This is going to devastate her.'

'I will,' Marlene agreed, suddenly feeling exhausted. 'And I agree. It will. This *will* devastate her.'

She wasn't going to say any more but couldn't help herself.

'Especially on top of what she's already had to deal with.'

Chapter Nine

Making herself a cup of tea and adding a good splash of brandy to it, Mabel slumped down in the chair by the kitchen table. A few minutes later, though, when the back door creaked open and Thomas came in, she immediately perked up.

'Oh, Thomas. Am I glad to see you. What a shock, eh?'

'It is that,' he said, walking to the sink and pouring himself a glass of water. 'Scary that life can be snapped away from yer in the blink of an eye.'

'I know . . . ' Mabel took a sip of her brandy-laced tea.

'Yer look as white as a sheet,' Thomas said, leaning back against the sink unit and taking another glug of water.

'It was awful.' Mabel put a hand to her cheek as though trying to bring back some colour. 'Awful taking the phone call. I just knew by the way they said what they said that Mrs Stanton-Leigh wasn't going to make it.'

'It was a good job you were here. Shirley was in a right ol' flap looking for you, not long before the call came through.'

'Ah, I know. I'd had to nip out on a quick errand,' Mabel said, glad that Thomas was not one for asking questions as there was no way she could tell the truth about where she had really been.

'You okay, Mab?' Thomas asked. 'You seem to be taking

this really badly. It's a tragedy, but none of us really knew Mrs Stanton-Leigh, did we?'

'No, I know.' Mabel was quiet for a moment. 'I think it's because it brings back how *my* mam died,' she said.

Thomas knew that Mabel's mother had passed quite some time ago, and that her father had since remarried, but nothing more. 'How did she die?'

'Not quite the same as Mrs Stanton-Leigh. We certainly didn't have a cellar full of wine to fall into . . . No, Mam died in an accident at the factory. She was working on the line shafts making leather belts . . . She got caught in the machinery . . . I was told she died before she got to the hospital.'

'God,' Thomas said, recoiling at the thought of such a mutilating death. 'I'm so sorry, Mabel.' He stepped towards her and patted her hand.

Mabel felt her heart soar and the colour rush back into her cheeks. She gave him a smile she hoped showed off her dimples, which she had been told were very attractive.

'You get some rest,' Thomas said as he made to go, stooping to give the dogs a quick pat.

After Marlene had given Angie and Cora a blow-by-blow account of what had happened in the hospital, the three ruminated on the here and now and how those at the manor were going to deal with having the man they all disliked, if not hated – and who Danny absolutely despised – under their roof.

'I suppose it won't be for long,' Cora said. 'He'll have to go back to Roeburn Hall tomorrow, won't he?'

'He will,' mused Angie, 'but it's not as if that's going to be it, is it? I mean, he's Lucy's father – and there'll be lots to sort out. He's going to be about, one way or another.'

'Exactly,' Marlene agreed, sipping her tea. 'And judging by the way they were at the hospital, and how soft-hearted and forgiving Lucy is, I think he's going to become a regular here.'

'Which means we'll have to accept him,' Cora said.

'Mmm,' Marlene mused. 'I think Danny might have something to say about that.'

When Marlene headed to the kitchen with a tray of empty cups and saucers, having said goodnight to Angie and Cora, it had gone midnight, so she was surprised, then immediately irritated, when she pushed open the door to see Mabel sitting at the kitchen table like the cat that got the cream, smiling at Thomas, her long, curly red hair free from the updo she normally wore for work. And despite the lateness of the hour, her blue eyes looked wide awake and vibrant. *And those dimples.*

'Everything all right?' Thomas asked. He'd been patting the dogs, but on seeing Marlene he stood up.

'Yes,' Marlene said, glancing down at Mabel, who was nursing a steaming cup of tea. 'Angie and I were just saying, one minute we're celebrating Lucy's pregnancy and the news of a new life – and the next moment there's a death. And a bloody one at that.'

Mabel's expression changed to one of disgust as she pointed towards a pile of clothes on the kitchen table. 'There's actual blood on his jacket. I said I'd try and get the stains out before they became ingrained.'

'That's very good of you,' Marlene said. 'Especially as you keep telling us you are no longer a scullerymaid.'

'Well, everyone has gone home – there was no one else.

And you know me, I don't mind getting my hands dirty.' She glanced at Thomas before turning her attention back to Marlene. 'Besides, when I took Mr Stanton-Leigh his tray, the poor man looked wretched. I felt sorry for him.'

'And is *Lucy* all right?' Marlene asked. It annoyed her that Mabel's sympathies always went to the man – never to the woman. '*She* was also feeling pretty wretched. Did she go straight to the cottage with Danny?'

'She did,' Thomas chipped in, feeling the familiar chill in the air that always came when Marlene and Mabel were in each other's vicinity.

'She's *so* lucky to have Danny,' Mabel said, a little dreamily.

'As Danny is *so* lucky to have Lucy,' countered Marlene. Lately, Clemmie had been chatting to her about how women had to be aware of being brainwashed from birth into believing the so-called 'fairer sex' were second-class citizens, and how 'we have to unpick the ideologies we've been force-fed.'

'Of course,' Mabel said, glad that Marlene was sounding so militant. For everyone knew that men did not like combative and opiniated women. *Very unattractive.*

Sensing the tension notching up, Thomas clicked the latch on the back door.

'Right, night, all,' he said. 'See you in the morning.'

'*Night!*' the two women chorused as he closed the door behind him.

'Thomas is such a lovely person, don't you think?' Mabel asked, standing up and taking the bloodstained jacket off the table.

'Mmm,' Marlene muttered as she quickly washed up the cups and saucers.

'I was a little upset earlier and he was *such* a comfort. He even went so far as to give me a little cuddle,' she lied. 'It was just what I needed.'

Marlene glanced at Mabel, hoping that the sudden reappearance of the green-eyed monster had not been obvious.

Just the thought of Thomas with his arms around Mabel made her blood boil.

Chapter Ten

Heading back out to his little flat above the stables, Thomas couldn't get the image of how Mabel's mother had died out of his mind. He had heard of accidents back then when there were next to no safety measures in place and many a person had been maimed or lost arms or fingers to machinery – but never so badly that the injuries had ended a life. Poor Mabel. It must have been tough.

As Thomas climbed the wooden steps up the side of the stables to his digs, which had once been Danny's before his marriage to Lucy, he realised that he didn't really know much about Mabel or her background, despite working together for such a long time. Opening the main door to his living quarters, which had recently been installed with electricity and plumbing for a kitchenette and some basic sanitation, he mused how Mabel had done well for herself. Like him, she'd left school at the first opportunity and worked her way up.

Everyone at the manor seemed to like her, apart from Marlene, who lately seemed to have this ridiculous notion in her head that he was sweet on Mabel, when nothing could be further from the truth.

But what really needled him was the way Marlene waved off his rebuttals as though they mattered not a jot either way. Before her impromptu London trip, he'd thought that Marlene had feelings for him.

Now he was far from sure.

Chapter Eleven

When Marlene left, Mabel relaxed against the high-backed chair and kicked off her slightly heeled shoes, which made her feet hurt like hell but were worth it as they made her taller. Almost as tall as Marlene when she was wearing flats. She then put her stockinged feet up on the adjacent wooden bench and sipped her tea, mulling over the frantic events of the evening – how she'd rushed back to the manor from her fabricated 'chore', dealt with an angst-ridden Shirley, then taken the 'death call' from the hospital.

She had lied to Thomas when she said she'd been traumatised by the news of Mrs Stanton-Leigh. It might well have made Mabel think of her own mother's fatal accident, but she hadn't been affected by it as she'd only been a toddler at the time. But it was a story worth telling when she wanted someone to feel not so much sorry for her, but more compassionate towards her. And Mabel wanted Thomas to feel compassionate towards her – and for those feelings to grow into love.

For Mabel had made up her mind that Thomas was the one. He was attractive, a hard worker, lovely natured and was doing well for himself, especially now he was Danny's right-hand man and earning a decent wage. She had kissed too many frogs in her life and had decided that Thomas was the man for her. The husband for her. And what Mabel wanted, Mabel got. It was an innate part of her nature.

Thomas would be hers.

And nobody – least of all Marlene – was going to get in her way.

Chapter Twelve

Danny was lying in bed, wide awake. Lucy had cried herself to sleep and was softly snoring on his chest. He wasn't the least bit tired, but didn't want to get up for fear of waking his wife. A wife he loved more than anyone else in the world, but also a wife – and he felt bad about this – he was annoyed with, for she had not just opened her heart up to her father again, but had gone so far as to offer him sanctuary here at the manor. *After everything the man had done!* But that was Lucy, he argued with himself. And it was one of the traits he had fallen in love with – her gentle nature, her soft heart, her ability to forgive and see the good in people. *So unlike himself.* He castigated himself for being so lacking in empathy. His wife had just lost her mother – suddenly and unexpectedly. She wouldn't be thinking straight. Hopefully, in the clear light of day, once the shock had worn off, she would remember what her father had expected her to do.

Lucy could not simply forgive and forget that her own father had expected her to marry someone she didn't like – never mind love. And then, when she had eloped and committed the mortal sin of marrying someone she *did* love, both he and her mother had disowned her!

Danny would never forget the state Lucy had returned in after going to see her parents. He had thought them unnatural.

And still did. He certainly did not feel the least bit saddened to hear of his mother-in-law's death.

Danny gently kissed the top of his wife's head. He hoped that, in the midst of her bereavement, she would not lose sight of her mother's true colours, as so often seemed to happen when someone was no longer in the land of the living.

Or lose sight of her father's true colours, which had been revealed to her the day he'd disowned her.

Danny worried that what had happened that day would be whitewashed over, and Lucy would default back to the way she had been with her father before then. Edward Stanton-Leigh had always had a strong hold over Lucy. She'd been forever grateful to him for sanctioning, against her mother's wishes, her move to a day school so that she could indulge her love of horses and ride in the morning before school and afterwards. And, of course, her father had cemented his daughter's adoration by buying Dahlia, a beautiful black thoroughbred, for her sixteenth birthday.

Danny supposed it was unsurprising that Lucy had refused to believe her father had another side to him, and that he could be a ruthless, mercenary bully. It had frustrated him immensely that Lucy would not believe him, even though he'd seen with his own eyes Edward Stanton-Leigh's 'other side'.

As Danny had become more immersed in the world of horses and the landed gentry, and those who worked for them, he had heard of too many incidents that showed Edward to be a good-looking, intelligent man who had no conscience. A dangerous combination, especially when you added into the mix wealth and his high-born family. He had seen how

Edward would do anything to get what he wanted – no matter how cruel, no matter how much hurt and damage it might cause.

Lucy had never seen this as all she ever wanted from her father – from anyone – was kindness, love and care, and to be allowed to indulge in her love of horses. Edward had given his daughter what she wanted and in return had been granted godlike status. It had prepared the ground for when he needed her to do something for him.

It pained Danny to remember that Lucy had been on the verge of giving in to her father's wishes and marrying Anthony Hetherington in order to save Roeburn Hall. Danny had told her that those who had gone up against Edward knew him to be a manipulative, controlling and selfish man, and that if you didn't do what he wanted, you'd be dumped like a ton of bricks. Which was exactly what Edward had done to Lucy. She had not carried out his wishes and therefore had been cast aside and disowned.

But now that Edward's wife was dead and he was in financial straits, Danny knew without a shadow of a doubt that he would try and wheedle his way back into Lucy's life. Danny just hoped to God that Lucy was now older and wiser and would be able to see through him, and that after tonight she would carry on with her life as before – without him in it.

Chapter Thirteen

Thursday, 2 September

Over the next week, Marlene's prediction that Edward would become a familiar face at Cuthford Manor was proved right. Despite Lucy stressing that she really did not mind riding over to see her father to discuss the funeral arrangements, Edward insisted that he should come to her. Especially in her 'condition'. Lucy had told her father that she was expecting, and he'd reacted as most parents were supposed to, congratulating her, telling her she would be a wonderful mother and joking that he was far too young to be a grandfather. He'd added in a more serious tone that this was 'a ray of much-needed sunshine' in a time of such darkness.

As though mirroring the passing of one life and the beginning of another, summer gave way to autumn, the arrival of which was heralded by the first fluttering of leaves littering the roads and pathways. The change in seasons also signalled the beginning of the end of the summer holidays, and although Bertie, Jemima and Bonnie fervently denied it, they were bored, which meant any new faces, or visitors who weren't guests, were jumped upon.

When Edward had been introduced to the children on the morning after his wife had died, he had shielded them from his grief with a big smile and a declaration of 'Haha! It's the Three Musketeers!' Naturally, Bertie, Jemima and Bonnie had loved their new nickname and later argued over which Musketeer they wanted to be. Thereafter, whenever Edward visited, which was just about every day, the children would race to see him as soon as they got wind that he'd arrived, which was usually no longer than just a few minutes after he'd stepped across the manor's threshold.

Usually, it was the roar of his sports car, a cream-coloured Aston Martin DB1, that alerted them to his arrival, causing them to race from wherever they were to the front reception room, where they knew they'd find him, usually sitting at a table by the window, smoking a cigarette. They'd thought it peculiar that he had to wait in the guests' lounge area, but they'd heard Angie tell Wilfred that 'the grieving widower' was not to be taken to the family room, despite the fact he was Lucy's father and Danny's father-in-law.

Unlike Angie and Danny, the three youngsters thought Lucy's father was the bee's knees, partly because he showed them attention, chatted to them, asked them what they'd been up to, but probably most of all because he always brought them a treat from the village sweet shop. Sometimes a liquorice pipe, or perhaps cinder toffee or barley sugar. Today, as he always did, he put his finger to his mouth to show that secrecy was called for and quickly handed them their contraband.

Although they knew Edward wasn't being serious, the children had learnt not to broadcast they'd been given treats as they had picked up the general feeling that, on the whole, Edward did not seem to be in favour with most of those who lived at the manor. They weren't sure if Marlene liked him or not.

Today when Edward arrived, he struck a swordsman's pose, as he always did, and declared, *'En garde!'* Bertie was too old to play along and Jemima too bashful, but Bonnie loved the short re-enactment almost as much as she enjoyed the treat that followed.

'Now,' Edward asked breathlessly, having succumbed to a fatal stab to the heart from an imaginary sword, 'would you all be so kind as to go and locate my darling daughter and ask her if she could spare her dear old papa a few minutes of her time, please?'

Each clutching their little packet of candy cigarettes, they rushed off to the stables, which was always the first place they'd look for Lucy. Either that or the downstairs bathroom, where she seemed to be spending a lot of time lately.

Five minutes later, Lucy and her father were sitting in pastel-pink cushioned fabric chairs at a little table for two. It was near to the window and away from a family of four who were playing dominoes while they waited to be picked up by friends and taken for a tour of the Bowes Museum in nearby Barnard Castle.

Judging by the children's faces, they were not champing at the bit to go.

'And how are you feeling, my dear girl?' Edward asked, thinking his daughter looked a little drawn as well as disgruntled.

'I'm fine, Father, fine, really.' Lucy tried to sound convincing, but it irked her that she couldn't take her father to the family room, where they could relax more and also have some privacy, but she knew better than to voice that annoyance; as much as she liked Angie, she was not keen to cross swords with her. This was Angie's hotel, so her wishes were adhered to. And Lucy knew that Angie had only welcomed her father to the manor out of courtesy and because it was the right thing to do as he was her sister-in-law's father and he had just lost his wife.

'Before we start going over the plans for the funeral,' Edward said, 'I just wanted to tell you something that I've wanted to say for a good while now.'

Lucy sat back, her attention darting to the young boy and girl. She didn't think she would drag her children off to the Bowes Museum, despite its magnificence. There were paintings in there by some of the greats, but she thought their importance would be wasted on the two children. They'd be bored rigid.

'Darling Lucy,' Edward drew her attention back to their tête-à-tête, 'I really don't want to speak badly of your dear mother, but I have to speak *my* truth. That day . . . that unforgettable day you came to Roeburn Hall and told us you had married Danny, it couldn't have been at a worse moment. You see, your mother and I had just been arguing about what to do. She just kept going on and on, prodding the bear – the bear being me, of course – and then, just as I was feeling as though I couldn't stand it any more, you came knocking at the door. Oh, Lucy, there was a part of me which just wanted to welcome you back home. I hadn't seen you for what felt like such a long time.'

He sighed.

'I'm ashamed to admit it, but I knew if I did as I wanted – welcomed you back with open arms – then your mother would never forgive me. And I needed her.'

Another forlorn exhalation of breath.

'And to my shame, I vented my anger on you. My darling daughter . . . I'm so very sorry, LuLu.'

Edward looked with pleading eyes at his daughter.

'Can you find it in your heart to forgive me? I'm so ashamed of being so angry. It's plagued me ever since. We've never fallen out before, have we?'

Lucy shook her head. It was true, they hadn't.

'And the worst part of all this is that just before your mother's accident, she had finally agreed for me to come and see you so I could make amends for being so horrible to you that day.'

Lucy could see the love in her father's eyes. As well as his deeply felt wretchedness.

'Am I forgiven?'

Lucy blinked back her tears, which seemed to come upon her as quickly as her morning sickness.

'Of course,' she muttered, taking her father's hand and squeezing it. She caught the mother of the two children glance in their direction, and again she felt annoyed about their lack of privacy. This time her annoyance was directed at her husband as he had made it plain that he did not want her father anywhere near their cottage – never mind be allowed in for a cup of tea and a chat.

'Did Mother also want to make amends? Like you said at the hospital? Or were you just saying that to make me feel better?'

Edward hesitated. 'I think in her heart of hearts she did . . . But you know your mother, stubborn as an old boot when she wanted to be.'

He took Lucy's hand and squeezed it. 'You know we've always been closer. We've always had a special bond. And your mother, well, she did love you, but I don't think she was ever cut out to be a mother. I think she knew that. Which was why she told me that she didn't want any more children after we had you.'

'Yes, she used to joke that even one was too many. Many a truth said in jest,' Lucy said with a sad smile.

After her father's visit, Lucy went to see Danny in the stables.

'Was that your father I just saw driving off?' he said. 'Doesn't he have work to do?' He opened the stable door and coaxed Ghost out of his stall. 'Oh, no, I forgot people like your father don't work. It's deemed to be beneath them.'

Lucy scowled at her husband. She'd always loved Danny's honesty and how he called a spade a spade, but lately she'd been wishing he'd sometimes keep his thoughts to himself.

'And he's not asked you for anything? Any favours, other than helping with the funeral?' he asked.

'Being involved in organising the funeral isn't a favour – I *want* to be involved,' Lucy said.

'Well, he certainly wants to get back into your good books. And there's likely something else he's after or wants.' Danny brought Ghost out of the stall, patting him on the neck and reassuring him that all was well as Ghost was swishing his tail – a telltale sign the horse had picked up on his master's ire.

Lucy sat down on one of the nearby bales of hay. She felt drained despite having barely done anything all day. So much for blooming in pregnancy; she felt and looked like a wet rag.

'Actually, there *is* something he wants,' she said, watching her husband's reaction.

'Why doesn't that surprise me,' Danny said sanctimoniously.

'He's asked if we can hold the wake here,' Lucy said tentatively.

'Here?' Danny couldn't believe what he was hearing. 'He wants to have his wife's wake here? At Cuthford Manor?'

Lucy nodded.

'He said it doesn't seem right to have it at Roeburn Hall. The place of her death. Her tragic and very bloody death,' she stressed, lest her husband forget the circumstances of her mother's demise, which, unlike *his* mam's death, had not been in anyway loving or peaceful.

Danny had to fight back his anger. Not only had Lucy embraced her father and taken him back after all his wrongdoing, she was now welcoming him into their home with open arms. Edward had been at the manor just about every day and Danny had noticed that he tended to arrive around teatime and stay until dinner was called. Danny could see he would jump at the chance of eating with them all, but thankfully, Angie's dislike for the man was almost on a par with his own and she made a point of not asking him to join them.

'Will he be able to pay for it?' Danny asked. There had been muted conversations between himself and others at the manor about how Lucy's father was managing to live. It was a subject that was far too delicate and, in the circumstances, inappropriate to bring up so soon after his wife's death.

Lucy nodded. 'Yes, that was one of the first things he said. That he was not to be treated like a charity case.'

Danny made a noise that told Lucy he for one would certainly not be treating him this way.

'He said he and Mother . . .' Lucy swallowed. She kept having waves of guilt rather than grief sweep over her, especially as she felt she wasn't mourning her mother's death as a daughter should. 'He said he and Mother had been keeping their heads above water financially by selling off the family heirlooms bit by bit.'

'Well, good to know that due to his misdemeanours you have been deprived of your inheritance and any heirlooms that might have come your way.'

Lucy took a deep breath. It was becoming harder and harder to talk to Danny about her father. If she could bring herself to forgive him, why couldn't Danny? He wasn't the one who had been badly treated – it was her!

'So, has there been a date set yet?' Danny asked. He was hoping that as soon as it was over and done with, they might be able to get back to some sort of normality, without Edward Stanton-Leigh being a constant in their lives.

'Don't worry,' Lucy said, reading his thoughts. 'We've managed to get the inquest pushed up, so we can hold the funeral next week. You're not the only one wanting this to be over with as quickly as possible.'

Danny didn't say anything.

'So, what do you think?' Lucy asked.

Danny pulled a puzzled expression.

'About the wake being held here?' Lucy repeated.

Danny pulled the harness a little tighter. 'If it's okay with Angie, it's okay with me. But you do know that I won't be there, don't you?'

Lucy pursed her lips. 'Yes, Danny, I'm well aware of that. You've made it perfectly clear you won't be within a hundred yards of my father. And that it would be *hypocritical* for you to attend the funeral, as Mother was a *cold and uncaring woman who wanted to sell her daughter off to the highest bidder for a load of old bricks and mortar.*'

And with that, Lucy did something Danny had only seen Marlene do – she flounced out of the room.

Chapter Fourteen

One week later

Thursday, 9 September

After almost a fortnight of dithering, Nurse Emma Jones still really did not know what to do for the best – whether to report Mrs Stanton-Leigh's final words to the police or not.

In the end, it was reading the report in the *Durham Times* on the inquest into Mrs Stanton-Leigh's death that made up her mind. She felt a little panicked that it had been ruled an accidental death. *Was it really an accident?*

The following day, she went in early, before her shift, to speak with the ward sister. She, too, was undecided about what to do, especially as she knew Nurse Jones walked around with her head in the clouds most days and was prone to flights of fancy. In the end, she decided to pass the buck and went to see her nursing supervisor, who immediately went to discuss the matter with the hospital's director.

The hospital director, Mr Stewart Dickenson, procrastinated. Edward Stanton-Leigh was well known, and everyone in the county knew that his family was mentioned in the Boldon Book. It was a difficult decision to make as, like the director himself, Edward was a Freemason, but in the end ethics trumped the bonds of brotherhood, along with the fact that no one would know that the decision had come from him and was merely the young nurse going to the police off her own back. And so the poisonous parcel was handed back down whence it came.

Which was why Miss Emma Jones was presently standing at the front desk in Durham Constabulary's headquarters, having just rung the little brass bell on the wooden counter.

'Good day, miss,' the rather rotund desk sergeant welcomed her as he appeared from a side door, wiping crumbs from the side of his mouth. 'And what can I do for you this fine day?'

Suddenly Nurse Jones felt ridiculous. The very thought of a murder happening in Durham, and at Roeburn Hall of all places, seemed ludicrous.

'I'm probably being far too diligent – and perhaps overly suspicious,' she began, unconsciously feeling the badge on her nurse's cape, 'but I wanted to report something which occurred on the Critical Care Unit the other week.'

'Oh, right, then, young miss, you'd better come this way,' the desk sergeant said with a welcoming smile. It wasn't every day they had a pretty young nurse walk through their doors.

Chapter Fifteen

As Marlene got ready for the funeral, she thought about how Mrs Elise Stanton-Leigh was one of the most well-known members of the county's gentry, which in turn meant there would be many mourners, and those mourners would undoubtedly have money – and, of course, elderly parents. As she applied her natural-coloured lipstick, she pressed her lips together and then smiled into the mirror, congratulating herself for suggesting that funerals could be a profitable sideline for the hotel. If they were expanding the potential for weddings by creating an exclusive honeymoon suite, then why not funerals as well? Her idea had also succeeded in lessening Angie's reluctance to hold the wake at the hotel. Her bleary-eyed sister had been sleep-deprived from being up most of the night with baby Juni when Marlene had gone with Lucy to ask if the wake could be held at the manor. Not normally one to dance around an issue, Angie had been even less inclined to do so after next to no sleep, and she had not disguised her aversion to accommodating Edward Stanton-Leigh's wishes. She also didn't hold back from asking how he was going to afford it.

Lucy had reassured Angie that her father would be able to

pay his way – and Angie's reticence was further allayed when Marlene had told her of her idea to expand the business and start catering for funeral receptions.

'Weddings tend just to be in the summer, but funerals – well, people die all the time, don't they?' Marlene had said. 'Becoming the county's top venue for wakes and memorials will be a smart way to boost our income with minimal outlay.'

She'd seen her sister's smile and known she was perhaps a little too excited about the subject of people dying – and making money from it – but she could also tell that Angie was sold on the idea.

Checking herself out in the full-length mirror, happy that she had achieved a demure but drop-dead gorgeous look, Marlene hurried downstairs to grab a quick cup of tea before she left for the crematorium with Lucy. The funeral car was due to arrive in ten minutes, which just about gave her time. Crossing the main entrance hall, with its palatial chandelier and suits of armour gracing either side of the reception desk, she had to dodge staff as they buzzed about getting the place ready for the wake, toing and froing between the kitchen or storeroom and the library, which was where the wake was to be held.

Flower arrangements were being carried through from the kitchen. Carl had started to grow flowers on an almost industrial scale, which was saving the business a great deal of money. Cora had commented that Carl's new-found vocation, along with his gift for writing poetry, was helping to soothe his aching heart, which she and the others didn't believe would ever truly recover from the premature loss of his darling Ida.

'You look nice,' Thomas said on seeing Marlene come into the kitchen, dodging Shirley, who was in an even greater state of anxiety than normal.

Marlene threw Thomas a scathing look as she walked over to the kitchen table to feel the belly of the ceramic teapot.

'*Nice.* I hope I look much more than merely *nice*,' Marlene retorted as she gestured with an outstretched arm for the dogs to go back into their basket for fear they might ruin her figure-hugging black dress with their trails of slobber and hair.

Thomas let out a heavy sigh. He just couldn't win with Marlene. What he had wanted to say was that she looked stunning. Amazing. Totally gorgeous. Watching her humming a tune as she poured herself a cuppa, Thomas had to laugh. Her mood was not that of someone off to a funeral.

'I want to make an impression,' Marlene continued her rebuke, stirring milk into her tea, 'not simply look *nice*.'

Thomas held back from telling the woman he was crazy about there was no question that she would most certainly make an impression. She would have all the men fighting over her. A sinking feeling immediately followed. He could never compete with all those handsome, moneyed and eligible young bachelors who would, without a doubt, be clamouring for Marlene's attention – and ultimately her hand.

'I'm going to be schmoozing with the county's finest,' Marlene trilled, 'telling them about the Cuthford Country House Hotel and how it's not just for those who need a bed for the night and some decent food, but for all other occasions – weddings, parties and now funeral receptions and the like.'

Thomas shook his head. Marlene had gone from being man-mad, and Marilyn Monroe-obsessed, to being consumed by business and making money.

Was this the reason she now seemed to be too busy for love, or was it that she no longer had feelings for him?

Had he simply been Marlene's schoolgirl crush and now that she was no longer a schoolgirl, her love for him had also been assigned to the past?

As Marlene had never been to a cremation before, she spent her time quietly observing how it all worked. If she were to branch out into this area, she needed to be fully conversant with all aspects of the rituals, ceremonies and behaviours following a person's death. She also used the time before the service and afterwards to introduce herself to the mourners and to offer her condolences, making sure she spoke perfect Queen's English and briefly mentioning that she was the former sister-in-law of Mr Quentin Foxton-Clarke, thereby killing two birds with one stone – associating herself with a family who were revered in the area and had been for many years, and also showing them that she, too, had experienced the sudden and unnatural death of someone she loved.

Being seated in the first funeral car with Lucy and Edward had helped, showing that she was very close to the Stanton-Leighs. By the time they had returned to the little church in the hamlet near Roeburn Hall to inter the urn in the family burial plot, Marlene had managed to charm just about everyone.

Afterwards, when they arrived at Cuthford Manor, Marlene was pleased she had decided on holding the wake in the calm environment of the manor's wood-panelled library, with its wonderful views of the landscaped front gardens. And as the funeral reception got under way, guests congratulated her on the wonderful buffet and exclaimed that a more beautiful setting could not be found. A few also mentioned they could understand why Edward would not want the funeral reception at Roeburn Hall, and how difficult it must be for him living there after Elise's 'terribly tragic' accident.

'Well, my dear,' Edward Stanton-Leigh said as he suddenly appeared from behind, 'you've done a brilliant job here today.'

Marlene smiled, but not too enthusiastically; this was a wake, after all, and Lucy's father had just buried his wife. Not that she thought Edward would have been offended if she had been a little too jolly, as he was either doing a very good job of keeping a stiff upper lip or, as Marlene suspected, he wasn't too heartbroken over his wife's passing. She had guessed, reading between the lines of what had been said by Edward and what Lucy had told her, that it had not been a marriage made in heaven.

Seeing Lucy chatting to one of her mother's friends, who looked as though she had already had too much sherry, she caught her sister-in-law's eye and gave her a sympathetic look. Not just because Lucy was clearly bored, but because she had confessed to Marlene while they'd made their way from the family burial plot to the waiting funeral car that she felt 'the most horrible person ever' as she had not had the slightest urge to cry. 'I can cry at the drop of a hat at the moment, but not at my own mother's funeral. I must be the worst daughter on this planet,' she'd told Marlene.

'Or perhaps it was your *dear mama*,' Marlene had whispered back to her, 'who was the worst mother on this planet – and that is why you don't feel tearful.'

Lucy had pursed her lips in disapproval, but was secretly glad of Marlene's disregard for not speaking ill of the dead.

'Lucy tells me that you also buried your mother not so long ago?' Edward asked a little uncertainly.

'Last October – almost a year ago,' Marlene replied. On seeing his look of sympathy and hearing his gentle tone, she added, 'It might sound strange to say this, but it was not a sad occasion.'

'Really?' Edward gave a guffaw of surprise.

'It's a long story,' Marlene said.

'I'm intrigued,' Edward said. 'And to be honest, talking about someone other than my wife – lovely though she might have been – will be a respite for me at this moment.'

Marlene could understand. And casting her eye around the mourners, it seemed that others had also exhausted the subject of Elise, and the more single malt or sherry that was consumed, the more she'd heard conversations turning to other subjects. A former headmaster was sounding off about his abhorrence for the new comprehensive schools that would soon be 'popping up all over the shop'. And one of the younger mourners, who Marlene had guessed was around her age, was telling another girl about the new *Romeo and Juliet* movie, staring Laurence Harvey and Susan Shentall, which Marlene hadn't had time to see yet.

'I'm sure Lucy will have told you about my mother,' Marlene said. 'Or you've heard about her through the county grapevine? I think it might have been a hot topic at the time.'

Edward nodded. 'But I never pay much heed to what people say about one another, unless I hear it from the horse's mouth.'

Marlene looked at her friend's father and not for the first time thought how different he was to the man she had imagined. 'Well, to cut a long story short, my mother left us all when I was about eight, which is why we came here with Angie and Quentin. She ran off with her "fancy piece"—'

'Carl Farley, who is now your chief gardener,' Edward interjected.

'That's right,' Marlene said, her eyes automatically going to two beautiful floral displays he had created for the wake.

As Marlene told Edward about her mam, how she had been absent for many years but had returned to make amends before she succumbed to cancer of the blood, she was surprised how genuinely interested he seemed to be about her family. About her.

'Well, I think if your mother is looking down at you now, she would be very proud of you.' Edward looked at Marlene. 'You are quite a rarity – and I mean that in the best possible way – and incredibly grown-up and mature for your age.'

Marlene smiled, although she wanted to say that she had always been grown-up for her age, even as a child. But that it hadn't been a choice – more a need to survive.

As Marlene looked at Edward, it struck her that for him the reverse was true. He looked much younger than his age – more late twenties than late thirties.

Just then, Bertie, Jemima and Bonnie came into the room, wearing expressions that befitted a funeral reception.

'Ah, it's the Three Musketeers,' Edward welcomed them,

ruffling Bertie's and Bonnie's short hair, but not Jemima's as he knew she liked her hair just so. Today it was in two plaits that had been crossed over her head. 'Do you know what I think you all need?'

The trio shook their heads.

'I think you all need a big slice of cake from the buffet. I do believe there is lemon drizzle, fruit cake and chocolate cake.' He put his hand to his chin and creased his brow. 'Now, I wonder which one you might want?'

Three beaming faces looked up at him.

'Mmm, I thought so,' he said. 'Come on, then, let's go and get Shirley to cut up three good-sized slices of Alberta's mouth-watering chocolate cake.'

Marlene watched as Edward, flanked by her brother, sister and niece, headed off to the buffet. Despite being upper-class, Edward still made an effort to remember the names of the staff, unlike many of his peers, who barely even acknowledged those who cooked, cleaned and generally did their bidding. Having seen Edward most days this past fortnight, she had started to see him in a different light to the one he had been cast in, and she began to wonder if he really was as bad as people made out. Lucy had told her what her father had said to her the other day. It was what she had suspected at the time – he had told a white lie to make Lucy feel better about her mother when she was dying, but had ended up coming clean that her mother hadn't actually intended to come and make up with her daughter. Marlene wondered if Edward had told his daughter the truth in order to try and lessen the guilt Lucy was very obviously feeling.

Marlene watched as Bertie, Jemima and Bonnie hurried out

of the room clutching their plates, each with a large wedge of heavily iced chocolate cake.

Sensing someone next to her, she turned.

It was Mabel.

'Oh,' Marlene said, surprised at her sudden appearance. She looked at her love rival and felt the familiar rush of jealousy. A jealousy that had grown of late as Mabel seemed to be looking more glamourous by the day. And taller. She looked down at Mabel's shoes, which had a higher than normal heel, making her almost as tall as Marlene.

'Cora sent me to see if you needed any help, or anything doing?' Mabel asked as they both watched Edward adjust his black tie, take a glass of whisky and walk to the fireplace, where, instead of logs, the grate had been filled with an abundance of white orchids and green foliage. He chinked his glass with a teaspoon, and once he had everyone's attention, he began his speech paying tribute to his 'darling wife and Lucy's beloved mother'.

'There's no need for you to stick around,' Marlene told Mabel, who was listening intently to Edward's speech.

Mabel looked at her watch. 'Oh, thanks for the push, I didn't realise the time. Thomas needs to see me about one of the guests who wants to go trekking.'

And with that, Mabel left, smiling as she turned away and walked out of the reception room.

Of course, there was no guest who wanted to go out for a ride, but with every interaction she had with Marlene, Mabel had a sole aim – to wind her up and convince her that she and Thomas were becoming close. And more than just close friends.

Which would soon be the case.

She just needed more time.

Seeing Mabel leave, Lucy came over to stand with her sister-in-law.

'You didn't want to say a few words about your mother?' Marlene asked, realising that Edward was drawing to the end of his speech. 'We are in an age when women are allowed to speak as well as men.'

Lucy smiled. Marlene had always been somewhat unconventional, but since Clemmie had been expounding her socio-political opinions and beliefs, she had become even more so.

Lucy shook her head. 'I wouldn't trust myself with what I might come out with.' She took a sip of her water; it was the only liquid she was able to imbibe at the moment. Even tea had started to taste different. She was looking forward to the end of what Dr Wright had called the first trimester, when her body should start to settle down and, even better, the constant nausea she was suffering from would be a thing of the past.

Marlene looked at Lucy and smiled. She too would not trust what Lucy might come out with were she to make a speech. How different to the Lucy she had first got to know when she had started seeing Danny. The Lucy back then wouldn't have said boo to a goose – was a complete walk-over, or at least she was with her mother and father. Marlene had wanted to shake some sense into Lucy when it looked as though she was going to kowtow to her parents' demands that she marry Anthony Hetherington. But Lucy had managed to find the strength to fight back and had done something that had been incredibly courageous – and also, in Marlene's opinion, very romantic: she had eloped and married the man she loved. Marlene had viewed Lucy very differently after she had returned to Cuthford Manor with her new husband, knowing that their marriage would probably result in her parents turning their backs on her, which was exactly what had happened.

'To Elise!' The acoustics of the library carried Edward's voice.

'To Elise!' the mourners dutifully responded.

Neither Lucy nor Marlene joined in, but both smiled at Edward as he made his way out of the library, presumably to have a moment on his own after his heartfelt speech.

'God, I'll be so glad when I wake up tomorrow and all this is done and dusted,' Lucy said. She was also hoping that she and Danny might get back to normal once the funeral was behind them. 'Anyway, tell me about you.' She gave Marlene a mischievous look. 'I saw you chatting to your favourite person just then. Anything of interest?'

'Oh,' Marlene huffed, 'only that she was off to see Thomas about some guest who wanted to go on a ride.'

'Mmm, I wonder which one. I didn't think any of our guests were keen on riding,' Lucy said. She sighed. 'Honestly, Marlene, I really don't know why you don't tell Thomas how you feel about him.'

'Because,' Marlene rolled her eyes, 'I won't be seen to be desperate like mooning Mabel, who might as well have it stamped on her forehead how she feels about Thomas.'

'Mmm,' Lucy mused. She had watched Marlene and Thomas dance around a courtship for the past few years and had thought them ideally matched. They were so at ease with each other and only a blind man could fail to see the sparks of chemistry between the two. When Marlene had been recovering after her traumatising London trip, Lucy had thought it would bring them closer still and they would finally get it together and start courting. But nothing had happened. If anything, it was the reverse. Lucy knew it was not because her sister-in-law was no longer interested in Thomas, but that the sexual assault had changed her. Lucy thought that Thomas might not realise this – and might well interpret Marlene's change in behaviour as a cooling of her amorous feelings towards him. Which was why Lucy thought Marlene should be straight up and simply tell him. And sooner rather than later.

Mabel might not hide the fact she was keen on Thomas, but since she had been taken on as Cora's assistant she'd given herself quite a makeover and had really made the most of her looks. Mabel was not an unattractive woman. And if Thomas thought it was hopeless with Marlene, he could be forgiven for falling for Mabel's charms.

Chapter Sixteen

Edward returned to the wake looking more relaxed, which Marlene put down to him finishing his speech and the wake drawing to an end. She watched as a few of the younger women caught his attention and started chatting. They were not so brash as to flirt outright with the widower, but Marlene could see by their body language and mannerisms that they would not be so restrained in the future.

Out of the corner of her eye, Marlene spotted Mabel appearing from the staff quarters. She looked flushed and a few strands of her strawberry-blonde hair had escaped from her French twist. Marlene wondered if she had exchanged more than just a few words with Thomas.

As the clock struck four, the buffet had just about been reduced to crumbs and several empty bottles of whisky and sherry were being carried out of the library by a frazzled-looking Shirley. The mourners started to seek out Edward and Lucy to offer their final condolences and say their farewells.

While Marlene chatted to her neighbours, Gertrude Fontaine-Smith and her son, Jeremy, she glanced out of the window and was surprised to see a police car coming down the long gravel driveway. She wondered if perhaps someone on the force had known Elise and was coming to pay their respects, albeit rather late.

Edward, who had just said his farewells to one of the old-timers, appeared next to Marlene and gently steered her away.

'Dear me, it's the boys in blue.' He spoke quietly as he watched the shiny black Wolseley with its police insignia across the large front grille pull up outside. 'I wonder who's been up to no good to cause the local plod to come knocking?'

'You don't think they're here to pay their respects?' Marlene asked, her eyes glued to the two officers as they put their peaked police caps on in unison.

'Elise had a long list of friends, but none as far as I know were members of the local constabulary. And if they were, they would only be from higher up the ranks.'

The chattering of mourners died down as their interest was drawn to the two uniformed officers from the Durham Constabulary now climbing out of their patrol car.

'Why do you think they're here?' Lucy said as she sidled up to her father and Marlene.

'God only knows,' Edward said, watching the officers of the law as they walked the short distance to the manor's entrance.

Turning to his daughter and Marlene, he declared, 'Well, we'd better find out.'

As he made his way through the guests, Lucy and Marlene followed.

'It's not exactly an appropriate time for a police visit,' Marlene said, annoyed. 'Surely they must have known there's a wake going on.'

Lucy mumbled her agreement. Everyone who was anyone knew about her mother's funeral. And if they hadn't heard, they would have read the announcement in the local paper.

They were making their way through the main hallway, where a small group of mourners were waiting for one of the maids to fetch their coats, when Wilfred pulled open the grand Gothic oak door just as the two coppers reached the top step.

'Good afternoon,' Wilfred said, forever the professional. Nothing ever fazed the manor's former butler, or if it did, he didn't let it show.

'May I ask who it is you are here to see?' Wilfred's accent bore few signs of a northern accent, despite him having rarely crossed the county's borders in his seven decades.

'We're here to see—' Sergeant Richard Routledge, the more senior of the two, started to say before stopping mid-sentence on seeing Edward Stanton-Leigh.

Stepping past Wilfred, Sergeant Routledge walked towards the person who had brought him and his colleague to Cuthford Manor.

'Mr Edward Stanton-Leigh?' Sergeant Routledge asked, even though he knew exactly who he was. The Stanton-Leighs were well known in these parts.

'Yes,' Edward said, puzzled. He was just drawing breath to ask them the reason for their visit when the sergeant stepped forward and put a hand on his shoulder.

'Mr Edward Stanton-Leigh, I'm arresting you on suspicion of murder. You are not obliged to say anything unless you wish to do so, but what you say may be put into writing and given in evidence. Do you understand?'

'No, I bloody well do not understand!' Edward exclaimed,

shrugging the police officer's hand off his shoulder. 'I've not heard anything more ridiculous! Is this some sick joke?' He turned around to look at those in the hallway and the rest of the mourners spilling out of the library, as though the culprit behind the prank was among them.

'I'm sorry, sir, but would you come with us now, otherwise I'm afraid we will have to handcuff you.' Sergeant Routledge surveyed the onlookers gawping at the scene with obvious disbelief. 'I'm sure you don't want to cause a spectacle in front of your family and friends.'

'I don't give two hoots about causing a *spectacle*. This is outrageous! I've never heard the like!' Edward gasped.

The younger police officer stepped forward and after a brief tussle managed to click the heavy metal handcuffs onto Edward.

'My God! This is unbelievable! I'll do the constabulary for slander!' Edward shouted at Sergeant Routledge and the young police constable as they grabbed his arms and frog-marched him out of the door and down the steps.

Marlene looked at Lucy, who was standing stock-still, the little colour she'd had now drained from her face.

'What's going on?'

Marlene turned to find Angie next to her. Cora and Lloyd were just a few steps away, followed by Bertie, Jemima and Bonnie, speckles of chocolate cake around their mouths, their eyes agog. It was not every day the police turned up at your front door.

They all watched as Edward was concertinaed into the back of the Wolseley.

'They've arrested Edward . . . For murder,' Marlene said,

turning her attention to Lucy, who stood rooted to the spot, her eyes fixed on the sight of her father still shouting his objections as he was squashed into the back of the police car.

'Come on, Lucy, let's go to the family room,' Marlene said, gently taking her sister-in-law's arm and guiding her away.

'Oh, my goodness,' Cora gasped when they'd gone. She turned to Lloyd, who was looking equally shocked.

'Murder?' Bertie piped up.

Angie, Cora and Lloyd looked down at the three young ones.

'Come with me,' Lloyd said, ushering them back to the kitchen. His tone ensured they did as they were told, although their heads remained turned towards the main entrance, desperately trying to capture a snippet of the unfolding drama.

With the children gone, Angie and Cora immediately got to work guiding the mourners to the cloakroom and, as quickly and politely as possible, showing them to the front door and their cars. There was a collective sense of shell shock as the mourners muttered their farewells and left.

Jake took as many guests as he could reasonably fit into the Bentley back to their homes or hotels or to the train station. Thomas was called upon to fetch the family saloon and take any remaining stragglers to where they needed to go, rather than have them hang about waiting for a taxi to turn up.

As the last mourners were being driven through the ornate black iron gates of the Cuthford Country House Hotel, they passed another police car as it made its way through the entrance and down the gravelled driveway. This time it was two plain-clothes officers from Durham CID.

Once they'd parked up, they got out and strode towards the main entrance whilst pulling out their credentials. They were greeted by Wilfred, who had seen their arrival.

After they had asked to speak to Mrs Lucy Boulter, Wilfred showed them down one of the corridors that led to the rear of the manor, where the family room was located.

Knocking on the heavy oak door, Wilfred heard Marlene's voice call out, 'Come in!'

'I've two detectives from the Durham Constabulary here to see you, Mrs Boulter,' he said as he opened the door and stepped into the room. He turned to show the two men in.

'DI Cassey, ma'am,' the older and portlier of the two men said as he walked into the room and extended his hand to Marlene, who had automatically stood up from her spot on the sofa next to Lucy.

'I'm *Miss* Boulter,' Marlene said, turning to Lucy. 'This is *Mrs* Boulter.'

'Apologies.' DI Cassey extended a hand to the young woman, who he could tell at a glance was in shock. Her eyes were glazed over, and when he shook her hand, it was as cold as ice. She had made no attempt to stand and the detective knew it was because if she did, it was likely her legs would give way.

'DC Adams.' The younger, lither of the two officers stepped forward, shaking hands with both women.

'I'm so sorry to have to do this now,' DI Cassey said, 'but I'm afraid we have to ask you some questions, Mrs Boulter.'

Lucy stared at the man wearing a smart navy blue suit with matching tie, but words seemed to have failed her.

'You can't seriously think Edward has murdered his wife?'

Marlene asked, instinctively becoming Lucy's mouthpiece while she remained dumbstruck.

'He's been arrested on *suspicion* of murder,' DC Adams chipped in.

Marlene let out a hollow laugh. 'And there's a difference?'

DI Cassey wanted to tell the ballsy blonde he had presumed was Mrs Boulter that, yes, there was in fact a difference, but he knew the question to be rhetorical.

'You couldn't have waited until the wake was over and the guests gone?' Marlene snapped. She couldn't help feeling annoyed, rather selfishly, that her first venture into hosting funeral receptions would be tainted by this shocking turn of events.

'No, we couldn't,' DC Adams said, his tone not as gentle as his colleague's. He would have preferred to interview Mrs Boulter on her own.

'Information has just been given to us and we needed to react to it straight away,' DI Cassey said, throwing his partner a warning look. 'We will make this as quick and as painless as possible.' His voice was soft and courteous.

'I'm so sorry to have to do this today, Mrs Boulter.' DI Cassey kept his focus on Lucy. He could not imagine being in her shoes. The poor woman had just buried her mother, then witnessed her father being arrested on suspicion of her murder.

'Do you mind if we sit down?' DC Adams asked.

Marlene nodded and the two men sat in armchairs that were positioned adjacent to the sofa. DC Adams pulled out his notepad and flipped it open, taking the pencil from the side holder.

'Can I just start by asking if you know why your father wanted to have your mother cremated rather than buried, Mrs Boulter?'

Lucy looked at both men.

Marlene took her hand and squeezed it. The gesture seemed to bring Lucy back to reality, or at least partially so.

'I think she'd put it in her will,' Lucy said, her tone flat, her general demeanour showing that she was still in a state of shock.

There was a moment's silence.

Marlene saw the looks the two men exchanged.

'Is that right? Did Mrs Stanton-Leigh put it in her will?' she asked, afraid of what the answer was going to be.

'She did not,' DC Adams answered before quickly continuing. 'And do you know why your father decided to have the funeral so soon after your mother's death?'

'Two weeks isn't that soon,' Marlene jumped in. She knew from her recent crash course in all things to do with funerals that most people had their loved ones buried or cremated within a fortnight of their death. Some within a week.

'It is when it is an unexpected death,' DI Cassey said. 'I was surprised to see that the inquest was pushed through rather quickly. I believe your mother's case jumped the queue. And holding the funeral just a few days after the coroner's court case seems rather hasty.'

'I think Father just wanted to get it all done and dusted,' Lucy said. 'I agreed with him – it was better than to drag it all out. We'd both have been happy to have had the funeral earlier still.'

Marlene looked at both detectives and the penny dropped.

They thought Edward had decided to have his wife's cremation and funeral post-haste in order to prevent the police from exhuming her body and looking for evidence that the death had not been an accident.

DC Adams was making notes in his little black book.

'And can I ask, Mrs Boulter, were you aware that your mother had life insurance?'

Lucy shook her head. 'No, they never discussed those sorts of things with me.'

DC Adams scribbled in his book.

'And were you aware that your mother had – quite some time ago – opened up a private bank account which had a very healthy balance running into the tens of thousands?'

'Really?' Lucy asked, clearly surprised. 'No, I didn't.'

She looked at Marlene and they exchanged looks, each knowing what the other was thinking. That kind of money could have paid off Edward's debts with plenty left over to help keep Roeburn Hall afloat for a while.

'And how much will the life insurance pay out?' Marlene asked, her mind whirring.

'That depends,' DC Adams said, choosing his words carefully.

'On what?' Marlene asked. This day was becoming more surreal by the second.

'Well, it all depends on the circumstances surrounding Mrs Stanton-Leigh's death – and whether or not there was any foul play involved.'

Lucy shook her head. 'Foul play? This is Durham we're talking about. Not some Agatha Christie film!'

Marlene squeezed her friend's hands, now worried that

Lucy would swing from shock to verbal outrage at her father's arrest.

'I don't understand why you would think my father has murdered my mother?' Lucy's voice was becoming increasingly high-pitched with each word she spoke.

'I am so sorry, Mrs Boulter,' DC Adams tried to placate her. 'There just seem to be a number of factors pertaining to your mother's tragic death which we cannot ignore.'

'There's more?' Marlene asked.

DC Adams looked at DI Cassey, who nodded. 'I'm afraid there is. It's come to our attention that your mother had recently gone to one of the law firms in Newcastle to find out about starting divorce proceedings.'

'Oh my goodness!' Lucy's hand went to her mouth. 'I had no idea they were so unhappy.'

Marlene looked at Lucy and then at the two detectives before surmising, 'Which gives motive. If Elise had divorced Edward, he would not gain from any death benefits, and also would not have the right to any money his wife might have stashed away.'

Both men nodded.

'I'm afraid your father, Mrs Boulter, stands to benefit financially from your mother's demise to quite a considerable sum.'

Marlene and Lucy were quiet as they digested what they were hearing.

DI Cassey put his notebook into the inside pocket of his jacket. DC Adams pursed his lips, put his hands on his legs and pushed himself up.

Marlene and Lucy stood, neither of them sure if they

wanted the two detectives to go or stay so that they could find out more and ask their own questions.

The two men had just reached the door when Marlene spoke up.

'There must have been something that triggered your suspicions? Something which made you look into Elise's will and finances? Something which made you wonder if Elise had really fallen down the stairs – or was pushed?'

DC Adams turned and regarded the stunning blonde friend of Mrs Boulter. He had been surprised not to see a ring on her finger. Even more surprised after this interview. For Mrs Boulter's sister-in-law had brains as well as beauty. It wouldn't be long, he was sure, before she was sporting a large diamond ring along with a thick eighteen-carat-gold band on her wedding-ring finger.

'Yes, you're right, there was, Miss Boulter. We became curious – *more* than curious – after the words Mrs Stanton-Leigh uttered during her final moments in this life came to light.'

'And those words were?' Lucy demanded.

'To quote exactly,' DC Adams said, getting out his black notebook and flicking back a few pages: '"This is *his* fault. This is *Edward's* doing."'

Chapter Seventeen

Within half an hour of leaving Cuthford Manor, Detective Inspector Cassey and DC Adams were sitting at an ink-stained wooden table in the windowless interview room at Durham police station, in the centre of the city. DC Adams sat next to his superior, pen poised over a large lined writing pad. The small box room was thick with swirls of grey smoke as both suspect and interrogator were dragging on cigarettes. DI Cassey noted that Edward Stanton-Leigh was smoking du Maurier cigarettes, one of the most expensive brands on the market.

'So . . . ' DI Cassey fixed Edward with a penetrating glare, one he had perfected over the years. 'This will go much more easily if you simply tell us the truth. Did you or did you not deliberately push your wife down the stone cellar stairs at Roeburn Hall with the intent of killing her?'

Edward let out a guffaw that expressed his sense of sheer incredulity. 'I most certainly did *not* push my dear wife down the stone steps to the cellar with the intent of killing her! I wasn't even there when she fell down the damned stairs!' He gave an exhausted sigh. 'How many times do I have to tell you? This is the truth.' Edward took another deep pull on his cigarette before stubbing it out in the small silver-foil ashtray. His attention was diverted by the DC's scribblings as he talked. 'This is beyond ridiculous. I think it's time I called my lawyer.'

'Really?' DI Cassey said, the slightest of smiles playing on his lips. 'I have to tell you, Mr Stanton-Leigh, that if you did, I would be even more suspicious about your involvement in your wife's death than I am already.' Without giving Edward time to respond, he continued. 'Tell me again – what happened to the clothes you were wearing that day?'

'As I've already told you, I burned them.'

'And you burned them because?'

'Because, Inspector, there was blood on them.'

'Not because there were any tears or any other evidence of a struggle between you and your wife?'

'No,' Edward denied, 'and if you don't believe me, you can go and talk to the member of staff at Cuthford Manor who tried to get the bloodstains out of my jacket on the night of my wife's *accident*.'

'And who would that be?'

'The hotel manager's assistant, Mabel Glendenning.'

DI Cassey threw a look at DC Adams, who immediately stood up and made to leave.

'On thinking about it, though,' Edward said, lighting another cigarette, 'I should say for the record . . .' he waited until the detective constable had stopped at the door '. . . that the jacket was old and therefore might well have had a little tear here or there.'

DI Cassey fought hard not to show he was riled. 'It looks like you have an answer for everything, Mr Stanton-Leigh.'

The detective inspector thought he saw a spark of amusement in his suspect's eyes – as though mocking him.

'Tell me about your wife's life insurance.' DI Cassey flicked open his small leather-bound notebook. 'For which, I believe, you have already made a claim, and which will mean you are set to receive the sum of twenty-five thousand pounds.' He paused. 'That is quite some amount.'

'What is there to tell?' Edward asked. 'Doesn't everyone have life insurance these days?'

DI Cassey had to bite his tongue. The man's arrogance was starting to get under his skin. It should have been *him* getting under *his* skin.

'Many of those who can afford it might well have life insurance,' DI Cassey forced the words out through gritted teeth, 'but not with such a large payout.' He paused. 'And I am curious as to why it was not long after your daughter eloped and married Mr Daniel Boulter of Cuthford Manor that you decided to increase the amount you would receive if one of you died.'

'Purely a coincidence,' Edward snapped back. 'My accountant suggested it was worth paying just that little bit extra in order to increase the payout by, as you say, a "substantial" amount. At least if one of us did die, we knew the other would be well cared for.'

'And whose decision was it to make this increase?' DI Cassey asked.

'It was a joint decision,' Edward said.

'Really?' DI Cassey asked, once again fixing Edward with a penetrating stare. 'The problem is we can't verify that as your wife is clearly not here to confirm or deny your claim.'

'Well, you'll just have to believe me,' Edward said, raking

his long fingers through his mop of hair, combing it away from his face.

'And the money your wife had in her own personal account,' DI Cassey continued, 'this was also a *substantial* amount.'

'Ah,' Edward sat up straight, 'yes, well, I only just got to hear about that *after* Elise's tragic death. And to be honest, it was a tad disappointing she chose not to share that information with me. But to be fair to my darling wife, I can understand why.'

DI Cassey furrowed his brow in question.

'Because,' Edward answered, 'I had a tendency to gamble – although I wish she had believed me that I had knocked it on the head. Stopped. Good and proper.'

'Mmm,' DI Cassey said. 'It just all seems rather convenient. You and your wife are on your uppers, you are having to sell your ancestral home due to your dire financial situation, and hey-ho, your wife has a "tragic accident" and all of a sudden your money worries vanish – puff – into thin air.'

DI Cassey looked down at his notebook and then back up at Edward.

'My inquiries have revealed that you have already reassured your debtors that they will be paid back in full as soon as probate is granted and you have access to your wife's bank account, and the money you will receive from the life insurance will enable you to keep Roeburn Hall up and running for some time, at least.'

Edward stubbed out his cigarette. 'Really, Detective Inspector, if that is all the evidence you have, then I think I will be leaving now and going back to my dear wife's wake, although I'm sure your presence will have brought the afternoon of free food and drink to a premature end.'

'There is one other piece of evidence I haven't yet imparted,' DI Cassey said, determined to regain the upper hand. 'Evidence that is rather compelling.'

DI Cassey looked at Edward and thought this was the first time he looked even a little worried.

'Which is?' Edward asked.

'It's what your wife told the nurse just before she died.'

Again, DI Cassey referred to his notebook.

'She told her that "This is his fault. This is Edward's doing."'

DI Cassey looked up and scrutinised his suspect's reaction, knowing he would be hearing this for the first time.

Edward looked stumped, but only for a fraction of a second.

'That,' Edward said, giving a short, bitter laugh, 'is something my darling wife would often declare. Everything was my "fault" in life. Everything was my "doing". Elise was always saying this to me. The reason we had to sell Roeburn Hall was *my fault*. The reason our daughter eloped was *my fault*. I don't know of anything, to be honest, which *wasn't* my fault. Elise, bless her, would never take responsibility for anything that didn't go her way.'

Edward shuffled forward in his seat. 'I did not want to disclose this about my wife,' he said, his voice lowered, as though there were others about who might hear him, 'but the drink had taken hold. It started when Lucy married "the son of a coalminer" – that's what she used to call him. So snobby, I know, but that was Elise, she never held back from saying what she thought. Anyway, the drinking got worse. I tried talking to her about it, but she simply blamed it on me. *Her drinking, she said, was my fault.*'

Edward shook his head, his expression now sad.

'As we'd had to let most of our staff go, she had to fend for herself. She had to fetch her own bottle of wine – or whatever it was she was drinking – from the cellar. That's why she fell down those wretched stone steps. She was drunk.'

Edward paused. 'Normally, by the time I got home she was usually passed out in her bed. That's where I thought she was that night. It wasn't until I went to her room and saw she wasn't there that I started looking for her.'

Edward sat back, his posture sagging as though he was weighed down by the remembrance of that moment.

'And that's when I found her.'

Another forlorn look.

'So, yes, in Elise's mind, I was to blame for what happened. It *was* my fault.' Edward sighed. 'Don't you think she would have said, "Edward pushed me," or something more direct?'

For the first time, DI Cassey saw an inkling of emotion. A trace of humanity. Still, his gut told him Edward Stanton-Leigh was guilty. And his gut was rarely wrong. But it didn't matter what his instincts were; they held no weight when it came to the lack of hard evidence.

DI Cassey's hopes of holding Edward for longer were further dashed when he took advantage of his right to have a solicitor present and, as luck would have it, called one of the worst – or best, depending on how you looked at it – criminal lawyers in the county.

By the time it was dark, Edward Stanton-Leigh was back home at Roeburn Hall enjoying a large glass of whisky.

Chapter Eighteen

Over the next week, it seemed that every man and his dog had an opinion on Edward Stanton-Leigh's guilt or innocence. The story had spread by word of mouth and then reached an even bigger audience when the local paper ran it on its front page. Many hours were spent discussing the subject over pints in the pub, or whilst sipping cups of tea at mothers' meetings. Country houses and stately homes across the county were abuzz with speculation, many of their inhabitants whispering about Edward's gambling habit and his wife's penchant for taking lovers.

The opinion, in general, appeared to be evenly divided – as was the case at Cuthford Manor. Not that anyone voiced their suspicions within earshot of Edward's daughter.

Meanwhile, Lucy's shock at seeing her father being hauled off in cuffs by the local constabulary had been replaced by outrage.

'It is *they* who are guilty. Guilty of *complete stupidity*,' Lucy said many times. 'I would laugh at the ridiculousness of it all, were it not so serious.'

Those at Cuthford Manor mumbled their agreement, even if they did not agree.

Marlene was unsure. She knew from personal experience how a seemingly respectful person could commit murder – and premeditated murder at that. Lloyd's ex-wife, Evelyn Foxton-Clarke, had taught her this. Marlene kept her thoughts to herself, however, and supported her sister-in-law in her time of need. She really was going through the wringer of late – and to top it all was not experiencing the easiest first few months of pregnancy. She looked almost grey some days. And because of the amount of time she spent chucking up in the toilet, she seemed to have lost weight rather than gained it. Dr Wright had reassured Lucy that this would pass; the question Lucy kept imploring to know the answer to was 'When?'

It didn't help either that Danny was not holding back when it came to voicing his belief in his father-in-law's guilt.

'I wish Danny would keep his thoughts to himself,' Marlene confided in Thomas the following Saturday. She had gone out to see him during his lunch break. Having thought about Lucy's suggestion that she should tell Thomas how she felt, she knew she could never be so forthright, and wasn't sure she wanted to be, but she did think she could try and convey how she felt more subtly, which meant going to see him when she knew he'd be on his own.

'I'm guessing you're meaning thoughts about Edward Stanton-Leigh?' Thomas said, quickly checking his watch as he set about making them both a cup of tea in the tack room.

'Who else?' Marlene said as she sat down on one of the bales of hay that, thanks to a horse blanket thrown over the top, doubled up as a chair. 'I just think Lucy needs Danny's support at the moment.'

'The trouble with Danny is that he can't lie. And he really does believe that Lucy's father deliberately killed his wife for the money.' Thomas handed Marlene her mug of tea, their hands briefly touching.

'He *really* thinks Edward would do that?' Marlene asked, wanting so much to feel the warmth of his hands on hers for longer. Much longer. They had always been quite tactile with each other, but since her return from London, that had abruptly ended. Marlene wondered if this was her doing, albeit unconsciously, or whether Thomas now preferred to be tactile with someone else.

Thomas nodded and looked at Marlene. It irked him the way she spoke of Edward Stanton-Leigh – with such familiarity. Just as it had irked him to see how much time she had spent with Lucy's father until his arrest. If she hadn't been overseeing the builders, making sure they were following her designs for the honeymoon suite to her exact specifications, she had been working hard to make sure the wake was a success, which had entailed many meetings with the merry widower. She had said it was because the wake would be a showcase for other potential funeral receptions, but Thomas believed Marlene was also trying to impress Edward. And it hurt him to even think it, but he wondered if perhaps Marlene was a little taken with Lucy's father – despite the age gap.

'Danny thinks it was either premeditated because of the money he'd get if she died, or in a fit of anger,' Thomas said, again checking his watch.

'Mmm.' Marlene had heard many arguments for and against Edward's guilt. 'And what about you? Do you think he might have done it?'

Thomas shrugged his shoulders. 'I don't know.'

'Why do you think Danny is so convinced of his guilt?'

Thomas took a sip of his tea and put his cup down on the overturned crate that acted as a makeshift coffee table.

'Danny knows a lot of people who have seen a different side to Lucy's dad – going back years. And he says he's all sweetness and light as long as you agree with him and do his bidding, but if you don't, he will either turn on you or dump you before you can say Jack Robinson.'

Marlene thought of what had happened to Lucy when she had not done what her father wanted, marrying Danny instead.

'Danny says if you do go up against him, he can get quite nasty. And everyone knows Edward's got a temper on him.'

Marlene was just about to ask Thomas more – who exactly was 'everyone'? – when she heard the sound of boots on cobbles. A few seconds later, Mabel appeared at the door to the tack room.

'Mabel, you're early,' Thomas said.

Marlene stared at her. Mabel was kitted out in brand-new riding gear. The dark grey jodhpurs she was wearing looked to be the same make as the ones Marlene wore, and though it pained Marlene to admit it, they showed off her petite yet womanly shape well.

'I didn't know you could ride?' Marlene asked.

'I can't,' Mabel said, flashing a smile at Thomas before returning her attention to her love nemesis. 'That's why I'm here. Thomas is going to teach me.'

Marlene gave Thomas a look that was the opposite of the one he'd just had from his new student. *So that's why he kept checking his watch!* He had probably just been making polite conversation whilst anticipating the arrival of little Miss Perfectly Proportioned.

'Oh, well, I'd better leave you to it,' Marlene said, trying to mask a sudden onset of anger as well as the burn of hurt and jealousy.

As Marlene walked back to the manor, she realised that her anger was at herself. She had been enjoying dressage lessons with Thomas, but they'd dwindled off after Angie had given birth to Juni and Marlene had convinced her sister that she was capable of taking over from her. She'd worked hard to prove to Angie that she could do it and she had learnt on the job, which had sapped all her energy and taken all of her time. Then, just as she was getting the hang of everything, she'd given herself even more toil and even less time for anything other than work by suggesting that they convert the attic.

This had given Mabel the perfect opportunity to step into Marlene's shoes, or rather riding boots, by asking Thomas to give her lessons – something Thomas wouldn't have had time to do had Marlene still been having hers.

Mabel had copied Marlene yet again, enabling her to spend more time with Thomas – and leaving her love rival with even less.

God, that woman can be a clever, conniving cow, Marlene fumed inwardly as she headed to the office to go through the plans for the honeymoon suite with Lloyd.

The irony of losing the man she loved whilst working on a suite for love-struck newly married couples was not lost on her.

Chapter Nineteen

Three weeks later

Friday, 8 October

After much deliberation by DI Cassey and his team, along with numerous discussions with the solicitor from the Crown Prosecution Service, it was decided that Edward Stanton-Leigh should not be charged with his wife's murder.

The news was relayed to Edward via his solicitor, Desmond Pyburn, who had once been employed by Farrell & Sons, the law firm used by the Foxton-Clarkes. Desmond had left after suspicions arose that he had been leaking confidential information to his mistress, Mrs Evelyn Foxton-Clarke, now ensconced at a high-security psychiatric unit after trying to burn down Cuthford Manor, and for unwittingly killing her own son, Quentin Foxton-Clarke, instead of his wife.

Edward had taken on Desmond Pyburn – once known as Dashing Desmond, although not any more as the moniker no longer fitted – because his reputation as someone not averse to bending the rules preceded him.

'So, why did they decide not to haul me in front of judge and jury?' Edward asked over drinks at the County Hotel bar in Durham.

'To be blunt,' Desmond said, taking a swig of his gin and tonic, 'they couldn't get enough evidence. The Crown Prosecution said that they wouldn't – couldn't – progress with so little to go on. Everything they had could be argued down.'

Desmond had made the crossover from civil to criminal law after his departure from Farrell & Sons and had not once rued the day. He had found his calling. His wife might have chucked him out of the family home and forbidden him from seeing his children, and his reputation had been left in tatters after his affair with a psychopath, but he was now enjoying life more than ever – both personally and professionally.

'For example?' Edward asked, keeping his relief under wraps.

'Well, the words your wife purportedly said on her death-bed could easily be interpreted as an indictment of your marriage and the fact that, historically, your wife had blamed you for everything that went wrong in her life – rather than a statement that you had purposely pushed her down the steps to the cellar. I also made it plain that I would argue that the fact she had suffered a severe brain injury would cast serious aspersions on the veracity of what came out of her mouth just moments before her death – especially as she wasn't even fully conscious. I would also have suggested to the jury, had we gone to court, that your wife could well be perceived as having had a drinking problem that had caused her to fall down the stairs when she went in search of more liquor.'

He took another sip of his G & T, picked out the lemon, sucked on it and then disposed of it in the ashtray.

'And the fact,' he continued, 'that you had the funeral

post-haste could be understandable, especially as your daughter had told the police it was something she was thankful for – she just wanted it over with.'

Desmond clipped off the end of an expensive cigar.

'Oh, and I did not refrain from telling them how ridiculous I thought it was when they suggested that you only accompanied your wife in the back of the ambulance out of fear that she would implicate you. Why would anyone in their right mind get in a car and drive to the hospital when they could be by their wife's side?'

Edward nodded his agreement. 'Exactly, old chap.'

Desmond clicked his gold lighter and let the flame burn the end of his cigar. 'The issue of the life insurance was not quite so easy to dismiss . . .' he blew on the end and then took a puff ' . . . but that would never be enough to convict, and there was no way of ascertaining whether you knew about your wife's secret bank account.'

Desmond looked at his client through a haze of swirling smoke. Edward had a reputation as a good poker player. His natural flair for bluffing and hiding his thoughts and feelings made Desmond uncertain as to whether Edward had, in fact, known about the money his wife had squirrelled away or that she was about to file for divorce, or if he was telling the truth in claiming that Elise Stanton-Leigh had become dependent on drink. No one else Desmond had spoken to seemed to think she had taken to the bottle.

But what did it matter whether or not Edward Stanton-Leigh was lying? Desmond had defended many a guilty man since his entry into criminal law. And saved many from the heart-stopping horror of watching a judge place a black

107

cloth on top of his wig. Not to mention saved himself from having to watch a client end his days swinging from a hangman's noose, the only hope being that death came instantly and wasn't painfully protracted, as was the case more often than not.

After enjoying another drink with his solicitor, Edward had made his excuses and returned to Roeburn Hall, where he had arranged a rendezvous with his lover. Neither had known if it would be an evening of commiseration or celebration. As it was good news, Edward went to the cellar, carefully making his way down the stone stairs, stepping over the bloodstain that the cleaner had not been able to completely get rid of, and retrieved a bottle of Dom Pérignon.

Once his nubile young lover had left, though, Edward realised that his latest, rather long-term dalliance had become more than simply a bit of fun, an enjoyable roll in the hay whenever it took his fancy, which made him wonder, as he drifted off to sleep, if it was time to bring their affair to an end. After all, he didn't want her to get any ideas now that he was a single man, no longer destitute and still very much in the prime of his life.

By the time he had fallen into a deep, contented slumber, no longer plagued by worries of swapping Roeburn Hall for a prison cell or, worse still, of his own life being cut short prematurely, he resolved to bring their relationship to an end.

It was time to move on.

Time to start making plans for the future.

Chapter Twenty

The following day, Edward drove to Cuthford Manor and asked to speak to Angie. He knew she was the person making the final decisions on everything that was permitted at the esteemed Cuthford Manor. She might have taken a step back in the running of the place after becoming a mother for the second time, but she was still head honcho. Asking him to follow her into the study told Edward that he was still viewed as an outsider, still hadn't been forgiven for disowning his daughter, and was still looked upon with suspicion with regard to his wife's death.

Still, Edward consoled himself as he watched Angie walk around the large cherrywood desk and sit herself down in the swivel chair, it was early days. There was plenty of time to win her over, along with the rest of those at Cuthford Manor.

'I've purposely kept away,' Edward told Angie, pulling out the chair opposite and sitting himself down, 'because I did not want to bring your rather wonderful and highly regarded establishment into ill repute.'

Angie nodded her understanding. She had been thankful that she hadn't had to tell him to stay away after his arrest. She couldn't help but bristle at his words and his manner, though, which she found to be a little sycophantic, and which she guessed had been said to butter her up before requesting some kind of favour.

'But now that I have been cleared of any kind of involvement in my poor wife's death,' he continued, 'I wanted to ask if you would be happy for me to come and visit my daughter occasionally.' He paused. 'Or perhaps you would prefer me to meet her elsewhere?'

Angie was right in her supposition that he wanted something from her. And she would have most definitely preferred Edward to meet Lucy elsewhere, but she knew that it would cause bad feeling and she didn't want to upset her sister-in-law, especially as she was still struggling so much with her pregnancy. It had made Angie realise how easy she'd had it with both Bonnie and Juni.

'No, no, that's fine,' Angie said, although her tone was far from enthusiastic and her smile strained.

Her brother, for one, would not be pleased to hear of his father-in-law's return, or that he was no longer facing a murder charge, for he'd made no bones about his conviction that Edward was guilty.

As the two talked about their prospective properties and Edward asked Angie how she had managed to turn a 'unique but tired' manor house into a very successful business, Angie wondered whether he realised that giving him a pass would have the knock-on effect of creating friction between Lucy and Danny.

Was Edward aware of just how much his son-in-law hated him? Angie pondered.

And more worryingly, if Edward *was* aware, then he must surely realise that *he* was the cause of the growing tension in his daughter's marriage.

Chapter Twenty-One

January 1955

Initially, Edward's visits to Cuthford Manor weren't too frequent. He seemed busy with Roeburn Hall and with employing tradesmen of various skills to start work on bringing his family's ancestral home back to its formal glory, or, at least, to pull it back from the precipice of dereliction. But as the weeks turned into months and they welcomed in the New Year, then celebrated Marlene's eighteenth birthday shortly afterwards, Edward's visits increased in regularity.

Most of those who lived and worked at Cuthford Manor seemed to have accepted Edward and had forgiven him for his past misdemeanours towards his daughter. Their forgiveness was encouraged by the fact that Lucy, although still suffering from morning sickness despite being almost at the end of her second trimester, was nevertheless clearly very happy about having her father back in her life. Although it was also evident that Lucy's joy had come at a price. That price being the closeness and contentedness she had always shared with Danny, from the time they had first met at a local gymkhana almost four years ago.

Angie tried to like her sister-in-law's father, especially as he was now part of their extended family, but she found herself failing.

'He just seems too jolly,' she said to Stanislaw one night when they were up with Juni, who still didn't seem to want to sleep through the night. 'God, when Quentin died, it took all my energy just to get out of bed and put one foot in front of the other, but Edward seems full of the joys.'

Stanislaw took their seven-month-old daughter from his wife's arms and gently laid her in the crib by the window. 'The difference between you and Edward is that you and Quentin were very much in love. I don't think it was the best-kept secret that Edward and his wife weren't. And that they were happy to overlook each other's indiscretions.'

They both climbed into bed.

'Mmm,' she said, shivering because the sheets were cold. 'And I think the man's spending too much time with Marlene – more so since she's turned eighteen.'

'Well,' Stanislaw mused, 'it wouldn't surprise me if he was a little sweet on her. Your sister seems to have that effect on men, and she does look and act much older than her age.' He took Angie in his arms and tried to warm her up.

'I don't like the thought of that. At all. It's a good job Marlene only has eyes for Thomas. If not, I do think she'd be susceptible to Edward's undoubted charm.'

Stanislaw let out a half-laugh. 'Poor Thomas. One minute you've got me warning him off going anywhere near Marlene, and now you're relieved – happy, almost – that she's *sweet* on him.'

'Ah,' Angie defended herself, 'that was another lifetime ago. Marlene was still just a girl. I didn't want *anyone* trying it on with her – not just Thomas.'

'That might seem a lifetime ago to you,' Stanislaw

countered, 'but I'm sure Thomas feels as though the order still stands. And that he will face your wrath should he make a play for your little sister.'

'Ha! Hardly little any more,' Angie laughed. 'And I think you underestimate the pair of them. I don't think me giving Thomas a warning by proxy two years ago will stop either of them courting, if that's what they both want. They're adults now.'

Stanislaw pulled Angie closer, casting his eyes over to the crib and feeling relieved that Juni looked settled.

'Call me suspicious,' Angie said, keeping her voice low so as not to wake their baby girl, 'but I think the main reason Edward is spending so much time with Marlene is because he's wanting to pick up some tips on how to run a hotel and, moreover, to learn the logistics of how to possibly convert Roeburn Hall into one – the attic conversion gives a perfect blueprint of how it's done.' Angie snuggled up to Stanislaw, enjoying the warmth of his body.

Stanislaw kissed her on her forehead. 'I think you worry too much. I don't think people like Edward consider actually working for a living. He'll have some accountant looking at investments and how to make his money work for him.'

'Mmm,' Angie mused, making a mental note to herself to find out exactly how Edward was going to keep Roeburn Hall up and running once the money he'd accrued from his wife's death inevitably ran out – or was lost at the bookies.

Like his older sister's, Danny's feelings towards his father-in-law had not warmed. But unlike Angie, he had not even attempted to like his father-in-law these past four months. He was resolute in his belief that his wife's father was a no-good user who was only out for himself and would trample on anyone who got in the way of what he wanted – or needed. Danny's inflexibility, however, had created cracks in his marriage as Lucy could not understand why her husband wouldn't let bygones be bygones, whereas Danny couldn't understand why his wife wasn't able to see the man behind the mask.

'I wish Lucy could see him for what he is,' Danny lamented to Thomas while they were grooming the two shires, Monty and Bomber, and polishing their bridles ready for a county show the following day. 'I keep telling her to be careful. That her father is a more complex man than she thinks. He's got two sides to him. The one most people see is a charming bloke who wins people over within minutes of meeting them. He's certainly got the gift of the gab. What they don't see is his other, darker, nastier side, which shows itself when things don't go his way. When someone doesn't do what he wants.'

Danny separated Monty's long black mane into strands and started to braid it.

'Which is why I'm sure he pushed his wife down those stairs. I reckon they argued and he lost his temper because she told him – or he'd found out – that she was going to divorce him . . . and that was the last thing he needed in his predicament.'

Thomas didn't say anything. He thought it unlikely that Edward had killed his wife. Danny was about the only person he knew who still mentioned it, never mind thought he was guilty.

As though reading his thoughts, Danny added, 'It's like

114

everyone has erased it from their memories that just last year he was arrested on suspicion of murder.' He shook his head as he finished the braid. 'I wonder if memories would be so short had Edward not been just one rung down from royalty.'

Thomas nodded. This he agreed with.

'He's got everyone running after him.' Danny continued what was becoming a familiar rant. 'The maids are all gooey-eyed when he's about. *Yes, sir, no, sir, three bags full, sir.* He's even got Marlene eating out of his hand.'

'Do you think so?' Thomas asked, trying to keep the concern out of his voice. 'He's a bit old for Marlene, don't you think?'

Danny let out a bark of laughter, causing Monty to twitch his head. 'I don't mean in that way. Blimey, the man's old enough to be her father.'

Thomas felt relieved, although only a little. Edward might well be old enough to be Marlene's father, but he certainly didn't look it.

'What I mean,' Danny said, starting another braid, 'is that my sister – like my wife – seems to have been totally taken in by the bloke. Am I the only one who can see the man for what he is?'

'It would appear so,' Thomas said. His own reasons for disliking Lucy's father were not so much because of his apparent dual personality, but because he worried that the rather debonair Edward Stanton-Leigh embodied all the traits that Marlene had once told him she wanted in a future husband. It was why, a couple of years previously, when Marlene had made it clear to him that she liked him, Thomas had never responded to her flirtations. He'd had his pride, and he had been determined not to be used for a bit of fun and then cast aside when along came Marlene's ideal man – a man like Edward, a moneyed aristocrat.

Why can't you get it into your stupid head – Thomas felt like physically banging his head against one of the stall doors to knock some sense into it – *that Marlene wants a man who is about as different to you as different gets?*

Marlene might well like him, both as a friend and as someone she found attractive, but he came from generations of poachers, and although he had not followed in their footsteps and was now a stable manager and Danny's right-hand man, he would never have the kind of money that Marlene had always hankered after. And he certainly didn't have the status.

As the two men put their energy into making the horses' coats shine, their minds were on the women they loved – and how the same man seemed to be scuppering their chances of happiness with them both.

Chapter Twenty-Two

February

As February got under way, so did the start of what the newspapers were calling the 'Big Freeze'. And for once, it wasn't just the north of England that was badly affected. By the middle of the month, deep snow and freezing temperatures had hit the length and breadth of the country. Temperatures had fallen four degrees below freezing – the lowest for thirty years. Roads had been blocked by snowdrifts as high as thirty feet, leaving many parts of the country cut off from essential supplies. The familiar sound of low-flying aeroplanes could once again be heard in the skies, bringing back memories of the bombing campaigns of the Second World War. This time, though, it was not the Luftwaffe but the RAF, and it was not high explosives that were being dropped from the planes' metal underbellies but food and medical supplies to affected areas. Concerns for the welfare of the country's thousands of sheep and other livestock mounted as many were completely cut off, without any food. Roads and railways had been brought to a standstill. Commercial flights had been grounded. The entire country had found itself having to survive nature's nosedive into treacherous and dangerous weather conditions. Weather conditions that showed no signs of abating.

Like most hotels in rural areas, the Cuthford Country House Hotel, as well as the Cuthford Manor Equestrian Centre, had been forced to temporarily close its doors, which meant everyone found themselves with time on their hands.

For Marlene, it meant that she finally had time to spend with Thomas – uninterrupted time, as Mabel had got stuck at her parents' home when their village had become snowbound.

Despite this, though, Marlene still couldn't help but feel that it was a little too late, as she had become convinced that the man she loved viewed her purely as a friend.

Which was exactly how Thomas had started to believe Marlene viewed him.

But Marlene couldn't give up, not just yet – she simply couldn't quell her feelings of attraction for Thomas, no matter how much she tried.

And so, whenever the opportunity presented itself, she would go and see him.

Fortunately, Lucy's concern about how the horses were coping with the extreme temperatures provided Marlene with the perfect excuse for spending plenty of time at the stables every day, helping Lucy in any way she could, whether that was fetching blankets to cover the horses or keeping them topped up with water and feed.

Today, as they did most days after their work was done, Marlene, Lucy, Thomas and Danny sat around the glowing brazier in the barn.

'Listen to this,' Thomas said, holding the *Daily Mirror* out in front of him.

'We're all ears,' said Marlene as she got up and stoked the fire. Sitting back down, she held out her hands to the warmth.

The glow of the coals momentarily took her back to her child-hood, when they'd been hit by similar icy blasts and she and Danny would follow the coalman's cart, snatching up any bits that fell onto the cobbles.

'Do tell us what is happening in the outside world,' Lucy encouraged as Danny went off to make the tea.

Thomas shook the newspaper out for effect and put on his newsreader's voice.

'"Yesterday more snow and sixty-mile-per-hour blizzards in the West Country paralysed many parts of Devon and Cornwall. Cornish police reported that seventy vehicles had been abandoned in ten-foot snowdrifts. There are concerns for livestock on Exmoor and Dartmoor, which are both cut off by snow."'

'Oh, gosh, that's heartbreaking,' Lucy said. Any kind of suffering endured by any animal always disturbed her greatly.

'And there's been bad flooding on the south-east coast, making "conditions almost unbearable", and the AA have described driving in the south as "treacherous".'

'No worse than here,' Danny said, shouting through the open doorway of the tack room.

'I guess it's what you view as worse – flooding or being snowed in,' Thomas mused. 'Not like them down south to suffer like us, though, is it?'

There were murmurs of agreement.

'Of course, it goes without saying that Scotland's got it the worst . . . ' Thomas looked down at the newspaper. 'It says here that Caithness in the Highlands has been totally isolated and without power or light for several days.'

Danny came out of the tack room with the tea tray and set it down on the upturned crate.

'Here we are,' he said, handing Thomas and Marlene their mugs of steaming-hot tea. 'And a glass of ginger ale for my very expectant wife.'

'Ah, my golden elixir,' Lucy said with a smile. They would both be forever grateful to Alberta, who had presented Lucy with a batch of her own home-made ginger ale and told her to drink it whenever she started to feel nauseous. It had worked like magic.

Danny smiled as Lucy took a sip, putting her hand on her bump, which seemed to have become considerably larger this past week.

Marlene caught the look of love between her brother and sister-in-law and felt relief. They were more like the couple of old. Happy and content. You could no longer cut the air with a knife. Although Marlene guessed that their ease and return to normality might well be because Edward had not been able to visit since the bad weather had set in. And he'd had the good sense to ring Lucy when her husband was not about.

As they drank their tea, Marlene and Thomas chatted away, both secretly relishing the time they had been gifted thanks to the atrocious weather.

As had always been the case with them, their conversation was seamless and peppered with the odd mickey take, which tended to be about Thomas's love of rock 'n' roll, or his crew cut, or the fact that nowadays his wardrobe seemed to consist of just jeans and T-shirts, or Marlene's sudden change from wannabe glamour girl to ambitious female entrepreneur. To an outsider looking in, the chemistry between the two was as plain as day and their banter touching on flirting – not that either of them saw it as that.

After the tea and ginger ale had been drunk and the plate of biscuits devoured, Danny gave his sister a look, which she returned with a barely perceptible nod. The two had always been very good at reading each other's minds.

'Right, then, I think we'd better get a move on,' Marlene said, standing up and moving the bale of hay she'd been using as a chair away from the fire. Both she and Danny knew that if he had suggested his wife should head back to the cottage, then Lucy would have argued against it. Danny, according to Lucy, was treating her with kid gloves, which was 'highly annoying'.

'So soon,' Lucy complained, but she pushed herself up all the same.

Danny whipped the hay bale away as soon as she was on her feet, making sure that his wife did not try and do it herself. Lucy tutted her disapproval but didn't say anything. Angie had told her that Stanislaw had been the same when she was pregnant with Juni. And hard though it was, Angie had told her sister-in-law, she had tried not to argue the point as she knew it was just because he cared. Stanislaw had later admitted he had spent the nine months of her pregnancy swinging from euphoria at the prospect of having a child to the most terrible anxiety over her and the baby's well-being.

As Marlene and Lucy made their way back to the cottage, which was about a quarter of a mile from the manor, they were both shivering, despite the many layers they were wearing.

'That was nice, spending some time with Thomas,' Marlene

said, clapping her gloved hands together. She was feeling particularly happy as the more time she spent with Thomas, the more she began to think there might be hope that his feelings for her were as they had once been.

'And it's really good to see you and Danny getting on so much better,' she added.

Lucy smiled. 'I know. I do love him terribly. There's just the one fly in the ointment.'

'Edward – your father,' Marlene corrected herself through chattering teeth.

'Exactly—' Lucy said, grabbing hold of Marlene's arm as she slipped on a patch of ice.

'Watch yourself,' Marlene said, linking her arm through her sister-in-law's.

The dirt pathway to the cottage was as hard as rock, with the occasional sheet of sheer ice where there had once been a small puddle. Rain had preceded the freeze, making it treacherous underfoot.

'And talking about flies in ointments,' Lucy said, giving Marlene a side look, 'it makes such a change not to have Mabel appear out of the blue on some premise or other.'

'I know,' Marlene said. 'I'm sure she's got an inbuilt radar which alerts her to whenever I'm within a hundred-yard radius of Thomas . . . Not far now,' she said, seeing that Lucy was becoming a little breathless.

'Blimey,' Marlene declared, keeping an eye out for any more patches of ice, 'I can hardly see one foot in front of the other.' The steam from her breath was now mingling with the freezing fog that seemed to have blanketed the area in the blink of an eye.

'I think I can just about make out the outline of the cottage . . . ' Lucy squinted. 'I can see—' She stopped dead in her tracks, gasped loudly, then bent over double, her hand on her waist.

'*Oh God, my back.*'

She gasped again, one hand gripping hold of Marlene, the other her lower back.

'You okay?' Marlene looked at her friend's face, which suddenly contorted in agony again.

'God . . . it feels like I've been punched in the kidneys,' Lucy gasped.

'Let's get you home,' Marlene said, panicking that Lucy might collapse then and there in the freezing cold. She might be quite strong physically, but not so strong that she could carry Lucy the remaining few hundred yards to the cottage.

Lucy tried to straighten her back.

'Take a deep breath,' Marlene said.

'I think I'm all right . . . ' Lucy managed to stand up straight, then inhaled and exhaled.

'Right,' Marlene said, relieved, 'let's get you home and get your feet up. I don't think you should have been out in this cold for so long – if at all.'

As they reached the gate to the cottage, Marlene saw Lucy wince slightly.

'Nearly home,' she encouraged.

As they walked down the path, Marlene kept her eyes on the ground, still looking for any ice.

It was then that she saw a drop of vibrant red on the pure white of the frosted pathway.

Another step and another drop appeared.

This time, Lucy looked down.

'No, no, no.' Her voice was barely a whisper.

Chapter Twenty-Three

Dr Wright had been busy morning, noon and night since the Big Freeze had taken hold and had been tending to a variety of injuries, from cuts and bruises to broken bones caused by people slipping on ice. Sore throats were in abundance, and there had been two cases of frostbite to deal with. So when Lucy started to bleed and Marlene rang for his help, the phone at his home went unanswered as Dr Wright was at the bedside of one of the village's more elderly residents, who had succumbed to pneumonia that had worsened because the poor woman lived on her own and had been too stubborn to ask for help when she'd run out of fuel. Dr Wright's wife, on hearing what had happened, had gone checking on all the other old folk in Cuthford, helped by her three children, who were very excited by the extreme weather, particularly because the school had been forced to close.

Marlene's call to the hospital in Durham *was* answered but proved fruitless, as she was told there was no way they could get an ambulance out to Lucy. Not only were all their vehicles busy with other emergencies, but even if they hadn't been, they'd still not have been able to since there was a good chance they'd get stuck in snowdrifts or be unable to navigate the roads, many of which were now just sheets of ice.

When Marlene rang the manor, the phone was constantly engaged, which caused her blood pressure to rocket. She'd bet her bottom dollar that Angie was chatting to her best friend, Dorothy. And if it was Dorothy who had rung Angie, they'd be gassing for ages as it would be the *New Yorker*, the magazine Dorothy worked for, that would be picking up the bill.

When the phone rang at Roeburn Hall, Edward didn't hear it. He was outside, breathing in the fresh, icy air and thinking about the rather passionate time he'd just enjoyed with his young lover – which would also be the last time they'd enjoy one of their rendezvous, as he had finally got round to bringing their affair to an end. He had wanted to put a stop to their regular dalliances since the evening of his reprieve from the charge of murdering his wife, but had never managed to put his thoughts into action. He'd known, though, that he couldn't leave it any longer. They'd had their fun – and for quite some time. And like he'd said as she'd left, *all good things must come to an end*.

He had, however, been surprised at how well she had taken the news. She was either putting a brave face on it all, and if so, it was certainly a very convincing brave face, or she hadn't been terribly upset about the end of their far-from-short affair, which made him wonder if perhaps she had found someone else.

He felt annoyed with himself that the thought irked him.

But, he chastised himself, if that was the case, then it was probably a good thing and it had made for an easier parting of the ways – no dramatic scenes, and no repercussions further down the line.

As he looked out at the expanse of white lawn, he knew the time had come to move on and start afresh.

And more importantly, to begin working towards a future that was starting to look as bright as the glistening, snowy landscape stretching out in front of him as far as the eye could see.

When Marlene finally gave up on calling for help, having repeatedly phoned Dr Wright with the same outcome, she sat in the little lounge, forcing herself to take deep breaths and trying her damnedest to make her hands stop shaking. She didn't think she had felt so powerless, so completely helpless, so hopelessly inept about what she should do in her entire life.

Lucy wasn't quite eight months pregnant. There was no way, if she had the baby now, it would live. And even more terrifyingly, there was a good chance that Lucy, too, might lose her life. Marlene had grown up hearing stories about how so-and-so down the road had died in childbirth. She felt another wave of gut-wrenching panic when she thought of Carl and how he had lost his wife and child in a matter of hours when she had gone into early labour.

It flashed through Marlene's mind to run back to the stables to get Danny and Thomas – or to see who was about at the manor – but what could they do?

What could anyone do if they weren't medically trained?

'Oh God. Oh God. Oh God,' Marlene muttered to herself, again feeling ill at the thought that no doctor, no ambulance, no kind of medical professional was going to come. And worse still was the thought that even if they did come, would they be able to save Lucy and her baby?

Much as Marlene desperately wanted support from someone, anyone, she knew she couldn't leave Lucy on her own. Knowing that she was the only person Lucy had, she forced herself to try to dampen down the fear rising up in her.

Come on, think! Marlene demanded of herself.

She balled her hands, putting them on her temples and squeezing hard, as if by doing so she could force out an answer.

But it didn't work.

It merely made her head throb even more than it was already.

'*Marlene?*' Lucy's voice sounded croaky and weak as it sounded out from the bedroom.

'I'm just going to get a jug of water from the kitchen,' Marlene said, standing up and shaking out her hands.

She could not let Lucy see how panicked she was.

You can do this, she told herself. *You* have *to do this*.

Walking into the kitchen, she turned on the tap and filled a jug of water.

Pouring herself a glass, she gulped it down in one go, hoping the ice-cold liquid would calm her.

It didn't; all it made her feel was breathless.

'Coming!' she trilled, hoping that Lucy could not hear the slight tremor in her voice.

Walking into the bedroom, Marlene looked at Lucy and saw the most painfully desperate look in her eyes.

'Did you get through? Did you speak to Dr Wright? Is the

ambulance coming?' she asked, the desperation in her voice mirroring the look in her eyes.

And it was at that moment Marlene knew what she had to do.

Lie.

And she had to be convincing. She could not let her sister-in-law know that no one was coming to her aid. That there was no ambulance, and that she couldn't even get through to Dr Wright.

For a fleeting moment, Marlene thought of her previous yearning to be an actress. Well, now was the time to put on an Oscar-winning performance.

Marlene forced a smile and made her eyes return Lucy's look of fear with one of confidence that all would be well.

'Yes! The cavalry is coming!' she declared, putting the jug of water down on the bedside table. 'Help is on its way!'

Lucy sank back into the pillows she had propped up against the bed's walnut headboard.

'Oh, thank God,' she said, expelling air and putting her hand on her huge belly. 'It's all right,' she said to her unborn baby. 'You're going to be just fine. Help's coming.'

Marlene heard the words and felt her own stomach turn and a wave of nausea engulf her. She swallowed hard.

'Dr Wright said you must rest and lie on your bed with your legs slightly elevated.' As she spoke, Marlene fluffed one of the spare pillows, gently lifted Lucy's legs and put them on top of it. She then went over to the wardrobe and retrieved a spare blanket, which she shook out and laid over Lucy.

'How long before they get here?' Lucy asked, pulling the tartan wool blanket close.

'Not long,' Marlene said, purposely vague. 'But Dr Wright said not to worry. He said this is not so uncommon, and for now, the best thing for you is to have a lie-down and rest.'

Lucy's eyes pooled with tears as she reached out and grabbed her sister-in-law's hand.

'Oh, thank goodness,' she said, visibly relieved. 'He'll know what to do.' She smiled at her sister-in-law. 'No offence, Marlene, but you're not known for your nursing skills.'

Marlene forced out a laugh, which came out a little hysterically.

'That's true. You know me. Not one for all that blood and gore.'

Realising that was not an image Lucy needed to have put in her head, she blustered on.

'I may not be Nurse Nightingale, but I do make a blummin' good fire.'

And true to her word, within minutes Marlene had stacked and lit and cajoled the fire to life. Crackles and smoke soon became a vibrant mass of dancing orange flames, and before long the small bedroom was as warm as toast.

Lucy watched her friend at work, and feeling the warmth of the room, she started to relax.

'I'm going to clean up,' Marlene said, showing Lucy her dirt-smeared hands, as if surrendering.

As soon as she was out of the bedroom, though, she headed straight back to the lounge – or rather, the Bakelite telephone. And, as quietly as possible, she dialled Dr Wright's number.

'Goddammit,' Marlene cursed under her breath. *Still no answer.*

After quickly washing her hands in the Belfast sink in the kitchen, Marlene headed back to the bedroom.

Spotting on the bedside table a book called *The Gallant Heart – The Story of a Racehorse*, she opened it where there was a bookmark and started to read aloud.

'Oh, I love this book,' Lucy said, a little dreamily.

Marlene felt the panic again step up a notch. Lucy looked and sounded as though she was fading away. Should she keep her awake?

Somehow, Marlene kept the screaming panic engulfing her out of her voice.

It was not assuaged when, within a few minutes, she saw Lucy's eyelids flicker and close.

Marlene's imagination ran riot with images of Lucy slowly bleeding to death right in front of her and drifting off into an eternal sleep.

And so she resolved not to leave Lucy's side, but instead to keep her eyes on the soft rise and fall of her sister-in-law's chest, praying all the while to a God in whom she promised she would believe – but only if he made sure that Lucy and her baby survived.

Chapter Twenty-Four

One week later

Sunday, 27 February

Marlene was sitting by Lucy's bed, sipping tea and coaxing her to try and finish the bowl of Scotch broth Alberta had made especially for her.

'You must finish it,' Marlene cajoled. 'There's herbs in there that Carl's been growing in pots in the kitchen and which are meant to be really good for you – and the baby.'

Marlene looked at the mound of Lucy's stomach, which was covered by layers of blankets and on which she had balanced her lunch tray.

'I'm trying. Really, I am,' she said. 'I just still feel so nauseous all the time.'

'Did you manage to keep your porridge down this morning?' Marlene asked.

'Yes, but only by sipping ginger ale after each mouthful.' Lucy looked over at Marlene with a faux-serious face. 'Honestly, I swear to God, when this little mite comes out, he or she won't want milk, but a bottle of blummin' ginger beer.'

The two women laughed.

Marlene put her teacup on the bedside table and got up to

add some more wood to the fire. The Big Freeze was finally showing signs of letting up, but it was still bitterly cold. Having stacked a few more logs on the fire, she turned and looked around the little cottage to see if there was anything else that needed doing.

When Dr Wright had finally come to see Lucy several hours after the bleeding started, he had quietly praised Marlene – telling her that the advice she'd given Lucy from their fabricated telephone conversation had actually been spot on and was what he would have told Marlene had they actually spoken.

'When something like this happens,' he'd told her, 'it really is in the lap of the gods. There's not a lot us medics can do.'

He'd examined Lucy and been heartened that the bleeding had stopped and she hadn't lost as much blood as feared.

'I think you've had a little tear, which has caused the bleeding,' he'd informed Lucy. His remedy was a simple one. 'You must stay in bed, Lucy, my dear,' he said, patting her hand. 'Possibly until the baby comes. Eat, sleep and keep warm.'

Lucy had agreed to do as she was told, convincing herself that her due date in the first week of April was really not that far off. She'd do whatever it took to reach the full term of her pregnancy – even if it meant going out of her mind with boredom over the next five to six weeks.

In order to stop that happening, Marlene had taken to popping in to see her sister-in-law throughout the day, something that was also determined by her need to reassure herself that Lucy and her baby *really were* going to be all right. The immense relief she had felt after Dr Wright finally answered his phone and managed to get to the cottage to tend to Lucy had been overwhelming. When he had come out of the bedroom after examining Lucy and told Marlene that the bleeding had stopped, she had promptly burst out crying. All the fear and dread of what might happen, and the horrendous anxiety of watching Lucy, expecting the life to leave her at any moment, had just been too much. Dr Wright had sat and waited until Marlene had expended her repressed emotions before telling her that she had done well, which merely caused another silent bout of heaving sobs as Marlene didn't want Lucy to hear her in the next room.

Marlene's regular checks on her sister-in-law more often than not coincided with Edward's visits to see his daughter. He'd been mortified he had not heard the phone ring when Marlene had called for help, but as Lucy and Marlene had reassured him, there was very little he could have done – and it was unlikely he would even have been able to get to them, due to the snow and ice on the roads. Still, Edward seemed determined to make up for not having been of any help by coming to see his daughter every day.

Marlene could see how much it cheered Lucy – but also how much it had the opposite effect on Danny.

'It's like the elephant in the room,' Lucy told Marlene one afternoon after her father had gone. 'Danny knows Father's been, but he won't mention it. Won't ask anything at all about the visit, or what we talked about, or what Father might have brought.'

Marlene listened, knowing how stubborn her brother could be.

'Honestly, the other day, Father bought us some steaks and I swear Danny almost choked on them because he knew, even though he didn't ask and I didn't tell him, who they were from.'

Marlene had to laugh. 'Oh, Lucy, he'll come round, I'm sure of it. It'll just take time.'

Lucy felt her stomach. 'I just want this baby to come into the world and be greeted by a united family – not one at war.'

Marlene didn't say anything, but got up and rearranged some flowers she'd brought. Her worry was not so much about family feuds as Lucy making it to her due date without any more scares. She knew Dr Wright had played down the seriousness of what he had called a 'minor uterine tear', but she understood why. It would not help Lucy, or her baby, to be in a state of high anxiety for the remainder of her pregnancy.

'And dare I ask about Thomas?' Lucy queried.

'Oh,' Marlene gasped dramatically. 'Still being pursued relentlessly by the woman who can do no wrong.' It was a constant source of annoyance to Marlene that she seemed to be the only person who didn't like Mabel. She was beginning to see how Danny felt; it was why she never took Edward's side when her brother sounded off about him to her.

'But the question is,' Lucy asked, 'if *Thomas* thinks that Mabel can do no wrong?'

Marlene slumped down on the side of the bed.

'When Mabel was at her father and stepmother's house during the two weeks we were cut off, I felt Thomas and I got back to how we used to be with each other.'

Lucy nodded. She had thought so too.

'But now that Mabel's back on the scene, every time I've gone to see Thomas, *she's* there. I've given up going now.'

Lucy tutted.

'It hurts me to admit this,' Marlene continued, 'but I *do* think Thomas has feelings for Mabel. I know he's always denied it, but feelings can change. I know he used to have feelings for me before, but I'm not sure if that's the case now – or whether his feelings have transferred to the marvellous Mabel. And it's not just because she's an attractive woman, but because they seem like they've actually become really good friends these past few months. I feel like she's stolen my place. Which sounds so childish. But Thomas has always been *my* friend. We've known each other for years.'

Lucy listened. It was true. Mabel had been spending a lot of time with Thomas lately. More since she had become a live-in employee.

'And you've still not managed to show him that your feelings go much further than simply being friends?' Lucy asked. 'I still reckon Thomas thinks that your feelings are purely platonic.'

Marlene sighed. 'I just can't.'

Lucy took her friend's hand and squeezed it. Neither of them said what they were thinking – that this would not have been the case before her trip to London. Marlene might have had a close call when she'd been conned into believing that the two Rossi brothers simply wanted to have a drink with her before getting a taxi to take her to the train station, but although they had not got what they'd wanted, they had still taken something from Marlene. Lucy couldn't quite put her finger on it, but it had left Marlene wary and without the confidence she had once had.

'It's frustrating.' Marlene got up from the bed and opened the window a little to let some air in.

'Because?' Lucy asked, taking a sip of her ginger ale as she felt yet another wave of nausea hit.

'Because I've changed a lot, and I don't think Thomas realises that.'

Lucy thought he *had* realised that, but didn't say so. Instead, she asked, 'Changed in what way?'

'Well, I'm older, obviously, and I'd hope I'm more mature.' She paused. 'I should be – I am now a fully fledged grown-up. I can go into a pub and have an alcoholic beverage without breaking the law, and I can join the army, navy, RAF or police force. Although I still have to elope to Gretna Green if I want to get married without parental consent.'

They both chuckled.

'But seriously,' Lucy said, taking another sip of her drink. 'Changed in the way you are? The way you think?'

'Both, I guess,' Marlene mused. 'Before, I was determined to marry someone rich and of the highest social standing. Whereas now that's not important.'

'Because?'

'Because I'm not so much in awe of their status or their wealth. I've been around them long enough now and they're just flesh and blood like the rest of us. And I'm not so fixated on being with someone who's rich as I'm really enjoying earning my own money. Having lots of money isn't the be all and end all.'

Lucy arched an eyebrow. Marlene liked the best of everything – from clothes to food and fine wine.

Marlene tutted. 'Okay, I do want lots of money, but *I* want to be the one earning it – and it's no longer my number-one priority in life.'

'So what is?'

'Love,' Marlene said. 'True love.'

Lucy smiled. Marlene mightn't have realised it, but love had always been her priority. And not just a priority, but a deep-seated need.

Chapter Twenty-Five

The arrival of March finally brought an end to the cold snap, and evidence of spring started to push its way through the once ice-hard soil. And with the thaw came a return to normality. The wheels of commerce creaked back into action, roads opened up, trains started to run again, people went back to work. The Cuthford Country House Hotel opened its doors when the first drops of melting snow and ice started to trickle from the lead-tiled roof and conical-shaped towers. And business immediately started to boom once again, as those who could afford it were desperate for a break after being confined to their homes during the Big Freeze. The children's return to school followed, with surprisingly few moans and groans. Carl went back to working around the clock on his vegetable patch and flower garden, his workload heavier still as the new cook, Mrs Trendle, was keen to see the pots of herbs and other saplings, which had been rescued when the bad weather started, returned to their rightful place. Outside.

Everyone who was a cog in the running of the hotel was working flat out.

Lloyd spent much of his time in the study, crunching numbers and doing the books, looking at the outgoings and income, and chatting to the bank about how best to invest any money that didn't go straight back into growing the hotel as a business.

Cora and Mabel worked well as a team, with Cora doing most of the hotel management from her little box room down the corridor from the kitchen, and Mabel physically implementing what needed to be done. She had a way of getting the staff not only to do what she asked with good grace, but often to go that little bit further. She had the older ones like Wilfred and Alberta wrapped around her little finger, as she'd always sneak them a little treat from the kitchen. Lloyd liked her because he saw how happy Cora was and how much less stressed she'd been since taking on Mabel as her assistant. The only staff who didn't really know Mabel were those who worked outdoors – Ted and Eugene, the groundsmen, and Bill, the old gardener, who now pottered about and helped Carl – for the simple reason that if Mabel had free time to go outside, she was not going to waste a minute of it on anyone but Thomas.

Marlene was working hard on planning and organising what she was calling her 'debut wedding', which of course necessitated buying Weldon's *Bride Book*, and any bridal-related editions of *Vogue*, *Harper's Bazaar*, *Woman* and *Woman's Own*. Seeing Clemmie's reaction on spotting such publications lying around on the kitchen table, anyone would have thought they were pornographic in nature, and they led to Clemmie having a 'chat' with Bonnie and Jemima about a life 'beyond getting married and being shackled to the sink'.

Marlene's debut wedding was not only going to be the hotel's first hosting of a couple's wedding breakfast and evening do, but the soon-to-be Mr and Mrs had booked the new honeymoon suite – as well as the rest of the hotel's suites for their family and friends. Their only lament was that there were not more rooms to accommodate more of their guests.

It was going to be a full house, with all the staff working every waking hour, making sure the rooms were immaculate, with fires stacked and fresh flowers in place.

Although she was thrilled with the success of her forays into both weddings and funeral receptions, which the hotel had become well known for, it did not leave Marlene with much time for a social life or even to see Thomas. If she had a spare hour or so, she'd go out to the stables to find that he had taken a group out on a trek or was giving a lesson in the paddock.

The success of both the hotel and the Cuthford Manor Equestrian Centre had come at a price. Gone were the days when Marlene, Danny, Lucy and Thomas would sit in the tack room and chat or listen to the wireless.

Lucy was the only one who had the time, but she was, in her words, a 'beached whale languishing on a bed', and was now so big she struggled to heave herself onto two feet – feet, she lamented, she could no longer see, never mind touch. With only three weeks to go, her due date was rapidly approaching, something that was causing mixed feelings – relief that she had not had any more bleeds or signs of going into an early labour, and high anxiety about the actual birth and becoming a mother for the first time.

Danny was on the go constantly, his reputation as head of one of the county's best equestrian centres and liveries growing all the time. And if he did have a minute to spare, he'd be hurrying over to the cottage to check on Lucy – provided, of course, that Edward was not there.

141

Thomas had become Danny's sounding board of late when it came to the subject of Edward. Danny's focus was no longer on his father-in-law's true persona, but on the fact that Edward seemed to be pushing him away from his own wife.

'I feel like there are three of us in this marriage now,' Danny lamented, 'and I'm fast becoming the spare part. When we first got married, I remember coming back from Gretna and holding Lucy's hand and feeling like we were one – it was just us two against the world. Together we were strong. Nothing could beat us. But now it feels like her father is taking my place. I reckon he actually sees more of my wife than I do!'

Thomas had wanted to say that this also seemed to be the case for him and Marlene but didn't. He didn't want to add to Danny's growing ire by confiding his own concerns that Edward seemed to be getting very pally with Marlene – too pally. The balloon would go up if Danny thought that Edward was not only coming between him and his wife, but also making a play for his younger sister.

Meanwhile, Marlene mourned the loss of those earlier, more carefree days when she, Lucy, Danny and Thomas had been a tight-knit group, but as life had shown her many times already, there were no constants and it was all about adapting to change. She did not, however, like or want to adapt to the changes that seemed to be happening to her relationship with Thomas – or to his burgeoning friendship with Mabel.

Today, not for the first time, she'd gone to see Thomas during a rare break and had walked out into the yard to see that Mabel had beaten her to it and was heading out for a ride with him. She watched them from the back doorway of the manor house. Mabel had on her figure-hugging riding gear, along with a new tweed jacket that was nipped in at the waist. Her back was straight as a rod and her chest pushed out. Marlene would guess that underneath the jacket she had a blouse on which showed off her bust, which she was sure had been boosted of late with one of the new conical-shaped bras she'd seen advertised.

She remembered a time she herself had dressed to impress, when Thomas had been giving her lessons as she'd heard that some movie star had said in an interview that her figure was down to riding horses and learning circus tricks. Marlene had also worn low-cut tops and tight jodhpurs, along with a layer of her trademark red lipstick. Again, she realised the irony that the fulfilment and happiness she felt at becoming part of the family business seemed to have come at the expense of no longer having as much time to spend with Thomas. And now someone else had jumped into the gap she had left.

But worst of all was seeing how at ease Thomas seemed with Mabel, which was evident now as they made their way out for a ride on Ghost and Starling, chatting away and laughing. Marlene thought of how she and Thomas had laughed and chatted and been at ease with each other. She'd always felt she could be herself with him. There'd never been any pretence from either of them.

Marlene saw Thomas and Mabel push their horses into a canter and watched until they had disappeared from view.

Only then did she turn and go back inside.

As she went to close the back door, she was stopped by the sudden appearance of an out-of-breath Edward.

'Oh, Marlene,' he said, 'I'm so pleased I've caught you.'

He gave his feet a good wipe on the coarse mat.

Marlene guessed he had been to see Lucy.

'Everything all right?' she asked.

'Yes, yes, couldn't be better,' he said. 'I've left my darling daughter making short work of a Victoria sponge I purchased in the village bakery.'

Marlene smiled. 'Safe to say that the morning sickness has finally run its course.'

'I'd say so. Better late than never.'

'So, if it's not about Lucy, what is it you want to talk to me about?'

'Well, it's a bit of a business proposition . . .'

Chapter Twenty-Six

When Thomas and Mabel made it to the turnaround point, they dismounted. Catching their breath, they stood, hands to their foreheads, shielding their eyes from the sun as they took in the picture-perfect panoramic view of the landscape laid out around them like a huge canvas of varying blocks of emerald and olive greens, interspersed with occasional patches of vibrant yellow rapeseed. To their left, the canvas turned a blue-grey, speckled with splashes of white, the telltale sign that today the North Sea was feeling lively.

Thomas let Mabel take in the county's natural beauty as this was the first time he had brought her to this spot, the ride here being more challenging for a relative beginner.

'There's Cuthford Manor,' Thomas pointed out.

Mabel turned around and squinted. She could just about make out its distinctive outline of castle-like turrets and fairy-tale towers.

She turned to look north.

'And is that Roeburn Hall I can just about see?'

Thomas turned and followed her gaze. The taller and more traditional shape of an English stately home could be seen.

'Yes, it is,' he said. 'I'd never really thought to look for it before.'

As they let their horses have free rein and munch on the

still-dewy grass, Mabel walked towards the top of the incline, took off her jacket and spread it down on the ground.

'I need to take the weight off. It's been non-stop today. Mind you, when isn't it,' she said, patting the space next to her. 'Not that I'm complaining. I wouldn't want it any different. Better to be busy than bored.'

Thomas sat on the jacket but ensured there was gap between them.

'Have you heard the latest scandal?' Mabel asked, shifting herself so as to be a little nearer to Thomas.

'Honestly, Mab, you're such a gossipmonger,' Thomas said, shaking his head.

As he seemed totally disinterested in knowing what she had to impart, Mabel answered her own question.

'Well, it concerns Marlene . . . '

'Oh, yes?' Thomas tried to sound nonchalant.

'Well,' Mabel said, widening her eyes, 'rumour has it that Marlene and Edward are secretly seeing each other, but have yet to be open about it because of the age gap.'

She paused, waiting for the news to sink in.

'And, of course, there's the fact that he's Lucy's father – and never mind that her brother hates the man's guts.'

Thomas felt a slew of anger and jealousy rise to the surface. *Danny wasn't the only one to hate the man's guts.*

When Thomas still hadn't said anything, Mabel probed further.

'What do you think? Are you surprised?'

He answered her question with a shrug of the shoulders.

Mabel gave him a playful nudge. 'A man of few words.'

'Suppose I don't really know what to say,' he muttered,

keeping his eyes focused on the view in front of him, although it was not the scenery he was seeing but an image of the woman he loved in the arms of another man.

'Well, apart from the age, I guess it's not so surprising,' Mabel said, turning her head and looking at Thomas. 'Those in the higher echelons of society generally like to marry within their set, don't they? Combine their properties and land and wealth.'

'Mmm,' Thomas said. 'They do that.' He thought about how Marlene had always made it quite plain that she would marry someone rich and upper class, but he'd thought she had changed since London. She didn't seem so materialistic or so much in awe of those with so-called 'standing' and money. He'd obviously been wrong. Very wrong.

'And to be fair, Edward and Marlene do look good together. You can see why they would be attracted to each other. He's tall and dark and good-looking – very Laurence Olivier in *Wuthering Heights*. And Marlene is well . . . ' Mabel had to force the words out, as it hurt her to say anything positive about her, ' . . . also good-looking. She certainly makes the most of herself.' Mabel couldn't help but be a little bitchy. 'And the age gap doesn't really jump out at you, does it? I mean, Marlene easily looks like she's in her early twenties – especially when she's all done up – and Lucy's father might be in his late thirties, but he could pass for ten years younger. Don't you think?'

Thomas wanted to snap back that he didn't *want* to think. That thinking about Marlene and Edward as being well suited, never mind romantically involved, was abhorrent.

'And they've been spending a lot of time together. First

it was planning the wake, and then, after all that nonsense about him killing his wife, once all that had passed, I'd see him with Marlene, chatting about how the new honeymoon suite was coming along and meeting some of the builders and labourers involved, seeing if they'd be available to do the work that needs to be done at Roeburn Hall.'

Thomas nodded. Since Mabel had been taken on as Cora's assistant, she knew everything that happened under the manor's roof. Especially since she'd moved into the staff quarters along from the kitchen at the start of the year.

'And now they always seem to meet *by chance* at the cottage when they go and see Lucy.'

Thomas couldn't stand it any more.

He stood up.

'Come on, let's get back,' he said, brushing himself down. 'Time's getting on and Danny wants me to take the beginners class this afternoon.' He was lying, which was something he rarely did, but he just needed to be on his own. Away from any more chatter about Marlene and Edward.

As he strode towards Ghost, who was munching on a patch of longer grass, he knew he would have to avoid Marlene at all costs. Not because he couldn't trust himself not to say anything, but because the heartache would be unbearable.

As Mabel mounted Starling and pushed the mare that had once been predominantly Marlene's horse into a trot, she congratulated herself on being so convincing. Thomas had believed everything she had said. Every word of which had been complete fabrication. But they were necessary falsehoods if she was to win Thomas over. For Mabel knew that

Thomas had to let go of any hope that he and Marlene could possibly be an item.

When Mabel started work at the manor and had seen how close Marlene and Thomas were, she hadn't thought there would be a cat in hell's chance of the two of them becoming an item. Marlene, being the total snob that she was, had made it clear to all and sundry that she was destined for great things – meaning she intended to nab herself some rich toff. Mabel had believed it was only a matter of time before she would be able to draw Thomas's attention away from Marlene, and for him to set his sights on her own good self.

But when Marlene had returned from London all battered and bruised, Mabel had seen a change within a fairly short period of time. Marlene had become less showy, more grown-up, and then she had packed in school to start work at the manor, which had really annoyed Mabel, and not just because it meant she'd be around more, but because it was clear her focus was no longer on being a Hollywood starlet who wanted high society and wealth. Instead, she was a woman who now seemed more interested in women's rights and earning her own money. She hadn't even dated anyone since the London trip.

Which was why Mabel had had to become more proactive.

She had begun by becoming a live-in employee, and with her new position paying more money, she had been able to give herself a makeover. She'd started wearing make-up, as well as clothes that showed off her figure to its full potential. The riding lessons had been a brilliant idea and meant she was spending a lot of time with Thomas; plus, she'd never have been able to wear something that left so little to the imagination in a normal social setting. She'd caught Thomas very occasionally glancing at her cleavage or looking away when she mounted her steed in her skintight jodhpurs.

The lie she had just imparted about Marlene and Edward's made-up romance was the final push. Soon Thomas would be hers. And not long after that, he would be her husband. If all went to plan.

She had no worries about Thomas repeating the 'gossip' she had just told him as that wasn't in his nature. And Mabel knew he also wouldn't mention it in case it got back to Danny. If Thomas told him that Lucy's father was courting Danny's younger sister, it would be like dropping a spark into a tinderbox.

Mabel could rest assured that her subterfuge would not be found out. And when the time came and Thomas did inevitably find out that this was not true, well, then it would be too late. She would have him in her thrall. He would be hers. She would just say that the person who had passed on the gossip had obviously picked up the wrong end of the stick, and Marlene and Edward were just good friends who were close because of Marlene's relationship with Lucy.

Mabel pulled back on the reins as they approached the paddock, dropping behind Thomas and Ghost. As they brought their horses to a trot and then a walk near the stables, she made sure one of the buttons on her shirt had come loose.

A few minutes later, when they were dismounting, she took off her hat, causing her strawberry blonde hair to come tumbling down. She had been told by someone she had been seeing a while ago that she reminded him of the Hollywood star Rhonda Fleming. After that, she had endeavoured to wear her hair like the actress and had even mastered the same sensual mannerisms and throaty laughter.

'Oh,' Mabel said, as though suddenly just remembering. 'I've heard there's going to be a bit of a do on at the Farmer's Arms this evening, if you fancy coming along? I don't know about you, but I think I need an evening away from this place. I do love living here, but sometimes you can forget there's a world outside.'

Thomas nodded.

'You're right.'

The thought of being somewhere – anywhere – other than here, near Marlene, felt like a godsend.

'I'll see yer down there,' he said. Not only would it be a respite from being so near yet so far away from Marlene, it would also mean he could sink a few beers.

If ever there was a reason to drown his sorrows, then this was it.

Chapter Twenty-Seven

Having said saying goodbye to Edward after he'd told her about his 'business proposition', Marlene went in search of Angie and found her in the family room with Juni.

'Oh, how's my gorgeous little niece,' she said, her attention immediately focused on the little girl who was trying to pull herself onto two feet by holding on to the coffee table. Angie had wisely removed anything that had been on there.

'I think she's had enough of crawling around on her hands and knees all day. She is determined to master the art of standing up – and staying up,' Angie said.

'Determined is definitely the word,' Marlene said, sitting down on the sofa and smiling at Juni's screwed-up red face.

Angie got up from the floor, sat on the armchair and looked at her sister.

'You've got that look,' she said. 'I feel you're going to pitch me an idea.'

'I am,' Marlene said, not at all surprised that her sister could read her so well. She'd always been able to.

'Go on, I'm all ears,' Angie said, keeping half an eye on her daughter, who had just thudded down on her bottom but was already preparing for take two.

'Well, you know the Thursby wedding?' Marlene said.

'How could I not . . . ' Angie glanced at her sister.

'Well, you know they were *ever so* disappointed we didn't have more rooms – and that it was *soo unfortunate* they'd have to *slum it in some B & B.*'

Angie smiled at Marlene's very convincing impersonation of the not-so-blushing bride who was organising her wedding like a military operation.

Seeing that Juni had once again almost pulled herself up to standing, they both clapped and made excited congratulatory sounds.

'Well, Edward has made us a business proposition which I think could work to our advantage,' Marlene said.

'Let me guess,' Angie said, her tone tight. 'He's offered to help us out and take the overspill?'

Marlene felt herself deflate.

'How did you know?'

'Because,' Angie replied, 'I've concerns that the man might have plans to start up his own hotel, and at the moment we have the share of the market in this area, which is how I'd like to keep it. This is a perfect "in" for him.'

'Mmm,' Marlene mused. 'I hadn't really thought about that, but it would make sense.' She thought of all those rooms at Roeburn Hall standing empty, doing nothing but gather dust.

'He *has* offered us a cut of the takings,' Marlene said.

'No doubt,' Angie retorted. 'And if he hadn't, I'd have asked.' She paused, knowing she had to be diplomatic. 'I know you get on with Edward and that you are trying to smooth the waters for Lucy's sake, which I think is very admirable, but just be careful. I don't want to sound like Danny's double, but I still don't entirely trust the man.' She paused.

'But regarding him taking the overspill, I don't think we have much choice.'

'What do you mean?' Marlene asked.

'Well, for starters, we couldn't stop him renting out rooms at Roeburn Hall even if we wanted to. And if we tried to, we'd be seen as vindictive, especially as Edward is now part of our extended family. Plus, it would not be fair on Lucy. He is her father, after all – and Roeburn Hall is her family home.'

Marlene nodded her agreement.

'So, how much is he offering as a commission rate?' Angie asked as she got up out of her chair and bent down to pick up Juni, who had just thumped down on her bum for the umpteenth time and whose face told her she was just about to let loose an ear-splitting cry of frustrated defeat.

'Ten per cent.' Marlene repeated Edward's offer.

'Make it twenty – and we'll see how it goes.'

Chapter Twenty-Eight

The Farmer's Arms was full to bursting as not only was it Friday night and pay day, but word had spread like wildfire that the landlord had bought a jukebox. Donald, who had been landlord of the village pub for many years, had had to fight hard to be granted a licence from the local council for fear it would be a noise nuisance and attract undesirables, but he had finally twisted their arms, arguing that jukeboxes were now in pubs all over the country and that it was important to keep businesses in the village alive. He didn't have to remind the parish councillors that Cuthford had been on the county council's Category D list four years previously – and that the future of the village had looked in doubt.

Mabel fought her way through the packed pub, her heart lifting as she spotted Thomas, then dropping when she saw it was three-deep at the bar. Managing to worm her way to him by a combination of fluttering her eyelashes and pressing herself up against the men who didn't have a girlfriend in tow, Mabel finally made it to the front and shimmied up to Thomas.

'Blimey, I can't believe how busy it is. It's taken me an age just to fight my way to the bar.' Mabel leant into Thomas on the pretext that she needed to in order to be heard over the noise.

Thomas made an attempt at a smile as Mabel slid onto the bar stool next to him, but it was hard work. His mood had dropped and had continued to drop ever since he'd heard that Mabel and Edward were an item. He'd thought a pint or two might help, but it had only made him feel more morose. Even the rock 'n' roll records the landlord was playing didn't do anything to lift him out of this quagmire of deep depression.

'Well, it's certainly a change of scenery, isn't it?' Mabel remarked, looking around and then focusing her attention back on the bar to catch the barmaid's eye.

Thomas nodded. 'It is that.' He tried to sound normal. 'What you having to drink?' he asked, leaning to the side to pull out his wallet from his back pocket.

Mabel shook her head vehemently. 'No way. I owe you more than a pint for the riding lessons you've given me.'

When the barmaid reached them, Mabel had to lean across to give her order as the music was so loud and the chatter louder still.

'Another pint for Thomas and a whisky chaser, and I'll have a gin and tonic, please, Mary-Anne.'

The barmaid gave Mabel a sceptical look. The two had grown up together and Mary-Anne knew that Mabel didn't shell out for anything unless she was going to get something in return.

After they'd grabbed their drinks, Mabel led the way through the throng waiting to be served. Seeing some friends from the village, she looked back at Thomas and nodded over to the small crowd in the far corner of the pub. As they had all been born and brought up in and around the village, there was no need for introductions and the usual banter followed, which tended to focus on Thomas and Mabel working for the swanky hotel while they did the 'real work' either on local farms or down the pit. They all knew, though, that they'd swap their jobs at the drop of a hat to work at 'the manor'. Angie and her extended family who ran the hotel were well liked and paid decent wages.

It was an effort for Thomas to be sociable, but he tried, hoping that the locally brewed ale and the whisky chasers he was drinking might help. They didn't. Nor did they help to drown his sorrows as he'd hoped. Instead, as the evening wore on, they remained resolutely afloat. Images of Marlene kept rising to the surface, reminding him of their history together, which had started shortly after he'd been taken on as a stablehand. Not long afterwards, the owner, Marlene's brother-in-law, Quentin Foxton-Clarke, had died in what was thought to have been a tragic accident, and Thomas had seen how Marlene had cared for the little ones when Angie had taken to her bed, unable to function under the weight of her grief. It was then that Thomas had seen Marlene through a different lens and had been struck by her strength of character and how she had naturally fallen into the role of mother hen with Bertie, Jemima and Bonnie. He'd learnt they weren't as different as he'd initially thought – they'd both come from working-class backgrounds, with Marlene's father a miner and her mother a former splicer in a rope factory, just as they'd both been outcasts in the communities in which they'd been brought up. Thomas's family were known poachers and as such were viewed as criminal and the lowest of the low. Marlene's father was a drinker and her mother a 'loose woman', which had led Marlene to suffer the same derision from her peers.

As the pub got noisier, Thomas made a show of listening to what Mabel was chatting about when really his mind was a million miles away, remembering the connection he'd felt with Marlene and how he knew she felt the same. He'd seen how she behaved around other people and how she was with him and knew that he was getting to know the real Marlene. When Angie had decided she would mend her broken heart by emigrating to the other side of the world to live with her sister and family in Australia, Marlene had been distraught and they had talked endlessly of ways to put a stop to it. He'd known then he was falling for her – that his feelings were much more than those of mere friendship. The thought of her leaving the manor, leaving the country, of never seeing her again, had caused him to feel his own kind of grief. And when it was decided, much later, that they were to stay put, he'd felt such incredible relief. He'd wanted more than anything to tell Marlene how he felt, having spent months believing that he was going to lose her, but he couldn't. Angie had instructed Stanislaw to warn him off making any moves on Marlene. He might have ignored the caution had he not known that Marlene liked him and definitely found him attractive, but he'd realised that if they did get it together, it would never have lasted as Marlene had made it plain that she wanted a wealthy husband.

A part of him thought that Marlene might change as time passed, and he began to believe that she *had* changed after the ill-fated London trip and the months she had spent with her mam before Ida passed away. He really thought that her yearning for a life of superficial materialism and the need to be revered socially had waned.

But had he simply seen what he wanted to see?

After what he'd heard today, it would appear so.

By the time the bell clanked, signalling last orders, everyone in the pub was more than merry and a little tipsy. Thomas wasn't exactly merry, but he was definitely tipsy, and much more than a little.

At chucking-out time, Mabel managed to cadge a lift from one of the local farmers who had to pass the manor on his way home. Mabel was pleased. She had not wanted to walk the half a mile back to the manor as it would give Thomas time to sober up. And that was not part of her plan.

Thomas was glad as it meant he would not have to make conversation with Mabel during the trek back home. He still didn't seem able to tear his thoughts away from Marlene.

He'd never forget seeing her blackened face after the West Wing had gone up in flames. He'd sprinted there on hearing that the fire engines, which had woken the entire village, were headed for the manor. His heart had been in his mouth and he'd been terrified something had happened to her. Spotting her on the lawn, as dirty as a chimney sweep, he had wanted to gather her in his arms, so relieved was he that she was unharmed. But, instead, they'd gone off with Danny to bring the horses in from the paddock, where they had been taken earlier for fear the fire might reach the stables. The three of them had stayed for a good while, keeping the horses calm as they were understandably jittery from all the commotion.

Listening to Marlene as she'd told how she and Danny had raced to fetch the ladder Angie had climbed to rescue Stanislaw, Thomas had heard the pride in her voice when she explained that her sister used to operate the huge cranes in one of the Sunderland shipyards during the war, and that was why she had gone up the ladder. But in Thomas's eyes, Marlene was the heroine. She had jumped into action and done what was needed. And the bales of hay that she and Danny had hauled from the barn had ended up breaking Stanislaw's fall from the ladder, thereby saving his life. That night, Thomas reflected, he had become even more in love with Marlene, something he had not thought possible.

'Come on, Thomas, I'll help you up these stairs.'

Thomas's thoughts were derailed by Mabel's voice. He hadn't even been aware of the short journey back to the manor, or even of walking down the long driveway, so lost was he in his thoughts of the past – and his love for Marlene.

As Thomas slowly put one foot in front of the other and made his ungainly way up the wooden stairs to his digs, Mabel followed, gently placing a hand on his back to steady him.

How he wished more than anything that it was Marlene's hand he could feel.

'I'll make you a nice cup of tea when we get up there,' he heard Mabel say. 'That'll sort you out.'

Mabel was glad she herself had resisted drinking more. She'd had just enough to give her a little Dutch courage.

Chapter Twenty-Nine

Thomas woke up shortly after six in the morning with a thumping head and an overriding feeling of nausea. He had hoped getting so inebriated would have given him a break from thinking about Marlene, but it hadn't. Not only had he spent the entire evening thinking about her until he'd passed out on his bed, *he had also spent the entire night dreaming of her*. And, cruelly, in the dreams he'd had, they had been together – he had actually felt as though her body was next to his; the kisses they had exchanged had felt so real. And he had felt so happy. But then a faceless figure, whom he knew to be Edward, appeared and she had left him. But it had felt wrong. Not only did he feel bereft at her leaving, it seemed as though Marlene was also not willing to go – to leave him. She had looked back with eyes that said she loved *him*. Not Edward.

Thomas opened his eyes and looked at the ceiling. His dream had obviously been a manifestation of his want. His desire.

As he tried to lift up his head a fraction, he suddenly heard the sound of someone breathing. A soft, gentle breathing.

He slowly turned his head as a feeling of realisation and dread began to filter through his body, along with memories of last night.

As his eyes focused on the naked body next to him, he felt his world crumble.

There was no doubting who it was. Long, curly, strawberry blonde hair fanned out across the white linen pillowcase. The porcelain skin. The faint freckles on the side of her face.

He vaguely remembered coming back home. The trudge up the stairs and the feel of her hand on his back, helping him to stay steady.

The offer of tea to 'sort you out'.

He remembered crashing onto the bed as though every last ounce of energy had suddenly deserted his being, pulling off his boots and jacket, the sound of the kettle boiling. Mabel talking, but Thomas not hearing what she was saying.

He had a vague recollection of her walking towards him holding two mugs of tea and handing him one as she sat next to him on the bed.

He remembered looking at her face and feeling as though the room was beginning to spin.

But after that nothing.

Feeling his own nakedness and seeing that Mabel was also not wearing any clothes, Thomas could only assume what had happened.

As if sensing his stare, Mabel slowly rolled over so that they were facing each other.

She shuffled forward and kissed him gently on the mouth.

Sheer panic filled every fibre of his being. *Had he slept with Mabel while his mind had been full of Marlene?*

He sat up with a start.

'Mabel, I'm so sorry,' he blustered. 'I didn't . . . I can't . . . '

Mabel sat up in bed and covered her modesty with the sheet.

'Please don't tell me you don't remember?' she asked, her tone not reproachful but playful.

'Well, I . . . um . . . ' Thomas climbed out of bed and pulled on his boxer shorts and his jeans, which had been cast onto the floor. His head was banging so badly he thought he might have to sit back down again.

'I didn't think you'd had *that* much to drink,' Mabel said, watching him as he looked around for his T-shirt.

Thomas fought back a surge of biliousness as he remembered downing a shot of whisky. Quite a few shots.

'I don't normally drink spirits,' he said, pushing his hair back and walking a little unsteadily towards the kitchenette. He poured himself a glass of water and drank it back in one go.

While he did so, Mabel quickly got dressed.

'Let me make you a cup of tea,' Thomas offered.

Mabel looked at her watch.

'No, I'd better get back before anyone notices I've been out all night.'

She picked up her coat.

Thomas put his empty glass on the counter, took a step forward and stopped. Unsure what to do.

Mabel picked up her shoes and walked over to him. She kissed him on the lips again, her hand lightly touching the back of his head. She didn't step back but instead went on tiptoes so that her mouth was near his ear.

'It's a shame you can't remember,' she whispered. 'But I hope you might. Because it really was worth remembering.'

And with that she turned and walked towards the door. She waited for a brief moment, glancing out of the small square window that looked onto the rear of the manor and the cobbled backyard before opening the door and stepping out into the fresh early-morning air.

As Marlene did every morning at seven o'clock on the dot, she went to check on Lucy at the cottage. It was a habit she couldn't break for fear of something happening if she didn't go, which she knew to be ridiculously superstitious, but she didn't care. She needed to be reassured that her sister-in-law was well and that her little nephew or niece was staying exactly where he or she should be, and not trying to make an early entrance into the world.

Stepping out of the back door, Marlene did what she couldn't help herself doing whenever she was in the vicinity of the stables: she cast her eyes over to the barn, and seeing that no one was there, she looked up at Thomas's little bedsit. He would probably be walking out the door any minute, stomping down the wooden stairs that had recently been built to make his living quarters into a proper flat with its own entrance.

Shrugging on her quilted jacket as the morning air was icy cold, a movement caught the corner of Marlene's eye.

She looked up, expecting to see Thomas, a smile already starting to play on her lips. But as her eyes fell on the person coming out of the door, she stopped dead in her tracks.

Any semblance of a smile disappeared in an instant.

It was not Thomas.

She watched as the person leaving Thomas's abode turned to quietly shut the door.

When the young woman turned around again and started to make her way down the wooden stairs, she too stopped dead.

Both women locked eyes.

Marlene felt a physical pain in her chest as she looked at the person who had clearly just spent the night with Thomas. Her long, naturally curly hair was tousled, the clothes she was wearing were creased and she was holding her heeled shoes in one hand as she walked down the steps in her stockinged feet.

Mabel!

The name of her love nemesis screamed at full volume in her head, blotting out all other sounds.

Marlene tried to move, walk away, escape from the vision of the woman who was causing her heart to break as comprehension sank in.

Mabel had spent the night with Thomas.

Mabel and Thomas were an item.

At that moment, Marlene felt all her hopes of love crushed into non-existence.

And the loss she felt was immense.

As was the anger that followed.

He'd lied. Thomas had lied to her.

And in that moment, the man she had believed she *loved* more than anything became the man she *hated* more than anyone.

Finally able to snap herself out of her temporary paralysis, Marlene looked away and walked across the cobbles, then along the perimeter of the paddock before her legs began to turn to jelly.

She just managed to make it to the front door of the cottage before the tears started to stream silently down her face.

And she felt the all-consuming pain of her heart breaking into a million pieces.

Chapter Thirty

After Mabel had left, Thomas sank down onto the leather sofa and put his hands on his head in despair.

What the hell had he done?

He looked across at the rumpled bed.

Stupid question.

God, how could he be so foolish? So dumb? So bloody brain-dead?

How had he managed to sleep with Mabel – with anyone, for that matter – when his head had only been able to think of Marlene and his heart felt as though it had been ripped to shreds?

He felt a sudden jolt of memory. Of his dream about Marlene – in which he had been kissing her. He again felt the rise of nausea. Had that really been a dream? Or had it been reality, only instead of Marlene, he had been kissing and caressing Mabel?

God, no, please, no.

He desperately tried to recall more. They had clearly made love; he just couldn't remember.

Again, Thomas cursed himself. His brother often had memory blackouts when he went out on the lash, but this was something Thomas had never experienced before. But then again, he had not downed so many shots of Scotch before.

They must have been the cause of the void in his head about his time with Mabel.

And Mabel, of all people. She was a friend. They worked in the same place. Lived in the same place. He knew she was keen on him, but he'd thought he'd made it clear that his feelings were purely platonic.

Thomas stood up and looked at the small bedside clock.

He needed to get to work.

Goddammit! He felt a sudden surge of fury. Wanted to snatch the clock and hurl it against the wall. He refrained. And as the anger waned, the dark cloud that had engulfed him after hearing about Marlene and Edward infiltrated every part of his being once again.

Chapter Thirty-One

As was Marlene's way, after she had cried all her tears and exhausted herself, never mind Lucy, with the relaying of what she had seen and her heartbreak and grief at losing the man she had believed was 'The One', her feelings returned once again to resentment and rebuke.

'Why lie to me?' she said in exasperation. 'God, I gave him enough chances to tell me that he had feelings for Mabel. Why not be honest? We've known each other for years. He should have said.'

Lucy nodded and made the right sounds, but she just wished Marlene had done as she had suggested and told Thomas how she felt. There had been no doubt in her mind that Thomas had been very much in love with Marlene – for years. She'd seen it with her own eyes. She and Danny had often wondered how long it would be before they got it together. They had danced around a courtship for so long. Lucy had believed that the two were on the verge of finally becoming a couple, but then London had happened – and Marlene had changed. Her feelings for Thomas hadn't, though Lucy knew that it might look that way. Which was why she had been encouraging Marlene to simply tell Thomas how she felt. Especially as any fool could see that Thomas and Mabel were becoming closer; they were certainly very chummy with

169

each other, even more so after she'd started to learn to ride. Which had coincided with how much busier Marlene had been at the manor and her taking on more projects.

'It makes you wonder how long it's been going on for?' Marlene stewed.

'It might have just been a one-off?' Lucy said, although she didn't really think it would be. Thomas was not the kind of person to have one-night stands. Nor was Mabel, from the little she really knew of her.

Marlene shook her head, dismissing the idea for the same reasons.

Seeing the time, and worried about bumping into people as the manor came to life, Marlene said her farewells to Lucy, telling her she'd pop in and see her later.

When she left the cottage, she walked around to the front of the manor so she wouldn't run into Thomas, who she knew would now be in the barn, seeing to the horses and their daily ablutions, or Mabel, who seemed to be everywhere lately. Hurrying so as to avoid anyone noticing her puffy red eyes, and not trusting herself to speak should anyone say anything to her, she breathed a sigh of relief on reaching her room in the West Wing.

After splashing her face with cold water – repeatedly – she sat at her dresser and carefully tried to hide the damage and mask any signs that she had been crying. She'd bitten down on her lip so many times to stop more tears from dripping down her face and undoing her work, she didn't need to apply any lipstick, just a slick of gloss.

Forcing herself to take a deep, shuddering breath, she then headed downstairs to start work.

After making herself a quick cup of tea and having the briefest of interactions with the staff, Marlene hurried to the sanctuary of the study and closed the door, glad that the little ones weren't yet up, and even more glad not to have seen Mabel. She was pleased she had plenty to do: there were menus to sort out, and a number of guests had made specific requests regarding their accommodation or their food, or both. There were lots of phone calls to make, but any direct, face-to-face meetings or discussions could wait until tomorrow.

By teatime, Marlene had organised a funeral reception and spoken to two couples over the phone about their vision for their wedding celebrations. She felt she should be in the running for a Best Actress Award with her ability to sound so carefree and happy. Feigning great excitement about the impending nuptials, she asked how they'd met and, with a heart that just seemed to keep on breaking, listened to their tales of how they had fallen in love.

Seeing that it had gone four, Marlene decided she had done as much as she could. Now she just wanted to go for a very long walk, tell the cook there would be one less for dinner, then disappear off to her room, where she could be morose without worrying that anyone would see her and ask what was wrong.

She also had to work out exactly how she was going to deal with Mabel when she saw her – and with Thomas, of course.

Marlene was just leaving the study when she saw Edward being welcomed by Wilfred. She grimaced inwardly. If she had known he was there, she would have stayed in the study until he'd gone. She guessed this must be today's designated time to spend with Lucy at the cottage, which made sense as Danny never made it back home until gone six.

'Ah, how's the budding entrepreneur doing today?' he asked, spotting his daughter's best friend.

Marlene plastered what she felt was a convincing smile on her face – but neither that nor her carefully applied make-up fooled her friend's father.

'Has something happened?' he asked, his face an open book, showing that his anxiety was for his daughter.

Marlene smiled for the first time since the morning's revelations.

'No, no,' she reassured. 'Lucy's fine. She's well. Honestly, nothing to worry about.'

Again, Marlene thought how lovely it must be to have such a genuinely caring father.

'Then if it's not my daughter,' Edward concluded, 'it is *you* I should be concerned about.'

'It's nothing,' Marlene said, looking at her watch. 'You'd better go and see Lucy. The clock is ticking.' She tried to sound jocular, though she was feeling anything but; her smile, however, was natural. Edward's words of concern for her had brought a slight warmth to her fractured heart.

'Okay,' Edward said, automatically looking at his own watch. 'But when my time with my daughter is up, I am taking you out. You need cheering up.'

Marlene opened her mouth to object. All she really wanted to do was to go for a walk, then crawl into her bed and stay under the covers until she had to get up again.

'And,' Edward beat her to it, 'I won't take no for an answer.'

He started to walk away.

'I shall see you in an hour,' he called over his shoulder as he headed off.

Chapter Thirty-Two

Thomas had felt wretched all day. His hangover he could endure; the fact that he had slept with Mabel, he could not. He had to see her, talk to her, try and put all this right. *God, who was he kidding!* There *was* no 'putting this right'. *Talk about shutting the gate after the horse had bolted.* Spotting Mabel heading over to the allotment with Winston and Bessie on either side of her, Thomas rightly presumed that she was going to see either Carl or Bill to find out what produce was available for the guests' evening meals. He waited on tenterhooks until she was on her way back to the manor before he jogged over to her. As soon as the dogs saw Thomas, they bounded towards him, making him stop in his tracks. Thomas responded by giving them robust pats and a good scratch behind their ears.

'Can I have a chat when you're free later?' he asked, straightening up and forcing himself to make eye contact with the woman he'd had intimate relations with – something he still couldn't remember. He wasn't sure whether in some perverse way he had blanked it out because he didn't want it to be real.

'Yes, of course we can have a chat,' Mabel said. '*I* was also hoping to see *you* later.' She paused. 'After last night.'

'Great,' Thomas said, hoping that Mabel wanted to see

him for the same reason he wanted to chat to her – to say it had been a mistake.

'I've just got to tell Cook there's leeks and rhubarb galore if she wants it – and also that there's one less for the family dinner.' Mabel looked at Thomas and raised her eyebrows. 'Apparently Marlene has just gone out with Edward. They're dining out this evening. Just the two of them.'

This caught Thomas unawares.

'So, they're being open about it?' he asked, his tone full of outrage.

'Oh, God, no,' Mabel said, quick to put Thomas right. 'They said they just wanted to go out and discuss an idea that he and Lucy have for Roeburn Hall. They both made a point of saying that Lucy would have gone with them were she not still having to rest up.'

Seeing the dogs were starting to wander over to the barn, Thomas called them back.

'Come on, you two,' Mabel said, using her sing-song voice for Winston and Bessie, who responded with wagging tails. 'Let's see if Mrs Trendle has got you any scraps.' She looked at Thomas. 'I'll meet you by the five-bar gate in ten minutes,' she said as she turned and headed back with the dogs padding before her.

Thomas walked over to the barn, wondering how he was going to carry on working there if he had to endure this terrible feeling in his chest every time Marlene and Edward were mentioned in the same breath. It was why he had to tell Mabel that last night was a mistake. How could he be with her, or someone else, *anyone else*, when his heart was still with Marlene? Just because she was now with Edward didn't mean he could stop how he felt about her – couldn't stop being *in love* with her. He'd thought about telling Mabel the whole truth – that he loved Marlene and it had been Marlene who had been in his head when they had slept together last night – but he knew that it would be unfair and incredibly hurtful. So, instead, he would tell her that he was truly sorry, but it really was a case of beer in, wits out. He would tell her that most blokes would give anything to have her on their arm, and that he liked her a lot, but just as a friend.

Chapter Thirty-Three

Danny sniffed the air as he walked through the little front door to the cottage they had unofficially called 'The Haven' when they had first moved in, though it now felt anything but.

'Does your father *have* to smoke when he visits?' he asked, pulling off his boots. 'It's so lovely and fresh out there, then you walk in here and you feel as though you've just stepped into the local boozer.'

Lucy sat on the sofa in the sitting room, her feet up on a pouffe, as directed by Dr Wright when she really had the urge to leave her bed. She couldn't wait for the baby to arrive so that she could once again start to see life from a standing position.

'Sorry, Dan, I *have* asked him, but he forgets,' she yelled in the direction of the hallway.

'Mmm, I'll bet,' Danny mumbled under his breath. 'God forbid he does anything he doesn't want to do.'

Lucy tutted. 'I might be incapacitated at the moment, but that doesn't mean my hearing is also out of action.'

She watched as her husband walked into the kitchen and went to the range, where there was a rabbit and black pudding stew that Cora had brought round earlier. He lifted the lid with a pair of oven gloves.

'Besides, I want him to feel at home here,' she shouted through to the kitchen, which was directly opposite the lounge. 'Not feel that there's all these rules and regulations he has to follow.' Lucy's voice went up with each word, betraying her ire and frustration that her husband could not get down off his high horse when it came to her father.

Danny put the lid back on the casserole.

'I see, or rather, I should say *I hear* there's nothing wrong with your vocal cords,' he batted back, giving away his own feelings of irritation and anger when it came to his wife's father – and lately to his wife. Which it pained him to admit. How awful that he could feel angry at his wife, the woman he loved and who was having his baby. But how could he not when she continued to take her father's side, refusing to see him for what he was and, worse still, unable to see how he was coming between them?

Which, he felt, was Edward's intention.

Not that Danny would admit this to anyone, as they'd think *he* was being paranoid and that *he* was the one who had the problem.

Chapter Thirty-Four

Marlene took another sip of her wine and smiled at Edward. 'Thanks for listening to me. And I'm so sorry for rambling on. I can't believe I've just chewed your ear off . . . Honestly, I'll bet you're sat there, regretting having ever asked me to come out for a meal.'

Edward shook his head. 'Quite the reverse, Marlene, quite the reverse.'

'Well, thank you for listening.' She let out a slightly sad laugh. 'I'm not sure if it's the wine or the fact I've just unburdened myself on you that has made me feel a little better.'

Edward gave a hearty laugh. 'I think both!'

They fell silent as the waiter came to take their plates.

'So, I want to talk about something different now,' Marlene said, once the table had been cleared and they had declined dessert.

Edward poured the last of the wine into Marlene's glass. 'Purely medicinal,' he said with faux seriousness.

'Well, then, how can I refuse?' Marlene replied equally earnestly.

'So, if we are to talk about *something different*,' Edward said, upending the bottle and putting it in the silver wine bucket, 'I'll let you pick a subject.'

Marlene took a sip from her refreshed wine glass.

'Roeburn Hall,' she said. 'I want to know what you are going to do with the place. I'm guessing you don't have a bottomless pit of money to keep it going for evermore?'

Edward spluttered on his drink. 'You certainly are a card, aren't you, Marlene? Did no one tell you there are some subjects which are a big no-no in polite conversation?'

'I seem to have skipped that part of my education – but I'm guessing money is one of them.'

'Ten out of ten,' Edward said.

'I think you're stalling,' Marlene said, 'which says to me that either you don't want to tell me, or you don't really know what you're going to do.'

'Ah, a mind reader as well as a veritable beauty.' Edward smiled.

Marlene felt herself blush, which might have been heightened because she had started to feel a little tipsy with the wine.

'So, which one is it?' she pressed.

Edward sighed. 'I'm stalling because I don't want to appear to be a man without a plan.' His shoulders drooped ever so slightly as he sat back in his chair. 'But I'm afraid that is exactly what I am.'

Marlene narrowed her eyes and looked at Edward. 'That surprises me.'

'Does it also disappoint?' Edward asked hesitantly.

'Not at all,' Marlene answered. 'I like your honesty.'

She took another sip of her wine.

'I'm sure you'll come up with something,' she said.

Edward suddenly sat up straight.

'I've a suggestion,' he declared. Turning to catch the eye of one of the waiters, he mimicked signing a cheque.

'Which is?' Marlene asked when he turned his attention back to her.

'Well, I might not have a business plan,' he said, his eyes sparkling, 'but I would like to talk you through my vision.'

Half an hour later, Edward was pulling up outside Roeburn Hall in his sports car. Marlene was in the passenger seat. Her mind went back to the last time she had been in a car with Edward, when she had been driving back from the hospital after Elise's death. That evening it had been Edward in the passenger seat, and she had felt uncomfortable with him so close. Her gut had told her to be wary of Edward. On top of which, her opinion of him had certainly not been high after the way he had behaved towards Lucy following her marriage to Danny.

How much had changed since that day seven months ago.

She certainly hadn't felt ill at ease during their drive from Durham to Roeburn Hall. And his car was even more snug than her Ford Anglia.

As Edward opened the car door for her, she took his hand and he helped her out, which was a necessity as well as good manners since the Aston Martin was so low it was practically touching the ground.

Walking up the front steps to the grand pillared entrance of Roeburn Hall, Marlene thought how easy it was to get the wrong impression of someone. And how you had to make up your own mind about people, find out what they were like for yourself. It was something she'd learnt from the time she'd spent with her mam and how much her opinion of her mother had changed as she'd got to know her. And although

Marlene had always been one to listen to her gut, perhaps getting to know Edward was showing her that her gut wasn't always right.

'Welcome to my humble abode.' Edward opened the door and moved aside so that Marlene was the first to step over the threshold. He followed and flicked on the lights in the hallway.

'Wow!' Marlene exclaimed as the massive wood-panelled hallway was suddenly illuminated. She looked up at the expansive ceiling to see a chandelier that made the one in Cuthford Manor look positively small.

'What amazing plasterwork,' she admired, her neck bent back as she marvelled at the intricate patterns and swirls of the ceiling and cornices.

'It dates back to 1891. The original lime plaster. Rococo style,' Edward explained. 'But it needs repairing and a repaint. Rather like the whole place.'

Walking over and opening the door to show Marlene the lounge, Edward began the tour around his ancestral home, sharing his vision, as they went from room to room, of what he wanted to do and how it was his dream to bring Roeburn Hall back to its former glory.

The tour, however, did not take in the cellar, although Marlene noticed the dark wooden door, which she knew opened onto the flight of stone steps that had ultimately led Elise Stanton-Leigh to her untimely and tragic death.

'You know,' Edward said when they were walking along the landing, the carpet of which Marlene noticed was practically threadbare, 'I feel that the old gal is crying out for life and laughter, and dare I say it – love . . . I know many might say that it is too early for me to be thinking about such things – about finding love and having another family – when it's not yet a year since Elise passed away, but . . .' he paused '. . . I think I can speak candidly with you, my dear?' He looked askance at Marlene, adding, 'I know you have seen more than most your age, and I would go so far as to say that you are far from shockable.'

Marlene laughed. 'Yes, I guess so. On both counts.' Although she had to admit to herself that she *had* been shocked that Mabel had spent the night with Thomas.

She forced her mind back to her conversation with Edward.

'So, go on,' she encouraged, 'what did you want to speak to me candidly about?'

'Well, you see, by the end of my marriage to Elise – actually, probably well before that – we were never really properly *together*, you know? We had gone our separate ways. It had become a marriage in name only. And I hope I can say this without seeming improper . . . ' another quick glance at Marlene ' . . . but, well, Elise and I were . . . we were not faithful to one another.' He spoke the last words quickly, all the time watching for Marlene's reaction. Seeing that she did not look either embarrassed or morally outraged, he continued. 'We both saw other people. Of course, we were discreet. But I think what I'm trying to say is that ours was never a great love.' He paused. 'And I must say it had always been my desire to have more children. Elise only ever wanted the one, which I have to admit was always a disappointment to me.' Another pause as he looked around him. 'I would love to hear these empty corridors filled with the squeals and laughter of children.'

Marlene was taken aback by Edward's confession – not the revelation that his marriage had been one of convenience, which was no surprise, but his honesty, his forthrightness and his heartfelt wishes.

Edward looked at Marlene and then at his watch. 'Gosh! And now it's me who is *chewing your ear off*. And look at the time!'

Marlene had been unaware of how late it was as she had been quite entranced by this incredible property. Especially its immense potential. It would have been a disservice to call it merely a house. *But what a home it could be.*

'Right, come on, let me get you back to Cuthford Manor. You must be shattered!' Edward declared. 'Especially after everything that's happened today.'

Those words immediately brought Marlene back to the reality from which she had enjoyed a brief reprieve. And as they drove back to Cuthford Manor, so Marlene's thoughts returned to Thomas. After saying goodnight to Edward and thanking him for a lovely evening, particularly for helping her escape her misery for a few hours, Marlene headed to bed, where her thoughts were given over to Thomas.

During the years they had known each other, he had been there through all the dramas life had hurled her way – Quentin's tragic death, the arson attack on the manor, the aftermath of finding out the unthinkable truth about Quentin's mother, and how Angie had been the intended target. Marlene had felt so guilty about her relief that it was Quentin who had mistakenly been killed instead. It was Thomas who had convinced her that it was normal for her to think that way as Angie was not only her sister but had been like a mother to her. Angie had been the one constant in Marlene's life.

As Marlene tossed in her bed, it occurred to her that in many ways Thomas had also become a constant in her life. Someone she knew she could go to at any time and say anything without fear of judgement. When her mam had turned up, just knowing he was there if she needed him had been enough.

She realised now how stable Thomas's life was in comparison to hers. Marlene had never known him to have any great dramas. He'd suffered prejudice, but his family were also kind and caring folk and they had brought up Thomas and his brothers with love. Perhaps that was what had drawn him away from her and towards Mabel. Unlike Marlene's, Mabel's life was not one catastrophe after the next but a content and happy one, from what Marlene could gather. Perhaps Thomas had decided that Marlene came with too much baggage and he didn't want to have a life filled with one upset after another, as seemed to be Marlene's destiny.

The irony was, though, that Marlene had felt more grounded since returning from London, and after spending time with her mam. Since then, she had realised so many things about herself and what she wanted and didn't want. She had thought she wanted fame and fortune and the bright lights of London, but when she had been in the capital for those two days, which had felt more like two months, she had yearned for the country, for the fresh air, for the green landscape, for the beauty of the flora and fauna. Most of all, Marlene had been overcome by the most intense feeling of homesickness. She had craved to be back at Cuthford Manor.

And most of all, she'd desperately wanted to be back with her family and friends.

Pulling the bedclothes tightly around her, Marlene recalled returning from her impetuous trip to London. She would never forget Thomas's look on seeing her black eye. It had spoken of his fury that someone had done this to her, but also of his love for her.

Where had that love gone?

Had she somehow pushed it away? She knew she had changed after London – was that what had caused Thomas's feelings for her to diminish?

Chapter Thirty-Five

Marlene was not the only one who was struggling to get to sleep. Mabel had given up wrestling with the bedcovers and had gone to make herself a mug of Ovaltine in the kitchen. She was now sitting in bed, her pillows plumped up against the headboard, blowing on her steaming-hot malt drink. It was rankling her that her meeting with Thomas this evening had not gone to plan. When she'd met him by the five-bar gate, she'd gone to kiss him. She'd taken him by surprise and he'd not had time to back away, but the kiss had been brief and chaste. She'd known then that it was not going to go as planned. She had hoped, perhaps foolishly, that the simple fact they had spent the night together would mean they would start dating. Even if he had been a little unsure, she had presumed he'd be courteous and ask her out. Once they were out on their own, she knew she could work her charm on him and capture his heart. She was attractive and could be quite the seductress when she wanted, but they also got on really well. They had become good friends.

He was the perfect husband for her.

She just needed to make him realise that she was the perfect wife for him.

She took a sip of her drink.

Her plan would have gone better had she not been forced

to show her feelings for Thomas sooner than she'd originally anticipated. She had clearly bamboozled him. He had stuttered his way through a raft of apologies and excuses, and claimed he only saw her as a friend. But she was convinced that wasn't true. As soon as his mind was free of Marlene, then he would be able to see his real future. *A future with her.*

She took another sip from her mug.

She should not bemoan Thomas's lack of enthusiasm. He just needed time to get over his broken heart. Then his thoughts and feelings would turn towards her.

She was sure of it.

Chapter Thirty-Six

Over the next few weeks, Edward made a point of seeking out Marlene for a cup of tea and a chat after he'd seen his daughter. Their conversations tended to focus on Roeburn Hall and how the work was coming on to convert more bedrooms into suitable accommodation to cater for the overspill from Cuthford Manor. He had joked that he hoped those who stayed would not be too disappointed, having seen just how amazing the suites at Cuthford Manor were, but they had agreed that guests would be glad of the more affordable rates – and also the authenticity of staying in such a historical building, even if it was a little 'battered around the edges', as Edward put it. Although he never asked how she was feeling, having learnt of Mabel's stayover, Marlene knew he was checking up on her, making sure she was all right, which she thought incredibly caring. Once more, she thought how he had been misjudged by so many people. She wished Danny could see this side of him, although, knowing Danny, he would probably just claim that it was because Edward wanted something, which was his response when anything in any way positive was said about his father-in-law.

Marlene had been thankful to Edward for their evening together, which had provided a wine-induced salve for her broken heart, but as the days mercilessly rolled on, so the rawness of her wounded heart continued to cause her unrelenting pain.

Purposely keeping herself busy so as to have an excuse not to have to talk to either Mabel or Thomas, Marlene would be the first to volunteer for any chores that had to be done in the village or which required a trip into Durham. But it was simply not possible to avoid them completely. The few times that Marlene had seen Thomas, there was an awkwardness between them that hurt Marlene almost as much as her broken heart. She was not just losing the man she had thought was 'The One', but a really good friend to boot.

She was thankful no one mentioned Thomas and Mabel's coupling, which she put down to the staff not wanting to be seen gossiping in front of her, and because those who knew how she felt about Thomas were being sensitive. She was surprised, though, that Mabel wasn't doing the opposite and rubbing her nose in it, but she realised with growing envy that Mabel didn't need to as she was positively blooming and looked better than ever. Clearly the benefits of being in love.

Not wanting anyone to feel sorry for her, and, perhaps a little childishly, wanting to show Thomas that she was not short on male companionship, Marlene started taking Edward with her when she walked the dogs at teatime. Marlene's teatime treks with Winston and Bessie had originally started after London, when she had needed to feel the earth underfoot and breathe in the smells of the season at the end of the day. She had also found it helped her to think up new ideas or find solutions to problems, either at the Cuthford Country House Hotel or, more recently, at Roeburn Hall.

Being accompanied by Edward after he'd dropped in to

visit a very bored and bedbound Lucy coincided with the last riding lesson of the day, when Thomas and his pupils would be leading their horses back to the stables. He could not fail to see Marlene out walking with Edward, deep in conversation, the dogs barking in excitement.

On a practical level, the walks also provided Marlene with the opportunity to chat to Edward about renting out the rooms at Roeburn Hall, if there were any problems and how it was going in general. Its success benefited both families, since the more money Roeburn Hall brought in, the larger the amount of the commission that was handed over to Angie, who was accepting of the situation as their own profit margins were increasing despite not having to do much at all.

On the few occasions that Marlene went over to Roeburn Hall to chat to Edward about the design and costing of the guest rooms, she would walk through the main doors into the hall and recall the wonderful picture of family life that Edward had painted on the evening he had taken her there for the first time. The kind of family life she had always dreamed of since she was a child. It was the life she had thought she might have shared with Thomas. Marlene would shelve those thoughts as she walked up the long, sweeping staircase with Edward to see what more could be done on the limited budget he had at his disposal. It was only when she was alone in her bed at night that Marlene would allow herself to indulge her heartache and grief over what might have been.

Little did Marlene know, though, that similar thoughts were going through Thomas's head as he, too, lay in his bed – alone – at night.

But his sadness was not quelled by tears but by anger. Having to witness Marlene and Edward's not-so-secret courtship being carried out right in front of him was agonising. He couldn't bring himself to mention it to anyone he worked with, and they were considerate enough not to say anything about the pair when he was about. He had mentioned it to Danny, but he'd said they weren't an item. Marlene was clearly keeping her romance from her brother, knowing what his reaction would be. It was probably for the best, as his friend certainly had enough on his plate with his worries about Lucy and their unborn baby's well-being – an anxiety that Thomas was sure would continue until his wife gave birth to a healthy boy or girl.

Dr Wright had told Lucy that he felt she was almost out of the woods as she was now just a week or so away from her due date. But he still insisted that to be on the safe side she needed to keep resting. A little stroll was allowed around her cottage garden, which was now starting to bud with a mix of daffodils, primroses and camellias, but that was all. Lucy had told Marlene that if she didn't follow the doctor's orders to the letter and lost the baby, she would never be able to forgive herself.

Dr Wright, who was forever expounding the merits of the country's National Health Service, had also told Lucy and Danny that he would recommend a short hospital admittance a day or two before the baby was expected in case there were any complications. The risk of further blood loss was a concern, especially if his original diagnosis had been right.

'At least it will be a change of scenery,' Lucy had only half joked.

But, in order to stop herself from going 'doolally', and having exhausted just about every periodical and book on horses she could get her hands on, Lucy had become an avid magazine and newspaper reader, and when Marlene came to see her at the cottage, she would update her sister-in-law on what was happening outside the world of the Cuthford Country House Hotel.

Today Marlene arrived a little later than usual as she had been on the phone offering her condolences to the daughter of a mother who had passed away aged just fifty-four. It was relatively rare to have a funeral for someone who was younger than sixty, and it had touched Marlene more than normal, as her own mam had also died while she was still in her early fifties.

As soon as Marlene walked through the door, she put on the cheeriest voice she could manage.

'So, what are the headlines?' she trilled as she headed down the hallway.

'There's just one headline today,' Lucy griped.

Marlene walked into the living room and saw that Lucy's face matched the sour tone of her voice.

'What's happened?' Marlene immediately went and sat by her friend.

'I'm angry,' Lucy declared.

'Yes,' Marlene said. 'That much is obvious. But why?'

'It's Dan,' she said simply.

'Oh, no, what's he done now?' Marlene said. The tension between the two was still as taut as a fiddler's string. It was why Marlene always hurried to the cottage before her brother came in after work.

Lucy pursed her lips.

'Go on, tell me,' Marlene cajoled. 'You can trust me.'

Lucy let out a long exhalation and put her hand over her now enormous belly. Marlene had wondered if Lucy's ire against Danny was really down to her frustration at being so huge and immobile and also so anxious about the pregnancy.

'Well, I wasn't going to tell you,' Lucy said, eyeing her sister-in-law, still unsure whether to confide in her.

'Go on,' Marlene encouraged.

'Well, a little birdie told me in a roundabout way that Danny might be playing away from home – or is at least on the verge of it.'

'No, no way,' Marlene said with total conviction. 'Danny would never be unfaithful. He's as loyal as they come.' She looked at Lucy. 'I don't know why anyone would say that. Who's the "little birdie"?'

Lucy shook her head as though it wasn't important.

'Apparently, Danny's been seen with one of the Travellers from Bishop Auckland. You might have seen her at events. She's got long, dark hair and is gorgeous, of course.'

'Mmm, I think I know who you mean,' Marlene mumbled. If it was the young woman she was thinking of, she was very attractive. She reminded Marlene of Hedy Lamarr, with her naturally thick, curly hair, olive complexion and distinctive bone structure. She had seen the Hedy Lamarr lookalike at a recent event. She had been very chatty with Danny, but nothing about their interaction had given her cause for concern.

'I wouldn't be surprised if Danny was tempted. Not only do I bear more than a passing resemblance to Humpty Dumpty at the moment, but we're just not getting on.'

Marlene didn't say anything, hoping her silence would encourage her sister-in-law to elaborate. She knew Lucy never liked to say anything bad about Danny because of the closeness between Marlene and her brother.

'It just feels strained between us at the moment,' Lucy said. 'I don't know if it's because of how he feels about Father and the fact he comes here to visit, even though there's no other option.' Lucy wanted to add that Angie didn't help either, as she had made it clear she wasn't overly keen on having Edward about. But she couldn't start badmouthing Marlene's brother *and* sister. 'Or if there's more to it.'

'More to it in what way?' Marlene asked.

'That we're growing apart. That Angie was right the day we came back from Gretna.'

Marlene furrowed her brow.

'She basically said we should have waited, and we were too young,' Lucy informed her, her mind going back in time. Recalling the happiness she'd felt then caused her pain when she compared it to how miserable she felt now. This should be a time when she and Danny were walking on cloud nine. Like Angie and Stanislaw had before, during and after Juni's birth.

Before Marlene had a chance to refute her older sister's words, Lucy's face flushed red. She stood up and started pacing the room, or rather waddling back and forth, one hand on her back, the other on her hugely extended stomach.

'Honestly, Marlene, I keep getting these whooshes of murderous rage every time I think about it. I honestly feel like a volcano spitting molten lava, ready to erupt!'

'Well, don't,' Marlene said. 'For starters, I really don't think there is any truth to Danny even having his head turned by another woman, let alone having some sort of affair. Just saying it sounds ridiculous. It's just been a trying time – all couples go through their ups and downs.'

She patted the sofa.

'Sit down. The last thing you need at the moment is to "erupt" – in any shape or form.'

Marlene's attempt at a joke was met by a thunderous scowl from her sister-in-law.

'I've got another week,' Lucy said, 'before I'm packed off to the hospital.'

She stopped walking.

'Which will give Danny free rein! He can spend more time with his bit on the side without having to worry about coming back home to me.' Her last words were spat out with venom.

Marlene was about to defend her brother for the second time when she stopped, seeing Lucy's expression change from murderous rage to absolute alarm.

She watched as Lucy took hold of the sides of her long maternity dress and slowly pulled it up.

'Oh. My. God,' Marlene said.

Both women's eyes were glued to the wooden floor of the living room where a small pool of water was forming.

Lucy was just about to speak when her expression changed once again, from shock to excruciating pain. She bent double, her hand flailing out to grab hold of something. Anything.

Marlene jumped up.

'Come here!'

She grabbed Lucy's hand. 'Let's sit you down . . .'

*

After ringing Dr Wright, who, much to her complete relief, was in, and a quick thank you to the God she had promised to believe in last time Lucy had been in dire straits, Marlene told Lucy to try to stay calm.

'He's calling the ambulance, but he said it might be quicker for someone here to take you to the hospital.'

Lucy looked at Marlene, who immediately read her thoughts. Her sister-in-law might be mad at Danny, but he would always be her first port of call in an emergency.

'Yes, of course, Danny. I'll go and get him. I'll tell him to get the car.' Marlene hesitated. 'Are you going to be okay on your own?'

'Yes, of course! Go!' Lucy ordered.

Marlene propelled herself out of the front door and sprinted as fast as she could towards the stables, glad that she was wearing slacks. Like Lucy, she presumed Danny would be there as it was the end of the working day and he liked to settle the accounts after the last rider had paid up and gone.

As she reached the paddock, she looked towards the barn. It seemed very quiet. All the horses must have been returned to their stalls. She saw a car disappear around the corner and presumed it was the last of the pupils being taken home.

By the time she reached the backyard, she started to slow down to a jog and then a walk. She was sweating, her heart was thumping and her breathing came in gasps. She put her arms akimbo as she walked towards the entrance to the barn.

'Danny!' she shouted out when she'd managed to catch her breath.

There was no reply.

She strode to the barn; both wooden doors were still wide open.

Jogging the last few steps to the opening, she squinted as the sun was dropping and had momentarily dazzled her.

She made to shout for Danny again, but stopped on seeing Thomas coming out of the tack room.

Before he had a chance to ask Marlene what was wrong, as there clearly *was* something wrong, judging by the state she was in, she beat him to it.

'Where's Danny? Lucy's waters have broken.' She gasped and took in another mouthful of air. 'We need to get her to the hospital as quickly as possible.'

'Oh, my goodness—' Mabel's distinctive voice could be heard before she appeared from the tack room. She was dressed in her jodhpurs and had either just been out for a ride or was about to go out for one.

For a split second, Marlene felt pain at seeing the two together, before panic reasserted itself.

'Where's Danny?' she asked, looking around the barn.

'He's not here,' Thomas said. 'He's over at the Travellers' camp.'

'What? The camp at Bishop Auckland?' Marlene asked.

'They've moved now. They're just past Bowburn.'

Marlene stood rooted to the spot. A hundred and one thoughts going through her head.

'I'll drive instead,' Thomas said. He started moving towards the door. 'I'll get the car.'

Marlene looked at him. 'No, you go get Danny. Get him to the hospital.'

'I'll go get Jake,' Mabel butted in, putting her crop and

riding hat down on one of the hay bales. 'I'll get him to bring the car round to the cottage.'

'Okay,' Marlene said, for once glad that Mabel was there.

'Do you want me to let Cora know, and Mr Stanton-Leigh?'

'Yes, yes, please,' Marlene said.

The three made off in different directions. Thomas to the stables by the paddock, Mabel to the front of the manor, and Marlene back to the cottage.

Thomas was praying that one of the Travellers would have a spare vehicle so that they could drive to the hospital.

Mabel was desperately trying to recall if Jake was out chauffeuring the guests, and if he was, who could drive instead.

And Marlene was frantically trying to think up a lie as to where her brother was. Lucy did not need to hear that her husband was at the Travellers' camp, not after the conversation they'd just had.

As luck would have it, Jake was free, having just got back from picking up some guests from Roeburn Hall who were dining with friends staying at the manor. He jumped into the Rover, which he reassured Mabel might look like a plodder but was the best car for the job. Having to take it slowly along the potholed track that provided a vehicular access of sorts to the cottage, Jake arrived at the same time as Marlene.

Waving frantically at Jake to come and help her, Marlene turned, flung open the front door and strode down the short hallway and into the living room, where she found Lucy sitting exactly where she had left her.

Breathing an almighty sigh of relief that her sister-in-law looked all right and did not appear to be in labour, she went to help her up, but immediately cursed herself for being so optimistic. Lucy immediately let out a slow, groaning moan that did not sound like anything a human should make.

'Come on,' Marlene said, 'we're taking you to the hospital.'

Lucy puffed. 'Danny?' was all she managed.

Just then, Jake appeared, took hold of Lucy's other arm and guided her out of the room, down the hallway and out to the car.

As Marlene helped to squeeze Lucy's sizeable girth into the back seat, Lucy gripped her arm so tightly it hurt. Marlene expected another feral sound, but instead Lucy breathlessly demanded, 'Where's Danny?'

Marlene opened her mouth to speak, but nothing came out.

'He's meeting us at the hospital,' Jake said, jumping into the driver's seat and turning the ignition.

'You in there, Marlene?' he shouted over his shoulder.

'Just!' she replied, flinging herself into the small space next to Lucy and twisting around to yank the car door shut.

And with that, Jake floored it, leaving dust and gravel in his wake.

Chapter Thirty-Seven

When the maroon-coloured Rover pulled into the bay area of the Casualty entrance, Jake was red-faced and sweating, his knuckles white from having gripped the wheel so tightly. His nerves were shredded after driving as fast as possible along winding country roads and through villages, and then, on reaching Durham city, blaring his horn as he bullied his way through teatime traffic, all the while his mind constantly aware that there were three lives at stake in the back of his car.

Marlene looked on the verge of throwing up. There had been no need to tell Jake to step on it.

Lucy's complexion was so white as to be almost translucent. Her contractions were just a few minutes apart and lasted about the same amount of time. She could also feel a wetness that she was praying was simply a continuation of her waters breaking.

When Jake yanked open the back passenger door and Marlene ran around the car to help him haul Lucy out, it was clear that Lucy's hopeful presumptions were wrong.

The wet feeling had not been caused by water.

'Oh, God,' Marlene blurted out, unable to stop herself.

Lucy looked back as she was being pulled from the car and saw the blood.

She wasn't given the chance to express her horror, as another contraction had her crumpling up in agony.

Marlene felt herself being nudged to the side and a voice telling her, 'We'll take it from here.' She had never felt so relieved in her life.

As Lucy was helped onto the gurney, Marlene put her hand on the roof of the car to steady herself and keep her legs from buckling beneath her.

She kept watching, all the time forcing herself to take deep breaths, as a doctor and two nurses surrounded Lucy and the burly porter pushed the stretcher up the short ramp and through the open doors of the Casualty Department.

'You okay?' Jake asked, breaking Marlene out of her stare.

'Yes, yes,' Marlene said. 'You?'

Jake nodded. 'You go in. I'll sort the car out and park up over there.' He pointed to the small car park. 'Just come and get me if you need me.'

'I will,' Marlene said as she hurried up the steps and into the hospital.

As soon as she was through the main doors, she looked around. Lucy and the team of medics were nowhere to be seen.

'Marlene – over here.' It was Edward. He was chatting to a doctor by a corridor signposted 'Theatre'.

Hurrying over, Marlene looked at both men. Their faces were deathly serious.

'Is she going to be all right?' Marlene blurted out as soon as she was within earshot.

'Of course she is,' Edward reassured her, but when Marlene looked to the young doctor for confirmation, he didn't look so certain.

'Your sister-in-law has been taken down to be prepped for

surgery,' he explained. 'She is haemorrhaging, which means we have two jobs to do here – safely deliver Mrs Boulter's baby and stop the bleeding.'

Marlene nodded, trying to take in what she was being told.

'The doctor is going to show us to a waiting room,' Edward added as the young medic in his white overcoat put his arm out to point the way.

'Danny . . . ' Marlene began, her brain feeling like mush. 'Is Danny here?'

Edward exchanged looks with the doctor.

'No, not yet,' he informed her.

'I've told the receptionist to call me when he arrives,' the doctor said. 'She'll tell him what's happening and then show him to the waiting room.'

'When will Lucy be going into surgery?' Marlene asked.

The doctor looked at his watch. 'Soon,' he said. 'I'd say within the next half hour. Mrs Boulter's GP rang and gave us the lie of the land, so we were able to prepare.'

'Can my brother see Lucy if he arrives in time?' Marlene asked, knowing Danny would be devastated at not being there for Lucy before she was operated on.

The doctor nodded. 'If he arrives in time.'

Half an hour later, Lucy was wheeled down to theatre. Her last words before the anaesthetic did its work were to ask if her husband had arrived.

Not wanting to tell her that he hadn't, the anaesthetist instead told his patient that he was sure her husband would be by her bedside when she woke.

If she woke.

Chapter Thirty-Eight

It had taken Thomas half an hour to find the camp. The last time he'd seen the Travellers they had been camped up near Bishop Auckland and he only had a rough idea as to where they had moved.

Thomas had taken Lucy's beautiful black thoroughbred called Dahlia as she was the fastest horse they had – apart from Ghost, which Danny had taken. As soon as he reached the camp, he didn't dismount but simply shouted out Danny's name.

His arrival and the panicked tone of his voice immediately caught the attention of those within earshot. Children stopped playing, women stopped tending to pots on the open fire or washing clothes in a tin bath, and the men seemed to appear from nowhere. Seeing it was friend not foe, their demeanour relaxed.

'Is Danny here?' Thomas asked, his eyes surveying the camp.

He spotted Ghost just moments before he saw Danny striding out from behind one of the more ornate traditional Romany vardos. He was followed by the dark-haired Traveller Thomas knew to be called Adriana.

'What's happened?' Danny demanded.

Thomas swiftly dismounted. 'It's Lucy. She's gone into labour.'

Danny immediately turned to go to Ghost.

'No, she's not at the manor,' Thomas said, looking around the camp, only this time for motorised transport. 'Dr Wright said to take her straight to the hospital.'

'Brogan, take 'em in ta van!' Adriana looked at one of the younger men, who was wearing a flat cap and black trousers held up by a pair of braces. He tossed his cigarette and signalled for Danny and Thomas to follow him.

'Don't worry about ta horses,' Adriana said, heading over to Dahlia and nodding at Ghost, who was grazing. 'They'll be fine here.'

Danny nodded his thanks as he and Thomas followed Brogan and climbed into a rusty, mud-splattered grey van.

Within minutes, they were on the main road to Durham.

'How long do you reckon it'll take?' Danny asked. He was leaning forward, his hands on the dashboard as though willing the battered old van to go faster.

'Ten minutes.' Brogan glanced across at Danny.

But as soon as the words were out of his mouth, the van started to make a loud whining sound, followed by deep metal clunking.

'No, no, no,' Danny said under his breath.

The van's grinding, knocking and squealing continued for another half a mile before it ground to a noisy halt.

The three men jumped out. Brogan opened the bonnet and inspected the engine. He shook his head. 'She's going nowhere. 'Tis the alternator.'

Five minutes later, Danny and Thomas had jogged a good half a mile down the road.

On hearing the noise of an engine, the two turned to see a car heading towards them.

They both automatically stuck out their thumbs. When it didn't slow down, Danny started to wave frantically, but the car simply sped past.

Chapter Thirty-Nine

Marlene was pacing the room.

'She's going to be fine.' Edward tried to sound reassuring, but didn't quite manage to pull it off.

'Oh God, honestly, it should be me telling you that,' Marlene said, wringing her hands.

'Come here.' Edward waved her over to where he was sitting.

Marlene went and sat down next to him, and he put his arm around her. 'My daughter is a tough cookie. Tougher than she lets on. Believe me.'

'Really?' Marlene said. 'I hope you're right.' *Tough cookie* were not the words Marlene would use to describe Lucy. She looked at her watch and Edward removed his arm and took her hand in his.

'It's been an *hour*,' she said, looking at Edward and seeing a mirror image of her own terrifying imaginings of what might be. 'And where the hell is Danny?' Her fear was morphing into anger. 'He should have been here by now.'

Marlene had explained that Thomas had gone to get Danny from the Travellers' camp near Bowburn. The fact that Edward hadn't made any comment, or asked why he was at the camp at this hour of day, spoke volumes to Marlene.

'God, I can't sit here and do nothing,' she said, standing

up. 'I need to know what's happening.' And with that, she walked the short distance across the small, windowless waiting room and yanked open the door.

Edward jumped up to follow, not sure whether he really *wanted* to know.

At the moment he had hope.

But for how long?

They left the waiting room and made their way along the corridor to find a nurses' station just as the young doctor who had seen them when they arrived came bustling through the swing doors at the other end.

Marlene and Edward stopped dead in their tracks.

Now it was Marlene who suddenly didn't want to know the news.

She could not even contemplate the worst-case scenario.

Neither Marlene nor Edward spoke. Both stood stock-still, all their concentration on the young doctor, or rather, on his face. Hoping upon hope to see the slightest upturn of his mouth signalling good news. Desperately hoping not to see a sombre expression and pity in his eyes, knowing that his words would devastate them.

As if in slow motion, Marlene watched the doctor walk towards them.

'Is she all right?' she asked, her tone a plea.

She saw the change in the doctor's expression.

It was the look she had prayed for.

'Yes,' he said as he approached them. 'Mother and baby are fine.'

He looked at Edward and put out his hand. 'Congratulations on becoming a grandfather.'

He then extended his hand to Marlene. 'And on becoming an auntie.'

Marlene felt as though her legs were going to give way, and they might have done had Edward not grabbed hold of her and hugged her tightly.

Marlene could feel the tears of relief sting her eyes.

'Thank God,' Edward said, still holding Marlene tightly. 'Thank God.'

The doctor watched, feeling almost as emotional.

'And is the father here?' he asked, looking over the pair's shoulders.

Edward released Marlene from his embrace.

'No, I'm afraid he's not,' Marlene said, wiping away a stray tear.

'Well, if that's the case, would you like to come and meet the latest addition to your families?'

They walked and the doctor continued talking.

'Mrs Boulter asked before she went into theatre if she'd be awake when the baby was born. On learning that she wouldn't, she asked for the baby to be placed for a moment on her chest before being handed over to the baby's father. I asked her what to do if Mr Boulter had not arrived by then, and she said that she would want the baby to be given to you, Miss Boulter.'

'Call me Marlene . . . '

'Your sister-in-law, Marlene, seemed very well read in all matters pertaining to childbirth.'

Marlene let out a slightly gasping laugh.

'The result of being bedbound for so long.'

'So I understand,' the doctor said as he walked quickly

down the corridor. 'Mrs Boulter said it's apparently important that a mother hold her baby straight after birth.'

They walked through another set of doors.

'Mrs Boulter also said that she didn't like the thought of her baby being on its own until she was brought round.'

Marlene felt fresh tears forming. *So like Lucy.*

'And here we are,' the doctor proclaimed.

He opened the door to the hospital's nursery, allowing Marlene and Edward to walk through first.

As soon as she stepped over the threshold and into the light-filled room, Marlene was greeted by a young nurse with a tiny baby swaddled in a hospital blanket in her arms.

'Miss Boulter?' the nurse asked, her face emanating joy.

Marlene nodded as the nurse held out the scrunched-up little baby boy and she took him into her own arms as though it was the most natural thing in the world. Looking down at his shock of black hair and startling blue eyes, Marlene fell instantly in love. She stood still, swaying the little bundle gently to and fro, whispering to him her welcome into the world.

As she did so, her ruddy-faced little nephew gurgled his own reply.

Turning to Edward without taking her gaze off the babe in her arms, she said, 'And say hello to your granddad.'

As she lifted the newborn child to show him, Edward simply stood and stared. Mesmerised.

Hearing a slight cough next to her, Marlene looked to see the nurse with her arm outstretched, indicating a couple of high-backed cushioned plastic chairs in the corner of the nursery.

'Why don't you sit down over there? It might be a little while before Mrs Boulter is fully awake.'

Marlene and Edward did as instructed, only taking their eyes off the newborn in order to navigate their way around the neat rows of cribs. Two nurses who were quietly checking the babies in each cot stepped aside to let them both past, smiling at the child who had been born with such a beautiful head of hair.

As Marlene carefully sat down, still swaying the swaddled baby, Edward waited until they were both settled before sitting down too.

'Just wave me over if you need anything,' the nurse whispered. This was the quietest the nursery had been all day and she didn't want to do anything that might disrupt it.

Marlene nodded.

'Isn't he gorgeous?' Edward said, his voice barely audible.

'He is,' Marlene said, taking her gaze away from the baby to look at Edward.

They were sitting close together, unified in their adoration of this tiny being in their care.

When Marlene looked at Edward, she saw that he had also drawn his attention away from the baby and was gazing at her.

Their faces were just inches apart.

And then he kissed her.

A soft, lingering kiss on her lips.

Chapter Forty

When the second car had passed them on the road to Durham without stopping – actually veering across the road to bypass them – Danny and Thomas started to jog in the middle of the road. When a third vehicle eventually came into sight, they stood next to each other like a human barricade and waved their arms. The small Morris Minor had no option but to stop. The elderly couple, their demeanour that of victims of a highway robbery, agreed to sit in the back while Danny drove and Thomas sat in the front passenger seat. When they arrived at the entrance of Dryburn Hospital, Thomas thought the two pensioners might need to be checked out by a doctor themselves as they looked as white as ghosts. The couple insisted they were 'fine, thank you very much,' and seemed beyond relieved that the pair they had believed to be akin to modern-day Dick Turpins had been telling the truth and really had needed to get to the hospital for an emergency.

Danny and Thomas burst through the main doors of the hospital like cowboys through the batwing doors of a saloon, then jogged over to the main reception counter. The receptionist, who had been primed to keep an eye out for Mrs Boulter's husband, guessed he must be one of the two frantic-looking men.

'My wife's been brought in . . . ' Danny felt as though he was tripping over his words, he was in such a rush to get them out, ' . . . the baby's come early.'

'Her waters broke,' Thomas chipped in.

'Mr Boulter?' the middle-aged receptionist asked.

They both nodded.

Looking at the two men staring at her with wild, desperate eyes, she smiled.

'Everything's fine,' she reassured. 'Mother and baby are doing well.'

'Baby?' Danny asked, his brain now struggling to keep up with what he was hearing.

The receptionist smiled again – this time even wider.

'Yes, Mr Boulter, I'm pleased to tell you that you are now the proud father of a healthy baby boy.'

Danny pushed his hair back and turned to look at Thomas, who was looking equally amazed and emotional – as well as exhausted.

Thomas threw his arms out and gave his friend a hug and a slap on the back.

'Congratulations!' he said, his voice cracking with emotion.

The receptionist dialled an internal number, muttered into the receiver and hung up.

'Your wife, Mr Boulter, is still in recovery as she had to go down for surgery, but she is fine. The doctor will explain everything to you when you see him.'

Danny's expression dropped to one of concern.

'And she *really* is fine?'

'Yes, she *really* is,' the receptionist reiterated.

'Now, if you would like to see your baby boy, take this

corridor on the right, turn left at the bottom and the nursery is halfway down. It's well signposted.'

Danny and Thomas didn't need telling twice.

A few minutes later, they arrived outside the nursery. Danny took a deep breath and was given a gentle nudge by Thomas, who opened the door and followed him in.

The two men stood there, startled by the sight of rows of cribs, almost all of which held a baby who was wearing a starched white romper suit and was either sound asleep or balling its tiny fists and making soft babbling sounds.

As the young nurse approached them, Thomas caught sight of Marlene in the far corner. She was cradling the baby boy in her arms and was sitting next to Edward.

As Danny chatted to the nurse, Thomas stared as Marlene and Edward turned their attention away from the babe in arms and looked at each other – before sharing the most intimate of kisses.

When Danny turned to Thomas, his friend was already pulling open the door of the nursery and leaving.

'Let me take you to meet your baby boy,' the nurse said. 'He's been well looked after.'

It was only then that Marlene noticed her brother.

She had not seen Thomas disappearing through the doors.

A little flushed, Marlene immediately stood up, a wide smile on her face.

'Congratulations, big brother,' she said, still keeping her voice low. She made to hand over the baby. 'You have a beautiful baby boy.'

Danny reached out and took the small bundle in his arms. It was a natural movement since, like Marlene, he had been tasked with looking after his younger siblings when they were babies.

As he gazed down at the tiny baby in his arms, his look was one of pure enchantment.

Bowing his head, he planted a soft kiss on his son's little crinkled forehead.

As though sensing that the person holding him was important, the baby-blue eyes fluttered open and his son gazed, equally enchanted, at the man holding him.

Chapter Forty-One

On seeing Marlene, a baby in her arms, sharing the most loving and sensual kiss with Edward Stanton-Leigh, Thomas could not have been more devastated. He had thought the hurt had been intolerable simply *hearing* that the woman he loved was with another man, but *seeing* it took that pain to an altogether different plane.

Fleeing the nursery, he ran along the corridors, through the entrance foyer and out of the main doors, nearly colliding with an elderly couple entering the hospital.

He stood catching his breath, his hands on his knees. It felt as though the shock of seeing Marlene – not just with Lucy's father but being intimate with him – had sapped the life out of him.

When he caught his breath, he stood up straight and spotted Jake smoking a cigarette by the Rover and chatting up one of the nurses, who looked to be on a break.

When Thomas approached, and seeing the state he was in, Jake quickly asked the nurse for her number and then walked towards him.

Once he'd been reassured that Lucy and the baby were well and there were no more emergencies or threats to life, Jake didn't probe further, although he guessed that Thomas's wretched demeanour might well have something to do with

Marlene. Instead, he drove Thomas to the Travellers' camp, as requested, and then returned to the hospital and his spot in the car park, glad that he was not a one-woman guy.

At the camp, Thomas sought out Adriana and informed her that all was well, although his dark, brooding look told her that this was not the case for his own heart.

Adriana told Thomas that she would ride one of the horses back to Cuthford Manor, and looking over to a red-haired woman who had come out of her vardo, she cocked her head at her own horse.

The three rode cross-country to Cuthford Manor. Thomas was on Ghost, who, sensing his rider's need to vent his emotions, galloped like the wind across the moorland; they were followed by Adriana on Dahlia, and the redhead on a dark bay horse.

On reaching the stables, the women didn't linger. The redhead reached down and pulled Adriana up onto the back of her horse and the two returned to the camp.

Thomas was not aware of taking off the bridles and heavy leather saddles, putting the two horses into their respective stalls, giving them water and replenishing their hay bales, as his thoughts were consumed by a myriad of emotions. Anger seemed to be the most predominant. Anger at Marlene for falling for Edward. Anger at Edward for stealing the woman he loved. And anger at himself for being such a fool for believing that Marlene might ever be his. How many times did he have to tell himself? God, Marlene had told him enough times when they were younger. *She wanted a rich, upper-class man*. Why had he allowed himself to think there might be a chance they could be together?

'You're an idiot,' he mumbled to himself as he dipped his hands into a bucket of cold water and scrubbed them with a bar of carbolic soap.

He heard the creak of the stable door and turned.

'They say it's the first sign of madness – talking to yourself,' Mabel said, her eyes fixed on Thomas.

'I think I am past the first signs,' he said, standing up and drying his hands on a towel he had thrown over his shoulder.

Mabel gave him a quizzical look. There was something different about him.

'Are you okay?' she asked, walking over to him.

Thomas looked at Mabel as though for the first time and nodded.

'Cuppa? You look like you need it,' she said, heading into the tack room.

Thomas followed and watched as Mabel unpinned her hair from the constraints of her bun and it tumbled down her back. He noticed she was wearing flat shoes and a summer dress, not her normal high heels and close-fitting outfits. She looked different.

Thomas sat on one of the hay bales and observed Mabel as she busied herself with making the tea, her face alight with joy as she chatted about Lucy and Danny's baby – and how everyone in the manor was celebrating. Thomas, though, wasn't really listening. His mind was dissociating itself from the memory of Marlene and Edward. Together. With a baby. Kissing. A portent of the future when they would have their own family.

And as he forced that vision of the future back, along with his boyish dreams of being with Marlene, he started to think of the present – and of his own future.

And how he had to get on with life.

His brother had said it enough times to him. 'Just move on, Tom. There's plenty more fish in t'sea.' He had berated Thomas, saying he didn't get out enough. That he had become too insular. That he needed to take off the blinkers and realise there were other lovely young women about.

His words came back to Thomas as he watched Mabel walking over with their tea.

Without thinking, he stood up, took the mugs from her and put them down on the upturned wooden crate.

And then he put his arms around her small waist and pulled her close.

Using one hand to move a strand of curly strawberry blonde hair away from her face, he then bent his neck and kissed her on the lips.

Softly at first, and then more passionately.

Chapter Forty-Two

April

When Danny had gone with his newborn in his arms to see Lucy, who had finally come round after the anaesthetic and was able to keep her eyes open for longer than a few seconds, all the suppressed anger and resentment that had caused the ever-increasing cracks in their marriage disappeared as though tapped by a magician's wand. Their love for their newborn child obliterated everything and anyone else. It was as though there were only three beings in their entire universe. Neither could quite comprehend the level of love they felt for their child. It knocked them for six, but in the most deliriously happy way.

Mother and baby had to stay in hospital for a couple of days, until the doctors were happy that Lucy was well enough to go home. The surgeon had been forced to perform a caesarean section because of the haemorrhaging and fears for the mother's life. Luckily, their patient had been able to get to the hospital quickly. If she had stayed at home or had not been able to get there for whatever reason, they were in no doubt that the baby would have lived, but not the mother. Knowing the mortal danger she had been in added even more to Danny and Lucy's feelings of being blessed.

Coming back to the cottage, Lucy and baby Felix, a name Lucy and Danny had chosen simply because it seemed to suit him, were overwhelmed by their reception. Everyone had pooled their time and resources to make the occasion special. Bertie, Jemima and Bonnie had all made cards and put up paper chains and streamers in the cottage, and had created a 'Congratulations' banner from cereal boxes that had been cut into letters and coloured in, then strung together. Bertie was particularly enthusiastic because the baby was a boy. *At last.*

Angie, despite originally having reservations about her brother and his new wife starting a family so young, was very happy that Juni now had a cousin who was just a year younger than her. Observing her daughter's look of delight on being introduced to baby Felix, Angie could see a future in which the two would be close. Angie also caught a look in Stanislaw's eyes that told her he would not be averse to adding another baby to their brood. A younger brother or sister for Juni and Bonnie, and another cousin for Felix.

Marlene had organised the party for Lucy and baby Felix's return home during any spare time she had outside of managing the hotel. She thrived on being so busy as it stopped her from thinking about Thomas and Mabel, and by the end of each day she collapsed into bed and fell asleep as soon as her head hit the pillow. It had been hard enough simply *knowing* that they were an item, but to actually *see* it in reality, on display, with Mabel using every opportunity that came her way to show they were courting, was tough. Really tough. She actually felt real pain in her chest when she saw them together and had to think quickly to make up an excuse to go off and do something *terribly important* that couldn't wait.

Avoiding them, whether they were on their own or together, was difficult, especially because Mabel was constantly buzzing around the manor, organising the staff and chatting to the guests to find out if there was anything they needed or were not happy about, which she would then feed back to Cora.

But there was also another reason Marlene was glad to be busy.

To stop her thinking about that kiss.

Edward had apologised profusely after his sudden burst of *amour* while they had been looking after baby Felix in the nursery. 'I don't know what came over me,' Edward had declared, clearly embarrassed by his spontaneous show of affection. 'I think this lovely little baby has just made me feel a little giddy.' Marlene had smiled and reassured him that she was not in any way angry with him for kissing her. She didn't say so, but it had actually been rather nice. But it was very obviously a mistake. A moment of madness on Edward's part. A moment of madness she was glad Danny hadn't seen.

Marlene had confessed to Angie that she was glad that Danny and Lucy had put their differences aside and seemed to be back to the couple they had been before Lucy's mother had died – and Edward had re-entered his daughter's life. She was also glad that Lucy had not asked her where Danny had been when she had gone into labour. Either she had forgotten or she had asked Danny and he had told her, although Marlene was pretty sure that he would not have told her the truth – he wouldn't have told her that he had been up at the Travellers' camp. The camp where the mysterious raven-haired Adriana lived.

Marlene couldn't help but wonder herself what her brother

was doing up there. There had been no mention of buying any horses from them, or of them doing any kind of trade. So why had he been there?

Marlene was pleased to see that Edward was taking a back seat. He had told her how anxious he was not to upset the apple cart in any way, especially as it seemed that his daughter and her husband were back on an even keel. He had told Lucy he felt it was important that she spend this special time with just Danny and baby Felix. Lucy didn't say so, but she was relieved as she didn't want to deal with any of the friction that was inevitable when her husband and her father were in close proximity. She was glad of her father's understanding and loved him all the more for it as she knew how much he wanted to see his grandson.

A fortnight after the dramatic birthday of Lucy and Danny's baby boy, they had a low-key christening at St Cuthbert's Church, followed by a little celebration at the manor afterwards. Neither Danny nor Lucy were big on parties or liked to be ostentatious in any way and they had only invited immediate family and close friends, who mainly consisted of those who lived and worked at the manor, as well as their neighbours, Geraldine and Jeremy Fontaine-Smith.

Lloyd, Cora, Alberta, Bill and Wilfred had watched Danny grow from a skinny young boy to an intelligent, hard-working young man. He had never tried to hide his lowly upbringing or been in any way ashamed of his roots – far from it. Like Angie said, her brother wore his class as a badge for all to see.

As Felix's grandfather – his only grandfather, since Danny's father was no longer in contact with his children – Edward was naturally invited to the christening. Marlene had seen the relief on Lucy's face when Edward had caught her as they'd all left the church and told her that he was only able to stay for the toast and then he'd have to head back to Roeburn Hall to check on the workers. 'You know how it is, my darling girl – while the cat's away, the mice will play,' he said in his usual jovial manner. But they both knew the real reason for leaving the celebrations early. Edward was keeping a low profile, not wanting to do anything to ruffle Danny's feathers, as he had done so successfully before baby Felix had been born. Lucy and her father knew that the party would be much more enjoyable and relaxed if he was not there. So, as soon as the toasts had been made and Felix wished a happy and healthy life, Edward was true to his word.

'I'm going to head off now,' he told Marlene, draining the last mouthful of champagne and placing it on a tray of full glasses that Shirley was taking around the room. 'I don't want to create a fuss, so would you mind terribly making excuses on my behalf when I'm gone?'

'Of course,' Marlene said. She felt a sudden rush of sympathy for Edward. Along with a stab of annoyance at her brother for not even trying to get on with his father-in-law.

'I don't suppose you fancy a stroll around the gardens before I go?' Edward asked a little apprehensively.

Marlene was momentarily taken aback. They had hardly seen each other – never mind chatted – since *the kiss*.

'Yes, of course – it'll be nice to get some fresh air,' she said, hiding well her own nervousness at his request.

Edward put out his hand to allow Marlene to go first as they left the party, which was being held in the front reception room and had been cordoned off with a thick red rope draped between gold-plated stands. A notice suggested that guests might enjoy a cup of tea or a drink in the library.

Walking quickly through the kitchen, which was busy since staff were tending to guests as well as making sure there was a flow of drinks and canapés for the christening, Marlene and Edward stepped out into the backyard, where they were hit by a blast of warm air infused with the smell of hay and horses.

Marlene did a quick scan of the stables.

Edward caught the look of relief on her face when Thomas was not anywhere to be seen. 'Is your heart still feeling irrevocably broken?' he asked as they walked towards the flower gardens.

'No,' Marlene said, her mind going back to the evening Edward had taken her out for dinner after she had spotted Mabel coming out of Thomas's bedsit early in the morning. 'I've had time to adapt to the fact that he is not *The One*.' She said the words in a self-deprecating manner.

Edward didn't say anything, but he took it as a good sign that this was all Marlene wanted to say on the matter, and that she didn't want to pick over the reasons why Thomas had not told her about his feelings for Mabel, which really equated to why Thomas had chosen Mabel over Marlene, something Edward really could not understand himself.

As they walked around the perfectly tended flower gardens, now in full bloom, Edward admired Carl's handiwork. 'It's like a real-life Monet painting,' he said. 'The man is a horticultural artist as well as a poet.'

'He is, isn't he,' Marlene agreed. 'And I think you can also see elements of his engineering background. The way he has plotted everything out so meticulously.'

Edward nodded as they walked. The heat of the sun was a natural relaxant. The melodic chirping of the commune of chaffinches that had nested nearby filled the air.

'Carl must miss your mother,' he said, more a statement of understanding than a question.

'Yes, he does,' Marlene sighed. 'He never says as much, but he doesn't have to.'

'And you? Do you miss your mother?'

Marlene thought for a moment.

'I do and I don't,' she answered honestly. 'I think it's easier for me than for Carl. He was with Mam for those eight years, and I was only with her for the last few months of her life. I don't really count the years when I was a child as she wasn't about much, and she was a different person back then.'

'Do you think you are like her?' Edward asked as they continued to follow the winding crazy-paving pathway, which provided a comprehensive tour of the different sections of flora.

Marlene laughed. 'Mam thought so. She said I had inherited her stubborn streak and could be as pig-headed – and impulsive.'

'But something tells me that – unlike your mother – you are naturally maternal. I could see it immediately when you were holding Felix in the hospital.'

They were both quiet. A slight awkwardness had suddenly nudged its way between them as the thought of what had happened while they were sitting with Felix in the nursery came to mind.

The kiss.

Neither of them had alluded to it since Edward had apologised. And it was something that Marlene had tried to push to the back of her mind.

'Mmm, I don't know about being naturally maternal.' Marlene batted the compliment away. 'Just used to having a baby dumped in my arms and told to look after it.' She gave a sharp laugh.

Edward looked at her as they slowed their pace. 'You really are quite an anomaly, Marlene Boulter.'

Marlene frowned. 'An anomaly?'

'A wonderful anomaly . . . '

He paused.

'I have to admit, Marlene, that I do find you rather fascinating.'

Marlene felt herself blush. No one had ever told her that before.

'Fascinating because?' she asked. The question was a genuine one, not fishing for a compliment.

'You really don't see it, do you?' Edward said. His question a rhetorical one.

Marlene gave him a slightly wary look, as though afraid of what he might say next.

'You're not like any woman I've ever known,' Edward said as they continued to follow the narrow pathway around to the left, towards an area filled with wildflowers. 'Lucy has told me a little about your upbringing, which by the sounds of it was positively Dickensian, and how you had to grow up well before your time.' Edward looked at Marlene to make sure he was not overstepping the mark, before continuing:

'And I know you've been through an awful lot since then, despite moving here.' He waved his arm around at the beauty of the Cuthford Manor estate. 'You've had different hardships to deal with – to endure.

'A woman of strength and substance,' he said, turning his attention away from the array of colourful flowers swaying slightly in the gentle breeze.

They were walking so closely, Marlene could smell Edward's aftershave and could sense his body almost brushing her own.

And that was when she felt the touch of his fingers on hers and the tingling of her body as he gently took her hand in his.

It seemed so unexpectedly natural.

Just as it felt natural when they stopped walking and Edward turned to her and traced the outline of her face gently and slowly before lowering his head and kissing her.

Chapter Forty-Three

Thomas had known he had made a big mistake almost as soon as he'd taken Mabel into his arms and kissed her on the day of Felix's birth, three weeks ago. He knew that it had been a knee-jerk reaction to having seen Marlene and Edward kiss in the hospital, but it was as though someone or something else had taken him over; this was the only way he could possibly assuage the searing pain he had experienced after seeing them being so intimate. A foretelling of what was to come – Marlene and Edward married, doting over their first child.

Thomas had tried hard to make it work with Mabel. She was a lovely person, so happy all the time, full of energy, love and light. He told himself that he should be over the moon to have found someone like her. Mabel was an attractive woman, and he got on with her. He enjoyed talking to her. And he admired her for how she had worked hard to get where she was. The two voices in his head had kept at it – arguing the cases for and against. One telling him that he just needed time to get Marlene out of his system and then he would see that the right woman was there in front of him. He had just been blinded by Marlene and needed to be patient while he slowly regained his vision. The other, contradictory voice told him that there was something missing with Mabel. That she was perfect for him in so many ways, but the essential ingredient was absent. He was quite simply not in love with her.

And so, this evening, he had suggested they go for a drink at the Farmer's Arms, where it had all started, in order to bring it to an end. He was dreading it. But he knew he had to nip it in the bud now, before it became too serious. It had been an odd courtship in many ways. Their relationship had started with a night spent together and then, as though wanting to rewind, they had gone on dates that had ended with just a kiss and a cuddle but nothing more.

Thomas had arranged to meet Mabel in the pub, rather than go there together, as he'd wanted to have a beer before 'the talk'. He had drunk most of his pint before Mabel arrived. Watching her face light up on seeing him, his heart sank with the guilt he knew he was going to feel.

He waved her over.

'I've got you your drink,' he said as she approached. 'Gin and tonic.' He looked down at the glass and then back up at Mabel as she pulled out the chair opposite him and sat down. Again, Thomas cursed himself for being the way he was – for feeling the way he did. Mabel looked radiant and very attractive. Still, he had to tell himself that she would have no trouble at all finding herself another beau; the looks she was attracting from a few young men at the bar were evidence of that.

'Thanks, Thomas,' she said, her eyes trained on his. She took the smallest of sips. 'I'm so glad you said to come here for a drink. I was going to suggest going somewhere private. Somewhere we could talk. Away from the manor.' Thomas was tempted to ask if there was something in particular she wanted to talk about, but decided to simply charge on. Rip the plaster off in one go.

'Actually, there was a reason for it,' he said, taking another slug of his bitter and draining the glass.

'Sounds intriguing . . . ' Mabel furrowed her brow and scrutinised Thomas's face. Concluding his expression was not one that boded well for the imparting of good news, and seeing his pint was almost empty, she jumped up. 'Well, you need another drink before my curiosity is satiated.' She turned and walked over to the bar before Thomas had time to argue the point.

He watched as Mabel chatted to the barmaid he knew to be an old friend of hers. He thought that Mabel had changed a little since they had started to date. She had now permanently swapped her heels for flat shoes and her tight modern dresses for floaty feminine ones. He actually thought her new look suited her, especially with her long, curly hair let loose.

As she walked back to the table with the pint, Thomas thanked her and took a deep breath. 'I—'

'Sorry, Thomas,' Mabel interrupted. 'I know you want to chat, but can I tell you my news first? I don't think I can wait . . . '

Thomas sat back in his chair. 'Yes, of course. Now you've got *me* curious.'

Suddenly the tables were turned and it was Thomas scrutinising Mabel's face, unable to discern if it was good or bad news. He really couldn't tell. It flashed through his mind that Mabel might well be wanting to tell him that *she* didn't want to court *him* any more. His heart lifted at the thought. He had wondered if she, too, had come to the same conclusion – that they were compatible in many ways, but just not *in love*.

'Go on then,' Thomas cajoled.

'Well,' Mabel took another small sip of her drink. 'I suppose there's only one way of telling you this.'

Thomas was suddenly engulfed by a heavy feeling of foreboding.

'So I might as well just spit it out,' Mabel said. *'I'm pregnant . . .'*

It took Thomas a while to get over the shock and actually be able to speak. When he did find his voice again, he asked falteringly and rather stupidly, 'How come?' His question was not quite so dumb as they had only slept together the once – the night he had got totally drunk after finding out that Marlene and Edward were secretly courting. A night he couldn't even remember! *He had fathered a baby and had no recollection of it.*

'It can just take the once,' Mabel said, looking at Thomas. She was not surprised at his reaction, especially as she'd had a good idea exactly why he had wanted to see her tonight.

Anticipating the question that she knew Thomas would be thinking but was too much of a gentleman to ask, she told him: 'No, it's not someone else's. I hope you know I'm not that type of girl. That night we were together took me by surprise as much as you.'

She paused.

'And, no, I'm not going to get rid of it. You know my family's Catholic. And even if I wasn't, I couldn't.'

Thomas nodded his understanding.

'And you're sure?' It was his last hope. 'That night doesn't seem that long ago?'

This time it was Mabel who nodded.

'I'm sure,' she said. 'To be honest, I had a suspicion a few weeks after that night when I missed my monthly and my body started to feel different.' Mabel knew all the signs only too well, as she had seen her stepmother go through pregnancy after pregnancy and she had not held back from giving Mabel every detail of every symptom and every twinge. Mabel had already decided to sail through her own pregnancy in a demure and dignified fashion.

Imagining himself with a baby, Thomas's mind started to spiral out of control. Seeing Danny with Felix was great, but Thomas had not felt the least bit envious. Unlike Danny, he was not ready for a family – and certainly not ready to start a family with a woman he liked a lot but did not love and was not in love with.

Chapter Forty-Four

Later on that evening, lying in her bed, her curtains open as she always liked to look out at the night sky, Marlene replayed her walk in the flower garden with Edward and found herself blushing. This time the kiss had not been brief, nor was there any apology afterwards. Edward's impromptu show of affection at the hospital had clearly not been a moment of madness but had come from a place of desire. A desire very evident as they kissed each other. And a desire that had also triggered physical feelings within herself that she had not felt for a long time. Since before London. It was as though his kiss and the way he held her, the way he had touched her face and run his hand down her bare arm, had reawakened her.

She felt herself blush again, which was ridiculous as there was no one to be embarrassed in front of. Just herself.

When she had finally pulled away from Edward, she had been at a loss for words. There were too many thoughts galloping around in her head for her to articulate how she was feeling about this line they had stepped over. Edward was Lucy's father. He was hated by Danny and viewed with varying degrees of suspicion by her family and friends. He was much older than her. Almost twenty years older. And he had not long lost his wife. Had only been a widower for just over eight months.

But if she was honest, she knew that all this didn't really concern her too much. She had a feeling that Lucy wouldn't mind. She could imagine she might actually be pleased. In hindsight, Lucy had positively encouraged their friendship, and had also declared that life was short and if her father met someone else, she for one would not disapprove, especially as there had been no real love between her mother and father.

Then there were Danny and Angie. They would disapprove. It would cause conflict, but she was a grown woman now and had her own mind. It was up to her whom she did or did not court.

The age gap was substantial, but it didn't feel so. He certainly didn't look his age. Their friendship had always been one of equals. He had never treated her like a little girl, as some older men did. And there was no denying his dashing, tall, dark and handsome looks.

On top of which he was a rather lovely kisser.

The words he had spoken before they had stopped and kissed had made her feel so special. She liked the thought of being 'an anomaly' and being proud of herself for overcoming the adversity in her early life.

When Edward had said his goodbyes, and kissed her again, he had said that he hoped Marlene might reciprocate his feelings and agree to a courtship.

But the question was, did she want to be with Edward?

She had just had her heart broken and then ground into the pavement like the stub of a cigarette. She had felt that love and romance would not feature in her life for a long time.

Marlene knew, deep down, if she was totally honest with herself, that as much as she had enjoyed that moment of

234

intimacy with Edward, she was not ready for any kind of relationship.

Not when Thomas still dominated so much of her thoughts. It wouldn't be fair on either of them.

Her mam had given her a wealth of wisdom during the months they had shared before her death, wisdom she said she'd gained from making so many mistakes. Mistakes she hoped her daughter would not repeat.

Ida had told Marlene that if she was ever unsure about something, then 'hold your horses'.

'Just wait a little while. Give that head of yours time to unravel its thoughts and work out what it wants or doesn't want,' Ida had told her.

Marlene had known that this was her mother's way of telling her not to be so impetuous – one of the traits that had led her to jump on a train and go looking for her father in London within hours of finding out he was still alive.

As she closed her eyes, Marlene resolved to tell Edward that she liked him a lot, but that she wanted them to be just friends.

Her mind settled, she was finally able to fall asleep.

Chapter Forty-Five

The next day, Marlene went to see Lucy and baby Felix at the cottage after work. She had woken feeling more positive about life. And love. Perhaps her kiss with Edward had put life – and especially Thomas and Mabel's relationship – into perspective. There was a good chance that their courtship would not last the course. And as time went on, she and Thomas might become close again – as close as they had been before Mabel got her claws in. They would be older and wiser.

Her step felt light as she walked up the path to the cottage, her mood lifting even more in anticipation at seeing her little nephew, who seemed to be growing by the day and who had kept his thick shock of black hair, making him even more adorable, if that were at all possible.

But as soon as Marlene walked into the lounge and saw the serious look on Lucy's face, her spirits dropped.

'Is everything all right?' Marlene asked, looking around to find Felix.

'Yes, yes, everything here is fine,' Lucy reassured her, shuffling uneasily in the armchair. 'I've put Felix down as he's just had his feed.'

Marlene breathed a sigh of relief. The various traumas leading up to Felix's birth seemed to have left her with an expectation that something else might go wrong.

Luckily, Lucy did not feel the same.

'The baby's fine. I'm fine,' she said. 'It's you I'm worried might not be so fine.'

Marlene pulled a puzzled expression and sat down. Lucy had the tea tray ready and had put it on the coffee table. Marlene poured them each a cup.

'Why would I not be fine?' Marlene said, taking a sip of her tea and sitting back.

Lucy stood up and started to wring her hands.

'God, Lucy, you're making me nervous, hovering about. Come and sit down. Have your tea,' Marlene ordered.

Lucy did as she'd been told and picked up her cup of tea and had a sip.

'Go on, then,' Marlene said. 'Don't keep me in suspense.'

Lucy took a deep breath. 'It's got to do with Thomas.'

Marlene felt her lightness of being starting to desert her.

'What about Thomas?' Marlene asked. 'Oh God, he hasn't had some kind of accident, has he?'

'No, no,' Lucy again reassured. 'Although I think there has been an accident of sorts.'

'Lucy, you are beginning to speak in riddles.' Marlene eyed her sister-in-law.

'Well, Danny came back later than normal last night . . . ' she began.

Marlene hoped his tardiness was not because he had been up at the Travellers' camp.

'You see,' Lucy continued anxiously, 'he'd been chatting with Thomas.'

Marlene widened her eyes. 'Which is not so unusual.'

'No, but what he told Danny was,' Lucy said, knowing she just had to come out with it.

'Mmm?' Marlene said, taking another drink of her tea.

'You see . . . ' Lucy hesitated. 'Oh God, Marlene,' she said, knowing she had to say it, 'I'm so sorry, but it looks like Thomas has got Mabel in the family way and they're going to have a shotgun wedding.'

Marlene felt herself become a little dizzy. The shock of hearing Lucy's words blindsided her as though she'd been punched in the head. It took her a moment to gather her thoughts.

'Thomas has got Mabel pregnant?' Another punch. This time to the stomach. The knowledge this time making her feel sick.

Lucy nodded.

'And they are going to get married?' she asked, needing to hear it confirmed.

'Yes, it sounds as though they're going to set a date before she begins to show too much,' Lucy said, repeating what Thomas had told Danny and Danny had told her.

'Oh God,' Marlene said, her mind finding it hard to accept the reality of what she was hearing.

Lucy's own heart hurt, hearing the devastation in her sister-in-law's voice and seeing it on her face and in her demeanour.

'That's it, then,' Marlene said, more to herself than to Lucy. 'There's no going back.'

The scandalous news of Mabel's condition swept through the manor. Mabel had not needed to tell them that she was expecting, just that she and Thomas were going to get married – and had decided not to wait. The date they had set was in six weeks' time. They just needed to check with the vicar at St Cuthbert's Church that he would agree to marry them.

Cora tried to keep the disappointment out of her voice – not just because of the situation Mabel had got herself into, but because she was going to lose her assistant. Despite Mabel's protestations that she would work right up to when the baby was due and would return as soon as possible after the birth, Cora thought it unlikely.

Angie was disappointed for the same reasons as Cora, but she agreed that Mabel could move in with Thomas after the wedding until they found somewhere more appropriate for a married couple with a baby.

Lloyd and Stanislaw privately admitted their disappointment in Thomas. They both liked him a lot and knew that his heart had always been with Marlene and they had not thought his relationship with Mabel would last. Now it didn't matter what Thomas felt; he had to do the right thing. He had to marry Mabel, regardless of whether he loved her or not.

But none of this was spoken of to either Mabel or Thomas. Rather, congratulations were expressed, and the offer was made to hold the reception at the manor.

That evening, Marlene did exactly the opposite of what her mam had advised, and she drove over to Roeburn Hall to see Edward.

When he opened the door, she walked over the threshold and stepped towards him.

She gently put her hand on the back of his head and drew his face down to her own and kissed him.

Edward had, of course, heard the news about Thomas and Mabel, but did not object.

Thomas's loss was his gain.

Chapter Forty-Six

After that night, Marlene and Edward became a couple. Although Marlene had no intention of following in Mabel's footsteps and was upfront with Edward that she intended to save herself for marriage. To which Edward replied, 'Well, it looks as though I'll just have to marry you, then.' They both laughed, although Marlene sensed that it had not been entirely a joke.

Leaving Edward that first night to head back to Cuthford Manor, Marlene suggested that it might be a good idea to stave off telling everyone about their romance for a little while. She didn't have to say why. Edward understood.

'People might well suspect, though,' he said, pulling her back into an embrace, 'when they see the change in me and how happy I am.'

Inwardly, Edward was glad of the time to work out how best to break the news to his daughter – and how he would deal with the inevitable wrath of Danny. He knew how protective his son-in-law was of those he loved – and how he had been Marlene's protector when they were younger.

When Marlene and Edward did tell Lucy the following week, they needn't have worried. Lucy was happy, although she privately asked Marlene about Thomas and suggested that perhaps she was on the rebound.

'You can't be on the rebound when you've not even had a relationship with someone,' Marlene declared, sweeping the notion away.

Lucy wasn't convinced, but gave her blessing to them both. She knew, however, that the news of her father and sister-in-law's courtship would not be so readily accepted by others. And she held her breath in anticipation of their reactions. Particularly her husband's. The news that his father-in-law was courting his sister would undoubtedly end their period of domestic peace, something she had known deep down was only temporary.

She had purposely not asked Danny where he had been on the day she had been taken into hospital because she had known she would not like his answer. She'd been proved right when she'd found out shortly after being discharged from hospital, when she'd wheedled it out of Jake. At that time, though, she had needed to focus on the baby, so she hadn't said anything. But she sensed that the time was coming when she would have to bring up the subject of Danny's frequent sojourns to the Travellers' camp.

Danny might not like his sister's choice of beau – but neither did she like her husband's choice of friends.

Or rather, *friend* – if, indeed, that was all Adriana was.

Chapter Forty-Seven

One week later

Thursday, 5 May

As Clemmie settled herself in one of the armchairs by the open fireplace in the family room at Cuthford Manor, she let out a long whistle, which aptly conveyed the sense of foreboding that not only she felt, but also all those settling onto the sofa and armchair opposite for an after-dinner drink.

'So,' Clemmie looked around the room at Angie, Stanislaw, Cora and Lloyd, 'it is as we all suspected.'

'Yes,' Cora agreed. 'I suppose it didn't take a genius to work it out. The two are rarely apart.'

'Mmm,' Angie said, her annoyance undisguised. 'This is something I wished I was wrong about, but I should have guessed. Marlene just seems to jump from the frying pan into the fire and back again.'

'I'd like to disagree,' Lloyd said, 'but it pains me to say you're right.'

Clemmie sighed. 'And I had really believed that Marlene was back on the straight and narrow. Focused on managing the hotel and being able to make the right decisions in both her working life and her personal life.'

Stanislaw smiled his thanks as Lloyd handed him a glass of vodka.

'Perhaps it will all end up just being a flash in the pan,' Lloyd said, 'to continue Angie's metaphor.'

'That man.' Angie shook her head. 'He's old enough to be Marlene's father.'

Stanislaw and Lloyd muttered their agreement and disapproval.

'And therein lies the problem,' Clemmie mused, nestling into the high-backed chair to get comfortable, her glass of Jack Daniel's in one hand, her other hand on the wooden armrest. Bessie had hogged the rug by the hearth, even though there were flowers rather than burning logs in the grate. Winston was lying by the armchair and had flopped his head onto Clemmie's stockinged feet.

'Remember when we found out about Marlene being bullied as a child?' Clemmie continued, now settled. 'How Danny had stepped in and warned them off – and we hoped he had managed to protect Marlene *all* the time, to ensure they hadn't been able to do what they had clearly wanted to do to her?'

They all nodded, their faces grim at the remembrance of the disclosure that day nearly two years ago. Even now, just the thought of what the older boys in the gang had wanted to do to Marlene as a girl still made them shudder.

'At the time it was my diagnosis that this was why, when she was younger, Marlene enjoyed dating boys and then dumping them. It was like she was getting back at those boys from her school. Making them suffer. Hurting them. As though she wanted all boys to suffer for the sins of those who had gone before them.'

Clemmie took a sip of her whisky.

'Well, I think that now she is older and has grown up so much since her trip to London – and, it has to be said, after spending time with your mam, Angie, and learning what she could from her in the short time she had left – well, I think now, rather than revenge, she wants love. Craves love. She's happier now and more mature and so hate has been replaced by love.'

'But she has *our* love,' Angie objected.

'She does, and that has certainly been Marlene's saving grace, but she's a woman now, and she wants that undivided love. The kind of intense love only romance and marriage can give.'

'Which is why you think she is falling for Edward?' Cora asked.

'I do,' Clemmie said. 'But it's not quite as simple as that.' She sighed. 'It's also because of her upbringing and because she was brought up in a household where, even though there might have been parents present, they were what's called in the business of psychoanalysis "absent" parents. They were there but they weren't. They were living under the same roof, but they did not give her any time, care or love. And so, in a way – although of course she is not aware of this herself – she is also seeking out that fatherly love in the man she is clearly becoming romantically involved with. It's similar to the Oedipus complex.'

She was greeted by three confused faces.

'Where the son loves the mother,' Clemmie explained.

'I think you're going a bit far now,' Lloyd said, shuffling in his seat, his discomfort obvious.

'Mmm,' Cora looked at Clemmie, 'I think that might be a bit beyond the pale.'

Clemmie dismissed their responses. 'I think Marlene *likes* Edward, but her need for a fatherly figure is getting confused with her need for love.' She sat up straight and leant forward, her arms now resting on her thighs, her drink clasped between her hands.

'Look how desperate she was to have a father in her life,' she stressed. 'She ran off to London to find her so-called "real" father without any thought for her own safety – so in need was she of a father's love.'

'Mmm,' Angie recalled, 'and she was let down big time when she did find him. Jimmy's not a bad bloke, but he's about as far removed from a father figure as you can possibly get.'

'So,' Cora said, 'what you're saying is that Marlene has a deep-seated need for a fatherly figure – as her own father was useless.' She looked at Angie. 'Sorry to be so blunt.'

Angie gave a sharp, bitter laugh. 'I'd be the first to admit it.'

'And then she's handed a second chance of getting the father she always wanted,' Cora continued, 'and that ends in disaster. Not only is Jimmy a bit of a cad, he actually came on to her.'

Angie shivered. 'Thank God he made it up to her when he realised she was actually his daughter.'

'No wonder the poor girl's confused,' Stanislaw said, shaking his head and taking a drink of his Polish vodka.

'She will grow out of it,' Lloyd said hopefully. 'It will just take a little time.'

'I wish I had your confidence,' Angie said. 'But what worries me the most about Marlene is that she's not one to do anything by halves.'

Chapter Forty-Eight

While the discussion continued in the family room at the manor, with Lloyd pouring another round of drinks and Clemmie filling the air with the sweet aromatic smell of her cigar smoke, the atmosphere in Danny and Lucy's cottage could not have been more different. The only positive was that husband and wife were not screaming at each other, as their baby boy had finally cried himself into exhaustion and was now asleep.

'Felix has never been as grizzly as this before.' Lucy's whisper was more a hiss as she threw Danny a scolding look. 'He's picked up on your foul mood, for which I am in no doubt of the reason.'

'Well, I think I have every right to be in a foul mood,' Danny defended himself. 'I have just found out that my younger sister, who is only eighteen—'

'But is in reality much older than her age,' Lucy butted in.

'Oh, so that makes it *so* much better?' Danny let out a bitter laugh. 'Well, then, that's all right.'

'There's no need for sarcasm,' Lucy said.

Danny paced the room.

'Marlene might appear very mature for her age, but there's part of her which is still very young.'

He stopped striding and stood with his hands on his hips, his eyes trained on his wife.

'It's not just the age gap.' He paused. 'I'm sorry, Lucy, but I really worry about my sister being with someone like your father.'

Lucy let out a frustrated garbled sound.

'Honestly, Danny, I could scream. It's like you want my father to be this horrible, self-centred person. You've not even given him a chance. You've not once tried to chat to him, get to know him.'

She took a deep intake of breath before the words she wanted to say rushed to be heard.

'I have sacrificed so much to be with you. I eloped with you, married you against my family's wishes, knowing that by doing so I was going to cause them untold grief – was going to be the cause of them losing Roeburn Hall.'

Danny was about to interject, but Lucy kept going. Now she had uncorked the bottle, there was no going back.

'Because of you – because I chose you over my family – I was shut out by my own mother and father and ostracised by everyone I knew.'

Lucy was becoming angrier by the second.

'I went against my own blood for you. By marrying you, I was showing I was prepared to destroy my family's legacy. Their ancestry.'

She took another breath.

'And after all that, after everything I have done for you, everything I have given up to be with you, you could not do one simple thing for me. You couldn't just try to get along with my father. Not once have you offered an olive branch. *Not once.*'

'I would have been a hypocrite if I had,' Danny defended

himself. 'Besides, he's not offered me any kind of olive branch.'

'That's because you've never given him the chance. Every time he's within spitting distance, you're off like the clappers!' Lucy said, her voice rising. She also thought there might well be another reason for her father not going out of his way to make peace with his son-in-law. Especially as the rumours about Danny and the Traveller woman had continued. She had tried to ignore them, tell herself that they were tittle-tattle, but deep down she knew they weren't. Just as she knew why she hadn't confronted Danny about them – she couldn't bring herself to spoil the magic of the first weeks with their gorgeous baby boy.

'And how do *you* feel?' Danny asked, breaking through her thoughts. 'Your own father dating someone the same age as yourself? Be honest, Lucy, it *has* to make you feel uncomfortable?'

Lucy sat down on the chair. Her husband's air of agitation and constant pacing were draining her.

'I've had longer to get used to it,' she said without thinking. 'They told me first. When it all started. About a week ago. They were worried about my reaction.'

'So, you knew before!' he said, flabbergasted. 'You knew and you never thought to tell me?'

'Yes,' Lucy said. 'Why would I tell you? It wasn't my place to tell you, or anyone else, about my father and my best friend's private life.'

Danny's mouth dropped open.

'Whatever happened to there being no secrets between man and wife?' he accused.

The words were the final straw for the camel's back.

Lucy had held off, but no more.

She let out a dramatic choking sound, trying to make it as quiet as possible, which was hard as her whole being wanted to scream at her husband at the top of her lungs.

'*Secrets?* You talk about keeping secrets from one another?' Another theatrical garbled sound.

'Talk about the pot calling the kettle black!' she heckled.

'What do you mean?' Danny asked, perplexed.

'Like you don't know!' Lucy lambasted. She felt a strange sort of elation at finally being able to say what she had wanted to say for the past few weeks.

'I don't think I'm the only one keeping secrets, am I?' she asked.

Danny still had the same look of puzzlement.

'Only,' Lucy said with a scary calmness, 'your secret is a little murkier than me not telling you about Marlene and my father.'

'Lucy, I have no idea what you are talking about,' Danny said. He had now stopped pacing and was staring at his wife.

'God, Danny, I never thought you were a liar, never mind a bloody good one at that!' Lucy stood up. Now she was the one pacing.

'Okay, you're starting to annoy me now,' Danny said, his voice rising. 'I'd love to know what it is I have been lying about so spectacularly.'

Lucy walked over to her husband and looked him directly in the eye.

'So, do you want to tell me where you were when I was

250

here, going into labour and for once in my life actually needing you?'

Danny fell quiet as his mind caught up with his wife's train of thought.

'I was up at the Travellers' camp,' he said. 'I thought you knew?'

'Why did you think I knew?' Lucy snapped.

'Well, you didn't ask, so I just presumed someone had told you!' he snapped back.

Lucy gave him a look of derision.

'Oh yes, someone did indeed tell me . . . ' Lucy recalled the insufferable hurt she had felt on hearing where he had been while she was giving birth to their son. 'Just like someone told me how often you've been sneaking off up there.'

Danny felt himself flush from the brewing anger. 'What do you mean, *sneaking off up there*? I've never sneaked off anywhere in my life.' His voice was low and thunderous. 'The only reason I ever go to the Travellers' camp is for trade.'

'Really?' Lucy said, her expression leaving Danny in no doubt that she did not believe a word he was saying.

'Well, why else would I be going up there?' he demanded.

'You tell me!' Lucy spat out the words, looking daggers at him.

'No!' Danny batted back, his face darkening. *'You* tell *me!'*

There was a silent stand-off.

The sound of Felix starting to stir could be heard from the next room.

'I know all about it,' Lucy said, trying desperately to keep her voice down.

'Know all about what?' Danny asked. He, too, desperately tried to keep his voice down, but it was hard. Very hard.

251

'Your new *friend*,' Lucy said. 'Adriana. I've been hearing all about you and her. And all the time you two have been spending together.'

Danny let out a bark of disbelief. 'What? You think I'm having some sort of affair with Adriana?'

Lucy bristled with the familiarity with which he said her name.

'*I know you are!*' she said, her anger and jealousy making her lie. She didn't know for certain that he was, but she was damn well pretty sure.

Danny went deathly quiet. His face was like stone. He looked at his wife as though he had never met her before in his life.

'Do you honestly think I would go with another woman?' he asked, his voice unnaturally calm.

Lucy glared at her husband; all her pent-up anger was making her feel as though she would burst.

'Yes!' She spat out the words. 'I do!'

Danny searched her face with his eyes, trying to see just a smidgen of the woman he loved.

'Well, if that's what you believe, I think you should leave!' His words betrayed both his hurt and his ire. 'You've got Roeburn Hall. You can go there and live with a father who you clearly adore. And who seems to make you happier than I do. And no doubt Marlene will be joining you there soon, so you can all live there happily ever after – and without you having to share a bed with a man you believe to be a liar and an adulterer.'

And with that, Danny walked out of the room and down the short corridor.

'I wish I'd never laid eyes on you, Danny Boulter!' Lucy shouted after him. 'You've brought me nothing but misery!'

Her final words were punctuated by the slamming of the front door.

Which was, in turn, followed by a whimper, then the beginnings of a wail as baby Felix expressed his own distress at his mother and father's war of words.

Chapter Forty-Nine

After Danny walked out that night, Lucy knew she could not live under the same roof as her husband while she believed him to have been unfaithful. It was bad enough that she believed her husband had been with another woman, but for that woman to be Adriana – the mysterious, beautiful bloody Adriana – it was too much. The jealousy she felt was on par with the hurt in her heart, especially as the woman Danny had chosen over her was so completely different to her. Whereas Lucy was blonde and blue-eyed with an English-rose complexion and aristocratic heritage, Adriana was olive-skinned, with long, curly, almost black hair and the most amazing deep brown eyes, her looks and way of dressing betraying her nomadic Romany roots. The only common denominator between the two was their love of horses.

So, Lucy hastily packed her bags, as well as everything she needed for Felix, and the two of them left. Marlene drove mother and baby to Roeburn Hall, where Edward was waiting for them with open arms.

Overnight, the lives of those who lived at Cuthford Manor were tossed upside down. And as the days turned into weeks, no one seemed to know how to put everything the right way up again.

'It's ever since that man ingratiated himself into our lives.

I honestly wouldn't put it past him to have orchestrated all of this,' Angie said, pouring herself another glass of wine.

Stanislaw glanced over at Lloyd and grimaced, but only because he knew Angie could not see him. Lloyd mirrored the look, sympathising with the man who had been his friend well before he had come to work at the manor and fallen for Angie.

'There is a lot going on at the moment, but everything will sort itself out,' Cora chipped in, aware of the need to calm the stormy waters and not churn them up more than they already were.

'I don't think we can put all of the recent troubles at Edward's doorstep,' Clemmie said. 'Now, don't play holy war with me, Angie. I need to be the voice of reason here.'

Cora threw Clemmie a warning look that she ignored.

'Edward didn't exactly cause the marital rift between Danny and Lucy,' Clemmie carried on regardless. 'They've both had a lot to deal with these past nine months. Lucy fell pregnant—'

Angie let out a loud huffing sound. 'I *said* they should have waited, but whoever listens to me.' She took a slug from her wine glass.

Clemmie ignored her and soldiered on. 'The poor girl's lost her mother, then had her father accused of her mother's murder, gone through the most godawful time with her pregnancy and been bedbound for weeks on end – it's enough to send anyone round the twist. The only solace she has had during all of this is from being reunited with her father.'

She looked at Angie, unsure whether she should commit the cardinal sin of criticising blood. As usual, though, Clemmie was unable to hold back.

'And it has to be said that Danny hasn't exactly been the perfect husband.'

Lloyd, Cora and Stanislaw froze. Angie was not in a mood to be crossed.

'He has resolutely refused to even attempt to build bridges with Edward,' Clemmie bulldozed on, 'and now there is a question mark over whether or not he's been having some kind of dalliance with this Traveller horsewoman.'

'Danny would never be unfaithful to Lucy,' Angie defended him. 'He's the most loyal person I know.'

Stanislaw and Lloyd coughed in unison.

'One of the most loyal I know,' she appeased, forcing a smile for her husband and the man who had become like a father to her. 'I do not believe for one minute that Danny has been with this woman.'

There was a slightly awkward silence. Conversations that had been conducted behind closed doors had speculated whether Danny had perhaps wandered. By all accounts, he had been spending more time than usual up at the camp, and there didn't seem to be any more trade with the Travellers than there was normally. On top of which, they shared a love for horses and, probably more importantly, were more akin when it came to their class. As the son of a coalminer, Danny would never totally fit into the society he was now a part of, just as Adriana, as a Traveller, would never be accepted by the wider community.

'If only Danny had denied it to Lucy – really tried to convince her that this wasn't the case – and explained why he had been going up to the camp so frequently,' Cora said.

'But that's not Danny,' Angie said. 'He's as stubborn as

a mule. And he was angry that Lucy could even think that of him.' She had talked to her brother, asking him the same question, and had received the answer she knew would be forthcoming.

Suddenly Angie expelled air and put both hands on her forehead, showing her despair.

'And then there's Marlene seeing a man her brother hates, and who also happens to be twice her age and her sister-in-law's father.' She sighed. 'It's times like this I wish Mam was still alive. I think she's the only person Marlene might have listened to.'

Stanislaw nodded. His strong disapproval of his mother-in-law had changed as he'd got to know her better.

'And if Danny is stubborn, well, I don't know what that makes Marlene,' Angie added.

'She's just strong-willed – and thinks she knows her own mind,' Clemmie appeased.

'Exactly. Marlene *thinks* she knows her own mind,' Angie stressed.

'Well,' Lloyd interjected, trying to offer up a shred of hope, 'my feelings are that this is just a stage Marlene is going through and she'll soon move on to someone more appropriate for her age.'

The silence that followed showed no one else shared his optimism.

'I think the best we can do,' said Cora, forever the peace-maker, 'is to try and hide our disapproval about Marlene's courtship. We don't want to alienate her.'

'Hmm, she's already spending much more time over at Roeburn Hall,' Lloyd said. 'As soon as she's finished work here, she's jumping in her car and is straight off over there.'

'A double lure of her new paramour and her heartbroken friend – and baby Felix, of course,' Clemmie mused.

'And,' Angie piped up, 'I don't like how this whole Edward scenario has the potential to come between Danny and Marlene – they've been thick as thieves their whole lives. It would not be good for either of them if they lost that closeness. And if things carry on the way they are, that's going to be inevitable.'

She sat up straight.

'Which brings me back to my initial point. This is *all* down to that man.'

'Well,' Cora said sadly, 'that might be the case, but one thing he cannot be blamed for is getting my wonderful assistant in the family way.'

Angie looked at Cora and had to concede the point. She knew Cora really liked Mabel and had taken her under her wing this past year. Never normally one to judge, Cora had confided in Angie that she was disappointed Mabel had been so 'careless' and doubted she would return to work after having the baby.

'How long is it now before the wedding?' Stanislaw asked.

'Two weeks,' Cora said. She had offered to help with the preparations since Mabel's stepmother had shown no inclination. The two didn't sound close.

'At least I was able to persuade the vicar to marry them in the church.,' Angie said. The vicar could not refuse. With the extra footfall St Cuthbert's had enjoyed since the manor had become a hotel, its coffers had swollen tenfold. 'And we can have the reception here.'

'And don't forget, we are here to help,' Clemmie said, looking across at Angie, who nodded.

They both knew that Cora would need a helping hand. Marlene, who would normally enjoy arranging any kind of celebration, would not want to participate in any way in the organising of Mabel and Thomas's nuptials.

Chapter Fifty

The two weeks leading up to Mabel and Thomas's wedding were busy for everyone – not just the 'happy' couple. Marlene found herself picking up jobs that Mabel would normally have done, as Cora had told her assistant that she only needed to work until mid-afternoon, in order to give her time to prepare for her wedding.

The subject of marriage, Marlene noticed, seemed to be inescapable. The manor was full of chatter about the impending wedding of two of its staff, whereas when she went to see Lucy, Felix and Edward at Roeburn Hall, it was the other, less joyous side of marriage that was being picked over. Marlene still couldn't quite believe her brother would have an affair, but she decided not to try and convince Lucy since if she were honest, she was not one hundred per cent sure herself. She was just glad that Lucy had agreed to allow Danny time with Felix, on condition that the baby was not taken beyond the manor's boundaries. There was no need to say why Lucy had stipulated this.

Marlene's evenings at Roeburn Hall quickly fell into a routine of seeing Lucy and Felix, chatting until her sister-in-law had worn herself out or her little nephew needed tending to, and then spending the rest of it with Edward.

'There is a silver lining to all this awful marital conflict,' he confided in her one night.

Marlene pulled a quizzical look. 'Which is?'

'Which is *you*!' Edward exclaimed, as though she should know. 'I get to spend more time with you. *Much* more time.' He took a sip of his wine. 'And because of that, I do wonder if perhaps you should have your own room here. We've certainly got enough to choose from. I do worry about you driving back late at night.'

Marlene batted the suggestion away. 'I think I can safely drive myself the one mile back home in the dark.'

But Edward's words did make her think that it might not be such a bad idea, as she was often tired when she left Roeburn Hall, and it felt a wrench leaving Edward and the warmth of his arms as they curled up on the sofa, chatting about their dreams and ambitions. She also liked the feeling of being cut off at Roeburn Hall, encased in her own bubble, away from all the chatter about Thomas and his impending marriage and, of course, the birth of their baby, which was apparently due sometime in November. Whenever the two were mentioned, Edward would inevitably turn the conversation away from the hurt and lost love he knew Marlene still felt and instead focus on their own burgeoning love affair.

One evening when they were both a little tipsy, Edward looked at Marlene as though appraising her and said, 'You know, if we were to have children, I wonder if they would have your blonde hair or my dark hair?' He chuckled. 'As long as they were to get your looks as well as your brains, they'd be fine.'

It was a topic of conversation that Marlene replayed while she lay in her own bed late at night. The news of Mabel's pregnancy, along with the time she was spending with baby Felix, seemed to have stirred up her own maternal feelings.

Just as all the baby talk seemed to have exacerbated Edward's paternal feelings too.

'You know, I have one great regret in my life,' he told her one evening when they were out for dinner in Durham.

'And what's that?' Marlene asked.

'I should have been a better father to Lucy,' he admitted. 'I wish I'd been stronger and not let Elise have free rein.'

'What would you have done differently?' Marlene asked. The more they got to know each other, the more she knew for definite that his marriage had been a loveless one.

'I'd not have let her send Lucy off to boarding school so young – if at all,' he declared, putting down his knife and fork; recalling his regrets seemed to have ruined his appetite. 'But it was what my father did with me, and his father did before that. So I guess I agreed because it was all I knew, but there was always something inside me that niggled, which was trying to tell me this was not right. And those niggles were proved well-founded when Lucy came to me and told me how unhappy she was there and how she was desperate to come back home and go to a day school so she could be with her horse.' Edward gave a crooked smile. 'You see, it was her horse she missed, not us. And that shocked me. And I decided I wanted to put it right.'

Marlene nodded. She put down her own knife and fork, having eaten most of what was on her plate. Lucy had told her how her life had changed after her father had stood up to her mother and allowed her to leave her boarding school in Harrogate and return home.

As they finished their drinks, Edward went on to express his remorse over the way he had been towards Lucy when she had married Danny, but again, he hoped he was now making it up to her. Another 'silver lining', he'd admitted, that had come from his wife's premature demise.

Marlene knew that Edward was smitten with her as he'd done nothing to hide it. There was no game-playing with Edward, which she put down to him being older and more mature.

'I'm falling for you,' Edward told her one evening. 'You know, that don't you?'

Marlene looked at him and gave the slightest of nods. At that moment, after the way Edward had spoken to her and looked at her, she felt such a wonderful infusion of love – of being loved – it momentarily overwhelmed her. Edward kissed her before she could tell him that she was also falling for him, which she was glad of. Their relationship was becoming quite the whirlwind romance, which she was revelling in, but at the same time something was holding her back.

Thomas's wedding was fast approaching, and she had seen next to nothing of anyone at Cuthford Manor. Normally she'd have caught up with everyone over dinner, but as she tended to eat with Edward and Lucy, or went out for a meal in Durham with just Edward, it meant that she was starting to feel a little estranged from her family and friends. But she convinced herself that this was what it was like when you met someone and started to fall in love with them. You just wanted to be with them and no one else. Something Edward also felt.

'It's crazy,' he told her another evening when he welcomed

her to Roeburn Hall, 'but I actually miss you during the day.' His declaration was followed by a self-deprecating laugh. 'God, I'm like a lovesick puppy,' he said, taking her in his arms and kissing her.

When they finally broke free, he smiled. 'But it's not just your beauty that I miss every hour of every day – there are so many times I also need that brain of yours to tell me what you think I should do with this room or that room.'

It was at that moment Marlene started to feel as though *she* was also falling for *him*. She had been told many times in the past how much a boy had liked her – loved her, even – but it was always to do with her looks. Edward saw beyond that. He loved her for her mind too.

'But I have to tell myself,' Edward said as they walked into the main hallway, 'that I can't have you every hour of every day.' He gave her a mischievous look. 'Just as I tell myself to be patient. All good things come to those who wait,' he said, subtly alluding to what he hoped the future might hold. 'In the meantime, would you indulge me this evening by taking a walk around my humble abode and sharing with me your vision of how you would transform Roeburn Hall back to her former grandeur?'

Marlene's eyes lit up. She had realised that the part of her work at the manor she loved the most was not so much managing the hotel as converting it into something even more special than it already was; as she had done with the attic, which was now a very beautiful, very popular and very pricey honeymoon suite.

As they walked down corridors and stepped into rooms, Marlene described her vision, which was full of colour and combined contemporary furnishing with the restoration of the original features.

'Honestly, Edward, you could make this place quite spectacular. As a hotel as well as a home.'

'You're right, my lovely, but I have to be careful not to upset your sister. I don't want her thinking I'm going to be competition.'

'Mmm, I understand,' Marlene agreed. Her sister and everyone at Cuthford Manor had worked their socks off to rebuild the West Wing, which had been severely fire-damaged after Evelyn's arson attack, and also to convert the rest of the manor into the very beautiful and exclusive country house hotel it was now. Not for the first time, she felt divided between her life at Cuthford Manor, and those who lived there, and this new life, which seemed to have very quickly, and rather magically, come into being.

'Yes, I think you're right,' Marlene agreed. 'It works at the moment as the rooms are really just somewhere for guests to put their heads down for the night.'

They continued their inspection.

'I do have one thought as an alternative to a hotel, although I am not sure if, or how, it could work financially,' Marlene said as she walked into the nearest room and over to the large sash windows. She looked out at the darkened outline of the vast countryside.

Edward followed and put his arms around her, then kissed her neck.

'Tell me what you are thinking,' he murmured.

'You'll think it's ridiculous and pie in the sky,' she said, enjoying the feel of his body against her own.

'Try me,' Edward said, again kissing her on her neck.

'It's something I've kept thinking about since my trip to London.' Marlene had never told Edward the details of what had happened there, just that she had gone in search of her real father and had found him. She wasn't sure why she hadn't elaborated. Perhaps because she felt embarrassed by her own stupidity.

Edward turned her around and kissed her on the lips. 'Tell me over a glass of Chablis,' he said, taking her hand and walking her out of the room, along the corridor and back down the long staircase to the living room. After he had poured them each a glass of wine, they settled on the sofa.

'Right, I'm all ears,' he said.

Marlene flushed a little. She had not told anyone what she was about to divulge.

'It might seem very idealistic,' she started.

'And what is wrong with idealism?' he encouraged.

Marlene took a sip of her wine.

'Okay,' she began. 'But you must not ridicule me.'

Edward adopted a stern expression. 'Never.'

Marlene took a deep breath, her mind pulled back to the short but traumatic time she had endured in London.

'When I was looking for my father, Jimmy,' she began, 'I came across two young children who were begging on the street. They must have only been about five and six. They were a boy and a girl, and they reminded me of Danny and I when we were little. We'd not beg deliberately, but often, if we were just sat on the kerbside or sitting up against a wall, watching the world go by, passers-by would drop a few coins at our feet. Anyway, I saw those two children again that day, a few hours later but at a different spot, outside a pub, clearly hoping that a few pints would make those coming out more generous with their pennies.'

She paused and glanced at Edward, who was listening intently.

'The thing is, those two children have stayed with me, as has the urge to bring them back to the manor – to clean them, feed them and give them a decent home. Which I know is ridiculous. I'd be arrested for kidnapping,' she added, trying to inject some humour into her story.

'I think what I'm saying is that I'd like to be able to do that for other children like them. Create a home for those who need a safe place to grow up in – a place where they can be nurtured.'

Edward didn't laugh, but instead took her hand and squeezed it gently.

'That is the most wonderful, kind and caring idea I have ever heard.'

With each day, Marlene began to believe that Edward – and not Thomas – was the man for her. Not that she had the choice. There was nothing like a baby on the horizon to obliterate any hope of ever being with the man you loved. Or had loved. Finally, Marlene felt as though she was starting to view Thomas as part of the past. And the more she did, the more Edward became her present – and also, possibly, her future.

Edward had hinted on a few occasions that he wanted to propose to Marlene. The hints came in the form of 'theoretically speaking' discussions on how long is long enough before a widower might think to declare to the world he has found the woman he wishes to make his betrothed. They always laughed, but Marlene knew that behind the banter and joking there was a very serious edge to Edward's comments.

Just as there was also a seriousness when Marlene discussed with him her take on men and marriage. Her chats with Clemmie had opened her eyes to the constraints of being legally bound to a man; how she would not want to be her husband's skivvy but his equal. After she had given her Clemmie-inspired view about all the sexist propaganda that was relentlessly spouted in all the women's magazines, and how she did not aspire to be one of those perfect-looking women wearing high heels and with her hands in a pair of oven gloves, about to serve her husband's dinner, Edward had barked with laughter.

'I could never in a million years even imagine you in such a scenario,' he declared.

They sat in a comfortable silence before Edward asked, 'But since you have told me you want to save yourself for marriage, that must therefore mean you are not averse to the *idea* of marriage? Or have I got it wrong and you are wanting to be totally emancipated and live in sin?'

Marlene gave him a disapproving look. 'Certainly not.' Under the light-heartedness, there was a granite determination that Marlene would never allow herself to be in circumstances that would lead to the name-calling her own mam had suffered, and which she, as her mother's daughter, had also had to endure.

Any talk of marriage, however, also led inevitably to the less palatable subject of Lucy and Danny. Because of the information Edward relayed to her after speaking to those with 'their ear to the ground', Marlene had begun to think that if what Edward was telling her was true, and she had no reason to doubt it, then it might be better for her brother and sister-in-law to separate officially. As Angie had said when the couple had arrived back from Gretna Green on the afternoon of Ida's wake, perhaps Danny and Lucy had married in haste, with the inference being that they risked repenting at their leisure. Perhaps this was what was occurring now. The night Marlene had taken Lucy and Felix to Roeburn Hall, there had been hope that her brother and Lucy would be able to work things out – but hearing the daily updates from Edward, she was now beginning to doubt it.

Marlene would have liked to have confronted Danny about it, but he seemed to be keeping himself busy and when he wasn't, she was at Roeburn Hall. Also, she knew that Danny would end up turning the conversation around to her relationship with Edward and would not hold back his disapproval as to who his younger sister had started to date. And she knew he would not listen if she tried to tell him how they had got to know each other well in a relatively short period of time, and how she felt that Edward understood her.

When Marlene and Edward occasionally chatted about Thomas, Edward admitted that he really did not see how she was in any way suited to him. And that he thought her feelings for Thomas were more those of friendship and a closeness borne of the fact that the two had known each other for many years.

'Sometimes it's easy to become confused and see the love of a friend as a romantic love,' he suggested.

Marlene was drawn to this theory because it helped her to

bury her feelings for Thomas, especially as there was no way they could ever be together – the wedding now just a matter of days away, and the birth of his baby a matter of months.

It annoyed Marlene that she still thought a lot about Thomas, but she hoped as soon as the damned wedding was over that would end. After that, she told herself, she just couldn't – *wouldn't* – allow herself to give way to any kind of feelings of torment when Mabel's pregnancy started to show or when the baby was born.

Thomas's baby.

Thomas and Mabel's baby.

Chapter Fifty-One

Saturday, 4 June

On the morning of Thomas and Mabel's wedding, everyone was up bright and early. Although it was just a small affair, there was still a lot to do. Cora had become the unofficial wedding organiser, something she did not mind because she liked Mabel a lot, and she did feel for her as her father and stepmother had told Mabel that they wanted nothing to do with the wedding. Mabel said they hadn't exactly disowned her for 'getting herself in the family way', but they had refused to play any part in her wedding because she had brought 'shame on the family'. It was why Lloyd was taking on her father's role and giving the bride away. When Mabel had originally told Cora, she had been shocked. She couldn't believe a father and the woman who had brought Mabel up were not even going to show their faces at the wedding. Mabel had put a brave face on it and said it didn't matter since she and her stepmother didn't 'really see eye to eye', but Cora could tell she was hurt. It was something Cora had discussed with Angie and the two had hummed and hawed as to whether or not to go and see Mr and Mrs Glendenning to try to cajole them into coming along.

Bustling into the kitchen to see how preparations for the

buffet were going, Cora bumped into Angie, who was jiggling Juni on her hip and trying to loosen the little girl's grip on her hair.

'Ah, just the person,' Cora said.

'Two seconds,' Angie said, finally succeeding in convincing Juni to let go of her hair, which she had just styled for the wedding. Angie looked at Cora and nodded over at the worktop by the range, where Mrs Trendle and Alberta seemed to be having an animated discussion about the sausage-roll mix.

'I'm just seeing if Nanny can take this little grappler off my hands for a while,' Angie said, cocking her head at the two vying cooks.

Cora nodded her understanding. There had been friction in the kitchen of late between the relatively new cook, Mrs Trendle, and the former cook, Alberta, who had been chief in the kitchen at Cuthford Manor for as long as anyone could remember, but who had hung up her apron last year in favour of becoming Juni's nanny. Or rather, she was meant to have. The problem was, whenever there was any kind of important do, Alberta seemed to forget she was no longer the kitchen's kingpin.

Cora watched as Alberta took Juni and agreed to take her out to see Lucky the pit pony and give him a 'nice carrot'. It was well timed as the steam coming off the pots on the hob was competing with that coming out of Mrs Trendle's ears.

'In the nick of time,' Cora mumbled as they walked out of the kitchen.

'I'd say,' Angie agreed, patting down her clump of tatty hair. She looked at Cora. 'You look a little apprehensive. What's up?'

'Well, I keep thinking about Mabel's dad and her step-mother and how sad it is they're not coming to the wedding. And from what I've gathered, they've not even met Thomas yet.'

'You're not thinking of going over there, are you?' Angie asked, looking at her watch.

'I thought it wouldn't hurt if we just nipped over quickly,' Cora said, 'to see if we couldn't persuade them to show their faces. I know it would mean the world to Mabel.'

Angie didn't think Mabel had been that put out, but then again, she didn't know Mabel like Cora did. She nodded, the corner of her eye catching a flash of colourful summer flowers. She turned to see Jake meticulously putting the finishing touches to the very beautiful floral arrangement in the hallway. He looked to be in his own little world.

Angie looked back at Cora.

'Let me just have a quick word with Marlene before she heads over to Roeburn Hall,' she said, wanting to add that she wished Cora had mentioned this earlier. They were going to be pushed for time.

'I'm guessing Marlene doesn't want to partake of the celebrations?' Cora asked, raising an eyebrow.

'She's apparently needed to babysit Felix as Lucy has some appointment or other she has to go to,' Angie said in a voice which did not hide the fact that she didn't believe a word of it.

'Nothing whatsoever to do with not wanting to suffer the heartache of seeing Thomas get married?' Cora said.

'Nothing at all.' Angie raised her eyebrows. '"Thomas is in the past," I've been told. And it's now all *Edward, Edward, Edward*.'

Cora knew what Angie was fearful of. 'You don't think there'll be another dash down the aisle coming up, do you?'

'Oh God, don't even think it, never mind say it,' Angie said, cringing. 'I'm praying she'll come to her senses sooner rather than later.'

Cora thought that unlikely but didn't say so. Marlene and Edward had probably squashed a year's worth of normal courtship into the space of the past month. She didn't know of a day they had not seen each other, which made her suspect that there might well be news of an engagement soon. Especially, as Angie had already pointed out, Marlene did not do things by half. And it was very clear that she was very serious about Edward.

Half an hour later, Cora and Angie were climbing out the Rover and walking down the little pathway to the home of Mr and Mrs Glendenning. The couple lived in a small village not far from Roeburn Hall, which was one of the reasons Mabel had said she wanted to 'live in', as a mile was a long way when you just had an old bicycle for transport. Particularly during the winter.

Angie knocked on the door.

'Coming!' sounded out a woman's gravelly voice, which they presumed belonged to Mabel's stepmother.

When the door swung open, Cora and Angie were somewhat taken aback as the rather gruff voice did not seem to tally with the petite woman standing in front of them.

'Can I help?' she asked, looking her two visitors up and down.

'I hope so,' Cora began.

After they had explained who they were and where they had just come from, Mrs Glendenning opened the door and ushered them in. Cora threw Angie a hopeful look as they had not been turned away.

'Can I offer yer both a cuppa?' Mrs Glendenning asked, showing them into the living room and nodding at a tatty old sofa. The cottage was small but uncluttered and as clean as a whistle.

They both declined politely, conscious that they were on limited time, but feeling more positive because of Mrs Glendenning's hospitality.

'We won't stay long,' Cora said. It had been agreed that she would do most of the talking as she knew Mabel the best.

'We really just wanted to come and have a chat to you about Mabel.'

'Cos it's her wedding day?' Mrs Glendenning asked.

Cora and Angie nodded.

'We were hoping that if we came to see you personally, you might reconsider your decision not to attend the service.'

'And, of course,' Angie chipped in, 'there'll be a lovely buffet afterwards at the manor.'

They each held their breath, fearful they'd be ushered back out with a flea in their ear as quickly as they'd been ushered in.

Mrs Glendenning's expression was one of confusion.

'Well, my dears, I'd love to come . . .' She paused. 'As would her da.' She looked from Cora to Angie. 'But we've not been invited.'

Cora and Angie were stuck for words.

They gave each other puzzled looks.

'Mabel didn't invite you?' Cora asked, needing it to be reaffirmed.

Mrs Glendenning shook her head, her face now betraying her hurt.

'She didn't tell yer?' she said, reaching for her rolling tobacco. 'To be fair, me and her have never really got on. It's difficult bringing up someone else's child.'

Angie nodded. It was something she knew only too well, having brought up her four younger siblings.

'She wasn't at all like my other bairns – or, to be fair, any of the other bairns she grew up with round here. She could be nice as ninepence, but as soon as she didn't get what she wanted, or someone crossed her . . . '

Mrs Glendenning licked the cigarette paper and tapped the end on her tobacco tin.

'Well, let's put it this way, you knew about it.' She pulled out a lighter from the pocket of her cardigan.

'But,' she continued, lighting up her cigarette, 'I thought she might have invited her da.' She blew out smoke and looked around the room, then through to the small kitchen that led out to the back. 'That's why he's not here. He didn't say anything, but I knew he just wanted to go out for the day and try to forget about it. He's at the allotment. He'll be there the best part of the day.' She sighed sadly. 'I just hope she brings the babe to see him when the little mite's born in October.'

'Oh, I don't think the baby's due until November,' Cora corrected.

Mrs Glendenning raised her eyebrows.

'Is that what she told you?' she asked, now curious.

'She did,' Cora said. 'Why would she lie?'

Mrs Glendenning shook her head, taking another draw on her cigarette. 'God only knows. But there'll be a reason. Mabel is a very cunning and calculating young woman. Course, I wouldn't say that if her da were about. He's always given her the benefit of the doubt.'

She took another drag on her cigarette.

'All I know is that Mabel got caught around February – around the time we had all that atrocious weather they kept calling the "Big Freeze".'

Angie looked at Cora and then back at Mrs Glendenning. 'But she wasn't seeing Thomas then.'

'She wasn't even staying at the manor then,' Cora mumbled.

'All I know,' Mrs Glendenning said, 'is that around the time of the thaw, I saw her and I said to her, "Mab, you've got yourself in the family way, haven't yer?"'

She took another deep drag on her cigarette.

'I might not be brain of Britain, but I know a pregnant woman when I see one. And don't forget, I brought Mabel up from when she was so high.' She stuck her hand out in front of her. 'I saw the change in her straight away.'

'And did she admit it?' Angie asked, her mind whirring with a plethora of thoughts. She looked at Cora, who seemed to have gone very quiet, then back at Mrs Glendenning.

'Oh, yes,' she said. 'She knew there were no kidding me. I've had a fair few bairns myself. All up and away now, thank goodness. Making their own way in life. They still visit their old ma, though.'

'So, just so I've got this right,' Angie said, 'you're saying that Mabel fell pregnant during the Big Freeze in February?

277

And that she knew she was pregnant a few weeks later, in early March?'

Mrs Glendenning nodded. 'Mab said she knew pretty much straight away. Could feel it in her boobs. Sore as hell, she said. And getting bigger by the day. Morning sickness as well, but she was lucky on that score. She didn't have it bad. It were gone before she knew it.'

Angie looked at the little wooden clock on the mantelpiece and saw it was nearing midday. The service was due to start in an hour.

'I'm so sorry to be rude,' Angie said, standing up and staring down at Cora, who looked as though she was stuck to the sofa. 'But we've got to get going now. I didn't realise the time.' She tapped Cora on the shoulder to break her from her trance.

'Yes, yes,' Cora said, standing up and extending her hand. 'Thank you for giving us your time.'

Mrs Glendenning pushed herself out of her armchair.

'No bother,' she said. 'Nothing else much to do today.'

She walked out to the hallway and opened the door.

'Yer moan about them when they're here, then you miss them when they're gone.'

Cora and Angie nodded as though they understood, which they didn't. Cora had never been fortunate enough to have children, and those under Angie's care were all still at home.

'Oh, my goodness,' Angie said as soon as they were out of the house and out of earshot.

She looked at Cora.

'Are you thinking what I am thinking?'

They climbed back into the Rover.

'I'm not sure what I'm thinking at the moment,' Cora said. She stared straight ahead as Angie turned the ignition and stuck the car into first gear.

They drove in silence for a short while.

'I suppose just because we didn't know they were seeing each other, that's not to say they weren't having *relations* with each other back then,' Cora said finally.

'That's true,' Angie agreed, slowing down for a horse and trap in front of them. It looked like there were a couple of Travellers in it, which made her think of Danny.

Was everyone having secret 'relations' with each other?

'But remember,' Angie said, 'we were pretty much cut off from the outside world. And like you say, Mabel got stuck at her dad and stepmam's because their village was snowed in.'

'When was it Marlene saw Mabel come out of Thomas's digs?' Cora asked.

'It was coming up to mid-March. I remember because the children were back at school – and it was the day after Marlene had come to see me about Edward's business proposition. Which, as you know, I was none too happy about.'

'I remember,' Cora said, recalling how she had patiently listened to Angie as she vehemently expressed her concerns that Edward was planning on turning Roeburn Hall into another country house hotel.

As they reached the sign to Cuthford village, Angie turned right, glad she could get out of third gear and into fourth.

Cora looked at her watch. 'It's quarter past twelve.'

'Oh my God,' Angie said, pushing her foot down on the accelerator. 'What should we do?'

When they reached the main gates of Cuthford Manor

and slowed down, Angie declared, 'Danny! He's the only one who could talk to Thomas about something like this. He can find out for definite.'

'And then what?' Cora worried.

Chapter Fifty-Two

As soon as Marlene pulled up outside Roeburn Hall, Edward was at the door.

'Come in, come in!' he said.

When she got to the top of the steps, she laughed. 'You look very excited?'

He pulled her into his arms and kissed her.

'You have that effect on me, my gorgeous girl,' he said.

'Hmm,' Marlene said, eyeing him suspiciously, 'I feel there's more to it than that.'

Edward gave a short bark of laughter.

'Nothing gets by you, does it! Now, come on in and say your hellos to Lucy and Felix, and then we are heading straight back out.'

He took Marlene's hand and led her across the threshold and towards the nursery.

'We're going out for a picnic. It's the perfect day for it!'

Marlene smiled. She knew Edward's intention was to take her mind off Thomas's wedding to Mabel. She wanted to tell him that she really wasn't bothered by it in any way, but that would have been a lie.

But it also wouldn't have been an untruth to say that those feelings were the dying embers of a lost love – and that Edward had brought her heart to life again. And dare she even admit it to herself, but she really did feel as though she was falling in love with him.

Chapter Fifty-Three

When Angie and Cora pulled up in the backyard of the manor, Angie jumped out of the driver's seat and ran up the stairs to Thomas's bedsit. She knew Danny, as best man, would be with Thomas, getting ready to go to the church. She knocked once, then walked in. It was empty. She saw a quarter-bottle of whisky with two empty tumblers on the coffee table. The obligatory shot or two before leaving bachelorhood behind.

Turning on her heel, she hurried back down the stairs just as Cora was starting to get out.

'They're not there! Get back in the car!' Angie shouted as she made her way down the rest of the steps as fast as she could.

As she turned the engine and started to pull away, she saw Alberta and Wilfred coming out of the back door.

'Damn!' Angie stamped on the brakes and then put the car into reverse. She had promised that she would take them to the church.

Stamping on the brakes again, she wound down her window.

'Hurry up!' she shouted.

Alberta and Wilfred walked across the cobbles to the car as quickly as they could in their best shoes.

'Come on! Get in!' Angie said, frantically waving her hands.

A rather flushed Alberta and disgruntled Wilfred clambered into the back of the car.

Angie was off before they'd had time to properly shut their doors.

Cora turned around in her seat and gave them an apologetic look.

'What's the rush?' Wilfred asked a little breathlessly. 'I didn't think we were meant to be leaving until gone half past?'

'We'll explain later,' Cora said. 'We'll let Angie concentrate on her driving.'

It took just minutes to get to St Cuthbert's Church in the village. Angie was out of the car in a flash and started jogging towards the church while Cora, Alberta and Wilfred were happy to remain seated and wait for their heart rates to go down.

Seeing Danny with Thomas and his dad and brothers standing chatting outside the church, Angie slowed to a walk and forced a smile on her face.

'Sorry,' she said to the all-male group, tapping her brother on the shoulder, 'but can I just borrow the best man for a moment?'

They all looked at Angie and thought she seemed a little frantic, despite her attempts to appear otherwise. Weddings, they had already agreed, brought out a different side of the fairer sex.

'The bride's not got cold feet has she?' Malachy, Thomas's older brother and the family joker, asked. Everyone chuckled.

Angie let out a peculiar noise that was meant to sound like laughter but came out more like she'd got something stuck in her throat.

Danny stepped away from everyone and followed Angie towards the graveyard. It was the only place within the small grounds of the church where there were no guests gathering.

'God, Angie, what's up? You look . . . I don't know – you look . . . *strange.*'

'Oh God, oh God, oh God,' Angie began before taking a deep breath. 'I really don't know how to say this – or how you're going to put this to Thomas – but here goes.'

Chapter Fifty-Four

Edward had told Marlene that they were going on a mystery trip and it would take about an hour to get there. During the drive in Edward's Aston Martin, which was just about able to accommodate the large Fortnum & Mason picnic basket he'd had sent up from London, Marlene decided not to try and guess where they were going but to enjoy the passing scenery as they passed through the city of Durham and continued down towards the south of the county. The sun was out, but there was a refreshing breeze. Not for the first time, Marlene wondered how anyone could live in a big city. Her roots might well be firmly planted in the industrial landscape of the biggest shipbuilding town in the world, but her heart was pure country.

When they took the turning before Barnard Castle, Marlene's face lit up.

'High Force,' she said. 'We're going to High Force.'

Edward smiled and nodded, slowing down to take in the amazing views as they approached the outskirts of the North Pennines.

'You're right,' she said. 'It *is* the perfect place for a picnic.'

And the perfect place for something else, Edward thought as he took his hand off the gearstick and gently squeezed Marlene's leg.

He just hoped he wasn't jumping the gun.

Chapter Fifty-Five

It was ten minutes before one o'clock and the vicar had started to usher the wedding guests into the church.

As Danny grabbed Thomas, he hoped that Mabel would be keeping with tradition and arriving a little late. He knew that Jake was chauffeuring her to the church in the Bentley.

'Thomas, can I have a quick word?' he asked, nervously scratching the side of his face.

Thomas looked at his friend. 'We should be going in now.'

'I know, but just give me two minutes,' Danny said, his face white and deathly serious.

'You've got me worried,' Thomas said as they started walking away from the main entrance. When Danny did nothing to reassure him, Thomas grabbed his arm. 'And your silence has got me really worried now.'

Danny stopped and faced his friend. He took a deep breath.

'I know this is going to sound – well – it's going to sound a bit weird,' he began. 'And . . . a bit improper.'

Thomas gave his friend a look. 'Improper?' He didn't think he'd ever heard Danny use that word.

Danny nodded, still wondering how best to phrase the question he needed to ask quickly. He had minutes before Mabel arrived.

'Well, go on,' Thomas said, glancing towards the road that

ran parallel to the church, which was where he expected the Bentley to be pulling up with his soon-to-be wife and mother of his child in the back.

'Okay, I'm just going to ask you one question,' Danny said.

'Well, get on with it,' Thomas said, again checking the road.

Danny exhaled.

'Okay, here goes.'

A brief pause.

'When did you first sleep with Mabel?' Danny rushed the words out.

Thomas's head snapped back to Danny.

'Why are you asking?' His attention was now totally focused on his best man.

'Just tell me,' Danny demanded. 'When was the very first time?'

Thomas let out a half-laugh. 'The first and only time.'

'You've only slept with Mabel the once?' Danny asked.

'Yes,' Thomas said. 'Why? What's this about?'

'Can you remember when?' Danny's voice became more determined.

Thomas gave him a puzzled look. 'It was on the second Friday of March. The night the Farmer's Arms got their new jukebox.'

'So, you did not have any relations with Mabel during February – when we had that really bad cold snap?'

'No, I didn't,' Thomas said. 'Like I said, we've only slept together the once.'

Danny took a deep breath.

'Then there's something I have to tell you.'

Chapter Fifty-Six

Edward and Marlene had walked the short distance from where they'd parked the car to a spot that gifted the most magical view of High Force, a spectacular waterfall renowned as one of the most impressive in the country. Reaching the patch of green at the viewing point, Edward put down the picnic basket and wrapped his arms around Marlene while they stared out at the incredible natural phenomenon.

'The whole of this area,' Edward said, pausing to kiss Marlene on the neck, 'used to be glaciated.' Another light kiss on her shoulder blade. 'But when the ice age came to an end, the waterfall was so forceful it carved out the Tees Valley.'

Marlene turned and kissed Edward.

'Thank you for bringing me here. It's awe-inspiring.'

Edward looked at Marlene and was about to say something but held back. Instead, he bent down and threw the tartan rug out for them to sit on.

'I think this is a *raison de célébrer*,' he said, opening up the picnic basket and taking out a bottle of Moët and two glass champagne flutes.

Marlene's eyes widened.

'Well, Edward Stanton-Leigh, you certainly know how to spoil a girl,' she said with a smile.

'Well, there is much to celebrate,' Edward said. 'You know,

when poor Elise had her accident and died, I really felt there was nothing but darkness and death in store.' His mind flickered to his arrest and how his future had looked worse still – with the threat of spending the rest of his life in a six-by-eight-foot prison cell courtesy of HMP Durham.

'But then the sun came out,' he said. 'I was reunited with my darling daughter and welcomed my gorgeous grandson into the world, but the cherry on the icing was you, Marlene. You've brought love back into my life. Something I never thought I'd ever experience again. On that awful day at the hospital when you brought Lucy to see her poor mother for the last time, who would have thought that just months later my life would change again – only this time for the better – and I would be falling head over heels in love with you?'

As she sat down on the rug and held the glasses while Edward popped the cork with aplomb, Marlene cast her mind back to the day she had met Edward for the first time and had not liked him.

How much had changed since then.

Marlene took a sip of her champagne and forced back thoughts of Thomas and Mabel standing by the altar in the small fifteenth-century church in Cuthford village, vowing 'to love and to cherish, till death us do part'.

As she chinked glasses with Edward, she repeated her mantra that she had to live in the here and now – not dwell on the past.

Or rather, on her past love.

Chapter Fifty-Seven

Danny had just finished telling Thomas everything that Angie had told him, and which Mabel's stepmother had told her and Cora, when Mabel arrived at the church in the Bentley, a few minutes after one o'clock.

Thomas walked up to the beautifully polished blue Bentley, which had white ribbons across its bonnet. Jake was dressed in his chauffeur's uniform and had just taken off his peaked cap and put it under his arm. He was opening the door for the bride when he spotted Thomas striding towards them.

Seeing Jake's attention diverted away from helping her out of her carriage, Mabel followed his gaze and was equally shocked to see Thomas – especially his demeanour, which in no way resembled that of a happy but anxious groom.

'Is everything all right?' Jake asked straight away.

'Thomas, you're not meant to see me until I walk down the aisle. It's bad luck!' Mabel reprimanded in a light-hearted fashion, though she felt anything but.

Thomas looked at Jake. 'Do yer mind giving us a moment on our own, mate?'

Jake nodded and immediately headed through the wooden lynchgate to the church, patting himself down to find where he had put his smokes.

'What's wrong, Thomas?' Mabel asked, searching his face for answers and getting none.

Thomas looked at his very beautiful bride in her ivory dress, which disguised her expanding waistline well, and the small bump that was just starting to show.

'Let's have a little walk,' he said, putting out his hand to help her out of the Bentley. 'We need to talk.'

Chapter Fifty-Eight

Edward and Marlene had nibbled on the perfect smoked salmon and cucumber sandwiches and sipped on their champagne, chatting and then breaking off every now and again to look out at High Force, which had been so aptly named. The natural power of the water could be seen and heard as it rushed over the jagged granite cliff and down the sheer drop before smashing onto the rocky bed of the river in an explosion of frothing white foam and residual mist.

Marlene watched Edward as he topped up their glasses, thinking how handsome he was, and how incredibly thoughtful, and she realised that what she was feeling was love – she was experiencing what it felt like to be loved. Truly loved.

'I've been thinking about your dream,' Edward said.

Marlene gave him a curious look. 'My dream being . . . ?'

'To create a place for those children who have no homes, or no real home to speak of – the lost and forgotten, the poor and neglected, children like the ones you saw begging in London.'

Marlene gave Edward another quizzical look.

'Go on,' she said, taking a sip of her champagne.

'I think that's what we should do with Roeburn Hall. I think we should make it into a home – a children's home. A rather lovely children's home, where they can run around the grounds, ride horses, come to places like this and see the true beauty of nature.'

Marlene sat and stared at this man who had listened to her and what she really wanted from life. And he hadn't just listened, he was prepared to act – to make her dream a reality.

And it was at that moment that Marlene realised she was not just feeling the love Edward had for her, but the love she had for him.

Chapter Fifty-Nine

After their walk, an ashen-faced Mabel climbed back into the Bentley while Thomas waved over to Jake, who was just about to light up his second cigarette. A few of the guests had come out of the church and were also having a quick smoke as Angie had told them that there was going to be a slight delay.

Jake took Mabel back to Cuthford Manor, where she managed to persuade him to wait until she had changed and packed up her belongings before driving her to her father's house.

She was furious with her stepmother and would subject her to a tongue-lashing to surpass all tongue-lashings. The real punishment, though, would be having her stepdaughter back to live with her – complete with all her worldly possessions, which didn't amount to much but would still impinge on her stepmother's hatred of clutter and chaos.

Mabel had tried her hardest to convince Thomas that the child was his, but it was no good. Her stepmother's damning words had obliterated the life she had lined up for herself. The life she had worked hard to attain.

How she was now going to dig herself out of this almighty mess, she did not know.

She had tried to convince Thomas that it didn't matter the baby wasn't his, that she loved him and believed they would be so happy together, but she'd been wasting her breath. It was clear the only reason Thomas was walking her down the aisle was because he believed the baby to be his.

She hadn't felt hurt or lovelorn over Thomas's rejection of her, just angry that her plans had been scuppered. Angry that, in the blink of an eye, she had gone from being a woman with a great job, a good wage and a husband whom she liked a lot, who was certainly very handsome and who, more than anything, would be the father of her baby, to suddenly being unemployed – there was no hope she'd be able to keep her job once Cora found out what had gone on – and, worst of all, a single expectant mother of an illegitimate child.

She would have to get her thinking cap on – and fast.

Chapter Sixty

For the next hour, Marlene and Edward talked excitedly about the future Roeburn Hall Children's Home. Marlene's eyes were alight with the vision of what could be: how many children they could accommodate, where the dining hall would be and how Lucy could be in charge of the stables so that the children could learn to ride and to look after the horses and any other animals they might have.

'Gosh, I feel quite dizzy just thinking about it all,' Marlene gushed. 'I can't wait to tell Lucy.'

'And, of course,' Edward added, 'this will pacify your sister's concerns that I'm going to convert Roeburn Hall into a rival country house hotel.'

Marlene smiled. 'Yes, it will.' Of that she was certain.

As the sun was just starting to drop, Marlene began packing up the picnic basket.

'Ah,' Edward said, 'there *is* something else I wanted to say before we headed back.'

Hearing a slight nervousness in his voice, Marlene broke off from what she was doing and looked at him. She thought he seemed a little unsure of himself, which was very unlike Edward.

'And what's that?' she asked.

He leant towards her and kissed her passionately.

When they stopped, Marlene narrowed her eyes at him.

'Was there a question in the kiss?' she murmured.

Edward cupped her face gently in his hand and kissed her lightly on the lips.

Then he took a deep breath.

'Marlene Boulter, would you do me the honour of making me the happiest man on this planet?' He paused. 'Will you marry me? Will you be my wife?'

Marlene's eyes widened.

'My goodness, Edward, that is about the last thing I expected you to ask,' she blustered, not hiding her shock.

'We're made for each other,' he said, taking her hand and kissing it. 'Surely you can see that?'

Marlene smiled at an image in her mind's eye of Roeburn Hall filled with the life and laughter of all those children they were going to give a home to.

'We can have our happy ever after,' he said, his eyes sparkling. 'Dreams can come true.'

A smile slowly spread across Marlene's face. 'You're right. Dreams *can* come true.'

And with that, she leant forward and kissed Edward before whispering in his ear:

'Yes, Edward. My answer is yes.'

Chapter Sixty-One

When Thomas walked back into the church to tell the vicar and the guests that he was very sorry but the wedding would no longer be taking place, a mass of thoughts and feelings were swirling around in his head, though *sorry* was not one of them.

As soon as the words had been spoken, there was a hushed silence. Thomas turned to leave, eager to go before people found their voices and started to quiz him about the whys and wherefores of it all.

Hurrying back down the aisle a free man, he heard Angie telling everyone they were still most welcome to come back to Cuthford Manor for a few drinks and a buffet. Everyone had made such an effort, it seemed remiss not to make the most of an unfortunate situation.

As Thomas walked back out into the sunlight, his whole being felt lighter. The sense of liberation that was now starting to sink in felt almost overwhelming. Hearing the sound of metal-tipped shoes on the flagstones, Thomas turned slightly to see Danny by his side.

'Pub?'

Thomas looked at his best man, who was already loosening his tie and undoing his top button.

'I'm up for that,' Thomas said, shrugging off his jacket and loosening his own tie.

A sense of happiness bordering on euphoria had started to bubble up through the shock of what had just happened. He hadn't realised just how unhappy he had been since that evening in the pub when Mabel had told him – lied to him – that he was the father of the baby she was carrying.

When it was clear to Mabel that he was not going to change his mind, Thomas had asked her about the night he had drowned his sorrows after hearing of Marlene and Edward's courtship.

'You knew then that you were pregnant, didn't you?' he'd asked.

Mabel had hesitated, but knowing what her stepmother had told Angie and Cora, she decided to come clean. Her situation certainly couldn't get any worse by telling him the truth.

She'd nodded.

'Yes, Thomas, I did.'

It was only later that Thomas wondered who the real father was.

News of the abandoned wedding and – especially – the reason for it tore around the village at lightning speed. At Roeburn Hall, Lucy was one of the first to find out when Angie called her as soon as she got back to the manor. Lucy had grown very fond of Thomas during the years she'd known him and when the news had first come out about the shotgun wedding, she'd agreed with Angie that it was a shame. Mabel was a 'nice girl', but Thomas was clearly not in love with her, which did not bode well for a happy marriage.

'Well, I wonder who the real father is?' Lucy asked now, keeping an eye on Felix, who was in his cot.

'Heaven only knows,' Angie said. After they'd chatted a little more, Angie asked if Lucy fancied coming over with Felix and enjoying some of Mrs Trendle's scrumptious buffet, washed down with a nice cuppa, or even a little tipple. 'Danny and Thomas are down the pub,' she added, knowing Lucy would be worried about bumping into her estranged husband.

'You read my mind,' Lucy said. 'I'll come after I've told Marlene – she's gone out with Father for the day.'

'Yes, of course,' Angie agreed. 'I look forward to seeing you and my gorgeous little nephew a bit later.'

After hanging up, Angie wondered how Marlene would react to the news. She tried not to get her hopes up, but with Thomas now a single man, Marlene might be tempted back to Cuthford Manor – and more importantly, away from Roeburn Hall and Edward's clutches.

Over the next hour, Lucy busied herself, all the time thinking how she could break the news to Marlene. It would have been better if she could have told her sister-in-law when they were on their own. It would feel a little awkward with her father there, as he knew how Marlene had felt about Thomas. And there would naturally be a concern that Marlene might want to ditch her father now that Thomas had suddenly become available and, furthermore, was not the man responsible for making Mabel pregnant. Her mind wandered to who had got Mabel in the family way. Whoever it was clearly didn't want anything to do with Mabel or her baby, otherwise she wouldn't have tried to trick poor Thomas into marriage.

301

Lucy really didn't know what Marlene's reaction would be. Just as she wasn't sure that Marlene was being entirely honest with herself when she claimed that she was over Thomas and he had been assigned to the past.

Hearing the familiar sound of her father's Aston Martin as it came down the driveway and parked up, Lucy braced herself.

Taking Felix into the front sitting room, she waited until she heard them open the front door and walk into the main hall. They were quiet for a moment, which meant that they were kissing. Lucy had tried to be accepting about her father and Marlene's romance, but she did struggle when she saw them being all lovey-dovey.

When the silence continued, she shouted out, 'I'm in here!'

'Coming, darling!' Edward's voice sounded raspy.

As soon as her father and Marlene entered the room, she knew something was up. They both looked flushed and happy. And perhaps also a little tipsy.

'Darling,' her father said, looking intently at his daughter, 'we have some news to tell you.'

Lucy looked from her father to Marlene and back again.

'Oh, yes?' she said. As her attention jumped between the two, she caught the twinkle of something catching the light. She looked to see what it was.

'Marlene and I are engaged. We're going to get married,' he declared, a wide smile spreading across his face as he looked first at his daughter and then to his future wife.

Lucy, her mind in a fog, was struggling to comprehend what her father was saying while she looked at what had caught her eye. It was her grandmother's blue sapphire engagement ring. A family heirloom that had been promised to her, but which was now gracing Marlene's ring finger.

Catching her look, Edward put his arm around Marlene and pulled her close.

'Darling LuLu, I hope you don't mind, but I just couldn't resist proposing with your dear grandmama's ring. I know it was promised to you, but I will buy you a bigger and better one to make up for it.'

Lucy waved away her father's words.

'Don't be silly,' she said. 'Of course it makes sense that . . .' she looked at Marlene and struggled to say the word '. . . that your . . . your future wife should have the ring.' She held up her hand to show her own, very modest diamond engagement ring. 'After all, I've already got one.'

Marlene walked over to Lucy and sat down on the sofa. 'Oh God, Lucy, you think we're mad, don't you?' She reached across and took Lucy's hand, wanting her to be happy, but at the same time knowing this must feel awkward for her. 'You probably think we're rushing into things, don't you?'

Lucy let out an awkward laugh. 'Well, yes, I do a bit.'

Edward came and sat next to Marlene.

'I know it's not that long since the death of your dear mama, but I've just fallen so terribly in love. And I do believe Marlene has with me.'

Lucy looked at them both, not knowing what to say.

'I know it's probably the last thing you want to hear with everything's that's happening at the moment, but I'm sure you and Danny will sort things out,' Marlene said hopefully.

'And if you don't,' Edward jumped in, 'there will be men queuing up at the door for the chance to take you out. You're young and beautiful. There will be someone else out there for you, my darling girl.'

Lucy felt herself stiffen.

'Perhaps, Father, I don't want *someone else*.'

She stood up.

'And in case you've forgotten, Danny and I have just had a child together,' she snapped.

Wanting to leave, but suddenly remembering why she had been waiting for them to come back from their day out, she looked at her father and then at her sister-in-law.

'I almost forgot to tell you why I was sitting here waiting for you both to return,' she said. '*Your* news ended up scuppering *my* news.'

'Sounds ominous,' Edward said. 'Does it concern your errant husband?'

'No.' Lucy felt another flash of annoyance at her father, something she had only started to feel since she had moved back in with him. 'It's not to do with my *errant husband*.'

'What is it?' Marlene asked, her concern growing. 'Has someone we know been hurt?'

'No, no,' Lucy said. 'Well, not in that sense.'

'Well, go on, then, LuLu, you're keeping us quite in suspense,' Edward urged.

'It concerns Thomas and Mabel,' Lucy said.

She waited a beat.

'*Their wedding didn't go ahead.*'

Now it was Marlene's turn to look stunned. 'Really?'

'Yes, really,' Lucy said, her focus on her friend, trying to gauge what she was thinking and feeling. At this moment, she simply looked shocked.

304

'Why ever not?' Edward asked, his own good mood starting to dip considerably. He cast a glance at Marlene. Like his daughter, he was also trying to determine how the woman he had just asked to be his wife was taking this totally unexpected turn of events.

'Apparently,' Lucy said, raising her eyebrows, 'Thomas is not the father of Mabel's baby.'

'What? He's not the father? I don't understand,' Marlene blustered.

'Well . . . ' Lucy said, seeing the beginnings of excitement in her sister-in-law's demeanour, ' . . . it would appear you were right about Mabel.'

Marlene's focus on Lucy was intense. 'What do you mean? In what way?'

'Well, there's clearly more to her than meets the eye. Very devious. Or very desperate. Either way, she was obviously pregnant before she started courting Thomas and very nearly managed to trick him into marrying her and, worse still, unwittingly bringing up a child that wasn't his own.'

'And do you know who the real father is?' Edward asked.

Both women looked at Edward – both having momentarily forgotten that he was actually there with them in the room.

'Not yet,' Lucy said. 'But I'm sure it'll just be a matter of time before it all comes out in the wash.'

Chapter Sixty-Two

Thomas and Danny had found a corner table in the Farmer's Arms, which was just starting to fill up with those who had been on an early shift at one of the local collieries or nearby farms. They had talked about Mabel's deceit, both admitting that the day's events were still taking time to sink in. Both stating that they were still shocked beyond belief at Mabel's scheming. Which had very nearly succeeded.

'I wonder if Mabel ever had feelings for me – or was I just an easy target?' Thomas mused.

'Easy target!' Danny laughed. 'No, honestly, mate, I really do think she was pretty stuck on you. Had been for ages. It used to rankle Marlene no end.'

'Yes, but that was only because she didn't like Mabel,' Thomas said, taking a sip of his beer.

'Not just because of that,' Danny said. 'You knew she was sweet on you.'

'Ages ago,' Thomas said, 'but all of that changed after she came back from London.'

Danny nodded, turning his pint glass around on the beer mat. 'But I don't think that necessarily meant she didn't still have feelings for you. I just think she put up a protective barrier around herself after what happened.'

Thomas felt a rush of resentment. 'So what happened to

that barrier when Edward bloody Stanton-Leigh came along?'

Danny shook his head in a show of exasperation. 'God only knows. But that's so like Marlene to let the wrong person in.'

'You still think he's not a good 'un?' Thomas asked.

'I do. I certainly do,' Danny replied.

Both men took a drink from their pint glasses.

'And do you still think he offed his wife?' Thomas asked.

Danny nodded as he wiped a white foam moustache off his upper lip. 'Which is why you need to get Marlene away from him,' he said in earnest. 'I know it mightn't seem like an appropriate time to be talking about this – you just finding out what you have – but I don't think there's time to waste when it comes to that bloke and my sister. I really think he's suckering her in. People like that always act quickly – before they're rumbled.'

'A bit like Mabel,' Thomas said. 'They sound uncannily alike.'

Danny nodded and took another long drink of his Guinness.

'You need to get Marlene away from him. And now you're single again, you'll be able to do it.'

Thomas spluttered on his ale. 'That's presuming she does still have feelings for me.'

'Oh, yes, that's a given,' Danny confirmed.

'Mmm . . . ' Thomas wondered if perhaps that was what Danny needed to be the case – but in reality it wasn't.

'So, are you going to tell her how you feel?' Danny asked.

'I will,' Thomas agreed. 'But what if she doesn't feel the same way?'

'We'll cross that bridge when we come to it,' Danny said. 'All I know is that my sister is making a massive mistake by getting involved with Edward. I'm worried about her. Nothing good's going to come out of it. Nothing good at all.'

Chapter Sixty-Three

When Marlene was driving back to Cuthford Manor, her head was all over the place. The initial rush of euphoria she'd felt after Edward's proposal had ebbed, or rather, had been flattened by the news that not only was Thomas *not* going to marry Mabel, he was also *not* the father of her baby.

Just the thought of it had her heart soaring. Which she knew was not right. Not when she was engaged to be married to another man.

As she turned right down the track that led to the manor, she knew she would have to talk to Thomas – wanted to talk to him – to see how he was, how he felt. Was he devastated? Hurt? Or perhaps, just perhaps, he might feel relieved. Or was that what she wished he was feeling?

The thought that Thomas would be heartbroken over Mabel had one end of the seesaw of her emotions thudding down hard on the ground. Just because he wasn't going to marry her did not mean that he wasn't in love with Mabel. It did not automatically mean that, with Mabel out of the way, the path had been made clear for Marlene to run into his open arms. Who was to say his arms would be open? She was just a friend, after all, wasn't she? And why on earth was she thinking such thoughts when she had just accepted another man's proposal?

She had thought herself to be in love with Edward. She *was* in love with Edward.

Wasn't she?

Or was she just in love with the thought of being in love?

The car jolted over a pothole in the road and she felt herself jolt too – mentally.

What did she really feel?

Was it love for Edward?

Or was it simply that she loved the fact that he loved and adored her?

As Marlene changed down a gear, she felt the rub of the engagement ring on her finger and had a sudden urge to take it off. If she kept it on, people would notice and she'd have to tell them. But if she took it off, that would be disloyal to Edward. And it would feel as though she was not sure about it. Which she was. Wasn't she? God, she'd never known her thoughts and feelings to yo-yo so much.

After Lucy and Felix had left to go to the manor, Edward had asked her straight if hearing that Thomas was now a single man meant that she wanted to call off their 'short-lived engagement'. She'd told him that of course she didn't, it was just that it felt as though their very romantic, very special day had been totally overshadowed by what had happened with Thomas and Mabel. Edward had nodded his understanding and they had also agreed that their joy had been tarnished a little before that by the way Lucy had reacted to their engagement.

Marlene hadn't said anything to Edward, but learning that her engagement ring was a family heirloom intended for Lucy had added to the dampening of her initial excitement.

Perhaps they could discuss getting a new one and give back to Lucy what was rightfully hers. She would talk to Edward about it tomorrow. Then they could have a day in Durham going round the jewellers to choose another one.

Driving through the gates to the Cuthford Country House Hotel, Marlene now saw no harm in taking the ring off as it wouldn't be her real engagement ring. Besides, it would be insensitive to announce the celebratory news of her impending nuptials on the same day that a wedding had just been called off – and for the most scandalous and scurrilous of reasons.

After she had pulled up at the front of the manor and turned off the engine, Marlene was just about to remove the ring when she spotted Danny and Thomas in her rear-view mirror, walking down the driveway. She was hit by a bout of nerves, which was ridiculous. They were her brother and her friend. It was then that she realised how much they had grown apart in such a short period of time. Something for which she had only herself to blame. She had purposely kept away from everyone these past six weeks because she was jealous of Thomas's wedding and was still hurting over his rejection of her in favour of Mabel.

Marlene tried not to feel a sense of satisfaction that she had been proven right. Underneath her butter-wouldn't-melt exterior, Mabel was an unscrupulous, selfish and conniving woman who would do anything to get what she wanted. Well, she hadn't got what she wanted this time. She'd been found out – but literally just in the nick of time.

As Danny and Thomas approached the car, Marlene started to panic as she was unable to pull the sapphire ring off her finger. She twisted and turned it and tried to force it over her knuckle, but it wouldn't come off. *Yet it had slipped on so easily!*

She was still trying to remove it when there was a knock on the car window. She looked up to see Danny and Thomas looking in at her.

She wound down the window with her right hand, keeping her left hand by the side of her seat.

'You all right, sis?' Danny asked. 'You look a little flushed. Have you hurt yourself?'

Marlene looked from her brother to Thomas, who also appeared concerned. And incredibly attractive in his morning suit.

'No, no, I just dropped something in the car and caught my hand. It's nothing.'

She pulled the door handle and the two stood aside.

As she climbed out of the car, she managed to keep her left hand out of sight. As soon as she was able to, she held it in her right hand as though she was injured.

'Let's have a look, Marlene—' Thomas reached out to take her hand.

Marlene snatched it away. 'No, I'm fine, really.'

Danny gave his sister a puzzled look.

'You're hiding something,' he said. Then, quick as a flash, he grabbed her hand as he had done many times when they were children and straightened out her fingers, turning them over so that the big blue sapphire twinkled in the sunlight.

There was a brief moment of shocked silence.

'Please tell me that's not what I think it is?' Danny demanded.

Marlene looked at her brother and then at Thomas, who

seemed transfixed by the ring and stood simply staring at it. She saw that a loose strand of his slightly curly hair had dropped just above his eye and had to stop herself reaching forward to push it back.

'Well,' Marlene stumbled over the words, 'it is, and it isn't.'

The damned ring!

Thomas had managed to force his eyes away from the ring and up at Marlene. The anticipation of her answer was making him feel ill.

'What do you mean, *It is, and it isn't*? Is that an engagement ring or not?' Danny demanded.

God, why did his sister always jump in with both feet when she had no idea how to swim?

Marlene felt herself slump with a feeling she was pretty sure you weren't meant to have just hours after being proposed to.

'Yes, it is,' she said simply.

Chapter Sixty-Four

Over the next couple of days, a quiet, almost pensive atmosphere seemed to pervade Cuthford Manor as well as Roeburn Hall. On the surface, life appeared to be carrying on as normal, and those who were staying at the Cuthford Country House Hotel were certainly unaware of the sense of underlying shock that was still very much present, with everyone going about their duties and their work as usual. But behind their smiles of welcome and professionalism, they were all still struggling to understand how someone they had known and worked with for such a long time, and whom they liked, could end up being such a master manipulator who had so ruthlessly nearly conned Thomas into marrying her. The relief they felt on Thomas's behalf was testimony to how beloved he was by those at the manor.

For Thomas, however, the immediate sense of liberation he had felt had quickly been replaced by a crushing feeling of depression when he had seen the sapphire engagement ring on Marlene's hand. All the hopes he had of winning her over and snatching her away from Edward had dissolved in that moment.

At the same time, the flames of hatred Danny felt towards his estranged father-in-law were fanned by the news of his sister's engagement. Whenever none of his riding pupils were around, he was like a bear with a sore head, his mind going over and over what he should do. Not just about Marlene, but about stopping the total disintegration of his marriage.

'I never thought Lucy was in any way stubborn,' Angie admitted to her younger brother, 'but she's giving you a run for your money at the moment – and that's saying something.' She told him to 'sort it out' as it had 'dragged on long enough', and Danny knew that she was right. Just as Lucy knew Angie was right when she gave her the same talk. It was time to take action, rather than stagnate at Roeburn Hall, stewing in her jealousy and resentments. The thought of Danny's alleged infidelity was eating her up. She was sick to death of arguing with herself over the truth of the matter. Of swinging from disbelief that Danny could be unfaithful to reprimanding herself for trying to pretend that he wasn't. It might well terrify her to hear the truth from Danny's own mouth, but she knew she had to.

Meanwhile, the mystery over who the father of Mabel's baby might be continued to dumbfound everyone. No one had the least idea who it was. There was even speculation that perhaps Mabel herself did not know.

Mabel, of course, knew who the father was. And she guessed that by now her former lover had a pretty good idea that he was the daddy. Although whether he would accept that was another matter.

Back at home after her cancelled wedding, Mabel barely ventured out of the front door of her dad and stepmum's cottage. In fact, she hardly left her bedroom, only coming downstairs to make herself a sandwich or to use the out-door toilet. Both Mr and Mrs Glendenning tiptoed around her, unsure what to say or do, which suited Mabel just fine as she didn't want them to say or do anything. She just wanted some peace and quiet so that she could think. And think hard, for she had found herself in the worst situation imaginable and needed to work out what to do next.

When she thought back to the walk with Thomas, Mabel knew she'd been lucky not to have been throttled for what she'd done. For the lies she'd told. For her deceit, which would have had Thomas bringing up someone else's child as his own. She wondered whether, if her lies had not been uncovered and she had managed to get Thomas down the aisle and then had the baby, he would have somehow known, or sensed, that the child was not his. Thomas was fair-haired, as was she, but the real father had very dark brown, almost black hair. If the child took after him, it might well have caused Thomas doubts. And then she would have been in an even greater mess. If that was at all possible.

Mabel had seen his anger, but what had been more evident – and even greater – was his relief at knowing that he no longer had to marry her. She'd been surprised that she hadn't felt hurt by his rejection of her. She had thought that she'd managed to win him over, that he did have feelings for her, but it was clear that his proposal had been made purely out of a sense of duty. God, she could not have chosen anyone more different from the father of the baby she was carrying. She knew now that she had to be honest with herself about her feelings for this man – and how very different they were to the ones she'd had for Thomas.

She thought back on the past nine months. So much had happened. And she had changed so much. She had really thought Thomas was the man for her, the husband for her, but those thoughts and feelings had started to wane a little before she had realised she'd fallen. Knowing that she was pregnant, and believing without a shadow of a doubt that the real father of the baby would not want anything to do with either her or the child, never mind marry her, she'd focused her attention back on Thomas. Looking back, it was quite obvious she had gone into survival mode – believing that by making Thomas think the baby was his, he would do the honourable thing and marry her.

As Mabel lay on her bed, her mind churning over, she began to think that perhaps what had happened was not so disastrous. Perhaps, just perhaps there might be a chance she could come out of this on top. And instead of living a modest life with a mild-mannered man she didn't really love, she could enjoy a far more exciting life, and certainly a far wealthier one, with a man she realised she did actually love. She just hadn't allowed herself to admit it because she had never seen it as anything more than an affair, had never thought they could be anything more than lovers. She admonished herself. Then, she had still been in the lowly frame of mind of a maid, but she had been promoted during their affair and had become an assistant manager of a prestigious hotel, known throughout the county. She should have had more confidence in herself.

By the end of the second morning of her self-imposed exile from life, Mabel was starting to kick herself for not going to her lover first and telling him that she was carrying his baby. Their love child.

She and her lover had conducted their affair for well over

a year and their desire for one another had not waned. And it hadn't been just physical. They'd talked and laughed and enjoyed each other's company. They were alike. In so many ways. Why hadn't she realised it? *He was the one she really loved.* Of course, it was understandable why she had not allowed herself to fall in love with her upper-class lover. They were from opposite ends of the social spectrum. But that was becoming less important these days. Society was changing and the boundaries of what was acceptable were changing. Her mind went to Cora. She had been a housekeeper when she and Lloyd had fallen for each other. And they had broken through societal constraints and got married. Angie had been a working-class girl who had married Quentin, lord of the manor. *So why could this not be the case for her?* Especially as her lover was no longer married. They could be a couple, like Cora and Lloyd. She put her hand on her stomach. *They could be a family.*

Mabel walked over to the little dressing table, sat down on the stool and looked at herself in the oval mirror. Pregnancy suited her. Her skin was glowing, her hair was thicker and glossier than normal – she was the epitome of 'blooming'.

As she brushed her hair and put on a little make-up – some rouge, mascara and lipstick – she knew exactly what she was going to do. And when she'd do it.

She would go and see him today. *Why wait?*

There was no time like the present.

Five minutes later, she was out of the front door, having told her father and stepmother that she was nipping out for a walk – a long walk – and not to worry about her. That she actually felt the best she had done in a while – certainly the past two days. She just needed some fresh air, and she might pop in and see an old friend for a catch-up and a cuppa.

Hurrying down the short pathway, Mabel started the half-mile walk. She had been going to take her bike but decided not to as it would give her more time to think about exactly what she was going to say.

Lucy was also in the mood for taking the bull by the horns and not putting off what could be done today. But unlike Mabel, she had not bothered with make-up, nor did she care that she looked the embodiment of the worn-out, sleep-deprived mother of a newborn baby. She had decided that morning she would go and see Danny. She would look him in the eye and demand the truth. She wanted him to say it outright. Admit that he had been having – and by the sounds of it was *still* having – an affair with the Traveller woman. That he clearly felt he had more in common with her than with his own wife – the mother of his baby boy. Lucy flushed with anger. And jealousy. She turned away from the mirror, not wanting to see herself, and instead got up, walked over to her bureau and pulled open the top drawer.

The day Mabel and Thomas had been due to get married – the day her father had proposed to her sister-in-law – Lucy had gone into town for an appointment with the family solicitor, when she had collected the document she had asked him to draw up.

She looked down at it now as she pulled it out of her desk drawer – the bold lettering of 'Petition for Divorce' making everything seem horribly real.

*

319

After saying goodbye to Lucy, who was heading over to Cuthford Manor with Felix to see Danny – a visit that, by the look on his daughter's face, was not for the purpose of reconciliation – Edward headed to his office. He had some drawings he wanted to look at that had been given to him by a local architect he'd shown around Roeburn Hall the other week. He'd not had a chance to really study them as the past few days had been quite busy – and had caused him a little anxiety, to say the least. But it looked as though his fears had been unfounded. Walking over to the small drinks cabinet, he poured himself a whisky to sip while he perused the plans and made some notes on possible costings.

He was just settling down at his desk with his Scotch and his plans for the future when there was a knock on the door. He looked at his watch. It had only just gone midday; Marlene wasn't due until two o'clock. Perhaps she'd come early. He certainly wasn't expecting anyone else. He quickly put the plans away, as they were something he did not want Marlene to catch sight of, then walked out of the office and across the large hallway.

'Coming!' he shouted out. He was looking forward to employing a butler. It wasn't becoming for a man of his stature to be answering his own front door.

But he must be patient.

All in good time.

Lucy had reached the right turn to Cuthford Manor when she realised that she had forgotten the divorce papers.

'Damn. Damn. Damn,' she muttered to herself.

She checked for traffic and, seeing none, did a U-turn.

'Mummy's such a scatterbrain,' she said, looking in her rear-view mirror, relieved to see that Felix was still calm and happily cooing to himself.

She looked at the clock on the dashboard.

It had just gone midday.

She had plenty of time.

There was no need to rush.

Reaching the front door of her former lover's grandiose property, Mabel took a long, slow breath, then gripped the large brass knocker in her hand and brought it down hard.

She waited a few moments, suddenly feeling depressed at the thought he might not be at home. She had presumed he would be, which was foolish. She looked around and her spirits lifted on seeing the bonnet of his sports car peeking out of the garage.

He was home.

And then she heard him.

Heard his familiar voice calling out.

'Coming!'

When Edward answered the door, his face dropped.

He should have known.

He had been kidding himself that there would be no repercussions after Saturday's aborted wedding.

'Ah, my dear Mabel, this *is* a surprise.' Edward fought to keep his demeanour devoid of any show of concern or anxiety.

'Is it, Edward? Is it really a surprise?' Mabel asked, straightening her back and looking him in the eye. His smile might be wide, but she probably knew Edward better than anyone and she could see right through his cool, unfazed façade.

Knowing it was pointless to pretend, Edward looked past Mabel's head and quickly scanned the grounds and driveway, making sure no one else was about to turn up uninvited.

'You'd better come in,' he said, standing aside and ushering his former mistress into the grand hallway. He was glad now that he did not have a butler, and that the cleaner and the cook would be arriving later.

He quickly checked his watch. Marlene wasn't due for another two hours.

'You'd better come into the office.' He turned and strode towards the open door of his study.

'Well, this is a change. I do believe that's one room I haven't had the pleasure of seeing,' Mabel said as she followed Edward through the door. She sat down on the proffered seat opposite his own, which was behind a large wooden desk.

'So, what can I do for you, my dear?' he asked, resting his hands on the embossed-leather top of the desk.

Mabel leant forward and put her hand over his, letting out a light, throaty laugh. 'I think you might be able to guess, Edward.'

Edward didn't take his hand away. Mabel's touch had always had a dual effect on him. Calming. And exciting. It was probably why their affair had lasted so long and why he had struggled to bring their relationship to an end.

Mabel took her hand away and sat back.

'I know what you are going to say,' Edward said, looking at Mabel properly for the first time. Pregnancy became her. 'You're going to say that the baby is mine.'

'Yes. Of course the baby is yours,' she said, watching the man she realised she had loved all along, hoping to see a trace of happiness at the thought of her expecting his child.

'Mabel, I don't want to cast aspersions on your character, but I can hardly know the baby is mine when you have such a – how should I say it – such a hedonistic streak.'

Mabel widened her eyes. 'I think you know that I was not being "hedonistic" with anyone else but you during our lengthy time together.' Another short laugh. 'Even if I'd wanted to, I'd not have had the time. If I wasn't working all hours at the manor, then I'd be making my way over to see you.'

Edward leant forward. 'But what about Thomas? How can you be so sure the baby's not his?' He knew he was clutching at straws, but he had to hear it directly from the horse's mouth. Lucy had only said that Thomas was not the father. It hadn't seemed proper to ask her for details.

'I'm sure the baby is not his because I didn't even sleep with Thomas,' Mabel informed him matter-of-factly.

Edward looked at her in disbelief. 'Mabel, the boy is far from the brightest button, but even he must have known he would need to have slept with you for you to be pregnant with his child!'

Mabel got up and walked over to the large sash window. 'I just made him think he had so he'd do the right thing and marry me.' She kept her eyes on the lawns, which were in need of a mow.

Edward's expression changed from mildly amused to confused. Very confused.

'How on earth could you make someone think that you had slept with them?'

323

'It's easier than you think,' Mabel said, turning around to face him.

'How?' Edward asked again.

Mabel smiled and perched herself on the window seat. She was nearer to Edward now and there was no longer a desk acting as a barrier between them.

'It really wasn't that difficult. I got Thomas drunk. Very drunk. So drunk that I had to help him up to his digs, where he promptly passed out on the bed. After that it was easy. I managed to get him undressed, got undressed myself, and hey presto, the next morning there was no reason for him not to believe it, especially as I confirmed that we had slept together – and said how unfortunate it was he couldn't recall it.'

Mabel stood up and walked over to the mirror above the fireplace to check her reflection. She could feel Edward's eyes on her.

'Of course, the plan had been to seduce him, which naturally I tried, but I had clearly coaxed him into having one too many whiskies. But I knew he would remember kissing me, or rather, me kissing him. And, of course, the feel of our naked bodies against each other.'

Edward observed Mabel as she preened in front of the mirror. She reminded him of a Pre-Raphaelite painting depicting Medusa he'd once seen. He hated himself for feeling a stab of jealousy at the thought of her naked in bed with another man.

He forced his own 'hedonistic' thoughts away – and back to the sobering conversation of him fathering Mabel's baby.

'I'm still not convinced that the baby's mine,' Edward said.

'Why?' Mabel asked.

'Because,' Edward said, 'we were always careful.'

'We were,' Mabel agreed. '*Nearly* always . . . But there was that once.' She paused, waiting to see the remembrance of that afternoon on her former lover's face. 'When I was staying at my dad's cottage during the Big Freeze and I came to see you that afternoon. When we had the place totally to ourselves. When our passion got the better of us both.'

Edward was quiet. He did indeed recollect that afternoon. How ironic that it was the last time they had been together – when he had told Mabel they had to call time on their very enjoyable and rather longer-than-expected affair. Looking back now, had he taken the risk because he knew it was the last time they'd be together? He'd told himself that the odds were in their favour. This was the one and only time of all the occasions they had been intimate with each other that they had not been careful.

Edward sighed to himself. Why shouldn't this surprise him, with his history of gambling? Or was it because he was not now a regular at the bookies that his addiction had led him to take risks in other ways?

'Okay, so let's just say for argument's sake that you are expecting my child – what do you expect me to do about it?'

Mabel looked at him as though he was the one who was far from the brightest button.

'Marry me, of course!'

'Marry you?' Edward asked. It was the last solution he had been expecting, but he now realised it was the most obvious.

'We are cut from the same cloth, Edward, you and I . . .' Mabel walked to the desk and perched on the side. 'We are one and the same.' She looked him in the eye. 'Sure, you have the so-called heritage and blue blood – and this place . . .' she stretched out her arm and looked around '. . . but our natures are akin. We're both pretty ruthless in our own ways. When we want something, we get it, regardless. We are two determined people who have the capacity to be a little manipulative when we need to be – some might say a little unscrupulous. It's just the way we are.'

Mabel leant forward and lightly traced her finger along his trousered leg.

'And physically, well, that doesn't need words. You can't deny the attraction. It shows in our lovemaking.'

Edward took Mabel's hand and held it. He had thought Mabel looked different because of the pregnancy, but he now realised the difference was in her manner. It was as though she was the one who held the power, was the dominant one. And it was something that made him feel ever so slightly fearful, but also more than a little turned on.

'I know,' he said. 'I agree with everything you've said. Why do you think it took so long for me to end our affair?'

Mabel withdrew her hand.

'But?' she asked.

'But,' Edward said, looking up at her from his chair, 'but I'm afraid it all comes down to money – and my position in society.' He paused. 'You know that. You *must* know that I could never marry you?'

Mabel stared at him, her stony glare disguising her hurt and her hopes.

'Besides,' Edward said, 'I'm engaged to Marlene. I thought you'd know?'

Mabel stood up in shock.

'You're going to marry Marlene?'

'Yes,' Edward nodded. 'It's the perfect match. The marriage of two of the county's most illustrious properties. Of course, Marlene isn't exactly loaded, but despite what they make out, the family are doing well. Very well. The dowry will help go towards getting this old gal back to her former glory.' Edward looked around the office at the beautifully carved wooden panelling that dated back to the sixteenth century and was in desperate need of being restored by skilled and therefore very costly craftsmen. 'But the bulk of the money will come from Lucy. I'm sure of it. She'll divorce that feckless husband of hers. She's already been to draw up divorce papers. And then she'll do what she should have done in the first place and marry someone her equal.'

'You mean, someone who's filthy rich.' Mabel folded her arms, shaking her head. 'You think you've got it all worked out, don't you?'

'I do, as a matter of fact.' He gave a self-satisfied smile 'But,' he added, looking at Mabel, 'you must know it goes without saying that I will make sure you and the baby don't go hungry.'

Mabel let out a laugh that was both hard and humourless.

'Well, thank you kindly, sir,' she said in an exaggerated West Country accent. 'I get thrown the crumbs,' she added, her voice now serious, 'and I'm meant to be grateful?' Her voice rose. 'I bring up your baby while you lord it here with a new wife who will no doubt give you the male heir I know deep down you've always wanted. Craved.'

'But that's not to say we can't still meet up?' Edward looked at Mabel with what he hoped were his best puppy-dog eyes.

'My God, Edward, you really are delusional, aren't you?' Mabel said, her anger momentarily usurped by her disbelief.

Edward looked genuinely puzzled.

'Delusional how?' he asked.

Mabel took a deep breath. 'Because Marlene won't marry you. It'll only be a matter of time before she gets wise to the real Edward Stanton-Leigh, and when she does, she won't want anything to do with you. And throw into the mix that Thomas is now a free man . . . '

Mabel looked at the man she loved and wanted to shake some sense into him.

'As for Lucy leaving Danny, well, I think you underestimate the bond they share. They'll get over this. The love they have for one another is a rare one. Even you won't be able to destroy that.'

Edward gave her a look that said he did not believe her.

'You just can't see what is staring you in the face, can you?' Mabel asked, deciding she had to give it her best shot.

'Tell me what I'm not seeing,' Edward said, tilting his head to look at his former lover.

'That I love you, Edward, warts and all, and I believe you do me – well, as much as a person like you can love. If you could just, for a moment, see beyond the money and the class divide, you'd see that we would actually be very happy together.' Mabel put her hand on her stomach. 'The three of us.'

Edward shook his head. 'I'm sorry, Mabel. You've made a good pitch, but I'm already halfway there. Marlene has agreed to marry me, and I do believe that Lucy is going to give Danny the Petition for Divorce documents today.' He looked at the clock. 'She is probably doing so right now.'

'Well, I'm not going to beg, Edward, but just so we're clear, that's a no?' Mabel asked. 'A definite no?' She had to be sure. She had to hear him say it before she initiated the next stage of her carefully thought-out plan.

'It's a definite no, Mabel, my dear,' Edward confirmed.

Mabel slowly nodded her head.

'Well, then, I shall get going. Things to do,' she said, walking across the carpeted floor.

Reaching the half-open door of the study, she stopped and turned to look at her former lover. The father of the baby growing inside her.

'I will tell you one thing, though, Edward Stanton-Leigh.' She gave him a piercing look. 'You will forever rue this day.'

And with that, her head held high, Mabel walked out of the office, across the grand hallway and out of the front door.

If Lucy had been coming down the driveway to Roeburn Hall two minutes earlier, she would have seen Mabel knocking at the door and being welcomed in by her father. But she didn't. And if Lucy had parked in her usual spot outside the main entrance, Mabel and Edward would have more than likely heard the car pull up. Mabel would certainly have seen it when she was looking out of the sash window. But Lucy didn't park in her usual spot because the sun was high and she'd wanted to keep Felix out of its glare, so she had instead parked by the side of the property, in the shade.

Lucy had also been very quiet as she climbed out of the car and gently closed the door for fear of waking her baby boy, who by the look on his little face was in a deep, contented sleep, which she'd hoped would stay the case until she came back to the car. She was only going to be a few minutes – the time it took her to go to her room, pick up the divorce papers from the bureau where she'd left them and then return to the car.

Walking quickly to the front of the house, Lucy had thought it unusual that the front door was ajar. She was sure she had closed it properly.

As she'd started to push open the heavy oak door just enough for her to slip in, she heard voices. One of them was her father's. The other a woman's she didn't recognise. Lucy couldn't remember her father saying that he was expecting anyone. Rather, he had commented that he would be glad of a couple of hours on his own before Marlene came over.

So, who was the woman?

Lucy could hear that the voices were coming from the office – and she could just about make out what was being said, since the door to the study had also been left partly open.

She stepped into the hallway to see if she could catch a glimpse of who was with her father, but she couldn't see.

She knew she should call out and announce herself, but something stopped her.

Instead, Lucy stood quietly and listened.

When she recognised Mabel's voice, she stood as still as a stone statue, barely breathing in order to catch exactly what was being said.

She stayed like that until it was clear that the two had reached an impasse, then, not wanting her father and Mabel to know that she had heard their conversation, Lucy turned and as quietly as a mouse stepped back outside, leaving the door as she had found it, and slowly tiptoed back down the stone steps.

Walking as lightly as possible, she made her way back to the car, now glad that she had parked in the shade and out of sight. Carefully opening the car door, she got in and started the engine, relieved that it was unlikely that they would hear it. Seeing that Felix was still sound asleep, Lucy breathed a sigh of relief and carefully reversed the car back onto the driveway and slowly drove away from Roeburn Hall.

Once again, she had left without her Petition for Divorce – but that was now the very least of her worries.

Chapter Sixty-Five

When Lucy arrived at Cuthford Manor, she was in such a daze that she walked away from the car having momentarily forgotten about her baby boy sleeping peacefully in his cot on the back seat. Luckily, she'd only taken a few steps across the cobbles when she remembered, slapped her forehead and did an about-turn. Carefully taking Felix out of his cot and cradling him in her arms, she prayed that he would remain in such a blissful state of slumber until she'd had her chat with Marlene.

Her intended chat with Danny would have to wait.

Opening the back door with her free hand, Lucy was hit by the instantly comforting smell of home-cooked food – something she had missed at Roeburn Hall. At the thought of her family home, Lucy immediately felt her stomach lurch and darkness cloud her head. Perhaps sensing his mother's upset, as soon as she shut the door, Felix woke up and started to cry.

'Oh, the little one needs a bottle,' Alberta said, walking over to Lucy and stretching out her arms. Lucy didn't think she had ever been more glad to see Alberta. Just as Mrs Trendle, who was standing stirring a pot on the range, thought she had never been more glad to see Lucy.

'Oh, thank you. Do you not mind?' Lucy said, not waiting for an answer but handing Felix over to her.

'You all right?' Alberta asked, eyeing Lucy. 'You look as white as a sheet.'

'Mmm.' Lucy didn't answer. All she could think of was Marlene. And how she was going to tell her what she had just overheard.

'You go into the family room and I'll bring a nice cup of tea in,' Alberta said, swaying Felix in her arms from side to side.

'Thanks, Alberta, but I need to see Marlene. Is she about?' Lucy's eyes darted around the kitchen as though she might find Marlene hiding in some corner.

Seeing the furtive, slightly deranged look in Lucy's eyes, Alberta became even more concerned. There was something wrong. Terribly wrong.

'Right, my love, let's get you in the family room and I'll find Marlene and bring her to you,' she said, gently pushing Lucy towards the kitchen door.

Five minutes later, Lucy was sitting on the chair by the sofa, wringing her hands, her eyes going from Marlene to Shirley, who had brought in the tea tray, which also had two glasses of brandy on it, a small sugar bowl and a plate of home-made shortbread.

Seeing Lucy's distress but not wanting to speak until Shirley had left, Marlene instead took hold of her sister-in-law's hand and gently squeezed it.

As soon as Shirley had hurried out of the room and shut the door properly, as she had been told to do by Alberta, Marlene looked at Lucy, concern in her eyes, along with a creeping anxiety that what she was to about to hear was in no way good.

'What's happened?' she asked. She knew Felix was well

as she'd just seen him when Alberta had come to fetch her. 'Please tell me no one's died?' she implored. That was always Marlene's first concern whenever there was bad news, which was understandable as in the past few years she had suffered the loss of two people who were close to her – Quentin, whom she had loved like a father, and her mam.

'No, no,' Lucy reassured. 'No one's died. Although you might wish they had after you hear what I've got to tell you.'

'Oh God,' Marlene said, pouring the brandy into both their cups of tea and handing one to Lucy. She definitely looked like she needed a strong drink. And Marlene guessed that she would, too, once she'd heard what Lucy had to tell her.

'Where to start?' Lucy mumbled, taking a sip of her tea and grimacing, but then taking another.

'From the beginning,' Marlene said.

'Okay,' Lucy said, staring ahead as she rewound to the reason she'd ended up going back to Roeburn Hall. 'I was coming over here with Felix – in the car – when I realised I'd forgotten the divorce papers.'

'The divorce papers!' Marlene exclaimed. 'You're—'

'Forget that for the moment,' Lucy butted it. 'I'll explain later. I just need to go through this step by step.'

Marlene nodded, forcing back a plea for Lucy to hang fire and give Danny a chance.

'So, I turned the car around and drove back to Roeburn Hall . . . '

For the next ten minutes, Lucy explained how she had parked up in the shade and entered Roeburn Hall, only to hear her father had a visitor. A female visitor. She repeated as much as possible of the conversation she had heard between her father and Mabel, trying her hardest to be as accurate. As she did so, she saw Marlene's complexion go from a healthy pink to a deathly white.

'So, Edward is the father of Mabel's baby . . .' Marlene said, still trying to process what she was hearing. 'And he was having an affair with her—'

'Until the Big Freeze,' Lucy said.

'Oh God, Lucy, this is so incredibly shocking.'

They each took a drink of their brandy tea.

'Oh, and apparently Mabel didn't actually sleep with Thomas,' Lucy said, suddenly remembering her own – never mind her father's – incredulity that Mabel had managed to convince Thomas they'd slept together.

Seeing the same confusion on her sister-in-law's face, Lucy explained how Mabel had managed to make Thomas believe he had bedded Mabel, which had therefore convinced him he was the father.

Listening intently, Marlene felt her shock starting to diminish as her spirits began to lift. *Thomas had not slept with Mabel.* Her fury at Edward was momentarily replaced by a feeling of euphoria. She knew it was ridiculous to have such an incredible feeling of relief and joy that the two had done nothing more than simply share a bed, but she couldn't help it.

'It was all a ploy to get Thomas to marry her, as I'm presuming she knew Father wouldn't even entertain the idea.' Lucy glanced at Marlene, who seemed to have regained a little colour, and decided to leave out the part of the conversation where Mabel had reminded Edward of the time they had not been 'careful'. Marlene didn't need to hear that particular detail, just as Lucy would have been glad not to have heard it either.

'There were bits I didn't hear,' Lucy continued, 'but the general gist of it all was that Mabel was demanding that Father marry her.'

Marlene's eyes widened. 'I'm guessing she didn't know that he'd just proposed to me?' She let out a burst of bitter laughter and shook her head. The more she heard, the more bizarre the reality of the past few months seemed.

'Father told her, but she just went on about them being similar – "cut from the same cloth" was how she described it.' Again, Lucy missed out the part about their sexual compatibility. And again, as much for herself as for Marlene. 'But obviously Father batted away the mere idea of it.'

Marlene shifted on the sofa. 'Why? I think Mabel has a point. They are well suited. Both devious, cunning liars who will do whatever it takes to get what they want.' She spat the words out. *Danny had been right all along.*

Reading Marlene's thoughts, Lucy put up her hand. 'I can't deal with anything to do with Danny at the moment. I have to shelve that for the time being, otherwise I might just go completely cuckoo.'

She leant forward, her demeanour suddenly very sombre. She hadn't wanted to repeat this part of the conversation, but she knew she had to. Marlene had to know all the truth – regardless of how unpalatable it was.

'Father said he couldn't marry Mabel because he was engaged to you. But the real reason he couldn't marry her was because of the class divide and because she didn't have any money.' Lucy took a deep breath and rushed on, just wanting to get it out. 'He said you and he were the perfect match as it would be the coming together of two of the county's most highly regarded properties. That it didn't matter that you weren't exactly loaded as your family were doing well and the dowry would go towards restoring Roeburn Hall.'

Marlene sat in shocked silence as she tried to tally the man she had agreed to marry with the one she was hearing about now. Her mind went over everything Edward had said to her, how he had told her how much he loved her – was *in love* with her – and about all his imaginings of how a child they might have would look, the charmed life they could have, the wonder of making their dreams a reality and having their happy ever after.

'God,' she muttered, more to herself, 'how could I get him so wrong? I must be a total imbecile.'

'Well, then, that makes two of us,' Lucy said. 'And I must be even more imbecilic as he's my father.'

She finished off her brandy tea and put her empty cup and saucer back on the tray.

'And if you think that's bad,' she added, 'Father told Mabel that it didn't matter too much that you weren't terribly loaded as the bulk of the money will come from me.'

Marlene looked puzzled.

'Apparently, I'm going to divorce my "feckless husband" and marry someone rich from the same class, as I should have done in the first place.'

Marlene didn't say anything.

'I know what you're thinking. The divorce papers,' Lucy said. 'And that's why I feel even more stupid. I was going to do exactly what he wanted me to do.'

Marlene took some consolation from the fact that Lucy had used the past tense; for now, it would seem, divorce had been put on the back-burner.

'It was like I was standing there, listening not to my father but to a completely different person,' Lucy said, her brow creased. 'And the really awful thing is that the man I heard today is actually my *real* father – not the father he has had me believe he is. God, Marlene, he even tried to convince Mabel to keep seeing him after he had married you. That he would see her all right for money for the baby, but he wanted a legitimate heir.'

Marlene closed her eyes for a moment as though not seeing would prevent her hearing the terrible truth.

'And what did Mabel say?' she asked.

'She called him delusional, but I could tell she was getting ready to leave and I didn't want to get caught, so I left and drove straight here.'

Marlene gave her sister-in-law the saddest of smiles, knowing the hurt she must be feeling. The hurt and anger she herself was feeling having been duped by Edward would not compare to the heartbreak that her sister-in-law must be feeling at having a father who was so lacking in love for her. Again, Danny's words came back to her.

Her brother was one of the few who had seen the real Edward Stanton-Leigh.

'Right,' Marlene said, standing up. 'Come on. We're going over there to give that pathetic excuse of a man and father a piece of our minds.'

For a brief moment Lucy hesitated, before she too stood up.

'Yes, we are,' she said.

338

Chapter Sixty-Six

Despite their initial reaction to head straight over to Roeburn Hall and confront Edward, Marlene and Lucy decided to give themselves a little time to think about what they wanted to say and to talk about how they felt. Seeing Winston and Bessie's excited faces when they went into the kitchen to return the tea tray, they agreed that a breath of fresh air and a walk with the dogs would be a good idea. Uncovering Edward's true character had caused them both to feel as though their lives really had been turned upside down and inside out – the reality they had perceived was actually a falsehood – and they needed a moment to adjust and to try to rebalance their equilibrium.

Glancing at Lucy as the dogs trotted ahead of them and then veered off when they caught a scent, Marlene thought back to the day she had driven her sister-in-law to the hospital after her mother's accident – and how she had watched as Edward had embraced his daughter, comforting her. Marlene had felt envious of Lucy, and as much as she hated to admit it, she'd also felt sorry for herself, having had no real father in her own life.

Knowing what she knew now, Marlene realised how much worse it must be to have a father like Edward and to have been conned your entire life, as Lucy had been. It had been clear from what Edward had said about Lucy divorcing Danny and marrying someone with money that he did not give two hoots about his daughter, that he was actually happy about the demise of her marriage, and was looking forward to her finally doing what he had wanted her to do all along – marry someone rich so that Roeburn Hall could be restored to its former glory.

'How are you feeling?' Marlene asked.

Lucy sighed. 'Incredibly disappointed. Betrayed. Sad. Angry. Unloved. Used.' She let out a sad laugh. 'And that's just for starters.'

Marlene put her arm around Lucy's shoulders and squeezed her. 'I feel for you. I'm so sorry this has happened.'

Lucy looked at Marlene as tears began to sting her eyes, but she was determined not to cry. 'And I feel it for you too. All your hopes and dreams have suddenly and brutally been dashed. My father has fooled you as well. Feigned love to get what he wanted – a beautiful young bride and the prospect of an heir on the horizon.'

Marlene hooked her arm into Lucy's. 'He fed me a dream and I was naive and stupid enough to gobble it all up. He really had me believing that I had met my Mr Right and could live "happily ever after". He actually said those words.' Marlene shook her head in disbelief, realising how desperate she had been to believe that this could actually happen to her.

Lucy glanced at Marlene. She had felt uneasy about how quickly Marlene's relationship with her father had gained momentum. She had intended to say something when she'd had some time with her on her own. She wondered if they would have seen through her father's deceit as time went on.

'And, of course, there was also your dream of starting up the children's home,' Lucy added. She knew this had been a big deal for Marlene. Probably as big as her anticipation of their marriage and having her own family.

Marlene nodded. 'So, do we just tell him we know everything?' she suggested.

'Yes, I think we have to combat his lies and deception with the truth. I'll tell him that I overheard everything when I went back to pick up my divorce papers, so it's pointless him trying to deny it. And then I think we just tell him how we feel – about what he's done to us, and how we feel about him.'

Marlene murmured her agreement.

They reached the small wooded area that marked the estate's boundary and Marlene whistled for the dogs to come back. As they waited, Lucy turned and said, 'There *is* something else I want to ask him, knowing what extremes Father's gone to in order to get what he wants . . .'

Marlene looked at her sister-in-law, the evening they had gone to see her mother at the hospital at the forefront of her mind. 'You're wondering if the police were right all along – that your father *did* kill your mother?'

Lucy laughed.

'*No*. Father's not a murderer. That's one thing I am sure of.'

Marlene was relieved she was so certain. Being lied to on such a colossal scale made you doubt just about everything.

'What, then?' Marlene asked.

'I want to know if he purposely tried to put a spoke in my marriage. Whether we'd be where we are now if Father hadn't come back on the scene.'

Marlene didn't say anything. She had wondered as much

herself, having heard how gleeful Edward was about the dire state of his daughter's marriage. Lucy's marriage to Danny had been a happy one until her father had come back on the scene. It seemed a bit too coincidental. 'But would I get the truth?' Lucy said as Winston and Bessie suddenly charged out of the copse, demanding attention and pats and praise for coming back when they'd been told to.

Returning to the manor, Marlene and Lucy were quiet. Both thinking their own thoughts. Both thinking about what they wanted to say to the man who had deceived them so.

When they arrived back, Mrs Trendle told them that she would sort the dogs out with water and some leftovers, and that Felix and Alberta were in the nursery with Angie and Juni. Lucy asked the cook if she could tell Angie that she and Marlene were just nipping out on a quick errand and would be back in an hour or so.

Marlene insisted on driving as she thought Lucy looked very pale. What Lucy had learnt about her father had been a huge shock, but Marlene also knew that her fallout with Danny was also adding to her upset. She had seen Lucy looking over at the stables and outdoor riding arena when they came back from their walk, and again when they'd been heading to the car, but no one had been about.

As they drove to Roeburn Hall, they agreed that it would not be right to tell anyone but those at Cuthford Manor that Edward was the father of Mabel's baby, and that it was up to Mabel if she wanted to disclose who the real father was.

'It's strange, though,' Lucy added, 'to think that I'm going to have another sister. Well, half-sister, but sister all the same.'

'Another?' Marlene asked.

'Yes, the other one's sat right next to me,' Lucy said, her eyes once again filling with tears she was unable to stop.

Marlene took one hand off the steering wheel and squeezed Lucy's hand.

'Yes,' she said, 'and one who will be here for you – whatever happens.'

Lucy knew what Marlene meant. Even if her marriage to Danny did not succeed, Marlene would always be there for her.

As soon as they turned into the long driveway that led to Roeburn Hall, Marlene and Lucy could see that Edward had visitors. It wasn't until they were halfway down the tree-lined drive that they realised the visitor's black Wolseley car had a blue police sign on the roof.

'What are the police doing here?' Lucy asked.

Marlene didn't answer, too many thoughts going through her head.

'Oh God, you don't think something's happened to him, do you?' Lucy worried. She, too, had a list of possibilities racing through her head.

Marlene pulled up next to the police car. Seeing it up close, with its worn but immaculate black-leather interior, she was taken back to the day of the wake when the police had turned up to arrest Edward, followed shortly afterwards by two detectives who had asked Lucy a load of questions about her father. Or rather, about her mother and father's finances.

'Come on,' Marlene said, getting out of the car, 'there's only one way to find out.'

Lucy climbed out of the car, part of her not wanting to know. She had already had enough shocks for one day.

As soon as they reached the bottom of the steps up to the

343

front door, they heard angry words, then saw the large oak door swing open.

Edward was in handcuffs, sandwiched between the same two detectives who had come to Cuthford Manor in September last year. They each had a firm hold of one arm.

Spotting Marlene and Lucy, Edward immediately started speaking.

'Thank God you're here!'

The two women were momentarily mute.

'Ring my lawyer – Desmond Pyburn – his name's in my telephone book,' Edward demanded.

Finally, Lucy found her voice.

'What's going on?' she asked, looking at the more senior of the police officers for an answer.

'I'm sorry to have to tell you this, Mrs Boulter, but your father's been arrested for the murder of your mother,' he said.

'No, no, no – not again,' Lucy said, shaking her head. 'We've already been down this road once.'

The two detectives hustled Edward into the back of the police car and slammed the door.

'And I'm afraid it looks like we're going down it again,' DC Adams said without any compassion as he walked round to the driver's side of the Wolseley.

Despite the restrictions caused by the handcuffs, Edward frantically wound down the window.

'This is insanity!' he shouted out as the car started to pull away. 'Get Desmond down to the station as quick as you can!'

Marlene and Lucy stood speechless, watching as the police car disappeared from view.

In a daze, they then turned and walked up the steps of the entrance to Roeburn Hall.

Lucy did as her father had requested and called Desmond Pyburn.

She could hear that he, too, was shocked and a little alarmed by his client's rearrest. Before hanging up, she told him to call her the moment he knew more.

As soon as Lucy was off the phone, Marlene insisted that she come back home – to her real home: Cuthford Manor.

'You're not staying here,' she ordered, again fighting her own shock at what they had just witnessed.

Marlene helped her sister-in-law pack before gathering up her own belongings, knowing she would never step over the threshold of Roeburn Hall ever again. They then drove slowly back to Cuthford Manor, their silence peppered with the occasional thought.

'They must have some kind of evidence to arrest him again,' Lucy murmured, staring out at the passing country-side but seeing only the desperate face of her father in the back of the police car before it pulled away.

'Mmm,' Marlene agreed. 'Something concrete – irrefut-able – for them to do what they've done.'

The pair, she thought, had had the air of victors.

As they turned off the main road, Lucy looked at Marlene. 'I know you think differently, but I really don't believe my father is capable of murder. I really don't.'

Don't or won't? Marlene wondered.

When they arrived back at Cuthford Manor, this time park-ing out the front and going in the main entrance, Marlene immediately walked over to Wilfred, who was on the phone at the reception desk. She waited until he had taken the booking for yet another Mr and Mrs Smith. As soon as he'd replaced the receiver on the black Bakelite phone, she asked him to 'gather everyone up' as she was calling 'an emergency meeting' in the family room.

Ten minutes later, Angie, Stanislaw, Cora and Lloyd arrived, all looking worried.

'No Danny or Carl?' Marlene asked.

'Carl's out foraging for mushrooms. He's on the hunt for a particular type called blushing wood mushrooms. They're meant to be very good for you,' Angie informed her.

'And Danny is not about,' Stanislaw added.

'Where is he?' Lucy demanded. 'No, don't tell me. Let me guess. He's up at the Travellers' camp.'

She reached over and put a good slug of brandy in her tea.

'Might as well move there,' she muttered as she picked up her cup and blew on it.

As no one denied Danny's whereabouts, Marlene presumed her sister-in-law was correct. If there was one time her brother really did not need to be up at the camp, it was now.

She handed everyone their tea and cocked her head at the bottle of cognac. 'You all might want to follow Lucy's example when we tell you the news.'

'I don't like the sound of this,' Lloyd said.

'Me neither,' Cora chipped in, taking her tea from Marlene and smiling her thanks.

'I think we've had enough shock and upset lately,' Angie said, wiping some of Felix's dribble off her blouse.

346

'Well, I think this is going to top it all,' Lucy added, sipping her second brandy tea of the day.

'Where to start?' Marlene said.

'From the beginning,' Lucy said, replaying their earlier dialogue.

Marlene looked at the four anxious, expectant faces.

'It started when Lucy had to pop back to Roeburn Hall as she'd forgotten something.'

Marlene purposely left out that it was her divorce papers she'd gone back for, knowing it would cause too much of a distraction. Instead, she stayed on track and related the shocking news that the real father of Mabel's baby was, in fact, Edward.

'He's the father?' Angie asked, not quite able to believe what she was hearing.

'My goodness,' Cora gasped.

'Dear Lord,' Lloyd blustered, 'never in a million years—'

'So,' Stanislaw said, 'they had been having an affair—'

Marlene filled in all the details – that the two had indeed been having an affair, which had started before Lucy's mum had died and had continued until the Big Freeze in February.

'So, it had finished by the time you and he started your courtship?' Angie asked, knowing that the news of Edward's affair and the paternity of Mabel's baby must have devastated her sister but that there would be some solace in knowing that she had not been cheated on.

Knowing what her older sister was thinking, Marlene said, 'It had – not that it's much consolation, as it also came out that his reason for being with me wasn't love, but because he thought he'd be getting a decent dowry and that it would mean the joining of "two of the county's most highly regarded properties".'

Angie tensed, pursing her lips, forcing herself not to let rip.

'Lucy, my dear,' Lloyd trained his attention on Danny's wife, who had already been through so much these past months with the death of her mother, her pregnancy and her marital strife, 'how on earth are you feeling about all this? He is your father. It must have come as such a shock?'

Lucy was taking another drink of her tea. She nodded as she swallowed, then grimaced at the strength of the brandy she'd sloshed in there.

'But that is not the most shocking news we've got to tell you,' Marlene said. She glanced at Lucy, who nodded, showing her sister-in-law that she wanted her to relate what had followed.

'There's more?' Angie asked, eyeing the brandy.

'Oh, yes,' Marlene said.

'I don't think I want to hear this,' Lloyd muttered, getting up and pouring himself a whisky from the drinks cabinet.

'After Lucy told me what she'd heard, we decided to go over to Roeburn Hall and confront Edward,' Marlene said. 'Obviously, I wanted to tell him where to stuff his proposal.'

'Too right,' Angie mumbled. Stanislaw took her hand and squeezed it. He knew that once his wife's anger subsided there would be relief that Marlene's courtship with 'that man' was now well and truly over.

'And obviously, Lucy also wanted to give him a piece of her mind – and had her own questions she wanted to ask,' Marlene added.

Lucy felt her heart constrict. She had hoped that her father was also to blame for the troubles in her marriage, but having heard that Danny was up at the camp, she realised that there was only one person to blame – *her damned, deceitful husband*.

'So, what happened when you arrived at Roeburn Hall?' Lloyd asked.

Marlene and Lucy looked at each other before returning their attention to their audience.

'What happened,' Marlene said, 'was that we saw Edward in handcuffs, being hauled away by the police. He'd been arrested.'

'Why?' Cora asked.

'Arrested? What for?' Angie asked.

'*Rearrested*,' Lucy said. 'For the murder of my mother.'

Chapter Sixty-Seven

'So,' DI Cassey began, 'this is how we think it played out.'
He looked at Edward sitting opposite, his face flushed red
with anger. 'You heard that your daughter, your only child,
Lucy, had eloped to Gretna Green and married Mr Danny
Boulter, and when you heard this shocking and truly devas-
tating news, you were angry. Very angry. And it was made
worse because this was something even you could not undo
or put right.'

Edward's mind spun back to that night more than a year
and a half ago. It had been Mabel who had come to tell him
the news. She had been breathless with adrenaline as she
had cycled the mile from Cuthford Manor to Roeburn Hall,
knowing he was on his own. He had been shocked and outraged on hearing the news, that much DI Cassey had got
right, although he had not been so consumed by ire that it had
prevented him from making love. Afterwards, though, his
energy spent, he'd lain in his bed, thinking about what to do.

'You therefore had to find another solution to your problem,' DI Cassey continued. 'Another way of digging yourself
out of the very deep financial pit you had put yourself in.' He
sat back in his chair as though to punctuate the point. 'And
you realised there was only one way forward. You had to
get rid of your wife. You knew there would be a substantial

insurance payout – and I'm guessing that, much as you denied it when we had the pleasure of speaking last, you also knew all about your wife's separate bank account, in which she had rather a large amount squirrelled away.'

DI Cassey paused to light a cigarette.

'It took you a while, though, didn't it?' he said, smoke billowing from his mouth. 'Which isn't surprising. I mean, plotting someone's murder and actually *doing* it are two very different things.' A puff on his cigarette. 'Aren't they?' Expelled smoke filled the small room. 'Or perhaps it was when you found out that your wife was planning on leaving you – divorcing you – perhaps that was the push you needed . . . ' He looked for a reaction from Edward, who was not giving anything away. 'I'm tending to go for the theory about the impending divorce.' Another deep drag on his cigarette. 'Yes, if I were a betting man, which I am not . . . ' He gave Edward a faux-sympathetic smile, knowing his collar's dire gambling form, ' . . . then that's the reason I would choose.'

Edward made a point of looking at his watch.

'Can someone see if my brief is here, please?' he demanded. He was trying his hardest not to say anything, but it was taking some doing. Desmond had drilled it into him that if ever he were arrested for anything at any time in the future, he was not to say a word until he had arrived and they had spoken.

'So, to continue,' DI Cassey said. 'In August last year – ten months after you had found out about your daughter's marriage – you decided to put your plan into action. But there was one thing you didn't bank on, and which I doubt you are even now aware of.' A deliberate pause. 'Actually, I'm sure you're not aware of it, as if you were, I believe that person might well have found themselves suffering a similar fate to your wife's.'

Edward sighed heavily.

'And what is this "thing"?' he demanded, not able to keep quiet for a moment longer.

'You didn't bank on a witness,' DI Cassey said, staring at Edward, wanting him to see the victory in his eyes.

'What?' Edward demanded. 'What *witness*?'

'That's right, Edward,' DI Cassey said. 'There was a witness. They have only just come forward, at considerable risk to themselves, because they fear there may be others in jeopardy.'

Edward couldn't hold back any longer. 'There can't have been a witness as there was nothing to bloody well witness!'

DI Cassey looked at DC Adams. He knew time was running out before Edward's solicitor turned up.

'It doesn't look good, does it, Edward? If you admit your guilt, it is going to go down much better with the judge, who will look favourably on your early plea. And I'm sure that, with a decent lawyer, there will be mitigating circumstances – that you weren't in your right mind, how remorseful you are. That should keep you from feeling the hangman's noose around your neck.'

Edward was just opening his mouth to speak when Desmond Pyburn came bursting into the room.

'Don't!' he demanded. 'Don't say another word, Edward!'

He turned and scowled at the two detectives.

'Right, *gentlemen*, you've had your fun, it's now time for you to leave.'

352

The two detectives slowly got up from their chairs.

'And be sure to shut the door behind you when you leave, thank you very much.'

When they had done as he asked, Desmond turned to look at his client.

'*Bloody hell, Edward! What on earth is all this about a witness?*'

Chapter Sixty-Eight

Thomas had heard about the 'emergency' family meeting when Wilfred had come looking for Danny. He'd told him that Danny had just nipped to the Travellers' camp as he needed to settle a bill, and as soon as he returned, Thomas would tell him. Thomas worried about what the family meeting was about, and he hoped more than anything that some catastrophe had not befallen the woman he loved. Which was why he was now loitering outside the stables, hoping to see Marlene come out the back. Hearing the latch click, he saw Winston and Bessie's heads pushing the door open as they bustled their way into the yard. Seeing Marlene, he strode over to her, his eyes scrutinising her face, trying to tell if something had happened that had caused her any kind of hurt, pain or distress.

'Are you okay? Is everything all right?' he asked before he even reached her.

Marlene looked up, surprised, as she'd expected him to be taking a lesson in the paddock or to be out on a trek.

'No,' she said. 'Everything is definitely *not* okay.' Her words, though, belied her joy at bumping into him. Despite everything that had happened today, just seeing Thomas had immediately made her feel better. *How she had missed him.*

'Do you want to chat about it?' Thomas asked.

Marlene looked around and was surprised to see how quiet it was.

'There's no lessons this afternoon,' he said, reading her thoughts.

'I was going to walk the dogs over to the cottage, if you want to come,' she said. 'Lucy's moving back there. I said I'd go over and see if there was anything she needed.'

Thomas didn't need asking twice. 'Yes, I'd love to.'

They started walking off in the direction of the cottage, the dogs keeping close as they had been trained to do when they were near the stables.

'I take it that's good news?' Thomas asked. 'That Lucy's moving back.'

'It is, but not for Danny,' Marlene said, frowning. 'Lucy's told me to tell him that she's moving back in with Felix and that he'll have to find somewhere else.'

'Oh,' Thomas said. 'I see.'

'I know,' Marlene said gravely. 'She's even had divorce papers drawn up.'

'Oh no.' Thomas pushed back his dark blond quiff with his fingers. 'That's not good news. Not good at all.'

As soon as they reached the grass field that was parallel to the paddock, Bessie and Winston charged off.

'So, what's happened?' Thomas said. 'I mean, only if you want to talk about it?'

Marlene wanted to say that he was the only person she really wanted to talk to about it, but didn't. Instead, she started to tell him all about the day's events for the second time in as many hours. As she had done during the emergency family meeting, she related the news chronologically. When Marlene reached the revelation that Edward was the father of Mabel's baby, there was a long silence. Marlene was quiet as they strolled, knowing that Thomas needed time to take in what she had just told him.

'So,' he muttered after a little while, 'Edward's the father.' He shook his head in disbelief. 'I must say, I'd never have guessed in a million years.'

'They're the exact words Lloyd used,' Marlene said. 'I think everyone has been totally taken aback by it all.'

They walked a little further. The cottage was now in sight and Winston and Bessie had expended their energy and were now walking slightly ahead, panting, their chops drooling with saliva.

'I did wonder who the real father was,' Thomas said. He shook his head. 'How bizarre that your fiancé ends up being the father of my fiancée's child.'

'Well, when you put it like that . . .' Marlene said.

'Looks like we both made bad choices, doesn't it?' Thomas said.

'We certainly did. And like you say, how odd that our bad choices are connected.'

Marlene eyed Thomas.

'So, you aren't upset?'

'Upset?' Thomas looked at Marlene with a puzzled expression. 'I was *relieved* when I found out the baby wasn't mine. Why would I be upset?'

Marlene let out a gasp of disbelief. 'Because she was your girlfriend, your fiancée – you must have loved her?'

Thomas shook his head. 'Don't get me wrong, I mean, I

did really like Mabel a lot – but not in that way. I never did.' He looked at Marlene. 'I don't think you ever believed me, did you?'

'It was hard to,' Marlene said, narrowing her eyes, 'when I saw her coming out of your digs first thing in the morning.'

'That was a mistake—'

Marlene laughed loudly. 'A *mistake*?'

'Yes, it was a mistake – and one I can't even remember,' he said, giving Marlene a sideways look. 'And actually, you were the cause of that mistake.'

'Now *that* I really don't understand!' she said, giving Thomas a look of astonishment. 'And I'm all ears as to how I was the cause of you spending the night with someone you claim you liked – *but not in that way*.'

As they reached the cottage, Thomas opened the gate and let Marlene walk into the little front garden first.

'Let's sit on the bench for a minute,' he suggested. 'And I can explain.'

The dogs followed Marlene, bumping past Thomas.

'I'll just get them some fresh water,' Marlene said, opening the front door and putting the doorstop in place. She returned with the dog bowl and put it down on the grass. Winston and Bessie lapped up the water as though they had been in the desert and had just discovered an oasis.

'Right, I'm all ears,' Marlene said, sitting down next to Thomas on the wooden love seat, looking out at the far-reaching views over the surrounding countryside.

'Well, I was upset,' Thomas began, 'and I decided to drown my sorrows, which led me into the situation whereby Mabel ended up staying the night.'

'Yes, but *why* were you upset? How was *I* to blame?' Marlene asked, genuinely puzzled.

'Because that day I found out you were seeing Edward – although I was told it was all very hush-hush.'

Marlene looked even more puzzled. 'I don't understand. I *hadn't* started seeing Edward at that point. In fact, I hadn't even started to see him in a romantic light.' She furrowed her brow. She wanted to say that the only man she had been viewing in any kind of amorous way at that time was the one sitting next to her now. But she didn't.

'Who told you that?' she asked instead.

Thomas looked at Marlene and suddenly the penny dropped and all the pieces of the jigsaw he had been trying to fit together these past few days suddenly slotted into place.

'Mabel,' he said. 'Mabel told me.'

Marlene looked at Thomas with wide eyes. 'But why would she lie?'

Thomas turned to look at Marlene, needing to see her reaction, even though he knew there was a good chance it would break his heart.

'Because,' he said, 'and I've only just realised this now, but Mabel must have worked out that I was in love with you.' He paused. 'So the only way she could trap me was to make me think that you were in love with someone else – not that I thought you were in love with me. And that was why she suggested we go to the pub that night, knowing I'd want to drown my sorrows and she could seduce me, then make me think I was the father of her baby, because by that time, of course, she knew she was pregnant, and knew that the baby's father – who we now know is Edward – would not make an honest woman of her . . . ' Thomas let his voice trail off.

Marlene felt her head spin with the sudden onslaught of information and insight.

'So, at that point in time,' she asked, 'you thought yourself to be in love with me?'

Thomas laughed and held back a strong desire to cup her face in his hands and kiss her. 'I didn't *think* myself to be in love with you, Marlene. I *was* in love with you.' He paused. In for a penny, in for a pound. 'And obviously, it goes without saying that I am *still* very much in love with you.'

'You are?' Marlene asked, her heart suddenly starting to thump in her chest. 'Even after everything that's happened?'

Thomas looked at Marlene and wanted to say so much, but this wasn't the time.

Instead, he did as he had just envisaged, and took her beautiful, slightly flushed face in his hands and kissed her.

Chapter Sixty-Nine

Marlene and Thomas were still sitting on the love seat, chatting and kissing and feeling as though they were the happiest, luckiest and most in love couple in the entire universe, when they spotted Danny and Lucy walking towards the cottage. Or rather, stomping.

'Oh dear,' Marlene said. 'They do not look happy.'

'No, they don't, do they? Far from it,' Thomas agreed.

They both shuffled on the seat, suddenly feeling awkward that they were there. And because it must be obvious to anyone but a blind man that they were deliriously happy and totally smitten with each other. But neither Danny or Lucy spotted them as they were both too busy scowling at each other and exchanging cross and hurtful words.

'Yes, all right, Danny, ten out of ten, you were right about my father, and I was wrong. Aren't you the clever one!' Lucy said, giving her estranged husband a thunderous look.

They stopped walking just before they reached the cottage and faced each other, both with their hands on their hips.

'It's not that I was right and you were wrong,' Danny said, his own look equally dark, 'but because you sided with him – *all the time* – and you turned your back on me, the one person who has loved you more than anyone else in your entire life.'

'Oh, and I'm meant to be eternally grateful for that, am I?' Lucy gasped.

'That's not what I meant,' Danny said, letting out a frustrated sigh.

Lucy ignored his denial. 'To be frank, Danný, you loving me more than anyone else doesn't take much when you consider I had a mother who didn't give two jots about me, and then died – and a father who has lied to me my whole life and is now accused of killing her.'

Lucy looked at Danny as though all the love she had felt for him over the years had turned to pure hatred. 'One thing, though, that I'm pretty sure my father is not responsible for is your infidelity— Oh,' she added in a faux-friendly tone, 'how *is* Adriana?'

'Do you really think I'm having an affair with Adriana?' Danny demanded.

'Yes, I do,' Lucy retorted.

'You see,' Danny said, shaking his head, his expression a mix of hurt and disappointment, 'that's what I can't understand – that you can believe that I would be unfaithful to you?'

'So, you're telling me that you're *not* having an affair?' Lucy asked, not sounding convinced.

'*No, I'm not having an affair with Adriana.* I'm not having an affair with anyone. Never have done and never will do!' Danny exclaimed, his outrage undisguised.

'If that's the case, why am I hearing that you are?' Lucy demanded.

'Who has been telling you that? Who's been spreading untrue and malicious gossip?' Danny retorted.

Lucy hesitated. It was only then that it hit her. The only

person who had mentioned Danny's closeness to Adriana and implied they were having an affair had been her father. Until that moment, she'd believed he had merely been reporting back to her what he'd heard others say. She didn't answer, but instead asked, 'So why is it that you seem to be over at the Travellers' camp every spare minute you have?'

'I'm not over there every spare minute,' Danny said, exasperated. 'I might have been over there more than usual, but there's been a reason for that!'

Lucy gave him a look of pure scepticism.

'And what reason would that be?' she asked.

Danny pursed his lips and stared at his wife, wondering whether to tell her or show her.

In the end, he put his hand out. 'Come with me. I'll show you.'

Lucy tentatively took it.

As they started walking towards the cottage, they both noticed Marlene and Thomas at the same time.

'Oh, all right,' Danny mumbled as he opened the gate.

'Hi,' Lucy said as they made their way up the short path.

Marlene and Thomas, who looked as if they would rather be anywhere else but there, attempted to smile but were unsuccessful.

Even Winston and Bessie, who ordinarily would have got up to greet the newcomers, instead chose to stay put and watch the warring couple warily from where they had settled on the front lawn.

When Lucy walked over the threshold, she realised just how much she had missed her home. Marlene was right. This *was* her real home. And so very different to Roeburn Hall. That was her father's home and his alone. She realised she had never been happy there; even as a child she'd preferred being out in the stables. As she stepped into the narrow hallway, she knew she should have told Danny that the rumours had come from the one source – her father. She would tell him later. For now, she needed to know why Danny had been spending so much time up at the camp. She needed to know without a shadow of a doubt that he had not cheated on her. She knew it was unlikely she would ever have questioned her husband's fidelity had her father not planted the seed of doubt, but nevertheless she could not uproot the distrust that had taken such a strong hold on her.

Standing by the lounge door, which had been left ajar, Danny pushed it open.

As Lucy took a tentative step into their living room, she stopped dead in her tracks.

At that moment, any lingering vestiges of doubt disappeared.

Positioned in the middle of the room – in place of the coffee table – was the most beautiful baby rocking-horse chair. On either side of the brocade-upholstered seat were two hand-carved and painted wooden horses – one black, the other a speckled grey – replicas of Lucy's beloved horse, Dahlia, and Danny's horse, Ghost. Along one side of the rocker, their baby boy's name, Felix, had been engraved and gilded with gold leaf.

Lucy stood and stared.

Finally, she turned, her eyes filling with tears. Unable to find the words, and unable to say them even if she could, she turned to her husband and stepped towards him so their bodies were touching.

Putting her arms around him, she tilted her head and kissed him.

And for a long moment, they stood and kissed and held each other close.

As Marlene glanced through the window to see Lucy and Danny in an embrace, she felt such an enormous sense of relief. And joy. Edward had not succeeded in causing their marriage to fail. Walking down the pathway with Thomas and the dogs following, Marlene realised that the love Danny and Lucy had for each other had overcome the lies and deceit that had been thrown at their marriage. Love had been the antidote to the poison Edward had been feeding his daughter.

As Thomas shut the little gate behind them, Marlene was brought out of her reverie.

'Did I hear correctly back there,' Thomas asked, 'that Edward's been charged with murder?'

Marlene's eyes widened.

'Yes, you did! Gosh, how could I not tell you? It's your fault – you distracted me,' she joked, before becoming deadly serious. 'But, yes, that's right . . . '

By the time they had arrived back at the stables, where they headed to the tack room for a cup of tea, Marlene had told Thomas every detail of her trip with Lucy to Roeburn Hall and how they had seen Edward being hauled off by the police.

'Then, just after the emergency family meeting, Lucy rang Desmond for an update and apparently there's a witness who saw Edward do it, but the police aren't saying who. They're claiming whoever it is has to be protected, although Desmond reckons he can reveal the witness's identity when he makes an appeal to the court.'

Thomas shook his head. 'Either way, the man's done for, then – whether or not the witness is named, someone's seen him do it. Danny was right. He always said Edward had done it – that it wasn't an accident.'

'I know,' Marlene agreed. 'That's exactly what I was thinking. It's Lucy I feel for, though.' She took the mug from Thomas. 'She's going to have to accept that her father has done the unspeakable.'

Thomas sat down next to Marlene and kissed her.

'And how do *you* feel about all of this?' he asked. 'I mean, you're engaged to the man?'

'*Was*, Thomas! *Was*! Past tense. And anyway, I don't think it really counted as I was only engaged to him for a few days!'

Thomas laughed out loud, partly because of the elation he felt from knowing that Marlene was no longer in any way attached to Edward, but also because he could hear the fight in her and knew that she would be okay.

'Honestly, though, I really don't know how I feel about it all at the moment,' Marlene said. 'I've spent most of the day trying to be a support to Lucy as it's so much worse for her. I mean, this is her father. And this time he's not just been arrested but actually *charged* with killing her mother. I just can't imagine how that would make me feel. And that's besides finding out she's going to have a half-sister.'

Thomas put his tea on the makeshift table and pulled Marlene close. 'What a state of affairs. Mabel trying to pass off Edward's child as mine – and having failed that, she's now facing the prospect of seeing the father of her baby jailed for life for murder, or worse still . . .'

Marlene shuddered.

Much as she might hate Edward for everything he had done, the thought of him being handed a death sentence was a disturbing one.

A while later, when Danny and Lucy were lying in their bed, the early-evening sun streaming through the net curtains, they started to chat. All Danny had wanted was to make love to his wife before the air was muddied with talk of her father. Lucy's response to his kisses and caresses told him that she, too, felt the same way. Their lovemaking had showed that their feelings for one another were as strong and as passionate and as loving as they had always been. And that now they were back together, they would be able to deal with whatever happened in the future because they had each other. They were united. Which was just as well, as they were now faced with the aftermath of the bombshell that had been dropped earlier in the day.

'I think the hardest thing for me,' Lucy said, recalling how she felt having heard the conversation between her father and Mabel, 'is how – ever since my mother's death – I've been fed lie after lie by my father. About everything and everyone. I don't understand how someone can do that? To *anyone*, let alone their own daughter.'

Danny was careful to hold back voicing his opinion that the reason Edward Stanton-Leigh could lie so well and so prolifically was because the man didn't have a conscience.

Life had taught Danny that this was simply the way some people were and there was no understanding why – it was just the way they'd been born.

'It's hard,' Lucy said, shifting herself around so that she was facing Danny, 'to accept that he feigned loving me – and Marlene, and probably Felix – all because he wanted something. He was happy to actively cause the break-up of his own daughter's marriage. And have me marry someone else for money.' She paused. 'And to marry someone himself not for love but for show, for money, and because of Marlene's connection to Cuthford Manor. Everything is about money and prestige and status. Without Roeburn Hall, he's nothing.'

Danny touched her brow and carefully brushed a stray strand of her blonde hair away from her eyes. 'I think you're dealing with this so well. With such strength.'

Lucy let out a garbled laugh. 'I don't think I've got much of a choice.'

She looked at Danny.

'I don't think I could do it alone, though,' she admitted. 'I need you by my side. To hold me up when I'm not feeling so strong.'

Danny kissed her. 'Always. I'll always be there for you.'

Neither of them said what they were thinking, neither wanting to vocalise their distress at the prospect of what would happen to Edward were he to be found guilty, which was looking highly likely. They might both hate the man for everything that he had done, but they did not believe in the ideology of an eye for an eye – or a life for a life.

Chapter Seventy

Over the next few days, Lucy was barely able to concentrate on even the simplest of tasks. She kept rewinding the conversation she had overheard between her father and Mabel. And the vision of her father in handcuffs being carted off in a police car seemed to have become stuck in a constant loop in her head. She talked to Danny when he came back to the cottage after work and she had put Felix down, and she would go back and forth over everything that had happened since her mother's death.

'There's so much I still want to know. I need the truth,' she said. 'My mind just won't let up.'

Danny had forced himself to listen more than talk, which was hard as he had much to say about Edward. But he was aware that Lucy's father had successfully managed to drive a wedge between the two of them, and he was not going to let him do so again.

Instead, he talked to Thomas about Edward's behaviour, how his father-in-law had the whole practice of 'dividing to conquer' off to a fine art, an art he had used mercilessly with himself and Lucy. And how Edward had also done the same, albeit to a lesser degree, with Marlene.

'He managed to get Lucy *and* Marlene away from all of us and had them practically living as recluses at Roeburn Hall,' he ranted. His anger towards Edward was still at its height as he could see how disturbed Lucy was by her father's incarceration – never mind his lies and manipulations.

'Talking about playing with someone's mind. The man had Lucy – and Marlene – believing a totally false reality. Lucy firmly believed I was having an affair with a woman who was making me a present for Lucy and Felix. A woman who must have been fed up to the back teeth of listening to me talking about Lucy and how wonderful she is.'

Thomas listened, although his mind was only half-engaged in the conversation as he could not stop thinking about Marlene.

Marlene had thrown herself back into work at the manor, but she would come and see him as soon as she was finished for the day and they would take the dogs for long walks. They had much to catch up on. And also to share. And the more they shared, the more they understood.

'That was why Edward was so keen to have the wake at the manor. It puzzled me, but that was the start of him ingratiating himself into the family – and the start of him hoodwinking me,' Marlene mused. 'I remember him saying to me, all good things come to those who wait.'

'He was playing the long game,' Thomas agreed.

Angie, meanwhile, was concerned about the effect Edward's arrest for murder would have on the children, who all thought him marvellous. It was decided to keep quiet about what had happened. For the time being, anyway. At the moment only a handful of people knew that Edward Stanton-Leigh had once again been arrested for the murder of his wife, and they all lived and worked at the manor and could be trusted not to give the county gossipmongers something that would cause a feeding frenzy.

Marlene was glad about this, not because of her own romantic connection with Edward but for Lucy's sake. Having your father's arrest for the murder of your mother splashed across the front pages of the local newspaper – and possibly the nationals as well – would only cause Lucy greater distress.

'I just need time to work out what I think,' Lucy told Marlene.

'Work out if you think he did it?' Marlene asked. Lucy was no longer expounding her heartfelt belief that her father was not capable of murder, but neither was she saying that she believed him to be guilty.

'Yes, I need to know. For my own sanity,' she told her sister-in-law and her husband.

Which was why Lucy and Marlene found themselves driving to Durham police station on the morning of the fourth day after Edward's arrest. They had been told by Desmond that there was a good chance he would be moved to Durham Prison before his first court appearance.

'We're lucky,' Desmond Pyburn told Lucy, 'that no one at the station has tipped off a member of the press yet.'

Desmond had facilitated the meeting and was there to greet Lucy and Marlene when they hurried through the front doors of the station. They were immediately ushered through the reception area and into the main hub of the police station, which was still relatively quiet due to the early hour. Normally visitors were not allowed to visit those being held in the custody suite, but Lucy had made a donation to the local police charity fund, which meant rules could be bent and Edward could meet with his daughter and her sister-in-law in the little cafeteria.

Edward was smoking a cigarette at a table in the canteen, which was empty bar a uniformed officer sitting by the entrance.

On seeing Lucy and Marlene, Edward's face lit up.

As soon as they reached the table, he stubbed out his cigarette and stood up to greet them.

'Oh, thank goodness you have come,' he said, looking from his daughter to Marlene. 'I've been told I am not able to hug you or have any kind of physical contact,' he said, his eyes conveying his desperation to do just that. 'Thank you so much for coming to see me. Both of you.' His attention went from his daughter to Marlene, then back to his daughter. He sensed animosity, which didn't surprise him. He just had to convince them that this was an outrageous miscarriage of justice with deadly consequences.

'Sit down,' he said, gesturing at two seats that had been pulled out from the Formica table in anticipation of their arrival.

'Before we go any further,' Marlene said, 'we have to tell you that we know all about your affair with Mabel, that you are the father of her baby, and that you only courted me because of Cuthford Manor and the misapprehension that you would be on the receiving end of some sort of dowry. You should know that working-class people don't do dowries.'

Edward looked gobsmacked.

He watched as they both sat down, words failing him for once.

'You knew Marlene was young and therefore easier to

371

manipulate,' Lucy said. 'You would have known her story – how she was brought up – and I'm sure you must have heard all about her awful experiences in London. I think that is what I find more abhorrent than anything else – that you used someone else's misfortune for your own benefit.'

She then looked at her father with eyes that told of her deep sadness and sense of betrayal.

'And I know all about your lies about Adriana. You wanted me back at Roeburn Hall, divorced from Danny and free to marry someone rich.'

Edward opened his mouth to deny the accusations, but Lucy beat him to it.

'Please, Father, no. No more lies. I heard it all from the horse's mouth. From your mouth – and, of course, Mabel's.'

Edward looked puzzled and still unsure if he was being conned into admitting the truth.

'I was there,' Lucy explained, knowing exactly what he was thinking. 'I came back for my divorce papers that day and heard everything that was said while you and Mabel talked in the study.'

Edward could not believe his own stupidity at failing to check that no one else was about when Mabel came by that afternoon. *God, this was all her fault.*

He looked at his daughter and then at Marlene, and desperately tried to portray a man who was deeply remorseful.

Edward again made to speak.

This time it was Marlene who stopped him.

'Don't,' she said, taking hold of Lucy's hand under the table. 'I think we might both scream if we hear another lie coming out of your mouth.'

'I'm sorry,' he said, 'I really am sorry for deceiving you both. But that's not to say I don't love you, Lucy.' He looked at Marlene. 'And I know I've been a total rotter to you, Marlene. But I did like you – a lot. And it goes without saying what an attractive woman you are . . . '

Marlene thought of all the times they had been intimate. She still couldn't shake the feelings of shame and anger at herself, which she knew were wrong, but knowing and feeling were two different things. At least she hadn't slept with him. She had that to be thankful for.

'But you liked what I could get you more,' Marlene said. 'Money, the joining of two great houses, an heir.' She paused. 'And I'm guessing that everything you said about Roeburn Hall and wanting to set up a charity for disadvantaged children was simply humouring me?' Marlene couldn't quite believe that Edward had been so convincing. She needed to hear it to really believe it.

Edward looked at Marlene, surprised that his feelings for her were mixed – one part of him felt ridicule for those with such philanthropic ideals, the other a peculiar kind of envy for possessing the compulsion, the kind of love, that drove them to help others.

'Yes, my dear, I'm afraid I was,' he said, lighting a cigarette.

Lucy squeezed Marlene's hand.

She then took a deep breath.

'The reason I've come here today,' she said, 'is because I want the truth.' She dropped her voice to a whisper. 'I just need to know, Father – ' she did not take her eyes away from his ' – did you kill Mother?'

Edward shook his head violently.

'No! No, no, my dear girl, I did not. Would not. Could not! I might be many things, but I am not a murderer.'

'So, why would someone say that they had seen you?' Marlene asked with scepticism.

Edward shook his head, more wearily this time.

'I really don't know. But what I'm trying to get through to you both now – and it goes without saying that this really is a matter of life and death – is that I am not lying about killing Elise. What I really want you to know, what I want everyone to know, is that I might well be a cheat and a complete cad – as well as a hopeless gambler and ridiculously inept when it comes to finances – but one thing I am not is a cold-hearted killer.'

Marlene sighed. 'The difficulty you have, Edward, is why would anyone believe you? I guess that's the problem being a compulsive liar – when you *do* tell the truth, no one will believe you.'

'You *must* believe me,' Edward pleaded. 'Both of you. I *did not* do this. I *did not* kill Elise.'

Marlene and Lucy stood up and pushed their chairs back under the table.

'I can't speak for your daughter,' Marlene said, 'but I'm afraid I don't believe you.'

Edward looked imploringly at Lucy, waiting for her verdict, but it didn't come.

As they turned and walked away, they heard the scrape of chair legs as Edward stood up.

'I didn't murder your mother, LuLu!' His voice was raised.

As the police officer opened the door and escorted the two women out, the other uniformed copper marched over to Edward to stop him trying to follow.

As Lucy and Marlene walked down the corridor, they could hear Edward's voice, louder and more desperate.

'I did not murder Elise!'

Chapter Seventy-One

Later that day, Edward Stanton-Leigh was taken to HMP Durham, where he was to remain until his first court hearing, which had yet to be scheduled. Desmond Pyburn had been by his client's side, explaining the process and trying to keep him calm, which was no easy task. Edward was beside himself, demanding to know who claimed to have seen him and declaring that they were lying and he was 'innocent'. Desmond had tried to explain to him that he would find out who the witness was, but it might well take time as the police and the Crown Prosecution Service were sticking to their guns about their decision to keep the witness anonymous.

Edward had naturally considered whether the anonymous witness could be Mabel. He had, after all, rejected her – and her baby. Their baby. But after arguing the case in his head for quite some time, and he'd had plenty of time to do just that, he had come to the conclusion that Mabel might hate him – despise him, even – for refusing to marry and make an honest woman of her, but he was sure she would not want to be responsible for his death. For killing the father of her baby. *Would she?*

Desmond had listened to Edward as he had racked his brains as to who, out of the many enemies he had accrued over the years, might want to see him 'swinging', but they both had to admit that none of those people had been so maligned by him that they would want to see him either publicly executed or at the very least sentenced to a life in prison.

Desmond himself was very nervous about the case, but tried his hardest not to let it show. He feared that a judge would not take kindly to a wife being murdered for purely materialistic reasons, and that it had most definitely been a case of malice aforethought. His plan was to try to coerce Edward into working on a defence that he had not intended to kill his wife, that it had been an accident: the two had been arguing and Elise had toppled backwards, having already consumed quite a quantity of alcohol.

But, in truth, Desmond did not rate his chances of success very highly.

The day after seeing his client transferred from a police to a prison cell, Desmond had a visitor. Not at his office on the first floor of a converted Victorian house on Old Elvet in the centre of Durham, but at his home, a small Georgian terrace on South Street, which overlooked the cathedral.

It was an impromptu visit, and he was not at all happy about being forced into conducting business at his home. It was not at all proper.

But by the time his unexpected visitor left, he saw the wisdom in it.

Mabel felt an adrenaline rush as she approached the side entrance of the prison, where she had been instructed to present herself before being allowed in on a visit.

The sudden swell of nerves was not because she had never

stepped foot inside of a prison before, or because she was going to see the man who had rejected her and her baby the last time she had seen him – her apprehension was because she had requested a visit under a false name, something that had been facilitated by Desmond, who knew he risked being disbarred if the subterfuge was ever uncovered, but who also knew that despite the gargantuan risk to his own career, there was no other choice. He might have a reputation as being a rather ruthless, cold-hearted criminal lawyer whose goal in life was as much about money as it was justice, but he did have one major, unwavering and passionate belief – that the death penalty should be abolished. It was why, when Mabel had come to see him the day after Edward had been trans-ferred to HMP Durham, he had agreed to what she had asked of him. He knew it was the only way he would be able to save his client. And so he had obtained some fake identi-fication, a dark brown wig, several rolls of bandages and a medical corset. The benefits of being a criminal lawyer were the contacts he'd made, and who could be called on as and when needed.

That morning, Mabel had gone to a house of a former client of Desmond's. She had entered the ground-floor flat as Mabel Glendenning, a woman with strawberry-blonde hair whose pregnancy was just starting to show, and half an hour later had left as Maureen Thompson, who had dark hair tied back in a ponytail, and no visible signs of impending motherhood.

Desmond had told Edward that he was to accept the request for a visit from a woman he didn't know, and that all would be revealed when his visitor was able to sit down and have a chat with him.

Having been shown into the visitors' room, Mabel looked around at the other tables. There were mostly women talking to their husbands or loved ones. She saw a woman crying into her hankie, trying to mute her sobs; another was laughing loudly. Mabel wondered how anyone could find anything in any way funny within these grey and depressing walls.

She had to survey the room for a moment before she found Edward, who was sitting at a table near the back, smoking. He looked right at her and didn't recognise her, which was a relief; if she had fooled Edward, then she could do this without being rumbled. She just had to concentrate on what she was about to do next.

Plastering a smile on her face, she waved at Edward and walked over to him. She could feel the tightness around her bump and her breasts, but the discomfort was worth it as the corset and bandages had done the trick.

'Ah, Edward,' she said, as he finally spotted her when she was just a few yards from where he was sitting. She kept her eyes firmly fixed on his. She saw the moment he recognised her. He stood up, his eyes taking in Mabel's disguise.

'Sit down. No need to stand,' she said in perfect Queen's English, pulling out the chair opposite him and sitting down.

Mabel was glad of Edward's inability to speak. It gave her time to talk while he caught up with what was occurring. She glanced around and was glad there were no prison officers nearby, and that the visitors sitting at the tables next to them were engrossed in their own conversations.

Mabel leant forward, putting her hands palm down on the table, enabling her to get near enough to speak quietly and yet still be heard.

'Edward, I need you to listen to me,' she said.

He started to speak.

'No, Edward, it's important you listen, then ask questions later.'

Edward was staring at Mabel as though he were hallucinating.

'First of all, the good news is that you're not going to be here for much longer. And you'll soon be back where you belong. In Roeburn Hall.'

'How?' Edward stuttered.

'I told the police that I saw you – or rather, heard you – arguing with Elise the night she ended up on the floor of the cellar. That I came to Roeburn Hall to see Elise about a job and heard you arguing, and that you pushed Elise down the stairs.'

Edward stared at Mabel. 'So, it was you – you're the witness . . .' he said, not taking his eyes off his former lover.

Mabel was glad Edward's voice was barely a whisper as she had been worried that he might lose it and start shouting and screaming.

'That's right,' Mabel said.

Edward leant forward, his brow creased.

'But I didn't do it. I *didn't* push Elise down the stairs. I wasn't even there when she fell down the damned stairs to the cellar.'

Mabel suppressed a smile. She loved Edward. Was in love with him, even though he could sometimes be a little slow on the uptake.

'I know you didn't . . . *I lied,*' she said, stopping herself from reaching out and touching him. They had always been so tactile with each other. Even when they weren't making love. 'I know you're not a murderer. You're a self-centred philanderer, a liar and a cheat – but you're no murderer.'

Edward slowly sat back as he started to comprehend what Mabel had done. He had spent hour after hour trying to work out who could be the false witness, who could do such a thing when his life was at stake. He shook his head. He had dismissed the idea that it might be Mabel. How wrong he had been. It was now glaringly obvious.

Mirroring his movement, Mabel sat back in her chair.

'I told you when I came to see you at Roeburn Hall that you would rue the day,' she said. 'I gave you the option, but you said no. Actually, you said no twice, so I was left with no other option. Like I said at the time, Edward, we're kindred spirits. I know deep down you pride yourself on always getting what you want, but, you see, so do I.'

Edward sat for a few moments simply looking at Mabel.

Then he did something that Mabel had not foreseen.

He laughed.

Loudly.

When he stopped, he got out his cigarettes and lit one.

'So, tell me, my dear, what do I have to do to get you to withdraw your "witness statement"?'

'Well, there is a bit of a list,' Mabel said, now all business. 'But I suppose the most important wish on this list of mine is that you marry me. You make me mistress of Roeburn Hall. And you admit paternity of your child.'

Edward narrowed his eyes as he observed Mabel, as though seeing her anew. 'You do realise that I don't have much money, don't you? You won't be living the life of the idle rich.'

Now it was Mabel's turn to laugh, although it was not so loud or so prolonged.

'Oh, I do realise, Edward. But the funny thing is, I think I'd be quite bored being idle. And I have an idea for Roeburn Hall which requires work, but is one I think will appeal to you, quite simply because it will mean you can stay King of the Castle – or rather, Hall. We might even end up being more than comfortably off.'

Edward took another drag on his cigarette and tapped it on the ashtray.

'So, do we have an agreement?' Mabel asked, her manner officious again.

Edward paused.

'You didn't tell Desmond that you lied, did you?' he said.

'Of course not,' Mabel said, as though this was so obvious there was no need to even ask the question. 'If I did, he would be straight to the police, telling them I was liar and a spurned lover who was further motivated because I'm carrying your baby.'

She took a breath.

'So, no, he firmly believes that you are guilty, that you killed your wife, and that I am going to save you by retracting my statement in exchange for a ring on my finger and a father for my baby.'

She paused, enjoying the moment.

'And by making an honest woman of me, this will prohibit any future change of heart I might have about what I witnessed . . . As I'm sure you're well aware, a wife cannot testify against her husband in a court of law.'

'You really have thought of everything, haven't you?' Edward said, stubbing out his cigarette in the little foil ashtray.

He knew he should be outraged about what Mabel had done, but at this moment he couldn't be angry as the thought of returning to Roeburn Hall a free man was like manna from heaven. The nightmare was about to end.

Mabel saw the life come back into her soon-to-be husband's face. The sallow, defeated countenance she had observed on arrival had gone.

'Good,' she said, 'I shall go now. I do believe Desmond will be in shortly with some paperwork you need to sign to ensure it's a done deal and that there will be no rescinding the agreement.'

Edward nodded.

'Of course he will. I would expect nothing less,' he said.

He stood as Mabel pushed herself to her feet. The way she did so was the only giveaway that she was pregnant.

'I'll see you again on the other side,' she said.

She made to turn, but stopped.

'Oh, and I thought it best if we go away for a while after you're released. We can get married somewhere with the least amount of fuss, and then we can return *home* when everyone has forgotten about this little episode of your wrongful arrest.'

'And the police?' Edward asked.

'What about them?' Mabel replied. 'We'll be married, so it doesn't really matter what they think or don't think – or suspect.' She smiled. 'Like you said, I really have thought of everything.'

She turned to go. Edward caught her arm, but immediately let go, knowing there was a strict no-touching rule.

'One last question,' he asked. 'What's your plan for Roeburn Hall?'

Now the smile on Mabel's face was wide and her eyes twinkled with a mix of excitement and ambition.

'Oh, that one's easy to answer. We're going to make Roeburn Hall the most amazing, expensive and exclusive hotel in the entire county. It's about time Cuthford Manor had some competition.'

And with that she turned and walked away.

Chapter Seventy-Two

Cuthford Country House Hotel

Six months later

December 1955

Everyone was enjoying the party to celebrate Marlene and Thomas's engagement, including Winston and Bessie, who had been allowed to sneak in and plonk themselves in front of the roaring fire, which had been well stacked to combat the drop in temperature.

Marlene was wearing a sky-blue cashmere top with a matching pencil skirt, her blonde hair styled into a double French twist.

Thomas might not have felt entirely comfortable in his tailored suit, which Marlene had matched with an open-necked white shirt, but he did look incredibly handsome. Something Marlene had not held back either telling or showing him. The pair had barely let go of each other's hands and whenever they got the chance, and no one was looking, they'd give each other a quick kiss.

'No second thoughts?' Thomas whispered into his fiancée's ear.

Marlene's smile was wide. 'I haven't if you haven't?'

Thomas chuckled. 'I do love you, Marlene Boulter.'

Marlene's eyes sparkled as she held Thomas's gaze, her look speaking the words of love she too felt.

The past six months had brought Marlene and Thomas untold happiness. A lightness of being that neither had ever truly felt before in their lives. And it seemed as though the joy of their courtship had infiltrated every nook and cranny of Cuthford Manor.

Cora had found a new assistant in Shirley, who seemed to be perpetually on cloud nine after being asked if she would like to train for the role. Lloyd was particularly pleased that Cora had been convinced by Angie to give Shirley a shot at the job as it meant he saw more of his wife, and he hoped to convince her to take a tour of Europe in the near future.

'It's time for us,' he'd said on more than a few occasions, 'to take a step back and go and visit all those places we've been promising ourselves we'd see.'

Cora had agreed that as soon as Shirley was fully trained, they would do just that.

Angie and Stanislaw were in particularly good spirits, which Marlene knew was because Angie was always more contented and relaxed when all those she loved and cared for were well and happy.

Marlene also thought that her sister's happiness might have something to do with Angie's comment to her the other day that if she and Stanislaw decided to extend their family, then she would be confident that Marlene would be more than capable of taking over the helm.

Marlene had taken this to mean that it would not be long

before her sister and brother-in-law would be giving her another niece or nephew.

Even Alberta and Mrs Trendle were not quite so fractious with one another of late, and were presently chatting to Bill, Carl, Ted and Eugene, who always looked ill at ease when they were indoors.

Marlene and Thomas waved over to Clemmie and Barbara, who had just arrived, followed by Wilfred, which meant everyone was there as otherwise he would not have left his post.

Looking at everyone as they sipped champagne or orange juice and nibbled on smoked salmon blinis, Marlene thought of the alternative life she might have had if Lucy had not overheard her father that day. She would have been living a lie, whether she was aware of it or not. Edward, she was sure, would have continued to have affairs with other young women, and he would have found some excuse not to start up the children's home she had been so excited about, and for which she still had hopes.

Knowing how calculating he was, Marlene was sure that Edward would have raced her down the aisle and coerced her into starting a family, and as soon as she had been bound to him by the laws of the land and, more so, by the birth of a child, she would have ended up being trapped and unhappy, standing in the mess left behind after all her dreams had been destroyed.

But much as she hated Edward for the trouble he had caused, not just for herself but for Lucy, and the worry he had caused others by default, she was glad the powers that be had decided not to prosecute. Even if the relief she felt was only for Lucy's sake. She did not want to think about how it would have affected her sister-in-law had she seen her father on trial and if that court case had culminated in a guilty verdict – followed by a public execution.

Lucy had admitted to Marlene that she had been hugely relieved when she had been told that her father had been released from Durham Prison and that the murder charge had been dropped. But despite his release, and despite choosing to believe that her father was not a killer, she still held fast to her resolve not to have anything more to do with him ever again. She knew she could never trust her father, nor could she have any kind of relationship with him. She had learnt that the hard way.

Edward had gone off travelling after his release and there had been quite a stir when he had finally returned to Roeburn Hall with a new wife – and that wife was Mabel – and another little chap, their baby boy, in tow. The news was quite scandalous and was pored over and talked about for quite a number of weeks. But Mabel had been right that day she had told Edward about their future. Their story was soon old news and the gossipmongers moved on to fresh fields.

Angie, though, had been spitting feathers when she had heard a few weeks after their return that they had been granted planning permission to change Roeburn Hall into a hotel.

'I knew it!' she had said repeatedly. 'I knew that was what he was after all the time.'

Cora was also furious with Mabel as she knew that the only reason Edward would be able to do this was because Mabel knew exactly how to run a hotel. She was sure that the motivation behind Edward's seduction of Marlene had in part been because he knew that she, like Mabel, would have the knowledge and wherewithal.

Danny never made any comment regarding his estranged father-in-law. He, too, had learnt lessons from the separation he'd had to endure when Lucy had left, but as he had told her, something good had come out of the bad – their marriage was now even stronger. *They* were now stronger as a couple. Nothing would ever come between them again.

Looking at her brother and Lucy as they sat on the cushioned window seat, chatting and watching the children taking it in turns to push Felix back and forth in his rocking-horse chair, Marlene thought the strength of their unity was clear to see – as was Lucy's bump, which this time, thankfully, had not come hand in hand with twenty-four-hour, seven-day-a-week sickness. This time her pregnancy was relatively trouble-free. Marlene had said it must be because it was a girl, which had caused much hilarity.

Lucy knew that she would never inherit her ancestral family home, since it would clearly go to the new male heir, but it didn't bother her in the least. In some ways she felt free and untethered by the knowledge.

When Marlene heard the news, she'd declared to Thomas, 'Well, it looks like Mabel got what she wanted in the end.'

Thomas had agreed. 'Although I think Mabel only ever set out to get herself a father for her baby,' he'd said, 'but that need – that determination – has ended up getting her so much more.'

'Unless Edward gambles it all away,' Marlene had laughed.

'Somehow, I don't think his new wife will allow that to happen,' Thomas had replied, thinking of his own experiences with Mabel.

'I guess Edward got what he wanted as well,' Marlene had

mused, 'a wife, an heir and Roeburn Hall, which he will be able to bring back to its former glory.'

'Looks like the bad guys do sometimes win,' Thomas had concluded.

'Mmm, perhaps not in all ways . . . '

Thomas's words had made Marlene think – which was why she was now tapping her champagne flute.

'This little celebration is not just about our engagement,' she declared, having got everyone's attention.

'And no . . . ' she looked at Angie ' . . . this is not an announcement that there's going to be another addition to our clan.'

She looked at the Three Musketeers, Edward's nickname for them having unfortunately stuck. They were playing with Juni, who was now not only walking but seemed to want to run everywhere.

'I just wanted to say,' Marlene continued, forcing back her emotions, 'how lucky I feel. Not just because I have this wonderful home . . . '

She looked around her at the intricately carved panelling and the ornate plaster ceiling, then at the views of the expanse of perfectly manicured lawns.

'Not just because of our engagement . . . ' She stretched out her hand and Thomas took it, giving his fiancée a reassuring smile. He knew this was as important as it was hard for Marlene to say, for she had never been one for showing those she loved how she really felt. Not in a good way, anyway.

'But because I have all of you in my life.' Marlene gazed around the room at those who were her family regardless of whether or not they were related by blood.

'You've helped me through many ups and downs over the years, and I know I'm probably the cause of more than a few grey hairs.'

Chuckles gently resounded around the library of Cuthford Manor.

Marlene looked at Angie, who had not just been the eldest sister but also a surrogate mother to her and their younger siblings, and she smiled her heartfelt gratitude.

'I love you all so much,' she said, holding up her glass of champagne.

'So, here's to love and an abundance of it – and may that love be present throughout all of our lives.'

She paused and forced back the tears of happiness that threatened to spoil her make-up.

'For I know, without a shadow of a doubt, that the love you've all given me has saved me several times over – and inspired me.'

She paused.

'Perhaps one day the love that I give can do the same for others.'

Thomas gently squeezed Marlene's hand.

'To Love!' Marlene toasted.

'To Love!' the chorus of voices agreed wholeheartedly – and even Winston and Bessie drew their attention away from the flickering flames of the log fire and thumped their tails loudly on the polished parquet flooring.

Dear Reader,

This book might well be the final in the Cuthford Manor series, but what I love about endings are the beginnings which come thereafter.

So, for all of you readers out there who have come to the end of a chapter in your life (whether that be one you have chosen, or have had unwittingly foisted upon you), I wish you much love, happiness and laughter in the chapter that will inevitably follow.

With Love, as always,

Nancy
x

Historical Notes

From the newsletter of the

Sunderland Antiquarian Society

One of our society's most illustrious members was the inspiration behind a recent riverside sculpture. Amanda Revell's bestselling book *The Shipyard Girls* (which she wrote under the name Nancy Revell) and the series of books that followed, featuring women working in the Sunderland shipyards, inspired the sculpture depicting a woman welder – 'Molly'.

During the Second World War seven hundred women were employed in the Wear yards with a further thousand in marine engineering workshops. Most of these were labourers but, as depicted by Molly, some worked as welders.

The unveiling ceremony on St Peter's Riverside was performed by Houghton & Sunderland South MP Bridget Phillipson, Secretary of State for Education and Minister for Women and Equalities. She said: 'The sculpture is a fantastic way to recognise our city's rich shipbuilding heritage and celebrate the women of Wearside who played a crucial role in the war effort.'

The sculpture was created by Dr Ron Lawson, a senior lecturer at the University of Sunderland. Ron started his working life as an apprentice sheet metalworker at the nearby North Dock. Appropriately, Molly is not made from bronze, the material traditionally used for statues, but is forged and welded from corten steel. This metal weathers, giving the sculpture an external protective layer of rust. Amanda Revell recalled how it was when stumbling across an article in the BBC archives about women who worked in the Sunderland shipyards during the world wars that led her to write about them. She said: 'I was in awe of what they had done, but also incensed that they had been totally forgotten – and never revered for the critical and crucial work they had done during such a hugely important period of our history.'

Discover Nancy Revell's bestselling Shipyard Girls series

Have you read them all?

On a station platform, with nothing to read,
and a four-hour train journey stretching ahead of him...

That's where the story began for Penguin founder Allen Lane.
With only 'shabby reprints of shoddy novels' on offer,
he resolved to make better books for readers everywhere.

By the time his train pulled into London, the idea was formed.
He would bring the best writing, in stylish and affordable
formats, to everyone. His books would be sold in bookstores,
stationers and tobacconists, for no more than the price
of a ten-pack of cigarettes.

And on every book would be a Penguin, a bird with a certain
'dignified flippancy', and a friendly invitation to anyone who
wished to spend their time reading.

In 1935, the first ten Penguin paperbacks were published.
Just a year later, three million Penguins had made their
way onto our shelves.

Reading was changed forever.

—

A lot has changed since 1935, including Penguin, but in the
most important ways we're still the same. We still believe that
books and reading are for everyone. And we still believe that
whether you're seeking an afternoon's escape, a vigorous debate
or a soothing bedtime story, all possibilities open with a book.

Whoever you are, whatever you're looking for,
you can find it with Penguin.